My Daug

ANNIE MURRAY was
lish at St John's College
novel, *Birmingham Rose*, hit *The Times* bestseller list
when it was published in 1995. She has subsequently
written fifteen other successful novels. Annie Murray
has four children and lives in Reading.

You can visit her author website at
www.anniemurray.co.uk

PRAISE FOR ANNIE MURRAY

Soldier Girl
'This heartwarming story is a gripping read, full
of drama, love and compassion' *Take a Break*

Chocolate Girls
'This epic saga will have you gripped
from start to finish'
Birmingham Evening Mail

Birmingham Rose
'An exceptional first novel' *Chronicle*

Birmingham Friends
'A meaty family saga with just the right mix
of mystery and nostalgia' *Parents' Magazine*

Birmingham Blitz
'A tale of passion and empathy which will
keep you hooked' *Woman's Own*

ANNIE MURRAY

My Daughter, My Mother

PAN BOOKS

First published in Great Britain 2012 by Macmillan

This edition published 2012 by Pan Books
an imprint of Pan Macmillan
20 New Wharf Road, London N1 9RR
Associated companies throughout the world
www.panmacmillan.com

ISBN 978-1-5098-3638-3

A CIP catalogue record for this book is available from
the British Library.

Typeset by SetSystems Ltd, Saffron Walden, Essex
Printed and bound by CPI (UK) Ltd, Croydon, CR0 4YY

Visit **www.panmacmillan.com** to read more about all our books
and to buy them. You will also find features, author interviews and
news of any author events, and you can sign up for e-newsletters
so that you're always first to hear about our new releases.

For my own mother, Jackie Summers, a great mom!

Thank you so much for everything.

Acknowledgements

A number of people were helpful to me in my research for this book. A particularly big thank you to: Gaynor Arnold, Brian Holtham and Ruchi and Gurmit Sandhu.

May–July 1984

One

May 1984

'Are you going in then, or what?'

Joanne jumped, her heart pounding in the violent way it kept doing these days. She had not heard the woman coming up behind her, the wheels of her child's buggy gliding across the dark-green lino.

In a moment of panic she realized she could also not remember anything about how she had got here herself, how she came to be peering through the reinforced glass window in the door of the church hall, her hand gripping the handle of Amy's buggy. Had she been here long? She had no idea.

The woman behind her was white-faced and plump, with jaw-length hair. She wore glasses in big red frames and a baggy purple T-shirt over a long denim skirt. In the buggy a dark-haired boy of about two was wrestling to get out.

'Sorry – yes, I'm going in.' Joanne pushed the door open. Sounds blared out.

The hall was strewn with toys and chaotic with the movements of small children. Some were pursued by their mothers, while other women stood talking in clusters at the edges.

The first time Joanne had come, a fortnight ago (she

had had to miss it last week, the state she was in), she had mistaken the time, come just after ten and found the hall almost empty. Only Tess was there, the woman who ran the group, carrying toys from the storage cupboard at the back and arranging them round the hall while her little boy ran up and down.

It was Tess who had given Joanne the courage to come back to the toddler group. Tess was freckly-faced with curly, straw-coloured hair tied up in a ponytail and had a kind, friendly way about her. She was carrying six months of pregnancy around in a pair of bleached denim dungarees with a bright-orange T-shirt underneath and purple desert boots.

She had seemed to sense how nervous Joanne was and spoke gently to her.

'It can be quite hard at first,' she said, then laughed. 'As if everything about being a mother isn't hard at first! But I sometimes tell people it might be better not to come until their children are already sitting up. Your little one's already on her feet, though, isn't she? So that's fine.'

She had smiled at Amy, who was in her buggy, sucking on a bottle of juice and watching everything with her huge blue eyes.

'She's beautiful,' she said warmly.

This kindness brought Joanne close to tears. She had felt a kind of adoration for Tess from that moment. Together they set up the rest of the room, and it had felt good to be involved. She had wanted to come back last week, but her mouth had been so swollen and the cut he had given her kept splitting open. She had been too ashamed to go out.

Today, though, it was all already in full swing – all the toys in use, a corner for painting, another for play dough (made at home by Tess), and even a little plastic pool on a table for water-play. Amy was squeaking with excitement.

'Out!' she insisted, tugging at the straps.

Joanne was glad to have Amy to deal with, as she felt shy and awkward among the other women. Some of them seemed so confident, as if they'd been mothers all their lives.

Unstrapping Amy, she kissed the top of her head, feeling her warmth through the cap of blonde hair. But Amy was in a hurry and jerked her head, banging against Joanne's lip where it had almost healed, so that her eyes filled. Faintly she tasted blood again. For a second it felt unbearable, like the last straw.

Amy headed straight for the painting table where one of the helpers, a cheerful young woman called Mavis, put a plastic overall on her.

'There you are, love. You can go and paint your masterpiece now, can't you?' she said, in warm Jamaican Brummie.

'Thanks,' Joanne mumbled. Amy looked lovely in the bright-yellow overall. She had met Mavis last time.

'She's loving it, isn't she?' Mavis observed. She stood watching Amy, her arms folded, neat in a short-sleeved grey top and black skirt. Round her neck she wore a little gold cross on a chain. Mavis must have been younger than Joanne – only about eighteen – but she seemed very mature. And Mavis was the sort of person beside whose neat slenderness, smooth brown skin and tidy, clinging hair Joanne felt like a wayward scarecrow.

Joanne was quite tall, at five foot seven, thin and long-legged like her father. She had ample-sized breasts (that was good), but otherwise she felt gangly and as if everything was bulging out in all the wrong places, especially now she'd had Amy. In the past Dave had always told her she was imagining it: 'You've got a great figure. That's the trouble with you girls – you're never satisfied.' That was the old Dave, who had loved her body, her pink-cheeked complexion and wavy brown hair; that was before he turned sour and critical. Now everything about her seemed to be wrong. These days she nearly always wore jeans, ripped at the knees, her hair hoicked back in a loose ponytail. She hadn't had it trimmed for ages – since before Amy.

'She'll be fine,' Mavis told her. 'I'll watch her for a few minutes, if you want to go and get yourself a coffee? You know where the kitchen is?'

'Oh yes, ta,' Joanne said, trying to sound relaxed and confident. 'I won't be long.'

Crossing the hall, she saw the stressed-looking woman who had arrived with her squatting beside a pile of Duplo, pleading with her son to stop whacking another child's head with his latest red-and-yellow creation.

'I'm warning you, I'll have to take you home,' Joanne heard shrilly, in passing. 'Look at Tom – he's not hitting other children . . .'

There was a gaggle of young white mothers in one corner. One whom she had met last time was thin and pale, with long black hair and a baby whose father was obviously black; another, dumpy and competent, was pregnant with her third child. With them was a mother of twin boys, who was as thin as a railing, with piercings round her ears and nose, which caught the light like a pincushion. There were a few nervy, educated women who were already fretting about primary schools (something Joanne had not given a thought to); a knot of black mothers who tended to hang out together; Mavis, who was hoping to move on to a career in childcare; and Tess, who sailed like a calm, reassuring ship among them all, spreading goodwill.

A couple of the West Indian mothers were in the kitchen, one arranging biscuits on a plate, the other pouring squash into little plastic beakers. They were busy chatting, so Joanne made tea for herself. Drinks were to be kept in the kitchen, away from any risk of scalding the children.

She took a few sips of her sweet tea, leaning against the kitchen doorframe, hugging the warm mug to her chest. Amy was still deep in her picture. Toy cars skittered across the floor. Joanne watched the groups of women talking.

I must make sure I get home on time, she thought. Her heart began racing again, with that sick thumping. He might come home to check up on her. It was never far away: every few minutes the thought of home came to her, and Dave. It had crept up on her, the way she was always waiting for something to happen now. Even in her sleep.

The main door opened and in came another buggy, pushed by the Asian girl whom she'd seen here last time. Joanne had been surprised. She didn't think Asians would come to these groups – not in a church. Wasn't it against their religion? She hadn't spoken to her, and the woman had seemed a bit left out. She looked very young, was fine-boned, delicate, and had a tiny daughter with huge eyes and a head of thick, wavy hair.

The Asian girl was lifting her daughter out. Joanne frowned, narrowing her eyes. It was the same girl, wasn't it? She certainly recognized the child. But there was something very different about her mother. It took her a moment to realize. Last time the girl had been wearing jeans and a T-shirt. Joanne remembered how its vivid yellow had flattered her, her long plait swinging darkly against it at the back.

This week the back of the girl's head was covered by a thin scarf. She was dressed in one of those Asian suits, baggy trousers and long shirt, all in a pale mauve, edged with gold. It made her look different, and Joanne found it puzzling. Wasn't she expected to wear one kind of clothes or the other? The Muslim girls at school, like her friend Mevish, had always dressed much the same: trousers under skirts, and scarves.

She rinsed out the cup and returned in time to find Mavis lifting the overall off over Amy's head.

'We've had enough of painting,' she said. 'There now, and what a lot you've done – look, three pictures! I'll peg them up on the line.'

Along the wall behind her exhibits with paint running down them were pegged along a piece of string.

Amy was already trotting across the room towards the pile of Duplo, and Joanne followed and knelt beside her, glad to feel useful at last. Beside her was the mother with the long black hair, who barely glanced at her.

A moment later Joanne felt something pushing in between the two of them. A pair of tiny brown hands appeared, then a face, as if the little girl was tunnelling her way in to get to the toys. Joanne leaned over to let her pass, and a moment later the child was absorbed in building something. She was wearing pale-blue trousers and a sugar-pink shirt.

'Sorry – did she push in?' Joanne heard a high, soft voice and turned to see the young Asian woman.

'Oh no, she's all right,' Joanne said. 'She just wants to play.'

Just then a voice called across the hall, 'Dani, come over 'ere and see this!'

Dani, the black-haired woman, heaved her daughter off the floor and disappeared. The Asian woman sat down in her place in a shy, almost tentative way and, as she did so, Amy leaned over and snatched a little Duplo fireman out of her daughter's hands. The other child gave a loud squawk of protest and held on for grim death.

'Amy, stop that!' Joanne said, breaking it up. 'You can't just take toys from someone like that. Now you let . . .' She glanced at the mother.

'Priya, but don't worry about it—'

'No, Amy, you let Priya keep it . . . I'm sorry,' Joanne said. Amy looked as if she was about to cry, but she let go, seeming bewildered. 'She hasn't been with many other children. She's not learned how to share yet.'

'Oh, that's all right. Priya's got cousins, so she's used to it.' The woman sounded amused. She seemed friendly, her face thin and pretty in a gentle way, with lively eyes that seemed to hold a hint of mischief.

'That must be nice,' Joanne said wistfully. 'The cousins, I mean.'

'Hmm, sometimes it is. But they're a bit older and they do push her about quite a lot. She's had to be tough, even though she's small.'

'How old is she?' Joanne asked. The girl looked so little and fragile.

'Just eighteen months, tomorrow.'

'*Is* she? I'd never've thought she was older than Amy – by two months!'

'Amy, that's pretty. What's your name?'

'Oh, Joanne. What about you?'

9

'Sooky. My name's Sukhdeep, but it sounds just a bit rude in English if you say it the wrong way, so everyone calls me Sooky.' She gave a surprisingly full-throated laugh and the mischief in her eyes increased.

'Well, I suppose – if you think of it that way!' Joanne found herself laughing too, and it was a nice feeling. When was the last time she had laughed?

Sooky looked as if she was about to say something else, but then Tess called from the kitchen door, 'Children's drinks are ready!' Everyone got up and headed for the squash and biscuits, and afterwards there was no chance to talk.

As they were all gathering up their children to leave at the end, though, Sooky pushed her buggy over to Joanne, with Priya already strapped in. Shyly she said, 'See you next time, maybe?'

Joanne found a smile breaking across her face. 'Yeah – probably. See you.'

Walking home she popped into the shops to buy bread and a bunch of bananas. She felt suddenly cheerful.

Two

She was in the back room, perched on a stool beside Amy's high chair, feeding her lunch, when the front door opened, then slammed shut. Joanne froze.

Previously Dave always used to shout her name when he came in. 'Jo?' Wherever she was in the house. Now, though, he'd taken to creeping in, as if he thought he'd catch her at something.

There was a long moment of silence, then his footsteps, Dave standing in the doorway, tall with close-cropped fair hair, vivid blue eyes, broad shoulders in a black T-shirt, his well-fitting jeans smeared with grease. Even when he was dirty he always looked neat.

'Dada!' Amy cried, looking up from smooshing carrots into the tray of the high chair. A band of sunlight through the window lit up her pale hair.

Dave's lips twitched into a half-smile. Joanne felt relief pump through her. It was all right. He seemed to be in a good mood.

'All right?' she said carefully.

The smile vanished. He leaned up against the doorframe, weight on one leg, a hand pushed into his jeans pocket, watching them. His expression was blank, but to her it felt menacing.

His eyes roved round the room as if gathering evidence, his glance taking in the table pushed against the wall opposite the window. None of what was on it

– yesterday's paper, a couple of bits of junk mail, Amy's red record book from the Health Visitor – had been moved since this morning. Joanne hadn't bothered to sit for breakfast; she had stood eating toast in the kitchen before she set out. Nothing about the rest of the room – the three chairs, two pushed in under the table and an old brown easy chair, Amy's toy box on the brown-and-fawn carpet squares or the spider plant on the windowsill – gave him anything to pick on.

He stared hard at her.

'Where've you been?' His voice was quiet, as if getting warmed up for something. He looked as if a dark cloud was hanging over him.

'Been? To the toddler group at the church.' She spoke lightly, feeding Amy a snippet of fish finger. 'I did tell you I was going.'

'You never.'

She knew she had; she wouldn't have dared not to. These days it felt as if he knew when she went in and out of the house, even when he was streets away, working at the garage.

'Maybe you've forgotten – you've got a lot to do.' She forced herself to sound good-natured, respectful; anything to defuse his mood.

'Where is this *toddler* group then?' It sounded contemptuous, the way he said it.

'Villa Road, the church at the end. She did some nice painting, didn't you, babby, eh? Look, you've still got a bit on your hands.'

Amy looked up at the mention of painting and clapped. There was proof in the rusty smudges between her fingers.

'So . . .' He kept his voice casual. 'Who d'yer talk to?'

'Hardly anyone really. A couple of the other moms. It's all women . . .'

'No men?'

'No – it's a *mother* and toddler group.'

He fixed her with that stare again. It was something he had started doing over the last few months, his face stony, his eyes wide, boring into her as if trying to nail her to the wall. It made her feel trapped and, increasingly now, afraid.

Ignore it, her inner sense told her, but her heart was already off on its sickening thump, thump.

Then the cloud seemed to clear. It was as if he had been struggling with something inside him and it had released. She saw him relax, move to perch on the arm of the chair and smile at Amy. Joanne's breathing came more easily.

'D'you want some dinner then?' She cleared Amy's tray away, wiping the child's hands and lifting her down. 'There's some chicken in the fridge; and I bought fresh bread . . .'

'Nah, been to the chippy; that Paki place.'

'Cuppa then? There's some cake left – chocolate.'

She'd baked it for him: he liked her to do womanish things like baking and ironing. If she tried hard enough, she felt, she could get things back to how they used to be, when everything was easy between them.

'All right then: a quick one. Then I'll have to get back.'

And everything was normal again, for the moment. She made him tea and they sat playing with Amy.

'Nice cake,' Dave said, through a big mouthful.

He told her they were having a slow day – that was why he had managed to get home. And that Al, who worked for him at the garage, was planning on getting married.

'What – him and Lesley, all of a sudden?' Joanne laughed. 'Why're they bothering?'

Al was in his forties, and he and Lesley already had three children.

Dave shrugged. 'Dunno – she wants to. Wants a wedding, I s'pose. The girls're going to be bridesmaids.'

'Oh,' Joanne said. She stroked Amy's head. 'Maybe we should've waited. Had Amy as our bridesmaid.'

Dave laughed, shaking his head. 'Nah. It's better to do things proper, like.'

They cracked some jokes about Al and Lesley, saying they might as well have waited to collect their pensions and paid for the wedding that way. Then Dave stood up, brushing crumbs off his jeans.

'Anyroad . . . Got to get back.' He put his mug down and stood up, saying lightly, 'You won't be going out again?'

'Well, it's a nice day. I thought I'd take her out to the swings and . . .' She hesitated. Things had been going so well, but she'd better prepare the ground now.

'What?' A dangerous edge was back in his voice.

'Tomorrow – you haven't forgotten? I promised Mom to go over and help get ready for her birthday. She's not feeling too bright . . .'

'When is she ever? She's like a bloody zombie, that woman.'

Joanne bit back an angry retort. It wasn't as if Mom was easy, either. Instead she said, 'She just wants a bit of help. I can take Amy over . . .'

He'd gone all tight again, full of resentment.

'We're only going to do a bit of cleaning,' she said. 'Amy can play – that's all.'

Again she saw the struggle going on in his head. What did he imagine? She could see that he wanted to stop her, tell her she couldn't go, but he managed to reason his way out of it. He shrugged.

'All right then. Here, give us a kiss.'

She kissed him and then lifted Amy up.

'Kiss Dadda goodbye.'

The front door slammed behind him. Joanne stood and took several deep breaths. Everything was all right. They had had dinner, talked. Nothing had happened.

Three

'Excuse me – can yer let me sit down?'

From her annoyed tone, Joanne realized that it wasn't the first time the woman had asked.

'Yes, sorry.' She moved her bag and pulled Amy in even closer on to her lap. The elderly woman dropped down into the seat, breathing chestily as the bus crawled under the Hockley flyover. Joanne faced the window. It was a hazy day outside. The woman beside her made clucking noises at Amy, but Joanne didn't turn and look. She hadn't the energy to talk.

It took two buses to get across town to her mom's. Joanne had grown up in Kings Heath and each time it was like returning to childhood again: Mom and Dad still in the same smoke-filled terrace near the baths, her younger sister Karen still living bossily at home. The place never changed. She never looked forward to going very much; it sapped her energy. But she felt responsible for Mom – always had.

As the bus swooped gently down into town she thought: well, at least last night was all right. In the afternoon she'd taken Amy out to Handsworth Park, where they'd fed the ducks. Bits of Mother's Pride and torn-up chapattis floated on the surface of the water. Amy had loved it. Joanne watched her adoringly, in grateful wonder at her daughter's settled, happy disposition. Once home, she'd made sure Dave's tea was ready – pork chops, which he especially liked. He'd phoned at six, apologetic, like his old, sweet self.

'We've had this bloke in with a flash BMW – wants it done straight away. He's made it worth our while. So I'll be late, can't say how long.'

'That's all right,' she'd said, relief flowing through her. 'Your dinner'll keep. I'll get Amy to bed – you take your time.'

There was a silence, then in barely more than a whisper he said, 'You'll be there, won't you, babe?'

'Course I will.' In that moment she was touched by his need of her, as well as confused by his moods. 'Where else'd I be going?'

'Love yer,' he'd mumbled gruffly.

She hesitated; she hoped not long enough for him to notice. 'Love you too.'

What fantasy world did he live in, she wondered as she put the phone down, thinking she might conduct some affair in the hour or so that he was out late, with a young child to get bathed and into bed? It was all so ridiculous, the way he tormented himself – and her – with his crazed fears.

It hadn't always been like this. It had mainly started since Amy, and this was the strange part of it. Looking back, Dave had had reasons to be downcast and angry with life. He'd had his shocks and disappointments: his dad dying the way he did, for a start. But he'd seemed to ride that and get over it. Basically he'd been a cheerful, lively lad, her Dave, the feller she'd given up everything else for. But then, just when something good happened – Amy arriving – he had started to change. Things began to happen that she would never have dreamed of before.

The first time he'd actually gone for her was nearly

six months ago. It had been fireworks night, and Amy was already asleep, oblivious to the noise. Joanne didn't know what had set Dave off. He'd been in a bit of a mood, but she didn't know why.

He'd gone out the back to their little patch of garden to put bagged-up nappies in the dustbin, and she'd come out to stand on the back step. The air smelt of gunpowder, or whatever that stuff was they put in fireworks. There was a blue tinge to the night and coloured sparks spraying high above the rooftops. Every few seconds there were bangs and voices cheering and 'ooooh'-ing. What with Guy Fawkes and Diwali, the whining and exploding of fireworks went on for weeks at that time of year, but this was the peak night.

Dave came and stood beside her. He was wearing jeans as usual and a big, dark-blue sweat shirt. She remembered that he had seemed disembodied: in the dim flashes of light, his face was the only part of him that was visible.

Except the fist that came swinging round when he hit her. Hard.

What had they been talking about? This and that, or so she thought. Pink sparks fizzed across the sky in front of them, lending a glow to the houses behind.

'Funny, isn't it,' Dave had said suddenly. 'All them people out there. All in their little boxes – thousands of 'em.'

'All getting into bed every night,' she'd said with a giggle.

She remembered he had rocked on his feet a bit when she said that, as if thinking about it. As usual he had his hands in his pockets. He was a big man – bigger now that he had stopped playing football and was drinking more. She had been standing with her arms folded, keeping warm.

'You won't be out there, seeing many of 'em, now will you? All those ... milling crowds of people.' He sounded disgusted. 'Not now we've got Amy.'

'Well, not till I get back to work,' she said.

He was standing on her right. When he twisted round and punched her, the blow smashed into her right collar bone. She didn't know if he'd misjudged in the dark, had meant to get her face or even a breast.

'Wha ... ?' She gasped as pain jarred through her, clutching at her neck, and staggered forward into the garden.

'You ain't going nowhere.' Even in her agony she could hear the extreme rage in his voice. 'I don't want you to. I earn the wages in this house, and you can bloody well stay at home like a proper wife and look after your daughter. That's how it's going to be. Got it?'

He disappeared inside. Seconds later she heard the front door slam.

Bent over, her teeth chattering, she prodded at her collar bone with her fingertips and tested it, flexing her arm. It seemed a miracle that it wasn't broken. She groped her way into the house. The lamp on the side table in the front room gave off a gentle light. She fell onto the sofa and curled up on her side, trembling with shock. With a fist pressed to her lips, she wept tears of pain and bewilderment. It was a long time before she stopped shaking. Eventually, oblivious to the faint bangs from outside, she fell asleep.

His coming back into the house jarred her awake. Still curled up, she lay rigid, listening for his breathing in the hall the other side of the wall as if he was an intruder. It was as if he had become the enemy, someone she didn't know at all. There was a chasm between them. Then he was there, kneeling beside her. She recoiled from him, but he almost fell on her.

'Bab? Oh, my babby – I'm sorry.' His voice was wretched. He was stroking her hair. 'I'm sorry. I'm so sorry if I hurt you . . .'

'Why did you hit me?' she sobbed.

'That wasn't me. I dunno who did that, but it wasn't me . . . I'd never hurt you, my little darlin', my babby.'

Longing to believe him, she had reached out and put her arms round his neck as both of them wept. His loud male sobs of contrition were like nothing she had ever heard and they moved her. She had never heard him cry before. He led her up to bed, unbuttoning her clothes in wonder, as if it was the first time he had ever seen her long, slim body, brushing his lips over her bruised collar bone in a way that made her overflow with tenderness for him. After they had made love she fell asleep with his warmth pressed against her back, and in the morning they acted as if nothing had happened. She told no one, though she couldn't move without pain for some time.

It happened again a month later: she had brought up the subject of work again. W.H. Smith were expecting her back, and she needed to get things sorted out. That time he had got her up against the wall, hand round her throat. Terrified, she agreed to give up her job. In any case she had dreaded leaving Amy, and Dave was adamant that his wages would cover the rent and everything else they needed. But that was when she told Michelle.

They had all been at the same school in Kings Heath – Dave, Joanne and Michelle – though Dave had been in the year above. Now that she and Dave were in Handsworth and Michelle had moved to Yardley with her mom and dad, they had only been able to meet now and then, for a coffee in town, and even less often now that Dave was so paranoid about her going out.

At first Michelle had been shocked and sympathetic.

'You want to watch it.' She spoke between drags on her cigarettes. Michelle was seldom seen without one, and a fog of smoke hung over her side of the little cafe table. 'Don't let him get away with any more crap like that.' She lit a new fag from the dying one, which she stubbed out in the glass ashtray.

'I'd never've thought it of Dave, but once they get like that, they can't usually stop. They're like horses going to the bad – and then you're stuck in the ditch with 'em, mate.'

But after the last few months, when Joanne had made excuses and cancelled meeting her several times, Michelle wasn't speaking to her.

'It's because of him, isn't it?' she had said the last time Joanne phoned.

'What d'you mean?' Joanne tried to shrug it off. 'No – it's just Amy's got a cold, and . . .'

'Has he hit you again?' Michelle's gravelly voice demanded.

'No! Well, once or twice – but only . . .' Only what? Her voice trailed off. *Only hit me* . . . ? In horror she realized that it was something you could get used to, that it might become normal. 'We'll sort it out. It's fine most of the time, really. Only I'd best not aggravate him.'

'You're a fool,' Michelle said, disgusted. 'You need to get out of there, mate: ring one of them phone lines – Rape Crisis or whatever.'

'He hasn't *raped* me,' Joanne pointed out.

'Well, whatever it's called. Look in the bogs somewhere – those stickers on the doors. Do summat about yourself.'

'You're a fine one to talk, Meesh.' Michelle had hit the bottle off and on over men and heartbreak.

'How d'you think I know the score?' she demanded.

Joanne kept out of Michelle's way now. She had grown more and more isolated. In fact, until she started going to the playgroup – she knew deep down that the cut lip Dave had given her last week was to stop her going there – she had barely seen anyone for several weeks.

She got off the number fifty bus carrying Amy and went into the indoor arcade to pick up some cheap chrysanths. It was a warm day, and by the time she had walked along to her mom and dad's house she was sweating.

'You're a heavy little dumpling, aren't you?' she said, nuzzling Amy's cheek. 'Never mind – we're at Nanna's house now.' She rang the bell, pinning a smile on her face.

There was no response for such a long time that she thought her mother must have gone out. Then at last she heard her rattling the safety chain inside.

'Hello, Mom! Look who's come to see you!'

Her mother, Margaret Tolley, was of a very different build from Joanne, who took after her father. Margaret was shorter, brown-eyed and well rounded. Her left eye wandered to the side, which gave her an eccentric look. She peered blankly at them through her specs. As usual she was in the middle of a smoke. Joanne saw little beads of perspiration on her forehead.

'Mom? I've come to help, remember? Get cleaned up for your birthday?'

Her mother passed her tongue over her lips, something she nearly always did before speaking.

'Oh – sorry, love. I'd sort of forgotten. Come in.'

'I like your hair,' Joanne said as they went in. The house stank of smoke as usual. 'Have you just had it done?'

'Yes, yesterday.'

Her mother's hair, a fading dark brown, usually hung round her collar in an indeterminate state somewhere between permed and straight. Today, though, it looked darker, and had been set in tight curls. It was good to see her doing something about her appearance.

'It's nice – ready for your party, eh?'

Her mother gave her vague smile again. 'Thought I might as well try and look my best.'

On Friday it was her fiftieth birthday, and on Saturday she was planning to have family and a few friends round for some tea. It was all she wanted, she said, no fuss.

'For God's sake, Mom,' Karen had argued, when she had announced this intention on another visit of Joanne's. 'You only live once – why don't you go out to a nice restaurant or something? It won't break the bank, you know.'

Karen, now nineteen, with her new admin job at the Poly, wore suits with shoulder pads, had even bought a little car and thought she knew everything. She had already thought she knew everything before, only a bit less so.

'Karen . . .' Joanne had said in warning. 'Don't push it.'

'But it's so boring – a little tea party! Anyone would

think she was an old lady!' They both felt that their mother dressed like one.

Mom had flared up, the way she did, sudden as a Roman candle.

'Don't you talk to me like that, you pert little bit!' Within seconds Margaret could be towering with rage over something that seemed minor to them. They had been in the kitchen, and Joanne was afraid she might pick up the kettle and hurl it at Karen. 'You're getting way above yourself these days, that you are. It's my birthday, not yours, and I won't be told what to do by you!'

'It's all right, Mom,' Joanne had said. She had always been the one to keep the peace. 'You do what you want – it's your birthday.'

'At least Dad could take her out,' Karen muttered, leaving the room. 'The boring old sod . . .'

'*Karen*.' Joanne hurried out after her. '*Shut – up* – just leave it. You know what she'll get like.' The eruptions of temper could end in a long reign of resentful silence.

'Let her,' Karen said. 'I'm sick of it.'

Thank goodness Karen was out at work now. She was always the one who wound things up.

While her mother was making a cuppa, Joanne slid the window open. Amy played on the rug on the front-room floor with the box of little toys that her grandmother had collected for her. Margaret brought the mugs in, got another ciggy out and was about to light up, but thought twice and put the packet back in her pocket. That was another thing Karen was forever on about. Mom and Dad both smoked like chimneys. *I go to work reeking of smoke. And do you want to give your granddaughter cancer?*

Sitting with her mother before they started on the

house, Joanne felt there was something different about her. At first she thought it was just the hair. Margaret was dressed in a faded navy skirt, a short-sleeved red-and-white checked blouse and her brown lace-up shoes. There was nothing new there. But it wasn't just that, or the way she kept licking her lips even more than usual, almost as if she had something difficult in mind to say and was working up to it. She seemed tense and strange, her fingers moving restlessly on the mug she held in her lap. Staring fixedly at Amy, she pulled a hanky out of her waistband and wiped her forehead.

'You all right, Mom?' Joanne asked.

'Why?' Margaret looked across at her, suddenly sharp. 'Why d'you ask?'

'Oh, you just seem a bit ... tired.' Maybe that's what it was, just tiredness.

'I didn't sleep very well. I was down here making tea at three in the morning.' She drained the mug and reached to put it back on the tray.

'Oh dear,' Joanne said. This was a common complaint. Her mother's sleep patterns had never been very good, and Joanne always thought this was the reason for her uneven moods. But it was hard to know what to say. 'At least I'm here to help.'

Margaret nodded. 'Dave all right?'

'He's fine, ta.'

'Good lad, that one.'

Dave could do no wrong in their eyes. She imagined it for a moment, her saying: *He hits me, Mom. Something's gone wrong. Sometimes I'm so scared of him.* They'd never believe her.

'Shall we get started then?' Joanne suggested.

Four

On Thursday Joanne stayed in nearly all day. Dave was in one of his better moods. When he came in from work she told him cheerily what she had been doing all day: it had been fine for hanging washing on their rack in the garden; Amy had played beside her with her little wooden trolley, picking up leaves and stones and carting them about. They'd watched *Sesame Street*, she'd ironed the clothes, had a short walk to the park . . .

'I got some sausages,' she said. 'Thought we'd have chips.' He loved her home-made chips, which were already browning nicely in the metal basket, dunked in oil.

'Sounds nice.' He came up behind her and lifted her hair to kiss the back of her neck. His hands smelt of Swarfega.

'That tickles!' she squirmed. 'Careful, or I'll have the pan on fire.'

Amy was calling 'Dada!'

'Fancy a video?' he said. 'I'll go down and get one in.'

'All right, yeah – say hello to Amy first, though, and I'll pop her into bed.'

She was full of relief. The evening was looking good. They could sit side by side, lost in a film. Nothing would happen. That's all she wanted now: for nothing to happen.

He came back after she'd settled Amy. The food was keeping warm in the oven.

'That smells nice,' he said. 'I could do with it – I'm starving.'

'What video did you get?' she asked, carrying the plates through. Dave was kneeling in front of the telly, feeding the video into the slot.

'*Quadrophenia*.' He sat back on the sofa. 'Here we go.'

'Is that the one where he goes off the cliff at the end?' She handed him his dinner. 'The one with Toyah in?'

'Yeah . . .' He moved his head to see past her.

'She grew up a few streets from me.' Toyah Willcox, one of the city's stars.

'Yeah, I know.' Everyone knew that, but she still wanted to say it.

They both ate hungrily. They'd got to the bit where the rockers are chasing round the London streets when the phone rang.

'Turn it down a bit,' she said, answering it, still watching the screen.

'Jo?' The voice was so tearful and panic-stricken that at first she didn't recognize her sister.

'Karen? Is that you?'

'You've got to come. It's Mom, she had this sort of fit – they've taken her into Selly Oak. It was terrible. Dad was out and I didn't know what to do. Can you come? We're both at the hospital – Dad's here with me now. They've not said anything yet, but I think there's something really wrong with her.'

Dave was the model husband and son-in-law that night.

27

'Come on, get in the car – I'm driving yer.' He only had a clapped-out old Fiesta, but a car was a car.

'No, I'll go on the bus.' She was dashing back and forth, trying to find her bag, some change. We can't leave Amy, can we?'

In a few minutes Dave had arranged for Mrs Coles from next door to come and sit with Amy. They crossed the city, through the underpass, roaring out along the Bristol Road. Why can't you always be nice like this? Joanne thought, examining Dave's profile in the flashes from the street lights, the outline of the handsome boy whom she had fallen in love with. The boy who was going to be a football star.

She was impatient to get there, but dreading it. Her hands gripped her bag hard. What was the matter with Mom? She had seemed a bit odd when she was there yesterday, distant – but then she often was; maybe unwell in some way? She had certainly seemed to be feeling the heat, sweat pouring off her, though it hadn't been extremely warm, just a sunny May day. She had sat down to rest several times as they cleaned, and instead of talking to Amy she had just stared ahead of her. But then she'd often been like that, hardly ever fully with them somehow. Maybe that was why Karen had turned out so hyperactive. You had to keep moving, so Mom didn't drag you down. Squabbling had been one of the ways the girls had kept their energy up.

'I should've stopped her,' she said.

'What, your mom? How d'yer mean?'

'Maybe she overdid it yesterday. I should have told her to sit down, let me do it.'

'She'd never've listened to yer.'

This was true, Joanne realized gratefully.

Joanne spotted Karen under the light outside the main door of the hospital, still in her work suit, pacing back and forth.

'Oh, thank God – at last,' she gabbled, seeing them. 'They're taking Mom up to the ward, I think . . .'

'How is she?' Joanne asked as they scurried along the brightly lit corridor.

'She hasn't really come round properly, I don't think. They've been doing some tests. I don't really know.'

Karen's normally immaculate pleat had half come down, a kinked ponytail lying across the back of her neck.

'I got home and I was in the kitchen getting a drink, and I heard this funny sort of scuffling . . . She was on the floor, just thrashing about, making this peculiar noise – it was terrible.'

'You poor thing,' Joanne said, touched by her younger sister's sudden vulnerability.

'There's Dad,' Karen said, slowing a fraction. 'That must be the doctor with him.'

Joanne saw her father's thin, sagging figure ahead in the corridor. The bright light made the bald top of his head shine between the longish hanks of faded brown hair that hung round his collar. His hands hung at his sides in a defeated sort of way. With him was a young Asian man in a white coat. When they reached the men, Joanne said, 'Dad?'

'Oh, 'ello, girls,' Fred Tolley said in a dazed way. 'All right, Dave? These are my daughters, Doctor . . .' He trailed off.

The doctor was also thin, with pimples and a prominent Adam's apple, which went up and down as he talked.

'Hello,' he said, nodding politely. Joanne thought he looked scared.

'They've done some tests,' Fred Tolley began to say, before deferring to the doctor. 'You'd better say it.'

'Would you like to sit down somewhere?' he asked.

'No, you're all right,' Fred said. 'There's no one much about. You just say what you've got to say.'

'We can't be certain yet – especially because your . . . Mrs Tolley hasn't fully regained consciousness. Obviously we'll need to see her tomorrow and we'll have a better idea what's happened.'

'But you think it could be serious?' Karen said.

The young doctor looked hesitant. 'We need to wait and see. But you should be prepared. The indications are that she's suffering from the early stages of multiple sclerosis.'

'Mom?' Joanne found the words tumbling out of her mouth. 'MS? She can't be . . . She was as right as rain yesterday – or at least, I thought she was. What makes you think . . . ?'

With all their eyes fixed burningly on him, the doctor looked increasingly helpless. He had his hands clasped together, rubbing one bony thumb along the other.

'There are certain signs,' he said. 'We haven't run all the tests yet, of course – it's early days. But all I can tell you is, your mother – wife – is quite unwell at the moment. You need to be prepared . . .'

They all stood in stunned silence.

'Should we . . . What should we do? Wait here?' Joanne heard her father asking, though her own mind couldn't seem to fasten on anything.

'She's sleeping now; they're taking her to the ward. To be honest, there's not a lot you can do. You'd be much better going home and getting some rest.'

When they walked, as if in a trance, out towards Raddlebarn Road, Joanne felt Dave's arm round her shoulders. She glanced round gratefully at him. They said they'd drop Fred and Karen back home, and drove along the dark streets in silence. When they got to the house in Kings Heath, Joanne got out as well to say goodbye.

'We'll ring in the morning,' Joanne said. 'Will you be all right, Sis?'

'Have to be, I s'pose,' Karen said. 'It's all right for you – you've got a nice husband to go home with.'

Joanne almost laughed. This was more like the normal Karen.

'See you tomorrow,' she said.

'It'll be her birthday,' Fred Tolley said. His voice was full of sadness.

Five

Joanne sat beside Margaret's bed in the long Nightingale ward, wondering when her mother was going to decide to open her eyes.

There had been calls to the hospital in the morning, requests that they come in a bit later on: 'A few things to discuss, nothing to be alarmed about.'

Dad and Karen had both taken time off work, and Mrs Coles was looking after Amy again.

This time they had seen a different doctor, older, with a comb-over of greasy brown hair and a slight air of impatience.

'We were told she might have multiple scelrosis,' Dad said. He never could pronounce it and he was in a dither.

'Well, there were indications,' the doctor replied. 'Some conditions, of course, share the same symptoms. But it's not that, I'm pleased to say.'

Since they'd been in to visit Mom she had kept her eyes clamped shut, as if in the deepest of comas. The three of them had taken it in turns to be the two allowed beside the bed.

'I don't see why we can't all stay there,' Karen had said in a loud, annoyed voice, nodding towards a group of Asians of all ages, clustered round a very large woman in another bed. 'That lot've got the whole flaming family there, kitchen sink and all.'

'It's part of their custom,' the nurse told them. 'The family unit is very important to them. We have to allow for different cultures.'

'Huh,' Karen said. 'And we don't have families, I suppose?'

'Shush, wench,' Dad said. 'Stop making a fuss.'

He took his wife's hand. 'Margaret? It's Fred. Can you hear me?'

'Mom?' Karen's voice was sharper. 'We're all here to see you.'

Joanne said nothing. The others kept this up for a few minutes, but their mother gave no reaction. After a while Joanne suggested they take it in turns to go and find a cup of tea. 'I'll wait here – you go first,' she offered.

As her father and sister retreated along the ward, she was certain she saw her mother's eyes open just a crack, to check who was there with her, before closing again.

Joanne waited, relieved to be alone, watching. Lying on her back made her mother's cheeks fall into a less creased, more youthful state. She had prominent, rounded cheekbones, the skin over them flecked with tiny red veins. With her hair away from her face and no glasses on, she seemed naked and vulnerable.

Who are you? Joanne thought, with a frightened, empty feeling. I don't know you at all. No one around her seemed to be who she thought they were. Dave had held her in bed last night, so tenderly. Now that she was vulnerable, in need, it made him feel strong. If only she could believe that would last. And now, almost with a sense of panic, she sifted her memory to find what she knew about her mother. She'd always lived in Brum, grown up in a back-to-back in a poor district, got a job, married. Her parents were dead, so the girls had never known their grandparents on either side, or many other relatives either to speak of. Mom was not one for anecdotes or for sharing herself much; she was a matter-of-fact, closed sort of person. And, as it turned out, there had been certain things she had never told anyone. Even Dad had been stunned by what the doctor said.

He had blinded them with science at first, with talk of benzodiazepines and dosages and symptoms. At last he had used a word that made more sense.

'Valium?' Fred had said, his lost look increasing. 'You're saying my missis has been on that Valium stuff – *for twenty years*?'

'So it would appear,' the doctor told them. 'I spoke with Mrs Tolley this morning and what appears to have happened is that, without taking any medical advice, she decided to stop taking it. Which, after such a long period of dependency, is a very bad idea indeed – as she has unfortunately discovered.'

'So, that fit?' Karen said. 'I mean she had a fit, a full-blown—'

'It can happen. It's variable from person to person, but that can be one of the consequences of trying to come off it too quickly.'

'But . . .' Joanne was struggling to take any of it in. 'Why was she on it?'

'I imagine she was prescribed it during a bout of post-natal depression,' the doctor said. 'She said she was put on it after the birth of her second child – it seems no one has thought to stop prescribing it.'

The doctor had to go: ward rounds to do.

'Dad,' Joanne said, out in the corridor again. 'You *must* have known she was on it?'

Fred Tolley looked as if he had been hit by a fast-moving vehicle. His old black jacket was hanging open and some of his shirt buttons were done up incorrectly. Scratching the side of his head, he said, 'Well . . . I did and I didn't.'

'What d'you mean, you did and you didn't?' Karen erupted shrilly. Joanne knew she was resentful at having to be away from work. She had her boxy navy suit on and a matching shoulder bag. 'How can you not know your own wife's a drug addict?'

'Karen,' Joanne hissed at her, 'keep your voice down. And there's no need to be like that with Dad – it's not helping.' Though she couldn't help wondering the same thing.

'I knew she was taking summat,' he said. 'I never thought to read the bottles; it was her business. She said summat about vitamins. I never thought to question it.'

'Vitamins, Valium,' Karen harrumphed.' Well. I suppose they both begin with V.'

But they were all too winded, too worried to say much more. The girls had watched their parents grow more and more distant over the years: Mom either blank, a bit like a robot doing housework, or now and then terrifyingly angry, tired, not sleeping well. They'd keep out of her way, as did her husband, a kind but shadowy presence, worn down to a silent kind of acceptance. And now Mom had suddenly erupted out of that predictable pattern, as someone with secrets, someone they knew and understood even less than they already thought they did.

'What the hell are we going to say to her?' Karen said. And for a moment, even with her immaculate pleat and office clothes, she looked like a little girl.

*

One of the nurses passed again as Joanne was sitting there.

'Has she still not come round?' she asked softly. She leaned closer. 'Mrs Tolley? Margaret? Maggie?'

'Oh, I wouldn't call her that,' Joanne said. 'She doesn't like it.' Mom went mad if anyone called her Maggie. It was always Margaret.

The nurse gave her a sympathetic look and began to move away. 'I expect she'll wake up soon and talk to you.'

Joanne sat rubbing her moist palms on her jeans, sneaking glances at her mother. She had to get Mom to speak before the others came back. She was the oldest – she had her own daughter. Imagine her lying there, with Amy sitting beside her as a grown woman. What would she want Amy to do?

She took her mother's hand. It felt small in hers.

'Mom. It's Joanne. You know I'm here, don't you? The others have gone to get a drink.'

Silence, but the hand twitched slightly.

'I know you're awake. I saw you open your eyes. Talk to me – please?'

Tears started to seep out from under Margaret's eyelids and roll down the sides of her face. She didn't sob, just released more and more silent rivulets of grief. The sight tore at Joanne. Her mother had never been the crying sort, either. Blarting, she'd call it, scornfully.

'It's all right, Mom. There's no need to get upset. The doctor told us what happened – it was a mistake, that's all. He said they'll help you . . .'

In fact he'd said no such thing, but they had to make sure she was helped and did things gradually.

At last Margaret's eyes opened. She pulled herself up on one elbow, looking round blearily. Her lazy eye showed more, without her glasses on. She was searching the little cabinet beside the bed.

'There are some Handy Andies somewhere. Pass me my specs.'

Joanne found them for her, and Margaret blew her nose, then raised her eyes warily.

'I'm so ashamed.'

'*Ashamed?* Why?'

Her mother looked desperately round the ward as if trying to find the words.

'All these years – keeping on taking those things. I mean the doctor gave them to me, but he never said when to stop, or how. It was after Karen was born – I couldn't seem to cope, didn't feel myself . . .'

Joanne calculated. Karen had been born in 1965. In fact it had been nineteen years that she'd been taking them.

Margaret shifted slowly into a sitting position, pulling the covers up.

'You take them, you see, and then the effect wears off, so you need a bit bigger dose. It never seemed to be quite right . . . And you get all sorts of things – you know, not sleeping well and all sorts. Feeling funny. But when you've been on them a while, the thought of coming off is . . . Well, it just seems impossible. I never thought I could cope without them.'

'Oh, Mom,' Joanne said.

Margaret dabbed her cheeks. 'I never wanted anyone to know I was on them. Not even your dad. And you know what he's like: he never really questioned after a certain time.'

She stopped for a moment. Joanne sat quietly, praying that her dad and Karen wouldn't come back – not just yet.

37

'I feel I haven't had a life. As if I've been living in a trance. I can't explain really. It's like living behind a sort of screen, where everyone else is getting on with life around you, but you're not really there, even though you are. And it got to this week and I decided: I'm going to be fifty, and I'm not going to live the rest of my life like this. I just thought, if I stop – this was last weekend – I'll be clear of them by my birthday. I never asked anyone, I just threw the bottle in the rubbish and that was that.' She swallowed. 'It was like jumping off a cliff or something.'

'It was brave,' Joanne ventured.

'It was bloody stupid, as it turns out.' The anger was returning. 'They talk about drugs all the time on the news: heroin and all that. And here I am, a drug addict like all of them – a dirty drug addict.' The tears started to flow again.

Joanne gripped her hand, feeling tears rising in her own eyes. All these years her mom – her strange, kind at times, but predictably unpredictable mother – had been suffering all this.

'So they've put me back on it again,' Margaret said bitterly.

'They can help you: you can come off it more slowly, like you would with any drug.'

Margaret crumpled, sinking further down into the bed again. 'I don't know if I can do it.'

'Course you can,' Joanne was saying. She sensed movement behind her and turned to see her dad and Karen approaching.

She watched her parents' eyes meet.

In a small defeated voice Margaret said, 'Hello, Fred.'

Fred looked down at her, his face lined with sorrow. 'Hello, love.'

He was about to sit down beside the bed, reaching out to take her hand, but Margaret turned her head away from him.

'Oh, go away, Fred,' she said. Her voice was full of weary contempt. 'Just leave me.'

Six

Joanne was perched uncomfortably on a miniature chair by the painting table, watching Amy, when she heard the soft voice again.

'She's really enjoying herself, isn't she?'

She'd been in such a daze that she hadn't seen Sooky come in, and turned to see her, dressed this time in a sunflower-yellow *salwar kameez* suit and smiling as she bent to put an apron over Priya's head.

'I can't seem to get her to do anything else,' Joanne said. 'She'd spend all day here, if I let her.'

There wasn't another chair, so Sooky knelt down.

'How're you?' she asked. She had a nice way of speaking, looking into your eyes as if she really wanted to know.

Joanne was relieved to see her, happy that someone – anyone – would come over specially to talk to her.

'I'm all right,' she said. She'd been miles away, her head full of all that was happening with Mom. 'What about you?'

'Oh,' Sooky said lightly, 'not too bad.'

There was a silence. Priya, with vigorous enthusiasm, was getting stuck into a pot of sky-blue paint. Joanne desperately wanted to talk, just to have a normal every-day chat, but it was hard to know what to say. The silence grew so long that she suddenly demanded, 'How old are you then?'

'Me? I'm twenty.'

'Oh, I thought you were younger.'

Sooky laughed, a sound that again Joanne found very cheering. 'Why – how old're you?'

'I'm twenty-two.'

'I thought you were older.'

'Thanks very much!' Joanne said. 'Mind you, I feel it some days.'

They were off after that, nattering away, finding out about each other. Sooky said she had been to school in Handsworth Wood, had two brothers and a sister, and her elder brother was already married with two children and another on the way. Joanne told her about Karen, about growing up in Kings Heath, then found herself blurting out, 'My mom's been poorly, you see . . . I've been back and forth to the hospital all weekend. She's back at home now, but it's been really hard, with Amy and everything.'

'Was it serious?' Sooky's voice was sympathetic.

'She just had a bit of a turn.' Joanne had no intention of explaining, so she made light of it. 'They think she'll be all right. Oh!' she smiled, pointing. 'Look at them!'

The two little girls were bent over the same sheet of sugar paper, making big strokes with their brushes and giggling, faces lit up with delight. Priya did a thick daub of blue, then Amy added bright yellow and they roared with laughter, as if this was the funniest thing in the world. They sloshed more and more colours on, both swirling their brushes round until there was a sludgy brown mess all over the soaked paper and they were cackling with joy in a way that made their mothers join in too.

'They're friends!' Sooky said. She sounded pleased.

'I'll give them some more paper,' Mavis the helper

said, laughing too. 'They're thick as thieves, aren't they? If you want to go and get a drink . . . ?'

'She always seems to be trying to get rid of us, doesn't she?' Joanne whispered as they crossed the obstacle course of toys to the kitchen.

'Who's complaining?' Sooky said, and they got the giggles too.

'So d'you live near?' Joanne asked hopefully, as they made cups of tea.

'Somerset Road,' Sooky said.

'Up in Handsworth Wood?'

'Yes, but the thing is . . .' Sooky hesitated, stirring sugar into her tea. 'I live back with my family. I'm divorced – well, nearly anyway.'

Joanne looked up from pouring milk. 'Divorced? What about your religion? I thought you weren't allowed that sort of thing?'

Sooky shrugged gently. 'Well, no. But I am. I was married at seventeen, you see . . .'

'God, that's young.'

'Not according to my mom and dad. But we made a deal that I'd be allowed to finish my A-levels. He was from Derby, so I was living there until six months ago and then . . . I came back to Birmingham.'

'Oh.' Joanne didn't know what to say. 'Did you do your A-levels then?'

'Yeah. English, politics and sociology.' She sounded proud. 'I got married, and I was expecting her towards the end, but I finished them. But I had to leave: my marriage, I mean.' Sooky stared ahead sadly as she talked. 'I was worried for – my daughter.'

Joanne had even less idea what to say now. What exactly did that mean?

'That's awful,' she ventured.

'Oh, it's not too bad. I didn't like him anyway.'

She looked at Joanne, and for some reason her frankness set them both off laughing again, even though Joanne found that it made her chest tight and she suddenly had to swallow down tears. She never seemed to know what her emotions might do, from minute to minute.

Tess appeared at the kitchen door and grinned at them both. 'It's all very jolly in here I see,' she said.

Joanne pushed Amy's buggy along the Soho Road, with plastic bags dangling on each side. She liked shopping in the Soho Road. Instead of going into one big shiny supermarket she could go into lots of little shops, though she wasn't sure about the whole halal thing or what to ask for, so usually she went to the one remaining old-fashioned English butcher right up near the top. But she liked buying bread and fruit and veg from all the small shops.

'I don't know how you can stand living over there,' her mother sometimes said. 'You might as well be living in India. All those people – none of them speak English. It's not right. I remember when Handsworth used to be a nice area.' And 'Ooh, no,' she'd say with a shudder if Joanne suggested her visiting them. 'I'm not going over there.'

So she'd only ever been once, just so that she could set eyes on their house. Dad had been a few more times, was more 'live and let live' about people who were different. And, Joanne knew, he missed her and was glad to get out of the home. She and Dad had always got along all right.

Joanne and Dave had moved there because of his

job. The garage had been his dad's business, on the borders of Hockley. She found she liked Handsworth: the old Victorian buildings, the park with its boating lake, and the sari shops displaying bright-coloured garments shot through with gold thread and scattered with sequins. And she liked the grocers crammed with oranges and mangoes, tomatoes and coriander and things she'd never heard of before, all spilling out over the pavement in their boxes, and music blaring out and the general bustle of things.

She also relished the fact that although the road was teeming with people, they would leave her alone, were not interested in her. In Kings Heath she was always bumping into people who'd known her since she was knee-high and seemed to have an opinion about anything she was doing. She felt freer living on the other side of town.

With difficulty she pushed the buggy through the narrow entrance to a grocer's.

'Leave here,' the shop owner, a neat middle-aged Muslim man in a little white hat, pointed to a space by the till. Joanne was a regular customer and there was no room to push the buggy round the shop. His wife, who could just see out above the counter's piled slope of confectionery, looked benignly at Amy.

'Hello, pretty girl,' she said.

Joanne already had bananas and spinach in her basket. Going to the back of the shop with its spicy smells, she added milk, a tin of baked beans and fish fingers from the little freezer cabinet, before going to pay.

'Lovely weather,' the woman said, adding, 'See you!' cheerfully as Joanne left.

Sooky had told her that she was not Muslim, as Joanne had assumed, but Sikh. She thought about

Sooky as she ambled back along the Soho Road, with Amy busy with half a banana and looking round at all the sights. There had not been much more time for chat, but after Tess left the kitchen, Joanne had asked Sooky what it was like living back at home again.

'Oh, not too bad,' she had said. 'It's quite nice for Priya. My sister-in-law's not very easy . . .' The side of her mouth twisted down for a second. 'I'm in disgrace, you see.'

'What about your mom?' Joanne asked.

Sooky hesitated. 'She doesn't speak to me.'

'What – never?'

Sooky lowered her head, and for just a moment there was something other than the tough, mischievous young woman.

'Not once. Not since I first came home.' She swallowed hard, then looked up again. 'It's upset her badly. But I expect she'll get over it, eventually.'

When she reached home, Joanne realized that for the first time in months she had not spent the walk home thinking about Dave, and getting more and more uptight with each step she took closer to the door.

Margaret had been allowed home from hospital on the Sunday. Until then they'd been back and forth visiting. Joanne had been once with her dad, pleased that Karen couldn't make it. Dad spoke more when no one else was there. Then on Saturday they'd all gone together.

'It's hard to get any sense out of anyone about what's going on,' Fred complained as they drove to Selly Oak.

'No, it's not – they told you,' Karen said. She picked a fleck of something off her smart navy trousers.

'They've put her back on the Valium again. She's to come off it slowly, instead of rushing it.'

'Have they told her how to do it?' Joanne asked. She'd left Amy with Dave. It would be all right, surely it would? For a moment she thought of Sooky: that she had been frightened for her daughter. But Dave never seemed to get angry with Amy – only her. And things were better now, weren't they? She tried not to think about it.

'They said to go to the doctor when she gets out,' Fred said. 'But what I want to know is, if it's the same doctor who has been giving her the stuff all this time, what bloody use is he going to be?'

'They know what they're doing, Dad,' Karen said. She took out a compact and peered at her face. Joanne looked down at the ripped knees of her jeans. Should she have dressed up for a hospital visit? Too late now anyway.

There was a quiet 'Huh!' from Fred Tolley.

Margaret didn't seem especially pleased to see them. Once again they took turns to be with her, but she seemed odd and distracted. Her hair needed a comb and she kept moving her head restlessly from side to side on the pillow on which she was propped, which didn't make it look any better. She had on her own flower-patterned nightie now.

'I don't know why there's had to be all this fuss,' she said ungraciously when they arrived. 'You don't need to keep traipsing over here like this. I just want to go home.'

They'd brought flowers and cake.

'We thought we'd have your birthday party,' Karen said chirpily. Her eyes were immaculately made up in shades of mauve, and the gold chain of her little bag gleamed against her navy jacket. 'You can have another one later, but we thought it'd be nice—'

'Oh, don't be so ridiculous!' Margaret erupted, with such force that they never dared get out the cake – a nice chocolate one that Karen had bought from Marks and Spencer – to cut up.

When Joanne was left alone with her, her mother lay looking across the ward as if there was no one there with her. Joanne felt very uncomfortable. Margaret's silence was not a calm one. She seemed to be lying there seething with emotion. Joanne didn't know how to talk to her, didn't know what it was all about, other than being in hospital, which she hated.

'How're you feeling now, Mom?' she asked gently, trying to break the spell that her mother seemed to be caught in.

'Terrible.' It was said in barely a whisper and her eyes filled. Joanne felt panic. This closed, emotionless mother she had known all her life seemed suddenly broken open, as if she couldn't stop the tears coming.

'D'you feel . . . ill?' she ventured to ask.

'I feel terrible,' she repeated. *Terrible in every way*, she seemed to be saying. *Sick in my body, my head, my soul . . . I can't bear being in my own skin*. She moved her head again as if to shake something out of it. Her perm was already coming loose and her face had changed, seemed slacker somehow.

'I can't seem to stop it. Can't stop my head. Everything's rushing by. I just can't . . .' And she dissolved into tears like a helpless little girl.

Seven

Worcestershire, September 1939

'Margaret? Well, that's a mouthful of a name. While you're in my house you'll be known as Meg, and that's that.'

It was the evening of Saturday 2nd September 1939, and her first sight and sound of Mrs Nora Paige at the door of her Worcestershire cottage: aged forty-something, with thick limbs, staring eyes and lank black hair strung up in a net day and night.

That morning had been the last time Margaret ever saw her mother.

The memories kept rushing in on her, scrambled and intense like dreams, except that she was awake and still couldn't stop them, any more than she could prevent the endless dryness of her mouth or her sleepless nights when she lay trapped by recollection, aching for sleep so that she could escape.

The morning of Saturday 2nd September 1939: each time it replayed, it was the same. Margaret was downstairs. The Old Man was up there, sleeping it off as usual. Her half-brothers, so far as she recalled, had not been there. Elsie, her half-sister, who was nineteen then, had already left for the factory. Margaret had been sitting on the bottom step of the stairs ('You'll get splinters in your bum,' Tommy kept telling her, but she always sat there anyway), picking at the scab on her knee. She'd tripped over on the way back from the wharf, when she and Tommy had been sent out for the coal. Tommy was her only full brother, two years older. She adored Tommy: he was her hero. She loved going to the wharf with him – or anywhere that he would let her tag along.

She must have been hungry, though she wasn't thinking about that until the door slowly opened and there was Mom, bent over, clinging to the door, a loaf under her arm. Catching a whiff of the fresh bread made the saliva gather in her mouth. Mom had her coat on, even though the morning was quite warm, and it hung on her, far too loose now.

Mom was scarcely more than a skeleton. Before she fell ill she had appeared careworn, older than her years. Now, at forty-two, Alice Winters looked like an old woman. She had been left a widow with three children, Margaret's half-sister and half-brothers, Elsie, Edwin and Cyril, and had worked her fingers to the bone in factories, cleaning, taking in washing, anything to keep them out of the clutches of the parish. Those years had drained away her youthful looks.

Alice had never moved far, either. Born in Cregoe Street – an old district packed with factories and jerry-built houses, edged by wharves and railway tracks, and a stone's throw from the middle of Birmingham – she'd ended up just round the corner in Upper Ridley Street. After those years struggling alone, Ted Winters, dark-eyed and stocky, had come along and wooed her. Ted was a widower with a son killed in the Great War, or so he said. Alice had had two more children with him in the 1930s: Tommy and Margaret. Hoping for rescue, for someone to share the load, Alice had found herself a man who looked sturdy and competent, who could turn on the charm all right, but who was in fact an idle boozer. He was out of work as much as in, and never lifted a finger to help her, even in her dying weeks.

'Alice?' Margaret heard a concerned voice from the yard. 'Oh, bab, you shouldn't be up and about like this! Oh my Lord, just look at the state of yer.'

It was Mrs Jennings from next door, a soft, rounded woman, swathed in a stained pinner, her pale-brown hair plaited and caught up roughly at the back and secured with kirby grips. She took Alice's arm.

'What on earth've you been doing? Have you been down the shops?' Dora Jennings sounded appalled. 'Come on – let's get you in and looked after.'

Margaret watched. Mom seemed unable to move. She was bent over, air passing in and out of her in shallow gasps, the skin stretched over her knuckles as she clung to the door. She didn't look the same any more. Her face was so pinched that her eyes and nose seemed to have grown and her cheekbones jutted, while the rest of her face had sunken in.

'I can't.' Alice's voice had gone high and reedy and it was almost a sob. 'Give us a minute. Just leave me . . .'

'Give me the bread – come on, take my arm.' In a moment Dora Jennings managed to steer the sick woman inside. The downstairs of these houses, which opened onto a yard and backed onto another row of dwellings facing the street, consisted of only one room and a minute scullery. The range and the table took up most of the space, so it was only a couple of steps to get the poor woman, now a bag of bones, onto a chair. Alice sank down with a moan, her head in her hands, having to give all her strength to drawing breath.

'I'll make yer a cuppa tea: you need summat inside yer.' Dora Jennings sounded severe because she was in a panic. 'My goodness me, look at yer – and where's that husband of yours? He wants stringing up, that he does!' The sight of Alice Winters was a disturbing one. Her neighbour hurried out to the tap with the kettle and came back to stoke the range. 'Where've you been, Alice, in heaven's name?'

Mrs Jennings hadn't noticed Margaret sitting there. Margaret watched as she pulled another chair close to her mother and gently clasped her bony hand.

Alice, lifting her head, managed to speak in between pauses for breath. 'I had to go to Auntie's – get summat for the little'uns. I took the blanket . . .'

'Off your own bed?' Dora Jennings was even more horrified. 'And you've been all the way down there in your state, carrying it? Why in heaven's name didn't you send Margaret?'

Weak as she was, Alice had managed somehow to go out of the yard, make her halting way down the entry and along, leaning against the fronts of the houses every other step, to the pawnshop near the corner. After that she had gone to the bakery, even further along the street.

She was shaking her head. 'No, I wanted . . .' Weak sobs shook her body, which was almost too wasted to cry. Margaret saw Mrs Jennings' face twist with a mixture of pity and horror. She stroked the almost transparent hand. 'I had to do summat for 'em. Today . . . Be a mom to 'em. I'll have to send them . . . It'll be – the last time . . .'

Margaret, with the dream-like perceptions of a five-year-old, had made no sense of this at the time. None of it made sense until years later. She didn't know that for days the lips of the adult world had been busy with the words 'war' and 'evacuation'. Nor did she know yet that she was going to school today, even though it was Saturday. Her mother's words made no sense, not then. But she did remember Mrs Jennings getting silently to her feet, tears in her kindly eyes, and going round to her mother, bending to embrace her, with Alice's pinched face cradled against her chest.

Mom had told her to carry the little bundle with some of the bread in it and a nub of cheese.

'You know what Tommy's like,' Mom whispered. Tommy was seven, big for his age and strong, but erratic. Alice couldn't stop the tears coursing down her cheeks as she sat, buttoning up Margaret's coat. 'He'll drop it or leave it somewhere. You be a big girl now and look after it. And put Peggy in your pocket. There's a girl.'

Peggy, Margaret's doll, was a rough little thing with brown wool hair and clothes made of scraps, sewn over a wooden peg. Her face had been put on with a blotchy fountain pen and was dreadfully smudged, but Margaret adored her.

And that was the last she remembered of her mother, taking the bundle from her that sunny morning, their rations for the journey tied up in a rag. Mrs Jennings appeared, having made them each a stera bottle – which had previously contained sterilized milk – full of sweet tea.

'Don't worry about your mother now,' she told them. 'I'll make sure 'er's all right. And, Tommy, you're a big boy now. You must look after Margaret.'

Then Tommy was with her and they were at school, gas masks in boxes over their shoulders. The string chafed her and made her shoulder ache. After that came the train, with them all crowded into carriages.

The day was hot and very long, the longest she could ever remember. There was no corridor on the train. Margaret was squeezed in next to the window where the sun streamed in, making her face red and hot. Over the other side was Miss Peters, one of the teachers from the school. She was nervous, but kindly, trying to deal single-handed with a carriage full of thirty or so young children. There was pushing and shoving, teasing. One of the girls was sick and the carriage took on a nasty sour smell.

Now and then Miss Peters thrust her head out of the window to call desperately to the teacher in the next carriage. She got them singing 'Ten Green Bottles' and 'Greensleeves'. The day grew hotter. What had seemed at first like an adventure became exhausting and bewildering.

Margaret dozed against Tommy's shoulder until he nudged her awake.

'Let's 'ave a bit of that bread, Sis.'

Margaret looked up at him, so glad he was there. If Tommy was with her, everything would be all right. He was a big, handsome-looking boy with brown eyes like hers, but darker hair, like the Old Man's. She knew Tommy would protect her. Tommy was seven and he had become very grown-up today. He'd said he wouldn't let anyone hurt her. Even though he teased her at home, outside he was her protector, chasing other kids off when they started on about her eye.

They ate some of the bread and drank some tea.

Soon an urgent feeling came on low down in Margaret's body. She hoped it would go away, but it didn't. She put her lips right up close to her brother's ear.

'I need to go, Tommy.'

She screwed up her face in misery as he looked down at her.

'What: number twos? Yer *can't*.' He looked round wildly for a moment. There were no toilets. 'You'll 'ave to hold it in.'

'I can't,' Margaret said, starting to cry.

Then for a few moments it went off and Tommy lost interest in her, assuming the problem was solved. But the feeling came back, more urgently. She waited, holding on until she couldn't any longer. She felt herself let go into her knickers and then she was sitting on it, like warm pebbles, alien and uncomfortable. She wanted to cry, but she was terrified the other children would notice her.

Letting a few moments pass, she slid from the seat and squatted on the floor, her face pressed against the knee of another child who was standing up. There was so much going on in the crowded carriage that she hoped no one would notice. Slipping her finger into her knickers at the back, she hoped to empty them discreetly onto the floor.

She was almost sure of her success when a voice cried, 'Phwoor! What's that pong!' It was one of the boys. ''Ere, look, uurgh! Old squiffy-eyes's shat 'erself!'

Margaret's mind seemed to have shut out all the details after that, except for the moment when every face in the carriage was turned to stare at her, Tommy's included, and she knew that she stank and wouldn't be able to clean her finger for the whole of the rest of the journey, and that of all the children there she was the most polluted. Miss Peters took over. Somehow, with the help of a newspaper, the offending mess was despatched out of the window. Everything settled. But the terrible swelling shame didn't, or the stench of her finger with its stained nail all that day.

Then it was evening and they were all in a big place somewhere, with a floor of scuffed boards and chairs with sagging seats round the walls and a little stage. A gristly-looking man in a cap came and fetched Tommy, saying that he looked a strong lad. Margaret waited for Tommy to say, 'My sister's coming too.' But Tommy got to his feet without a word and she saw that his face was set, the way it looked when he was trying not to cry. He looked very small next to the man, who led him away holding his shoulder. He glanced back, just for a second, looking frightened. And then he was gone.

The other children were collected in ones and twos. But Margaret was left in the gloomy village hall, cross-legged on the floor, clutching Peggy Doll in her pocket with her clean hand, rubbing her dirty finger round and round in a knot in the wood in front of her.

'There's just the little girl with the lazy eye,' she heard someone say. There were two other teachers with Miss Peters. 'She's very young. We must get her a billet tonight somehow.'

A discussion ensued. Then she was walking with Miss Peters, surrounded by the strange smells of the fields and a whiff of wood smoke and soon afterwards, out of the darkness, a door opened, showing a room lit only by a hurricane lamp on the table, and she had her first sight of a yellow-eyed cat and of Mrs Nora Paige.

Eight

'You'll sleep down here,' Mrs Paige said in her grating voice. An exhausted Miss Peters had disappeared off into the darkness after a brief introduction. 'There's no room for you upstairs – those rooms are mine and my Ernest's, so I can't go putting you up in a bed. Not even for ten and six a week.'

The cottage was a two-up, two-down. They had passed through a dark front parlour into the back room, which was dimly lit by the oil lamp. In the gloom Margaret could make out an iron range in the chimney alcove. A deal table took up much of the room and on it was a chaos of plates and books around the lamp. At the back, in front of the window, was the stiff, upright piece of furniture to which Mrs Paige was pointing. It had wooden arms, but on the seat lay some very firm-looking oblong cushions covered with dark material.

'Here's a blanket. If you need to do your business I've left a bucket there by the door. The privy's outside for the daytime. And Seamus usually sleeps up here, so you won't have to mind if he gets up with you.'

She eyed the cat, which was standing by a leg of the table, eyeing them back. He didn't look friendly, Margaret thought. She wasn't used to cats.

'Now you lie down. I'm going to my bed.'

With no offer of food, drink or any word of comfort, she left, taking the oil lamp with her. The room melted into darkness. Margaret lay her aching body down on the hard settle with its lumpy horsehair cushions, too tired to care where she slept. She clutched Peggy Doll in one hand and pulled the blanket over her, which was made of a patchwork of knitted squares and gave off an aroma of mothballs.

There was a mix of other smells in the room: the bitter whiff of coal, which she was used to, mixed with a ripe, fruity scent, which she wasn't. The next morning she saw that it came from a basket of cooking apples on the quarry tiles by the back door, fallers with bruises and wasp holes. Far away outside she heard a shriek, which must have been a bird. Her head was throbbing and her eyes already closing as she settled.

A second later something thumped down on her feet and she leapt up, whimpering with fear. It made a tiny mewing sound. The cat! She couldn't see anything, but she didn't like the memory of its staring yellow eyes and the feeling that it could see her when she could see nothing at all. For what seemed an age, she waited. Eventually she heard a rhythmic, purring noise from the cat, which sounded much more friendly and reassuring. She eased her weight down along the settle again until her feet, still in their dirty-white socks, met the creature's soft body. She snatched her legs away again in a panic, but nothing happened. Drawn by the warmth, she let her feet slide back against the purring cat.

She thought of her mother: not the frail woman clinging to the door that morning, but Mom as she had been before, hard-pressed, but kindly and comforting. Then she thought of Tommy, of seeing him being led away by that rough-looking man – Tommy looking lost and frightened. She began to snuffle and cry.

'Mom . . . want my mom . . . Want Tommy . . .' But soon she was overcome by sleep.

Miss Peters came to fetch her the next morning. Margaret burst into tears at the sight of her. Mrs Paige had given her thin salty porridge and kept talking about something called the Other Side, while peeling apples at the table.

'The border between life and the Other Side is as thin as a chiffon scarf,' she had said, her hank of tarry hair lolloping from side to side in the hairnet as she moved her head. 'Not everyone understands that. But the dead are all around us, reaching out, longing for communication, if we would only hear them. Eat up your porridge – you won't be getting anything else. That teacher'll be here for you soon.' Muttering, she added, 'Interfering harridans, the whole lot of them.'

The rank taste of the food had settled in Margaret's mouth.

'Where's my brother?' she howled as soon as Miss Peters appeared, seeming like a piece of home because she was at least familiar. 'I want Tommy. 'E said 'e'd be with me! 'E was s'posed to look after me – our mom said!'

Miss Peters was wearing a navy hat and coat, which made her look rather smart, especially beside Mrs Paige with her baggy beige cardigan and flopping hair. Miss Peters was thin, long-nosed and nervy, but she had a kind heart and a protective sense of responsibility to her charges. Looking upset, she bent down towards Margaret – this poor, unfortunate-looking little girl with her lazy eye and threadbare, cut-down clothes, her dark brown hair cut roughly in the shape of a pudding basin. She was the very youngest of the evacuees and certainly the most wretched-looking.

'I'm sorry, Margaret dear, we had to let the local people choose who they wanted staying with them, when we arrived. And Tommy was taken to stay on a farm a few miles away because the farmer wants him to help them.'

'Is 'e coming to school?' Margaret sobbed.

Unhappily Miss Peters replied, 'I do hope so, but I'm afraid I really don't know for sure.' She rallied herself. 'Come along now, dear, wipe your face and we'll go along to the school ourselves and then perhaps we'll find out?'

She reached out and took Margaret's hand, nodded coolly at Mrs Paige, who stared back with an air of insolence, and they set off. Margaret looked up at her teacher with adoration. The feel of Miss Peters' hand was a great comfort that morning as they set off along the lane between the dripping trees.

Days merged in her memory after that. There was no sign of Tommy, though Miss Peters said to Margaret that she would see if they could arrange to visit him on the farm. She and the two other teachers struggled to educate and keep an eye on their charges, who were a variety of ages and were scattered across three villages and the surrounding farms. There was a tiny school in Lowick village, to which Margaret had been sent, which was quickly overwhelmed by the number of evacuees. They had to overspill into a room at the vicarage some days in the week where they sat round a huge table, or into a nearby barn, perched on bales of straw.

After Margaret, the next-youngest evacuee was a

little girl called Joan, a few months older. Miss Peters took special care of Margaret, while another of the teachers looked out for Joan, though she was more fortunate, having been billeted with her eight-year-old sister.

On those glowing autumn days the hedges brightened with berries, and at one point on the walk to and from school, orchard branches hung over a wall, dipping down towards the verge and bearing the reddest of apples. Every so often they shed fallers with a little thump and rolled along the grass, which could be munched straight away, so long as you got there before anyone else.

Walking home from school with Miss Peters was always interesting, seeing the carts go past drawn by horses, which seemed gigantic to Margaret; and hens pecking in the road; and the older village children hurrying past, sometimes friendly, sometimes not. Some days an elderly lady sat on a low stool outside her cottage door shelling peas or topping and tailing gooseberries and they would stop for a few words.

One day, as they were walking back to Mrs Paige's house, an apple fell from a branch with a small thud right in front of them.

'Look!' Miss Peters hurried to pick it up. 'That one's hardly got a mark on it.' She polished it on her sleeve and handed it to Margaret. 'You eat that, dear – it'll bring the colour to your cheeks.'

Margaret reached out for the shiny red globe in wonder. When she bit ravenously into it, the flesh was a sweet, tangy taste of heaven. She had never had an apple like it. A smile spread over her face.

'S'nice,' she announced through her mouthful.

'Good!' A smile appeared on her teacher's tense

features as well. 'Oh, look, and there's another one come down – we're in luck today!'

Hand in hand they continued on along the lane, past the church, the last cluster of houses and the old field gate, to where Mrs Paige's down-at-heel cottage nestled at the fringe of the village. Its whitewashed front was stained green and the roof sagged.

Margaret remembered Miss Peters' questions as all one conversation, though perhaps it wasn't.

'Do you have any other clothes, Margaret? Has Mrs Paige washed them for you? Have you been able to have a wash?'

A shake of the head to all these questions. Words must have passed between the two women after this, as Mrs Paige did start, grumblingly, to pull up water from the well in the garden and heat it to wash Margaret's clothes occasionally, hanging them on the range to dry overnight. She made Margaret wash out of a bucket. (There was another snatch of conversation that Margaret overheard between the two young teachers one day: 'The woman doesn't have the first *notion* how to care for a child . . .')

'Does Mrs Paige have many visitors?' Miss Peters asked, barely above a whisper.

Margaret shook her head. She had never seen anyone come to the house.

After another pause Miss Peters said, 'Have you heard from your mother?'

Another shake of the head.

'Is . . .' Miss Peters hesitated. 'Is Mrs Paige treating you well?'

This question brought about a vague, floating feeling in Margaret's head. It was a question she barely understood. *Treating you well?* It was not something she

61

knew how to think about. As for finding any words to begin on Mrs Paige, with her strange rooms and her cat pouncing on Margaret's feet in the dark, and Ernest's riding crop (which had been pointed out to her more than once, a thin, black leather thing with a loop at the end) hanging on the back of the door. ('It can lash you,' Mrs Paige had told her, staring hard at Margaret, 'so beware. It can lash you badly, that can') . . .

Miss Peters stopped. 'Look at me, Margaret. That's right, dear. Is everything all right? You would tell me if you were worried about anything?'

Having no idea what other answer she might give, Margaret nodded her head.

'I'm going to show you round,' Mrs Paige said, the afternoon after Margaret's arrival. 'The abode of Mr and Mrs Ernest Paige.'

Her eyes stretched wide for a second, as if they might pop out of her head, then she blinked hard. It was something she did every now and then. 'You take note, my girl.'

She bent down suddenly and put her face close to Margaret's. Her breath smelled of old onions. Margaret saw, close up, that the mole on Mrs Paige's left cheek had dark hairs sprouting out of it and that her skin was like old cheese rind. She was dressed in a sagging combination of wool and tweed.

'I don't have to have you here, you know – it wasn't my desire to have you. They think ten and six is enough to make a person do anything. Huh! I didn't want you in here, disturbing Ernest and me. You'll have to fit in with Mr Paige and me, or there'll be trouble. And listen to me . . .'

She grabbed Margaret's shoulder so hard it hurt and her face was menacing. Margaret had to cross her chubby legs to stop herself spending a penny out of fright.

'I don't want any gossip, or there'll be trouble. You'll be sleeping out in the shed with the rats if I have a peep out of you. Not a word – d'you comprehend?'

Rubbing her shoulder, Margaret nodded. She didn't know what 'comprehend' meant.

Mrs Paige straightened up with an apparent shift in mood. 'But I'll show you my house – and the sickroom, so you know what's what.'

Margaret had still not met Mr Paige. She had wondered if he had already gone out to work, but now she realized he must be ill in bed.

She was already familiar with the back kitchen, with the dusty range that looked as if no blacklead had been near it for years. Mom had been forever cleaning theirs, when she was well. Mrs Paige didn't seem to bother. It was the warmest room in the house, for which Margaret was grateful, as she slept there with only the thin blanket.

'I don't use this room.' Mrs Paige led her to the front parlour through which they had passed in the dark the night before. Margaret walked into the middle of it and stood looking round. There was the front door and a window looking out onto the street. Two wooden chairs stood by the empty fireplace, and between them a worn-looking bodged rug. Apart from these, the room was empty.

'I don't come in here. I don't want nosy parkers looking in on me and my life,' was all she said.

The staircase ran up between the two rooms, its treads half-covered by a runner of faded carpet in crimson and black. At the top a narrow landing divided the two rooms.

'I sleep in the small room at the back,' Nora Paige said, pushing the door open just enough for Margaret to peer in. All she could see was a boxroom with a single bed and chair in it and pale-blue, cheerless walls. There seemed to be some dark curtains hanging each side of the window, but there was no covering over the floorboards, which also had a dusty look to them.

'I let Ernest have the main bedroom – it means he can be comfortable and it's the lighter of the two rooms. You see, Ernest fought in the Boer War and he got so used to the sunshine in the southern climes of Africa that he's quite miserable without it. He thrives on sunlight.'

Closing up her room, she unlatched the door opposite. As she predicted, late-afternoon sunshine was pouring in through the front window, falling on the white sheets of a large bed. The bedstead was of carved oak.

'There's a lovely view of the fields,' Mrs Paige proclaimed, going to the window. Her shoes were black, with thin laces, and very down-at-heel, and her brown lisle stockings wrinkled round her ankles. 'Oh, I think we need a bit of this late-summer air in here!' She unfastened the casement. 'Come and see, Meg.'

Her voice was softer than usual now. Margaret stood on tiptoe to look over the sill. Between the bushes edging the other side of the lane she saw the gold of a recently harvested field stretching before her.

'They've got those so-called Land Army girls work-ing on the farm now,' Mrs Paige said with contempt. 'As if they'd have any idea what it takes.'

Margaret turned round slowly. The bed had thick

pillows propped against the bedhead, and on the near side the covers were thrown back as if someone had just got out. The eiderdown was made of a cheerful fabric of tiny pink roses. On the little table beside the bed Margaret saw a pair of spectacles, a candle stub in a holder, a glass of water and a book. Fascinated, she also made out a set of false teeth. There was a chair near the bed with a pair of trousers hanging over the back and, beside it, a chest of drawers on which rested various objects of male toilet: a tooth mug, shaving brush and razor. In the far corner stood a dark-wood cupboard.

'There we are. I keep Ernest nice and comfortable,' Mrs Paige said. 'You can see that, can't you – have you ever seen a more comfortable-looking bed?'

Margaret shook her head, for that was the truth – she hadn't. She wondered if Mr Paige had just popped out to relieve himself.

'There, you've seen our abode,' Mrs Paige said. 'I keep it spick and span in here, as you can see. We'll leave our Ernest in peace now – out you go.'

As Margaret went obediently to the top of the stairs she heard Mrs Paige ask very quietly, 'Is there anything you need, dear?' Then the door closed and she followed Margaret downstairs, seeming more cheerful than usual.

'So,' she said, putting the kettle on to boil. 'That's us. You see, don't you?'

Margaret stared at her, then nodded her head. She wondered if Mr Paige had been hiding in the cupboard.

Nine

Fragments of memory kept firing through Margaret's mind. They'd sent her home from the hospital, on a slightly lower dose of Valium than before, but she was not free of it – not by a long way. She felt despair at the thought that she might never escape it. Now that she was back home, it felt as if she ought to be able to take up her life again, humdrum and familiar, no more fuss. Just get on with it. Be the same old Margaret. It wasn't as if Fred expected much.

But she couldn't concentrate on anything. It felt as if her head had been plugged into the mains, with flashes of electricity sparking through it.

'Maybe you need to rest,' Fred kept saying. He was doing his best to be helpful. 'If you need to go to bed, go. There's nothing that can't wait, is there?'

So most afternoons she found herself up in bed again, under the blue-and-white duvet, hearing noises from the street. It was all she could cope with – shutting herself away while her mind raced.

The alarm clock on her bedside table ticked loudly. She lay on her side watching it. She liked the way it broke through the endless silence. If she stared hard enough, she thought she could see the black minute-hand moving round.

And then she would move onto her back, close her eyes and the jolting assaults of memory would return like snatches of a film playing in her head. Certain images burned intensely in her mind: Mom clinging to the door that morning, with the last food she would ever give her children; the door of the shed slamming shut; Nora Paige's eyes widening, then blinking convulsively. It happened, Margaret had learned, when a strong emotion was brewing in her, her thick body charging up with it.

These were memories she thought she had buried forever, the years of evacuation sealed in her as in an airless tomb. And now she couldn't stop them. It was hard to set anything in order, confused as things had been by her infant mind; and now, in her half-waking state, she was powerless even to try.

'She's quite an educated woman, I believe . . .' That was Miss Peters' voice, half-whispered to another teacher when they were in the vicarage for their lessons. There was a blackboard with sums on it. 'Or she was once. There are books in the house.'

There were: volumes with dark-red and black covers. Nora Paige sat by the range at night, squeezed into the straight-backed armchair that was pushed into the corner in the daytime, reading by the light of the oil lamp. She did not possess a wireless to break the silence. Margaret was expected to make herself invisible.

'You sit quiet there,' Mrs Paige would instruct her, pointing at the settle with its hard cushions. 'Not a word, d'you hear?'

The aching boredom of those evenings! Somewhere, within a couple of days of arriving, Margaret had lost Peggy Doll, dropping her from her pocket, never to be seen again. There was nothing whatever to do, and no Tommy to make her laugh or invent games. Margaret would sit, sometimes with Seamus beside her, who would at least let her stroke him. Other times he was moody and lashed out with claws that drew blood.

Margaret would draw her legs up and pick at her knees, or at a thread in her old grey skirt, or at the piping at the edge of the cushions. The clock ticked, round-faced on the mantel, its pendulum swinging, and she watched, half-hypnotized. Mrs Paige turned the pages of her book, cleared her throat, scratched her scalp, a finger questing delicately through the hairnet.

Earlier on in these endless evenings she always prepared food to take up to Ernest.

'The poor man needs my company, lying alone up there all day.' Only one plate of the thin stew would go up with her. 'I have to feed it to him, you know,' she would say.

As Margaret ate her own meagre ration of food, picking up the plate to lick off the last traces of gravy, she could hear Mrs Paige's voice through the floorboards, though not what was said. She strained to hear Mr Paige's replies, but could never make them out.

School was a pleasant dream in comparison: the warm bodies round the table at the back of the vicarage; the bustling vicar's wife, Mrs Bodley-Fisher; the crackling fire in the grate. Had they been worried about her, she wondered now? There had been odd snatches of conversation that she overheard, their eyes fixed on her face as they talked with heads close together. But each day Miss Peters brought her from Nora Paige's house to her classes, then took her back again. New billets were not easy to find.

Winter drew in and their breath was white on the air. She had worn out her pumps and the *Birmingham Mail* charity boots, which had once been Tommy's, were still too big. She clumped along in them, her legs bare in all weathers under the old skirt and vest and royal-blue jumper. All the time she was hungry – so hungry.

One day, in the vicarage, during the mid-morning break, when they were each given a beaker of milk and a biscuit, Margaret had wolfed hers down in two bites. Joan was sitting next to her, taking tiny nibbles of hers. Margaret felt saliva rush into her mouth. Quick as a snake she leaned round, snatched the biscuit and stuffed it into her mouth. Joan set up a shrieking.

'Whatever's wrong, Joan?' Miss Cooper asked. She was the tall redhead who stomped through the snow to fetch Joan to school each day.

'Margaret took my biscuit!'

'Margaret!' Miss Cooper bore down on her. Margaret chewed and swallowed quickly, as if the disappearance of the biscuit could make it not have happened. Everyone was now staring at her. 'What d'you think you're doing, snatching Joan's biscuit?'

Margaret stared back in silence. Her appearance seemed to aggravate people. 'Well, say something, child.'

'I dunno,' Margaret said through her adenoids.

Miss Cooper clicked her tongue. 'Well, don't do it again. That's *greedy* and it's *stealing*. Now, Joan, there's another biscuit for you. Eat up.'

Mrs Paige fed her less and less. Because Margaret was a sturdy child it took a while before anyone noticed, though Miss Cooper often urged her to buck up and listen. But one day soon after she arrived at the makeshift school, blackness suddenly closed down on her like a lid. She came out of the faint feeling sick and confused.

Then it started snowing. On the way to school Miss Peters coughed, bending over, eyes streaming.

'Oh dear,' she kept murmuring as she straightened up. 'How am I to manage?'

Soon afterwards Miss Peters disappeared. Miss Cooper arrived the next morning in a great hurry, having already walked to collect Joan.

'I'm afraid Miss Peters has been taken ill,' she said, peering curiously in at Nora Paige's cottage door. There was nothing to see: just the unlived-in parlour. 'They've had to take her home – she's developed pneumonia.'

'Oh dear,' Mrs Paige said. 'I'm sorry to hear that.' Her eyes widened, then blinked hard.

What did the teachers say among themselves about Nora Paige, Margaret wondered now? Did the vicar's wife say, 'Oh, she's been a recluse since her husband died'? These things she only found out later. 'TB, you know, soon after the war ended. He must have been dead fifteen years by now at least.'

'Well, she's an odd one all right,' she heard Miss Cooper mutter as the door closed.

Margaret, cold and weak, her feet already so chilled that she could barely feel them, followed Miss Cooper through the snow. The wind bit into her cheeks. Each meal she had was smaller than the last. She was eternally hungry.

It was almost impossible to steal food. Everything in the low cupboard was in tins or jars, and the big meat safe with its mesh door, where Mrs Paige kept bread, cheese, meat and butter, was locked and the key removed.

'Don't think I don't know your cunning,' Nora Paige would say, slipping the key into her pocket. 'I'm not having you taking the food out of my poor sick husband's mouth.'

There were no more free apples, or blackberries in the hedgerow, now.

One evening Mrs Paige was standing by the table in her flat shoes, the beige wool of her sleeves pushed up her brawny arms as she spooned out a portion of food to take to Ernest. On a small plate she put a helping for Margaret – two morsels of meat, a spoonful of gravy, a mouthful of boiled potato.

'You see, Meg,' she announced, going to the door with her plateful. 'What I have discovered is that death is a state preferable to life for some people. No more pain and suffering, no more cold and anguish. I believe Ernest finds it so. After death has occurred, once they have passed through the eternal portal, it's so much easier for all concerned. I have come to the conclusion that this is how it is supposed to be. You'll find it to be true, I'm sure.'

Margaret pushed the tiny meal into her mouth. She had no idea what Mrs Paige was talking about.

She didn't know what devilment had driven her to it. It was a Saturday, a mild day during a temporary thaw. The two teachers who were left now that Miss Peters had gone had decided to gather their charges for an outing.

It was noon. Mrs Paige had given Margaret her midday meal – half a slice of dry bread – and gone out to the garden with a rake to gather up the skin of sodden leaves in between remaining patches of snow. Margaret watched her for a moment from the back doorstep and saw the movement of her sturdy calves, encased in a pair of man's boots – perhaps Ernest's? – across the grass, the rhythmic movements of the rake.

The air was damp and mild for late November. It was ages until the teachers were coming to collect her for the nature walk. Margaret wandered through the house and went to sit on the stairs. Much of the time now she was lethargic and hazy in the head. She never seemed to learn much at school. Mostly she just wanted to sink into the warmth and go to sleep. But they had all been cooped up and bored because of the snow, and the bit of bread had given her a spurt of energy.

Without willing it, she found herself climbing the stairs. She knelt on the last step from the top, looking from door to door. She didn't know what to feel about Ernest. She believed that he was in there – every day he was given meals, his room was cleaned, his opinions sought. But she had never even so much as heard him clear his throat. How bored he must be too! Maybe he'd like someone to come and see him.

Listening carefully, she could hear nothing. He must be asleep. To her surprise she saw that the latch of the door was not fastened. She would be able to peep at Ernest, the way she used to peep at her father, Ted Winters, when he slept drunk by the hearth. She'd found a fascination with his sagging mouth and dark stubble.

She crept across the landing and pushed the door open, her heart thumping. Supposing he woke up and shouted at her, and told Mrs Paige what she'd done? Putting her head round the door, she relaxed, seeing that the bed was empty. Had he gone down to the privy? Was he hiding in the cupboard again? Perhaps he had heard her coming and was watching her. The door of the cupboard was shut tight, but this didn't mean he wasn't there . . .

Seconds passed and, as nothing happened, she crept forward. The best thing in the room was Mr Paige's false teeth, grinning at her from the bedside table. She'd never seen any before and they held a fascination for her. Daring herself, she picked up the teeth and pulled them apart, then let them snap closed. The clacking sound and the sight of them made her giggle. After a few goes she held them in her hand and wandered round, picking up other things. The bristles of the shaving brush were stiffened by soap into a solid mass. She looked in the slanted mirror, saw her white, thin face, her dark eyes, one looking back at her directly, the other wandering to the side. Her hair was longer now and straggly.

Margaret went to the window. Now that the leaves of the hedge opposite had died back there was a clear view of the field, ploughed up for winter, a few lines of snow still caught in the furrows. She clacked the teeth between her fingers, staring out.

She didn't even hear Mrs Paige. She was caught from behind by the hair and was swung around, with a burning yank on her scalp that made her scream.

'What are you doing, you crossed-eyed little brat?' Mrs Paige was demented with rage. 'You monster! You filthy vermin! How dare you touch my things, my Ernest's things? Out, you little rat – get out!'

The dentures fell to the floor and several of the teeth jumped out of them. Margaret was dragged downstairs by the hair, mewling and crying.

Mrs Paige shoved her out of the back door and the few steps across to the wooden shed behind the house . . .

She struggled, crying, begging. In with the rats, Mrs Paige had threatened. Desperate, she tried to pull away, to get out of the woman's grasp, but Mrs Paige was so big, so enraged, that all Margaret could do was jerk and pull, crying, 'No, no, don't – not in there . . , No-o-o!'

'Mom?' The voice cut through her terrified remember-ings. 'Mom, it's all right . . .' A hand soothed her shoulder. 'I think you've been having a dream – don't worry.'

Margaret stared up at the face, the dark eyes like her own, the familiar voice. Of course, her own daughter, Karen! Here she was in her room. It wasn't 1939 – it was now. She almost wept with relief.

'Must've been dreaming,' she said muzzily.

'It's all right, Mom.' Karen struggled to sound in command, though she was frightened. 'Look, I've just got home. I'll make us both a nice cup of tea. Dad'll be back soon, and I can get the dinner on, so don't worry – all right?'

'Thanks,' Margaret said. She sat up, reaching for her specs, feeling stunned and foolish. 'Thanks, love.'

Ten

May 1984

The next Tuesday morning Joanne pushed Amy along to the playgroup, very relieved to have somewhere to go. I need a break from family, she thought guiltily. As she turned into Villa Road she took deep breaths of the warm air, feeling as if she had been let out of a lock-up. Karen had been on the phone again last night, on about Mom having bad dreams and seeming frightened and not herself. And Dave's mood had slid down again. She badly needed to get out.

While Margaret had been in hospital, Dave had been as kind and supportive as it was possible to be, minding Amy while Joanne went to visit, sending a get-well card to his mother-in-law, and treating Joanne as if she was fragile and needed his care and protection. But she could feel it beginning to wear off. Nothing had happened, but she could sense she was back to walking on eggshells, that his mood was building up again, until some unpredictable moment when he would explode.

She hurried along, anxious not to be late, realizing how much she was looking forward to the toddler group, to seeing Tess and, even more, Sooky and Priya.

'Who're we going to see – d'you remember?' She

leaned over the buggy while she was still moving to talk to Amy.

Amy twisted round to look up at her.

'You're going to see your little friend Priya.'

'Piya!' Amy couldn't manage the 'pr' yet. She jiggled against the straps in excitement. 'Piya!'

It felt wonderful to Joanne to think they had friends. Michelle had always been her best mate before, but Michelle didn't have children and lived so far away – not to mention the rift between them over Dave. She couldn't count on Michelle for everything now; she needed to make other friends. She walked much more confidently into the church hall, said hello to Tess and helped her finish getting the things out. She was pleased with the way Tess almost seemed to expect her now to come early and help. As the other mothers arrived, she found it easier to talk to them too.

'Where Piya?' Amy asked.

'She'll be here in a bit, I expect,' Joanne said. 'What d'you want to do, Amy?'

Amy immediately pointed at the painting table.

'How about waiting for that till Priya gets here – shall we go and play with the dollies instead?'

But no, nothing else would do. Joanne sat beside Amy again, talking to Mavis. She kept looking at the door. Sooky was often late. But after the first hour had gone by she realized Sooky and Priya were not coming. She was surprised by just how disappointed she felt.

When it was over they all spilled out onto the pavement. Despite Sooky not turning up, Joanne felt quite cheerful. She had had a chat with a few people and hadn't felt so crippled by shyness as she had the first few times. A nervous new mother had come, and she had been able to show her what to do. Just a bit of conversation and company made the whole day seem so much brighter. Humming, she turned to cross the road.

She stopped with a jolt. Dave was standing there on the other side, by the big *gurdwara*, the Sikh temple, staring straight at her. He was waiting, hands pushed into the pockets of his jeans. In those seconds she was struck again by how good-looking he was – blond, strong and athletic. And how frightening.

As she pushed the buggy across the road, her heart was hammering and she had to force a smile back onto her face.

'Look who's here, Amy – Daddy's come to meet us!'

She could see some of the other women turning to look. *Why the hell is he here?* she thought. But she knew the signs. He hadn't come out of interest in Amy: he'd come to spy on her.

'Hello!' she greeted him. 'What're you doing here? Have you got an early dinner break?'

He didn't smile back. He looked fed up and angry.

'Yeah,' he said sulkily. 'Thought I'd come down.'

'That's nice.' But it didn't feel nice at all. It felt as if he had intruded on her day. 'We can have something to eat together.'

As they walked home she chattered away about what Amy had been doing. She could feel the vibes of his bad mood, but she couldn't think of anything she'd done to cause it.

'Shall I make you a sandwich?' she called through

from the kitchen once they were inside. He'd sat down at the table, looking through the paper. 'There's cheese – and a bit of ham.'

His voice came through to her, hard and sarcastic. 'Yes, all right – make me a sandwich then. If it's not too much trouble for you.'

She went to the door.

'Well, which d'you want: ham or cheese?'

'Ham,' he said savagely. 'With mustard. And tomato.'

Oh no. Joanne rummaged frantically through the fridge. No tomatoes.

'I'm sorry, love.' She went back to speak to him. 'We haven't got any tomatoes in . . .'

He stared at her, then leapt up, kicking the chair back so that it tipped over.

'For ****'s sake. All I want's a bit of dinner – that's all. Not too much to ask, is it?' He picked the chair up and slammed it under the table. Amy started to cry. 'Forget it, I'll go to the chippy. At least I can get a decent bite to eat there.'

A moment later he had gone, slamming the door.

Joanne went to Amy and picked her up. Could Amy feel her shaking?

'Sshh, babby – it's all right. Don't worry. Daddy's just a bit grumpy 'cause he's hungry.' She kissed Amy's forehead. 'Shall Mommy make you an egg with soldiers?'

She settled Amy in her high chair with a little board book and went to put a pan on the gas. Staring at the orange-and-mauve flame, she was shaking with upset and anger. At other times when he got worked up she had blamed herself, convinced she must have done something to make him so upset. He was so sure everything was her fault that she had started to believe it as well. But this time she knew it wasn't true.

'I never asked you to come home and spoil everything, did I?' she whispered. 'Why couldn't you just stay at work and keep out of the way? You can get your own bloody dinner.'

Even her own anger upset her. She had always loved Dave, felt tender towards him for the hurts and difficulties of his life, his trying to be the big man when his father was dead and his mother like a childish hippy, with her magic crystals and scented candles and ridiculous theories, completely wrapped up in herself. But over these months he had become like a stranger and she was gradually losing respect for him, as well as the fondness that made her keep forgiving him.

Later he arrived home with a bunch of flowers – roses – which he must have had to go out of his way to buy.

She saw him come through the door with them and for a moment her temper flared again. So you think you can just buy me off? Why can't you just not be so nasty in the first place? All afternoon she'd been churned up, not knowing if he was suddenly going to come home again, afraid of what was going to happen next. But she wanted to keep the peace, wanted things to be better. What choice did she have? They needed things to be right for Amy.

'Here,' he said gruffly, in the hall. 'Bought yer these. Sorry about earlier.'

Sorry about earlier. Was that it? At least he hadn't hit her. She swallowed.

'Oh, they're lovely. Thanks. I'll put them in that nice vase – remember the one Karen gave us for our wedding?'

He held out the flowers, but as she went to take them he didn't release them, so they ended up staring at each other, both holding the bunch of crimson roses. He studied her face.

'I need to know . . .' He trailed off and looked down.

'What?' She stifled her impatience.

'I just need to know you're my wife.' He still couldn't meet her eyes.

Joanne let go of the flowers, sighing. She suddenly felt tired to the core. 'What d'you mean?'

'I dunno.' He was upset now. 'Here, look, take 'em – they're for you.' She obeyed, raising them to her nose, almost for comfort. They were tight buds and didn't smell of much. 'I just get these thoughts . . . I'm sorry. Look,' he said wretchedly, 'give us a kiss, will yer?'

She obliged, holding the flowers out to one side. Dave closed his eyes and held her close, breathing her in. His lips reached for hers, then he pulled back.

'Say yer love me?'

'Oh, Dave – you know I—'

'Say it!' The anger was back, quick as striking a match.

'I love you – you know I do. I'm your wife.'

The evening was quiet and fairly harmonious. They ate their dinner and watched TV. Later Dave wanted to make love to her, so she let him. She lay in the dark afterwards trying to decide what she felt about him, about all of it.

Eleven

Early that morning Sooky had crept downstairs, carrying Priya.

'We get you some milk, shall we?' she whispered. The little girl was wide-eyed, still dazed with sleep. 'Milk and toast?'

She always spoke to Priya in English. She wanted her to be good at English, to be quick-witted and get it when someone told a joke. It would help her fit in and make friends easily at school. Priya, like most children growing up soaked in more than one language, had taken her time to say anything at all except Mama and Baba. Now she was beginning to untangle the threads of words, to work out what to say to whom and in which language.

Sooky's mother, Meena Kaur, didn't speak English, even after more than twenty years in the country, so she always spoke to her grandchildren in Punjabi. To Sooky, these days, she didn't speak at all.

Sooky hoped she was the only one up and about, that there would be a bit of peace – before it all started off again. Even today, though, despite what was happening in India, Dad would have left for the factory by seven. He liked to work on the accounts before the other workers came in, said he couldn't think straight to handle figures by the evening. Mom claimed the factory was his mistress, but these days this was said in teasing, not complaint.

All day yesterday the house had been in a ferment: phone calls to friends in London, from the uncles in Delhi, Sikh friends and neighbours calling round, the hall full of '*Sat Sri Akal*' greetings as people came and went, with heated conversations and debates and the TV on – everyone glued, horrified, to the news reports.

Things in Punjab had abruptly reached a head. After the long lead-up to the movement for Khalistan, a separate Sikh homeland, the leader of the movement, Jarnail Singh Bhindranwale, and his followers had occupied the holy of holies, the Golden Temple in Amritsar. The army had closed in on them and now Prime Minister Indira Gandhi had ordered government forces to storm the temple and flush out the rebels. For all Sikhs, whatever their politics, 'Operation Blue Star' (this assault on the temple) was a horrifying outrage. It represented total sacrilege.

Rajdev, her elder brother, was the most explosive of all. He was obsessed with Khalistan. He was forever on at Dad for not wearing a turban the way he did himself now.

'What is wrong with you?' Raj would rave. 'Call yourself a Sikh? How can anyone tell you're a Sikh? They want to make Hindus of us, and you play right into their hands! You could be anything – Hindu, Muslim; you could be a Christian, for all anyone can see. Have you no pride?'

Khushwant, their dad, a sagging, cuddly-looking man, would sigh.

'Look, I leave all this politics to others – I've got a business to run . . .'

He'd take the cup of sweet tea that Mom would make for him when he got home, with a small stack of chocolate digestives on a plate, and keep as far away from Raj as possible. Raj seemed to be everyone's conscience these days, along with his sharp-nosed wife Roopinder, who was like a glove puppet, echoing everything he said.

'Why d'you have to push it all the time?' Sooky had said to Raj, before everything blew up in India, so that you couldn't just ignore it. 'You've got your politics – Dad's got his. Why make trouble?'

Raj had turned to her, his thin face with its long, straggly beard full of contempt. 'What do you know, *Besharam*? I was the one born in India – it's *my* country. They owe us. Sikhs have always been an oppressed people. We'll have our own land: a *Sikh* land.'

And *then* what? Sooky had thought bitterly. If the land was full of 'holy' people like you and Roop, I certainly wouldn't want to live there.

Not once had he, her brother – with whom she'd grown up and played, who'd walked beside her to school every day – ever given her a hearing about her marriage to Jagdesh or tried to see her point of view. He used to call her *Veer-ji*, the term of affection for his younger sister. Now all he ever called her was *Besharam* (shameless one) and condemned her for bringing dishonour to the family.

And Roopinder, smug with her two children and another on the way, just liked being nasty. It was a sort of hobby with her, Sooky realized, the only real outlet she had for her intelligence, and a way of making herself feel superior.

Sooky pushed the kitchen door open and, to her dismay, saw that she was not the first up after all. Raj was there, already dressed, his blue turban neatly fastened. He was standing by the sink, hunched up with the radio pressed to his ear.

'All I can get is bloody Mark Tully!' he fumed.

The Indian government had imposed a news blackout across Punjab as soon as the crisis developed. It was hard to get the full picture of what was going on, let alone anything from Bhindranwale's people. Jarnail Singh Bhindranwale, the leader of the separatists occupying the Golden Temple, was Raj's hero.

Sooky felt a powerful stab of loneliness. She held Priya on one hip and filled the kettle, looking at her brother's intense face out of the corner of her eye. He was such a stranger to her. He had grown his hair and insisted on observing all the religious rules. But it didn't seem to make him any happier or nicer. What had happened to that warm, mischievous little boy she had known, who had giggled like a burbling stream, watching *Dr Who* and sharing his sweets with her? Now he was hard-faced, rigid and cruel – to her, anyway.

Last month he had joined the rally in London, marching with thousands of Sikhs demanding a Sikh homeland – Khalistan. He had pinned up a Khalistan flag on his and Roopinder's bedroom wall and spoke in slogans. He seemed to feel contempt for anyone who did not feel exactly the way he did.

'Don't you care?' he erupted, clicking the radio off in frustration. 'They're slaughtering our brothers . . .' She could see he was close to tears.

'Of *course* I care,' she said. The situation had been in everyone's mind, on everyone's lips, building up over the past weeks. The army storming the Golden Temple, tanks pointed at the *Akal Takhat* – it was unthinkable, horribly distressing for every Sikh. 'But, Raj, I don't know what I can do. And . . .' She knew it was a mistake even as she said it, 'I just don't think Bhindranwale is necessarily—'

She had lit the blue touchpaper.

'You don't think he's *what*?' he sneered savagely. 'What would you know, you stupid *woman*? Sant Bhindranwale is our only hope.' He slapped his hand on the table.

'What do you know about politics: about having any kind of ideas, stupid? You can't even keep a husband. I bet you don't even know what to do in bed – look at you, thin and dried up like a dead stick!'

His face twisting with disgust, he crossed the kitchen. For a moment she thought he was going to hit her, but he went out.

'I've got to go to work.' The door slammed.

Priya started to snuffle, sensitive to the aggression in his voice.

'It's okay, baby, it's okay,' Sooky soothed her, sitting her in her high chair. 'Mommy's getting you a drink.'

But as she turned away, tears rose in her own eyes. She tried to be tough and resilient for Priya's sake, as well as her own, and not to be miserable. But living back at home, with the hostility of so much of her family, felt lonely and bitter. Dad was kindly enough in a distant way, but he didn't know how to treat her now. She'd always been his favourite, but now she seemed only to fit into the framework of 'disgrace'. Anyway, he was always so tired. He left what he thought was women's business to the women – which turned out, in Dad's book, to mean almost anything going on within the four walls of the house.

Raj and Roopinder were sanctimonious and spiteful.

But it was Mom's reaction that hurt the most. Her endless silence seemed to contain such pain and conflict that Sooky had no words for it. It was all the more confusing because Meena had seemed to agree that Sooky needed to get Priya away from Jaz, her husband.

'He keeps taking her off into the bedroom,' she explained, weeping once she arrived back from Derby. 'He was doing things to her. He locks the door. He's not normal.'

She had speedily realized that her husband was a superficial, money-obsessed oaf without a hint of sensitivity to anyone else. That was bad enough, but as his wife she would have had to live with it. But his sexual weirdness was another thing altogether. Relations with her were a cold duty. He seemed far more interested in his small daughter. When she told Meena this, her mother turned her head away from her in horror. Even at the cost of the family *izzat*, or honour, she agreed, painfully, that Priya must be kept away from Jaz.

Sooky was so desperate to be rid of him that she had taken the quickest way out and shouldered the blame. Jaz claimed that they were divorcing on grounds of adultery – hers. So far as everyone else was concerned, she had done the thing that no wife was supposed to do: she had broken the marriage and behaved like a whore. She had grossly shamed her family in the community. *That daughter* – she was someone to be whispered about behind hands, the eyes boring into her, in the street, the *gurdwara*. She never went there now. She knew she was a cruel embarrassment to her mother.

And now, at home, all she got was this endless wall of silence, almost as if Meena believed the charge of adultery to be true.

Handing Priya her bottle of milk, Sooky looked down at her. *My daughter ...*

She remembered Mom as she was growing up, rough and ready with her Punjabi village ways, but fond.

Meena had proudly borne her sons, as a dutiful wife, but she had shown as great a joy in her daughters. They were company and comfort, she said. Daughters-in-law could not be guaranteed to be the same – an unknown quantity. Tears running down her cheeks now, Sooky remembered the hurried touch of her mother's hands when she was little, the way she barked out commands. But that was just Mom. She'd not had much education or gentleness herself. But she had been like a rock, always there: the clink of her bangles as she moved round the house; her soft silky suits that you could snuggle up to while watching the television that she barely understood a word of (she had loved *Tom and Jerry*: anyone could understand that); and her food, the spicy smells wafting from the kitchen, the way she sang little snatches of Punjabi songs while she was cooking.

Stroking Priya's soft hair, Sooky whispered, 'I'll never do this to you. I want you to choose your life – be free as a bird . . .' But with a pang of misgiving she wondered: what if Priya chose to be different, to veer off the narrow track that women were permitted – would she face a lonely life, full of disapproval?

The best thing about home was her other two siblings. Pavan, her brother, who was eighteen, was a studious boy, in the run-up to his A-levels. He was doing science, and unlike Raj who had left school at eighteen, wanted to study to be an engineer. He never said anything about what had happened, about Sooky's marriage, except sometimes he'd just look at her and say sweetly, 'You all right, Sis?' And she'd always say, 'Yes thanks, Pav.' That was enough: to know he was not against her. And her sister Harpreet, fifteen and doing her GCSEs, was obviously delighted to have her home, even though she was worried for her.

'There was such a *fuss*,' she said when they were chatting soon after Sooky came home. They were sitting on the bed in the room they would now share again. Harpreet's school jumper was flung across the pillow, her old stuffed rabbit and teddy still on the bed, posters of Wham and Spandau Ballet on the wall. 'I thought something *terrible* was going to happen to you.'

'Oh, there was a fuss all right,' Sooky said, patting Harpreet's hand fondly. Her little sister was a sweet, stolid and rather fearful girl. 'But I'm okay – still alive and just as ugly, you see?'

Harpreet giggled. 'You're not ugly; you're pretty.'

'Why, thank you, my dear!'

'What will you do?' Harpreet was serious once more. 'Will you have to get married again?'

Sooky tried not to think about this. Attempting to be cheerful, she said. 'Oh, maybe they'll find me a rich sugar-daddy. But I could study some more, maybe do a degree.'

Harpreet's eyes widened. 'You think they'll let you?'

'Maybe, part-time. You can do that at the Poly now. Mum used to like me studying.'

'Yes, but that was before you got married. Oh God, Sooky.' Harpreet looked haunted. 'I just hope they find *me* someone nice.'

'We'll try and make sure they do,' Sooky said.

She didn't share her misgivings about how difficult this was. She knew her parents hadn't chosen Jagdesh with any bad intent. He had seemed polite and competent, looked good on paper, even had his own business cards. How could they know what a ridiculous, feeble bully he really was, his true colours coming out almost the instant they were married?

Priya banged her bottle on the table, interrupting Sooky's thoughts. She made some toast, then took Priya upstairs.

'It's the toddler group today,' she told her as they had a shower together. 'You can see your little friend – Amy, isn't it?'

Priya squirmed with happiness. 'Amy,' she said, stamping her feet excitedly in the water.

Sooky liked the toddler group. She had announced to her mother that she was going to start going a few weeks ago and received a puzzled-looking frown – but no words of course. She wanted it: for Priya to meet a mixture of children, not just Asians and Punjabi-speakers; and for herself. Brought up in England, in an English school, however many Punjabis were there too, Sooky had an English side to her. Punjabi in the house, English out of it, she thought, though of course it was never as simple as that. Most white people seemed to think that 'English' could only mean 'white'. But she'd never be like Mom, mixing only with Punjabi women, with no need to learn English for her everyday usage. Her life was very different. And she liked to get out and about, not be stuck in the house all the time.

At school and at work she'd always been drawn to the naughty ones: not the really screwed up and harmful, but the ones with a subversive sense of humour, the ones she kept being told to keep away from. Like Gemma, who'd done fantastic imitations of the teachers and got mostly As in her O-levels. And Suze, who worked in Dad's factory making leather goods – jackets and bags. Sooky had worked there sometimes in the holidays.

'Why d'you mix with the *gorees*?' Mom had asked her, puzzled.

Of course she had Asian friends, but she liked some of the white girls too. Suze was in her thirties, divorced with three sons, and smoked like a stack. Her situation was chaotic, but she was kind and funny and had a force of life in her, and that was what Sooky liked. She felt that vitality in herself, burning through her veins in a mad kind of energy. It was good to talk to someone else who had that sort of energy in them.

She liked Joanne too. They could laugh together and she was kind, and somewhere in her there was a liveliness that seemed to be trying to get out, and Sooky was drawn to her because of it.

Once she and Priya were ready and went downstairs, the TV was on again. Pavan and Harpreet had left for school, and Dad and Raj were long gone. She could hear Roopinder getting Amardeep and Jasmeet dressed upstairs, nagging at them as usual.

Mom, dressed in a suit the colour of milky coffee, the scarf loose on her neck, was sitting bolt upright on the sofa. Sooky noticed suddenly how much grey there was in her plait now. Both her parents seemed older than their years.

There were adverts on the TV and Meena was obviously waiting for the news. She watched TV a lot, often the videos of the most recent wedding they'd attended, going over and over events, relishing it all. Sooky wondered what had happened to the videos of her own and Jaz's wedding.

'*Mata-ji*?' She spoke in Punjabi. 'I'm just going out, taking Priya to the toddler group.'

All she expected from her mother was a vague nod out of her stony silence. For a moment Meena didn't react at all. Then she turned and Sooky saw there were tears on her cheeks. As she did so, the news came on. Meena nodded towards it. 'Look!'

'Events at the Golden Temple in the Indian city of Amritsar, the holiest shrine of the Sikh religion . . .'

The gold of the *Akal Takhat*, the Seat of the Timeless One, glittered onto the screen, its reflection shimmering in the green pool around it. Sooky felt upset, sick in her stomach at the thought of harm coming to it. Her eyes met her mother's.

'Don't go,' Meena said in a low, humble voice. 'Not today. Stay here with me.'

Sooky could hear the deep distress in her voice. In all the six months since she had re-entered the house, it was the most her mother had said to her.

She went and unstrapped Priya from the buggy and together they sank down on the sofa in front of the news. After a time Meena let out a trembling sigh and, in a distraught voice, said, 'Oh my God – such terrible things. It's going to happen all over again.'

Twelve

Sooky waited until the end of the TV news. Priya, to her relief, after a few squeals of protest, forgot all about where they had been going and started playing with some plastic hoops.

Sooky sat at the other end of the sofa, half-taking in the news, half-watching her mother's thin, careworn features. Meena stared at the screen, straining to understand the English. Pictures passed in front of their eyes: Jarnail Singh Bhindranwale in his blue turban, arm raised, rallying a crowd. Mom could understand him at least. She tutted at his words.

An ache rose in Sooky's chest. She felt tender towards her mother, so vulnerable in her big house, in this country that was still so foreign to her. She felt a sense of honour for the journey her parents had made, from the wide farmlands of western Punjab to this city full of factories, chimneys and strangers. They never talked about any of that much, but she knew how important the community here was to them. It was their place, their people, a bit of home preserved in a foreign land. To feel disgraced was to be outcast: a nobody.

Sooky's marriage had been a disaster. They all knew it, but it had upset everything. Mom was clinging to the ways she knew, where anything in marriage was endured. Your husband was as God: it was your duty as a wife to care for him, however he treated you. And yet what Jaz was doing went beyond this, and this seemed to lie at the root of the conflict. She also knew her parents blamed themselves for what had happened. Everything seemed to be about blame. Can't we just stop it? she thought. All this blame?

How long was Mom going to keep this up, she wondered despairingly? She sat waiting for the news to end. Maybe then her mother would switch off the TV and turn to her: they would talk, the way they used to. They sat through the weather forecast – warm days ahead. Roopinder brought the children down, taking them into the kitchen.

Meena got up with a grunt. Her body was stiff, prematurely aged. Barefoot, she went and searched for a video and fed it into the player. Images appeared from a wedding the previous week – Sunny's and Jaswinder's. Sunny was the son of a family friend; the wedding had been in Smethwick. Even Sooky had gone: the *mehndi* patterns were still fading on their hands, the henna turning rusty after a few days.

'*Mata-ji*?' She couldn't bear it any longer.

'Make me a cup of tea, Sukhdeep.'

This was a hopeful sign. Maybe if they both sat down for a drink together . . .

Roopinder was putting Weetabix into bowls in the kitchen. She was wearing a cerise *salwar kameez* suit and lipstick, and the pink material seemed to glow against the white kitchen cupboards. As usual her handsome face wore an expression of snooty disdain.

'I thought you'd gone out *somewhere*,' she said, turning away, as if Sooky was a bad smell. The way she said *somewhere* made it sound dirty and bad.

Not looking at her, Sooky smiled at her nephew Amardeep, a beautiful three-year-old boy, and niece

Jasmeet, his one-year-old sister, who was in the high chair. Sooky was very fond of Raj's children; they couldn't help what their mother was like, she thought.

'Mom asked me to stay,' Sooky said, pouring milk into a saucepan. 'I'm just making her some tea.'

Roopinder's head turned. 'She asked *you* to stay?'

Sooky ignored her and ruffled Amardeep's hair. He squirmed and giggled.

'Stop, Auntie . . .'

'What are you doing today?' Sooky asked in a mild voice, determined not to sink to Roopinder's level.

'Oh, I'm going to see *my* mother.' Her tone suggested that her mother was nothing short of royalty. Roopinder was also from Birmingham and her parents lived only a short distance away.

'That's good,' Sooky said sincerely. Great: Roopinder was going out. The stupid bitch would be out of the way.

She poured two cups of sweet, milky tea and carried them to the front room.

'Here you are, *Mata-ji.*'

Meena took the tea without meeting Sooky's eye. She nodded her thanks. Sooky could see she was very tense, was not sitting back comfortably.

Sooky sank down beside her.

'Look, *Ma-ji* – it's a nice day. Why don't you come outside with Priya and me? We can go to the park, walk round the lake. We could talk . . .'

There was no reply. Meena turned her head away with a slight gesture of recoil from her and fixed her eyes on the dancing wedding guests. Her silence went on.

*

Sooky went to the park anyway. I might just as well have gone to the toddler group, she thought, as she strapped Priya into the buggy, hurt and let down after those moments of hope that Mom might be softening towards her.

Why did she ask me to stay, when all she wants to do is ignore me again? She'd even dressed in her yellow suit again, not jeans and a T-shirt. She was trying to be a dutiful Punjabi.

It was sunny and warm outside. She turned out of their street of tall, gabled Edwardian houses, past her old school and then down towards the park. The streets were quiet and it was a pleasant walk. But Sooky could not feel peaceful, even when the green space of the park opened out in front of her. All the old doubts came back.

The first time she had seen Jagdesh, her prospective husband, she had thought he looked all right. Well, all right-ish. He and his parents had come over from Derby and they had gone through the rituals of tea and snacks and introductions. She had waited on them and been stared at and commented on. Jagdesh had been polite, though Sooky had been sure she could detect a smirk on his face, as if he thought himself superior to everyone there. He was clean-shaven, quite trendy in a smart suit. He worked with computers, or something like that. She hadn't taken too much notice because she wasn't really interested in that sort of thing. She was keener on people, dreamed of training as a social worker.

The parents had talked amicably enough.

'Sukhdeep is a good student,' her father had told Jaz's parents. 'She's a good girl.'

Her mother, of course, laid it on about how she

95

could cook, which was the truth. Mom had taught her well.

She and Jaz had a few minutes to talk alone.

'What d'you like to do in your spare time?' she'd asked him.

'Oh, you know. Films, music, that sort of thing.' Obviously neither the drinking and being insulting nor the inclination to be sexual with small children was laid out in his CV.

'You'd like Derby,' he'd told her assuredly. 'It's better than Birmingham – smaller and not so ugly.'

She hadn't liked or disliked him. She had been seventeen: Mom and Dad had started looking for someone for her. Now she wondered why she hadn't expected more, demanded more. They wouldn't have forced her. Jaz was only the second man who came; there could have been more. It was almost as if she'd known it was inevitable and just wanted to get it over. She realized later that Jaz, who was then twenty-two, had felt the same.

'You marry as strangers,' Mom had counselled her. She seemed in her element, the wise older woman who had been through it all, passing on her knowledge to her daughter. 'But you are not strangers for long. You live together, work together, have children. You look after him properly, do cooking, cleaning, bedroom things – he will respect you.'

After she'd met Jaz she'd crept upstairs to where Harpreet was waiting. Harpreet had been twelve then, and so shy that she'd begged to be let off the family meeting, but she was fit to burst with curiosity. She grabbed Sooky's hand and yanked her into the room.

'So, what was he like? What did you *say*?'

'He's all right. I said yes.'

She hadn't felt anything much. It had been a bit like going to the dentist for a filling. It just had to be done. And at that time the wedding itself seemed quite far off.

She'd missed Harpreet terribly once she had moved in with Jagdesh's parents. He had no sisters, just two brothers, one already married and living elsewhere, the other a year older than Sooky, but silent and unsociable. Jaz's mom was glad to have a girl in the house, and Sooky quite liked his parents. Everything had felt strange and lonely, but that was to be expected. It was bearable. With other people around, the fact that she and Jaz already disliked each other could be disguised. But once they moved out into their own little terrace in Derby, two months before Priya was born, things had gone quickly downhill and there was no one else to hide behind.

Sooky pushed the buggy along the path by the boating lake, relieved to see that Priya had fallen into a doze. She stopped, staring out over the water. There was a thin sheen of oil on the surface close to her. No one was out with a boat at the moment, and the only other person she could see was a man sitting up at the other end on a bench.

They'd never had much to say to each other, she and Jaz. There was nothing in common. She found him arrogant, insecure and limited, driven solely by the desire to make money. What intimate life they had was cold. Their rare lovemaking – and that was no name for it – happening mechanically in the dark, with no words or kindness. Maybe it would get better, she'd thought. He didn't hit her, he earned his money. She knew she could not say anything to anyone. No one would take her complaints seriously.

Once Priya was born, it all changed. After the initial excitement of the birth, his attitude to her hardened. He became colder and insulting.

'Where's my food, you skinny bitch,' he'd say, arriving home at night. When she gave it to him, sometimes he would hurl it back at her, the spices seeping into the carpet, staining it. He turned his back on her at night as if she was invisible, treating her as if everything about her disgusted him. All he wanted was Priya, in a cloying, overblown way, as if she was a new toy brought on Earth especially for him.

At first Sooky had been pleased when he wanted to help, to change Priya and spend time with her. But her suspicions grew. One day, when Priya was about six months old, she had come into the room to find Jaz holding her, kissing her on the mouth, and not as anyone kisses an infant – his eyes closed, and she could tell by the movement of his mouth that he was pushing his tongue between Priya's lips. The baby was squirming, starting to cry, struggling to breathe. Jaz didn't realize she had been standing watching as long as she had. He laughed it off.

He started taking Priya off into the bedroom, enraged if Sooky came in. Sooky felt like a servant, not a wife.

'What are you doing in there with her?' she asked.

'Just having a lie down with my daughter! What d'you ****ing think I'm doing, you nagging bitch?'

She couldn't say – not then. Thinking about it now, she searched her soul to see if there was anything else she could have done. She knew girls in marriages where they were cruelly beaten, shrunk into silent shadows of the bright girls they had once been, who felt they had no choice but to keep quiet. They were married: this was how it was. If they left they would be turned out of the community in disgrace – outcast, penniless and treated as nobody. In comparison, she knew she was lucky.

One Sunday afternoon when Jaz had taken Priya upstairs, telling her she'd better not disturb him, she crept up and listened at the door. There was no sound for a time, though she thought she could hear little movements inside. Then she heard a cry from Priya. Her stomach tightened with dread. Very quietly she opened the door.

Priya was lying on a towel, completely naked, kicking her legs in the air at the freedom of it. Jaz was on all fours on the bed over her, his flies undone, a hand working at himself.

Sooky closed the door very carefully, then opened it again, rattling the handle.

Jaz jumped away from Priya, too shocked to be angry.

'Sorry,' she had whispered. 'I just came up to get my cardigan. Oh,' she pretended to be surprised, 'she's not asleep yet then?'

'I was just changing her,' he said.

That Monday, once Jaz was at work, she packed a bag and took Priya back to Birmingham on the train. She told her mother everything. Meena stared at her as she spoke, sobbing as the words poured out. Meena's face was very grave and every so often she rolled her eyes up to the ceiling as if silently imploring God. Then she turned her face away. Sooky waited for her to say, 'You must go back. It is your duty. He is your husband.'

Instead – and even now Sooky found this the most puzzling aspect of everything that had happened –

Meena seemed to be in shock. It took an age before she said anything. At last, in a very quiet voice, she said, 'What are you going to do?'

'I think I'd better stay here for a bit.'

Sooky knew she meant forever, but it seemed too big a thing to say.

'What if he comes?' Meena said.

'He won't.' Jaz must know that she knew about him. He didn't want her any more than she wanted him.

She wrote to him, telling him that if he came anywhere near Priya she would personally tell his parents what she had seen, and would contact both the police and Social Services in Derby. She had no idea what he had told his family, but it all went quiet and stayed quiet. Two months later he wrote back saying he wanted to divorce her on grounds of her adultery, which he expected her to admit. She decided to agree, knowing that it would bring shame upon her own head, but she wanted to be rid of him. And who would believe her if she said anything else?

Now she was tormented by doubt again. Why had she agreed to something so unjust? And should she have told someone? What if Jaz started his behaviour with some other child?

A pair of mallards drifted past on the water below. Sooky tried to think sympathetically about Jaz. Should she have been able to help him, to do something to make things better? But she knew it would have been impossible. Jaz hadn't liked or trusted her. They had married as strangers and become enemies. And if she ever heard that he had married again, she ought to warn his new wife. That was something she promised herself to do.

She moved further along, away from the patch of oil,

and knelt down on the bank. Leaning over, she looked down at her reflection in the water, her yellow *chunni* pulled over her head. Her eyes stared sadly back at her. She knew she was glad to be away from Jaz, though she was sorry about his parents, about not being able to explain. And living back here, even in disgrace with Raj and Roopinder on at her, was better than the desolation of her marriage.

But what broke her heart was her mother. This stony, complicated silence, which made her feel so hurt and desolate. Would she ever see her mother smile at her or hear her talking to her properly ever again?

Thirteen

Meena drew up her legs, sitting cross-legged on the sofa, and stared at the television: the dancing after a wedding on the back patio of a house, a swirl of women's clothing, purple, orange, turquoise, and everyone chatting and eating sweets. Usually she found watching the wedding videos soothing. They showed her things as they ought to be, everything fitting into the right place, the old traditions handed down over centuries, tying them to home.

She gazed for a long time at the flickering images, soon ceasing to see them. Her mind was elsewhere completely. Eventually she picked up the remote control, and the red button folded the pictures away into darkness.

Silence. Roopinder had gone out with the children. It was very seldom the house was this quiet.

Meena looked down into her lap, fingering the hem of her *kameez* with its edging of coffee-coloured sequins, which felt rough, like tiny pieces of shell. Emotions boiled inside her. Her limbs were aching and heavy and a swelling sensation rose in her, as if she might vomit.

The past was all mingled with the present. Having her daughter Sukhdeep anywhere near kept her in a state of permanent turmoil. Her outrage with Sukhdeep could barely be contained: that she had dared to challenge her husband, to leave him and overturn everything that was expected of her, to disgrace her family. She was a woman – her duty was to accept her fate, her *kismet*, to bear everything, forgive everything.

And yet, there was the reason she had left . . . There were some things that could not be forgiven – at this thought the feeling of sickness became doubly oppressive – some things a young child should never have to experience. Then her rage turned like a white flare on Jagdesh, her serpent of a son-in-law, so smooth and deceitful in his smart suit with his Western ways and his computers and business talk. The feelings came so strongly that her body began to tremble and she had to breathe hard to calm herself.

And now, with the upset in Punjab, what the Indian army had done . . . She began to rock back and forth in distress. 'And my own son, my foolish Raj,' she muttered. He had become so savagely angry, so uncompromising. She was afraid for him – of him. And that Bhindranwale whom he worshipped. He was supposed to be a holy man, but why had he filled the holiest of all places with bullets and grenades? It was all so horrific, so confusing. And all of it began to revive those memories of the deep past, of the Punjab of her birth, which she had tried to bury forever, never to look at or speak of, even in the very darkest places of her own heart.

Western Punjab, April 1947

She remembered the rhythmic creak of the bullock cart, the brightness of the stars in the vast canopy of sky and the merest shred of a moon.

Lying in the cart, she had felt the itch of straw against her bony back, smelled the dung fires as they stole through the lanes at the edge of the town and heard the barking of dogs, which at last faded to a silence broken only by crickets and that rhythmic creak, creak . . .

Every so often there would be a whimper from her little sister Parveen and their mother urgently silencing her, 'No crying! You must be quiet.'

Before this there had been the thick darkness, the smell of fear, sitting all together in the *gurdwara*, showing no light, everyone deadly quiet. Then they were all squashed onto the cart, women, children and her Uncle Gurbir, because of his crippled foot. It was a cool night. Gurbir had been wearing a brown knitted hat instead of a turban.

Meena's mother Jasleen, with Parveen in her lap, had shivered beside her with cold and fear. Jasleen had been heavily pregnant, as had her sister-in-law Amarpreet, Meena's auntie. Meena's father had walked alongside the cart, as had Nirmal. Her beloved *Mama-ji* Nirmal, her mother's youngest brother, had been only fifteen then and he was always kind and looked out for others.

The journey had lasted a very long time. Meena slept, her cheek pressed to the back of her hand, breathing in the smell of the night.

They were heading for the border – or at least the border that would be officially drawn in four months' time, in August 1947, between Muslim Pakistan to the west and Hindu India to the east. Just then no one was completely certain where this slicing line across Punjab would fall. Would Lahore be part of Pakistan? Would Amritsar?

What they did know, the Sikhs whose homes fell to the west of the line (as the Hindus knew), was that they were no longer welcome. Those who were about to find themselves in Muslim Pakistan when the border fell would have to fight for survival or leave. The Muslims on the east side faced the same dire choice.

Only much later did Meena hear the stories that had made them flee. All over this western area Sikhs, Hindus and Muslims, who had shared the streets of towns and villages for generations, took violently against each other. More and more blood was being shed. Sikhs were now terrified of their Muslim neighbours.

But it was the news that came from the north, from villages in the Rawalpindi district, that chilled their blood. Villages where the Sikhs, often themselves gathering their forces for violence, were vastly outnumbered and had gone into hiding from the gangs of Muslims who came raiding their villages, taking away their women and making them convert to Islam, slaughtering anyone who was not one of them.

There were villages where fathers, to defend the honour of their women and stop them falling into Muslim hands, took up their *kirpans*, their long knives, and beheaded daughters, wives and sisters. Another where the women of the village had committed acts of communal suicide by throwing themselves and their small children into the village well. This would be their future if they did not get away.

Meena sat, still rocking herself, remembering, fiddling with the hem of her *kameez*. She found herself agitating at questions which could now never be answered, which didn't matter, except that they kept her thoughts away from confronting what actually happened that night as they fled their district of Gujranwala, a place that neither she nor any member of her family had ever seen again.

Whose was the bullock cart? There had only been a dozen or so Sikh families in their small community, all Jat farmers, living on the western edge of the town. What had happened to the cart? Because the next thing had been boarding the train: where? Gujranwala? Lahore? A bullock cart was a valuable thing. And not everyone who had been in the cart with them was on the train – certainly not everyone, because ... Because ...

Her thoughts were sucked towards the events of that night – or rather to the shame of not being able to remember, because as a little child she had been asleep, and that sleep had betrayed her.

Somewhere on the journey, while it was still dark, her mother, Jasleen, had asked them to stop so that she could relieve herself. A number of the other women got down also (not Meena who was asleep), among them their aunt Amarpreet and Meena's sister Parveen, clinging sleepily to their mother. They took themselves a modest distance away, to the rocks and scrub at the side of the road. Had her mother strayed further than the others? She had been an excessively shy, modest woman, and was eight months into a pregnancy.

Meena was woken by her father's cries. 'Jasleen? Jasleen? Wife, where are you? Come back now – don't move so far away from us! JASLEEN!'

His cries, becoming more hoarse and frantic, would echo forever in her head. Some tried to silence him, but Nirmal joined in the shouting for his sister. There was confusion, then utter panic. The other women were weeping hysterically, crying out that they had seen nothing, only darkness around them. Meena began to cry as well, terrified, not understanding what had happened.

The men searched every possible spot. Then they found her pink *chunni* a little distance away, as if she had thrown it down as a marker. But of mother or child there was no other sign.

Meena's father was distraught, twisting the pink scarf round and round in his hands, crying out, running this way and that.

'We must move on,' the others said fearfully. 'If they come back here they will kill us all.'

Meena remembered the sound of muffled weeping, of being forced to lie back down against the thighs of her *Bhabi-ji* Amarpreet, her aunt's hand unusually firm on her head as if holding her down, as they continued the journey without her mother and Parveen.

And then they were on the train, crammed in in the oppressive heat, squatting on the floor, pressed against the wall, faces of strangers all around them. For hours there was no water. Amarpreet, who was a timid, passive person, her legs spread wide to accommodate her belly, let out little moans of terror that her baby would start coming here in this crush. Meena sat clenched up, her chin on her knees, eyes staring blankly in shock. No mother, no sister. Only Nirmal beside her, his arm around her as they tried silently to comfort each other.

Meena rocked herself harder now, her head bending right down to her lap, hands over her face, the tears running out between her fingers.

Fourteen

Two weeks passed.

Joanne faced each day as if it were a mountain, glad only if she could get up and over it and safely down the other side before tackling the next one. Gradually, everything had come to depend on Dave's moods, so that she had to think hard to remember anything different. What had happened to the man she used to know and love?

When she opened her eyes in the morning, she was immediately tense. She usually woke first, roused by a cry from Amy. Sometimes it was difficult to ease herself out of bed without waking Dave, as his arm would be lying heavily across her. She would inch up into a sitting position and slide out, to find Amy standing in her cot, warm and adorable.

'Don't wake Daddy,' she'd whisper, lifting Amy out, smelling her sweet, yeasty smell. As long as Dave was asleep, peace could reign. 'Let's go and get you some milk, shall we?'

Most mornings she warmed a bottle for Amy and made cups of tea, carrying one up to him, hoping desperately to begin the day on a good footing. Quite often he was all right first thing, as if sleep had washed him clean of whatever had made him snarl at her the day before. Now and then, though, he woke in an ugly mood, his face clouded and aggressive even before his eyes were open, and she was tiptoeing around from the very start. Nothing she could do was right. If it was raining, it was her fault; if he couldn't find the shirt he wanted, she was the one to blame.

'Why can't you put anything away in the right place?' he'd growl. 'I'm out at work all day – just a shirt, that's all I ask.'

She had learned that it was not worth arguing.

The times when he hit her were almost always in the evening, as if all his rage and suspicion had built up through the day like gas under pressure. Afterwards she would try not to think about that, either – about anything. Just get up, face the next day, the next climb. See if you can get down the other side without disaster. Keep Amy safe. To start thinking would be too frightening.

As soon as he had gone to work, she could breathe. Her day revolved around Amy, her meals and naps and taking her to the park. Instead of dwelling on Dave, on what he had done or not done, she banished him from her mind, almost as if he didn't exist.

'This is our day now – our lives,' she sometimes whispered to Amy. 'And he can't do anything about it.'

Sometimes, when he was there in the evening, watching TV and caught up in the football and wouldn't notice, she looked carefully at him. She saw a strong, good-looking man with a head of thick, cropped hair, which had darkened slightly, but was still blond. In those moments she might see something else that twisted her inside: his tension and bitterness. She could sense it in the way he sat, in the way his eyes looked out at the world.

The boy she had first known, when they were teenagers, had been bright-eyed, full of it, keen and bouncy as a spring. He was going to be a footballer, had been selected for training with the Juniors at the Villa; he was *good*, he was going somewhere. He'd gone through life with a force that had carried her with him, away from her A-levels – 'What d'you need them for?' – into work and a life with him. He'd been the leader then, the lad taking life by storm. She'd adored him. And now, at times, she felt heartbroken for him.

Still, mostly she had to look at him with detached, wary eyes. Anger was like a demon in him. He was starting to drink more now as well, and to bring home a rack of cans on a Friday night and get stuck into them and end up asleep, snoring on the sofa so that she had to go up to bed without him. All these things increased the distance between them. Trying to talk to him about it was impossible. He had shut down.

In the daytime when he was not there, though, she didn't want to think about it, about what might happen or what she should do. She just kept climbing, one foot in front of the other, looking out for pitfalls and trying to avoid them.

Sooky had come to the toddler group both of the next two times. The first time Joanne felt a big smile spreading across her face when she arrived, and Amy ran to Priya, squealing with excitement.

'That's nice!' Tess remarked. 'She really remembers her, doesn't she?'

'Hello,' Joanne said shyly. 'Amy, give Priya a chance!' Amy was trying to throw her arms round her little friend.

Sooky laughed. 'Let me just get her out, darling.'

The two little girls ran off together, holding hands.

'She really missed her last week,' Joanne said. *And I missed you*, she thought, but didn't say it.

Sooky looked pleased. Pushing the buggy tighter in against the wall she said, 'I know – I wanted to come. It's just, there's all the trouble in India and my mom was a bit upset.'

'Oh, I see,' Joanne said as they wandered across to join their daughters. She racked her brains. She watched the news every day. It was full of the miners, pickets and police – and, yes, India. 'The ... is it ... the Golden Temple?'

'Yes.' Sooky looked suddenly uncomfortable, as if it felt wrong talking about it. She seemed tense.

'It must be upsetting,' Joanne said. She knew she had barely taken in what was going on, but that the Sikhs were very angry and upset about it all. Phrases from the news were coming back to her: '... the Sikhs' holiest place ...', '... leader of the rebels found dead ...', '... angry demonstrations in London'.

'It is,' Sooky agreed. Sensing that Joanne was not sure what to say next, she went on, 'Let's go and see the painting, shall we?'

After that they talked easily about day-to-day things, the children and how they were eating and sleeping. They drank cups of tea together, standing at the kitchen door. Sooky told Joanne she was a big fan of *Star Trek*, and asked her if she'd ever seen a UFO.

'No, I mean I'm not sure they really exist, do they?'

'Oh yes, I think so,' Sooky said. 'There must be something out there, mustn't there? There've been all those lights and spaceships seen in America – there's got to be something behind it. In fact there was one seen over Smethwick, in 1962. Apparently it looked like a cigar. My dad was there then.'

111

'Did he see it?' Joanne asked.

'No, but everyone was talking about it. One of his friend's cousins says he saw it.' Sooky hugged herself. 'I always look out for them; and I'd love to go up in a spaceship, wouldn't you?'

'*No!*' Joanne said. 'Oh no, I don't think I'd like that at all.'

'Oh, I would – go and explore other planets, see what's on them, like in *Star Trek*. It'd be really exciting.'

Joanne laughed. 'You've got a pretty funny idea of exciting!'

'I know . . .' Sooky shrugged. 'But life's boring most of the time, isn't it? You know last week, when there was that storm?' There'd been a thunderstorm with dramatic lightning and torrential rain.

'Yeah?'

'Well, I went out in the back garden and held my hands up.' She showed Joanne her wrists, gold bangles tinkling on each. 'I thought, as they're metal and everything, I might get struck by lightning—'

'*What?*' Joanne started to laugh, especially because she could see Sooky was being serious. 'You're a proper case, you are, aren't you? What the hell did you do that for?'

'I thought it'd be exciting.'

'What – being burnt to a crisp? You must be *really* bored!'

Both of them were laughing now, so much that everyone was looking at them.

'Don't tell anyone,' Sooky hissed, half-smiling, half-serious. 'I s'pose it is a bit strange.'

The time flew past. As they were packing up Sooky said, 'Would you like to come round one day: bring Amy to play?'

'Oh, I'd really like that; and Amy'd love it, wouldn't you? And you could come to ours – we only live round the corner from here.'

Sooky promised that she would, though neither of them had got round to it yet.

The next week they nattered away again. To their surprise, just as everyone was getting settled in, the door of the hall opened again and a buggy appeared, pushed by a man. Tess went forward to welcome him.

'Seems funny seeing a bloke, doesn't it?' Joanne said to Sooky. 'Good for him, though. You wouldn't catch my husband coming down here.'

The man had quite a young baby in the buggy and another small child walking alongside. Both he and the little boy had bright-ginger hair in a similar state of chaotic waviness. All the time he carried the baby in his arms and produced a bottle to feed him, and guided the toddler round to play with the toys. Tess told them quietly that his name was Kieran and that the children's mother was going through a difficult patch, so he had taken time off to help out.

When he worked his way round to where Joanne and Sooky were with their girls, on a slide, the little boy shyly came and joined in. The girls looked suspiciously at him at first.

'You let him have a go,' Joanne told Amy. 'What's his name?' she asked the father.

'Billy,' the man said, gently pushing the boy forward with his free hand. He nodded down at the baby. 'And this is Charlie.'

He seemed a friendly, gentle person and soon the children were playing happily. The man told them his name. He was a primary-school teacher and had asked for leave to help support his wife.

'She's not been too good since Charlie was born,' he said. 'But she's getting help. We just have to get through it.'

They chatted for a while. The conversation moved on to what had happened the day before, at Orgreave coking plant, and the mounted police and riot gear used against the picketing miners.

'When they did it at Saltley, back in '76, they won,' Kieran said. He explained that then the workers had managed to stop the coke deliveries to the gasworks. 'But they're not going to win this time – not the way the police are carrying on. It was really shocking.'

Joanne agreed. It had been chilling, seeing the violence of the police, the charges on horseback.

'He's sweet, isn't he?' Sooky said when he moved away.

Joanne was cheered as well. Kieran seemed like another nice person to talk to. It was a good feeling to be making friends.

Fifteen

That Friday evening Joanne was cooking dinner: liver and bacon, one of Dave's favourites. Standing at the cooker, she could hear Amy murmuring to herself happily in the next room and smiled. But every second that passed made her feel more wound up. What mood would he be in? How the whole evening would go depended on that.

With a surge of resentment she saw how much her life was under his control.

The doorbell made her jump violently. Cursing, she pulled the pan off the heat. Outside seemed very bright when she opened the door. On the step was a young woman, smartly dressed in a navy trouser suit. It took her a second to recognize that it was her sister.

'Karen?' Immediately she was panic-stricken. 'Why're you here – what's happened?'

Karen held up a hand to stop her. 'Nothing, don't worry. I just wanted to talk to you.'

As she turned to lead Karen into the house, Joanne registered that her sister looked pale and strained.

'I was just doing our tea – sorry about the smell.'

'No, it's nice.' Karen sniffed. 'I s'pose you're quite a good cook now.'

Joanne chuckled. She realized suddenly that she and Karen were having to find a new way of being sisters, as adults. Everything was shifting. 'I wouldn't exactly say that. Cuppa tea?'

'Oh God, yes please.'

Leaving the food to simmer, Joanne carried mugs in to join Karen, who was playing with Amy.

'Usually I'd be bathing her,' Joanne said. 'But she can stay up a bit later. It's Friday.' Stirring her tea, she said, 'It's nice to see you.' She realized she felt pleased, honoured almost, that Karen had deigned to come. She only worked over in Perry Barr, but she never normally bothered to call by.

Karen tilted her head as if to acknowledge that she should visit more often.

'Dave not back yet?'

'No, any minute though.'

'Thing is, Jo – I wanted to talk to you about Mom.'

'I thought she was on the mend?'

Joanne had seen her every weekend. They took Amy over on a Saturday or Sunday. Her mother had seemed to her to be more or less back to normal.

Karen looked troubled. 'I don't know. I mean, I really *don't know*.' After hesitating a moment she went on, 'Thing is, I feel a bit bad about this, but I was talking to someone at work about it. It just came up – she was talking about someone she knew who had been addicted to Valium. So I asked her a bit about it, and she said how hard it had been for this person ever to come off it after they'd been taking it so long, and how all the problems she'd had, which had put her onto it in the first place, had all sort of come back – as if the drug had just covered it up. And it had been horrible: she'd felt really ill and everything.'

'I thought the idea was that they'd get her off it really slowly. I mean, she just stopped overnight, didn't she? That must've given a terrible shock to her system – like coming off anything: heroin or whatever . . .'

'I know, there's that. She'll have to get off it somehow. But it was just that what that lady said made me think. For a start, how do we know what "normal" is for Mom? How does *she* know? If she's been on that stuff all my life and most of yours, we don't know what she'd be like without it. And the awful thing is . . .'

Tears filled Karen's eyes and she rummaged in her pocket for a tissue to wipe them away.

'She's always been there, physically at least – but in another way she hasn't – at all. What I suddenly thought is: how much do we know about Mom anyway? I mean my friend Josie's mom talks a lot about when she was a little girl, stories about her family and the things they all got up to. When's Mom ever talked about anything like that?'

Joanne considered this. It was true, but she was so used to it that she'd never questioned it. 'I thought all her family were dead – or miles away somewhere. Hasn't she got those nieces. Susan? She gets cards from a Susan. And Heather's the one is Australia. I think they're sisters . . .' She frowned. 'We've never met them, though, have we? D'you remember meeting them?'

'No. I've never met anyone – there was only Auntie Joan, Dad's family.'

'Didn't she tell us . . .' Joanne was struggling to recall now. 'She worked in factories, didn't she? In town somewhere.'

'And what about the war? Everyone else is always on about that, but I've never heard her mention it.'

'Have you tried asking Dad?'

'Well, sort of.' Karen sounded a bit impatient. 'But

you know what he's like. Like blood out of a stone. You wonder if he's even asked her himself.'

Joanne couldn't help laughing. 'Bless him. Look, I'll be over tomorrow with Amy. Are you going to be around? Maybe we could take her out somewhere, just for a cup of tea in the High Street or something – see if we can get her talking a bit?'

Karen's face fell. 'I'm really sorry. I said I'd help Josie tomorrow. She's decorating that new flat to move into . . .'

'Okay. Well, I'll take her anyway, if she'll come.' Joanne jumped up. 'Let me just check on the tea . . .' She went and stirred the liver and turned it off. Going back to Karen, she said lightly, 'Drop in when you like, won't you? Work's not far.'

Karen looked up from watching Amy. 'All right. I will when I can.'

And the sisters exchanged a smile.

Margaret had been back to the hairdresser's and her hair was tightly permed. She seemed to be having quite a good day. But when Joanne suggested a little trip out, she shook her head.

'Oh no, I don't think so, love. Let's sit in the garden. Amy can play – and what's the sense in paying for a cup of tea when I can make you one here?'

'All right then, it was just a thought,' Joanne said.

Her dad was bumbling about in the garden: a long strip, walled on one side, fenced on the other. He was sorting out raspberry canes at the bottom. Amy was carrying a red bucket about, as usual putting in any-thing she could find: stones and petals and sycamore aeroplanes.

Joanne made tea for everyone and carried it out on a tray. She took her dad a mug down the garden. He had his sleeves rolled up and bits of stuff in his hair and there were beads of perspiration on his forehead.

'Everything all right, Dad?'

'Oh yes, ta, love. I won't mow the grass till later, when you've gone. You go and keep your mother company.'

They sat with their mugs of tea and some Mr Kipling's fruit pies. Joanne broke off a bit to give to Amy. She didn't know how to start the conversation with her mother. Margaret was very touchy these days – even more so than usual.

'You starting to feel a bit better, Mom?'

'Better than what?' Margaret asked sourly.

'Well, you know – I mean since you've been in hospital?'

Margaret turned away to put down her plate with its little silver pie-case on it. She finished her mouthful. Joanne thought she wasn't going to answer, but after a sip of tea she announced, 'They gave me those pills – all that time ago – because I was a bit low after having Karen.' Her voice was very bitter. 'And instead of making me better, they gave me an illness: a worse one. That wasn't what I wanted. I never asked for this. That doctor did this to me without a thought.'

'Oh, Mom,' Joanne said. She wasn't sure what else she could possibly say. Amy trotted up to them then, pointing at the silver pie-cases.

'D'you want those in your bucket, bab?' Margaret handed them to her. 'There yer go, you take them for a ride.'

Joanne had had what she thought was a brainwave

on the bus on the way over. She'd remembered the book that Dave's mom had been telling her about.

'Oh yes, Mom – I meant to ask you . . . Wendy was on about this book she's found about Birmingham and the war: the Blitz and everything. She said you could have it to look at, if you like. She could remember bits and pieces, although she was quite young then. It was ever so interesting when she talked to us about it: her and her mom sitting in the cupboard under the stairs. It sounded like hell, really, with the bombs dropping and everything. And I suddenly felt bad because I've never known much about it, and I don't remember you ever telling us about the war . . . I know you're a bit younger than her, but you must remember some of it? The bombs and that? What did your mom do?'

Margaret had pulled her lips into a tight line. Once again, for no reason Joanne could understand, she seemed to be seething with emotion. What was the right thing to say?

'Will you tell me what you can remember – about Birmingham in the war?'

'No,' Margaret said. 'I won't. Because I wasn't in Birmingham through the war. I wasn't here, so I never knew anything about it. They sent us away, and by the time I came back, it was more or less over. So it's no good asking me, is it?'

She stood up, mug in hand and disappeared into the house.

Sixteen

Worcestershire, December 1939

Margaret sat with the patchwork blanket round her, hugging her knees. Against her back was the hard leg of the workbench.

It was dark and bitterly cold outside. The ground had frozen before sundown and in the bright mornings the trees were encased in glittering ice. But now it was night, a freezing eternity in front of Margaret before there was hope of the sun coming up.

She pressed her forehead against her knees, her teeth chattering and her whole body shaking. Little sounds came from her, trailing off into wordless whimpering that no one could hear: 'Mo-m, mer ... mer ... mer, Mom ... mer ... mer ... meeer ... Eeeer.'

The first time Nora Paige threw Margaret into the shed, after she had trespassed in Ernest's room, it had not been anything like as wintry. It had still been afternoon when the woman had dragged her by the hair, shrieking insults. Margaret spun into the murky shed, hearing the key being turned.

'You can stay in there. And don't touch anything!'

Nora Paige's barmy voice hissed through the wall. Margaret heard her moving away.

It was a sunny afternoon and she was not afraid. Not yet. In fact she was curious. She had never been in the shed before, although she had seen Mrs Paige go into it to fetch the rake and fork, which she would bring out and rest across the old wheelbarrow. Margaret had tried to peer through the window once, when she was alone outside, but it was too high. Now she had a good look round. The only thing that made her shudder were the thick, dusty cobwebs in the corners of the windows. She was sure she saw a movement in one of them and dragged her gaze away.

In the darkest corner, against the back wall, was a jumble of planks standing on their ends, some decaying logs and rusty tins. Near the door were the gardening tools and wheelbarrow and beyond, leaning against the wall, was a man's bicycle, black and heavy, the chain dried up and the frame and handlebars corroded by rust. Under the window on the other side was the workbench, and this looked by far the most interesting thing to explore. Each side of the window, on the wall, were fixed a host of tools: saws and spanners, chisels and screwdrivers, all brown and shrouded in cobwebs. There was a vice fixed to the edge of the bench and she spent minutes rotating the handle, loosening and tightening it.

She found a galvanized pail and turned it upside down, standing on it so that she could explore all the things on the bench. There were more tools, and a collection of St Julien Tobacco tins, which rattled promisingly as she picked them up. She spent some time shaking them, making different sounds as if they were maracas. They were hard to open and she didn't manage with all of them. When she removed the lids, inside she saw collections of screws and nails and nuts of different sizes. She took some of them down onto the floor to play with.

Soon she'd had enough of that and sat staring. Eerie shadows appeared. The sun went down and no one came.

Margaret's bladder grew tight and heavy and she relieved herself in one of the buckets and placed it far away from her. She sat on the earth floor, leaning against the leg of the bench. A terrible loneliness welled up in her and she started to cry, with her face against her knees. After a while she stopped crying, but still no one came.

The darkness thickened and she grew more frightened. The only light was from a husk of moon. There were rustling sounds. She knew it was the spiders and rats. Goosepimples of cold and fear came up all over her. How big were they? They swelled in her mind and she sat as still as she could, a scream locked in her throat.

A light came, bobbing across the garden. The key turned. Nora Paige's face was made up of odd blocks of shadow in the glow from the hurricane lamp. She threw the patchwork blanket through the door, and Margaret felt it slither down her shins.

'I've given Seamus your supper. Ernest and I didn't consider that you deserved it tonight. And you'll be staying here. We felt you should be punished.'

'I want to come in . . . Don't make me stay here!' Margaret begged. But the door was already closing again.

At first she just sat, paralysed by terror. Every sound made her heart pound. There were scuttlings across the roof, whether of mice or birds or something more sinister she didn't know. And it was cold: no snow or frost, but cold enough.

Eventually she wrapped the blanket right round her, and lay down, her head resting on her arm. The ground was so hard and cold. Through the night she slept and woke, longing for a drink of water. At last the sun came up.

Nora Paige appeared early in sludge-brown clothing, fed Margaret a meagre helping of salt porridge and made sure she was ready when Miss Cooper arrived.

'If you tell anyone about your punishment, you'll be in here every night, d'you understand? No sly words to the teachers. Not a one. Or remember where you'll have to sleep.'

That day it was such a relief to be in the warm room at the back of the vicarage that, almost immediately, Margaret slumped forward on her arms at the table and fell asleep. No one woke her.

Twice more she had been banished to the shed, before this, the coldest night of the year so far. Nora Paige was eager to punish her for the least thing: lifting her plate to her face, desperate for the last lick of gravy, had been one offence. And she was giving Margaret less and less to eat in any case. Her stomach ached for food.

'Are you feeling all right, Margaret?' Miss Cooper asked her, more and more often it seemed. And their hostess, the birdlike vicar's wife, Mrs Bodley-Fisher, also showed concern.

'The child doesn't seem to be quite all there, does she?' Margaret heard her murmur to Miss Cooper. 'Is this what she's like normally, poor little soul?'

'I don't think so – I'm not sure,' Miss Cooper replied. 'She was Miss Peters' charge, of course. Better keep an eye out, I think.'

Margaret felt distant and very sleepy through most of school, as if she wasn't really there. She had no energy to join in anything. Even when Mrs Bodley-Fisher opened up the gramophone and put on some of her crackly seventy-eight records, which was Margaret's favourite thing, she could barely keep awake.

And now the freezing dark seemed to fall on her, pressing her down as if it was made of iron. She couldn't even think what it was that she was guilty of this time. Already that day her throat had been agonizingly sore and her head was throbbing. She scarcely knew where she was, was too poorly to feel afraid.

Wrapping herself up as usual, she curled up as tightly as she could, shaking with fever. Her throat felt closed, as though there was a hand gripped around it. The night was quiet, all the creatures tucked in the warmest places they could find, and in the deadly cold all Margaret could hear was the banging of her own blood in her ears.

All night she boiled and shivered, half-waking to feel the hardness of the ground against her hip or shoulder, then lapsing back into feverish dreams.

Outside, everything froze: water butts and ponds, grass and trees.

By morning Margaret was unconscious.

What had gone on that morning in the mind of that crazed woman, Mrs Nora Paige?

Miss Cooper arrived at the door to collect Margaret, as usual. The sludge-brown apparition appeared.

'I'm afraid the little girl is no longer here,' Mrs Paige announced with an almighty blink of her eyes.

Impatiently Miss Cooper asked what she meant.

'She is no longer with us.'

Miss Cooper's heart must have started to pound in extreme panic at this point.

'Where is she? Let me see her.'

'I'm afraid that isn't possible,' Nora Paige said. 'She's no longer in the house.'

'Don't be idiotic: what have you done with her?' Miss Cooper's red-haired temper began to flare. 'Get out of my way – I insist on seeing my pupil.'

She pushed past Nora Paige's slack body and passed through the bare front room. At the back there was no sign of Margaret.

'Right,' Miss Cooper declared. 'Tell me where she is – now – or I'll search the whole house.'

'Don't go upstairs!' Nora Paige snarled, guarding the foot of the staircase. 'She's not up there, I can tell you that. Don't you dare intrude on my privacy.'

Her face at that moment convinced Miss Rebecca Cooper that the woman was completely insane. However, this confirmation only made her more determined. She came up close, smelling Nora Paige's oniony smell. '*Tell me* where she is, then.'

The woman gave a convulsive blink. 'Out the back.'

A few moments later Margaret, barely conscious, was lifted into Miss Cooper's arms. The teacher, stuttering with rage, said to Nora Paige, 'I'm going to get the police onto you.'

There was a period of weeks while Margaret recovered in the vicarage, on a little put-you-up bed, which felt comfortable and secure. The Bodley-Fishers were already hosting three other evacuees, but they made Margaret welcome over Christmas while she recuperated.

Mrs Nora Paige was reported to the police. Eventually she was fined five pounds. Later still she was taken away to a local asylum.

Margaret was amazed by the days of Christmas. Though still weak, she gazed at the decorated tree and was able to go into the church with the other children, see the crib and hear the carols being sung. It was the most lovely thing she had ever seen. Mrs Bodley-Fisher, a darting woman with china-blue eyes, fed her plenty of milk and was kind to her. She gave Margaret a handmade teddy bear as a Christmas present. It was made of brown felt and was wearing a red scarf. Margaret loved him immediately and called him Tommy.

When she told Mrs Bodley-Fisher that her brother was called Tommy, and that she didn't know where he was, Mr Bodley-Fisher, a fleshy-faced, cheerful man, made enquiries. He found Tommy on a far-flung farm, said he was happy there and that one day he would come and see his sister. This cheered Margaret up no end.

And then Margaret was told that a new home had been found for her, in another village five miles away called Buckley. Soon after the New Year she was collected by horse and trap, travelling well wrapped up through a freezing morning to meet the two sisters and the two other evacuees they had already taken in. After the bite of the cold air on her face throughout the journey, Margaret always remembered walking into the parlour of Orchard House in Buckley and feeling the delicious warmth of the fire.

That day, she had walked into heaven.

Seventeen

As Margaret gradually allowed herself to remember the past, of her years in Buckley she could only recall happy, blissful things. In reality there must have been dull days – wet, cold, boring days – the way real life was. But all the memories glowed in her mind like the leaves, every autumn at the end of the paddock at Orchard House filling the eye with yellow and copper brightness.

These thoughts would fill her with such an ache of longing that she would try to force them from her mind before they were snatched away from her somehow, the way Buckley and Orchard House had been snatched away.

For more than four years she had lived in this wonderful place. It was the family home of the Clairmonts, who ran an agricultural supplies business in Worcester. Miss Jenny Clairmont had stayed on in the house with her parents until each of them passed away, only to be joined soon afterwards by her elder sister, Mrs Lucy Higgins, recently widowed.

Now the household consisted of the two sisters – Lucy Higgins' two sons were both away in the navy – a younger woman, Emily, who had stayed on as maid to help run the house, and the two other evacuees, ten-year-old twins, the children of a cousin who lived in Birmingham. There was also an elderly man, known as

Sissons, who lived in a cottage nearby and attended to the outside things: garden, paddock, stable and hen coops. It was Sissons, the smoke from his pipe trailing sweetly into Margaret's nostrils, who had brought her to Buckley.

The morning she first set foot in the house, eyes watering from the bracing journey, Margaret was still convalescent, numbed by all the changes that had happened to her. Her feet, still in Tommy's old *Mail* boots, clomped across the crimson patterned rugs covering the uneven brick floor of the hall, into the main parlour with its bright log fire in the inglenook, its rugs and comfortable chairs. She found her knees being sniffed by the moist nose of a brown-and-white dog.

'It's all right, she won't hurt you!' said a tall, angular person. 'Now now, Dotty, leave our little friend alone.'

The dog wagged its feathery tail.

There were people, all waiting for her: the tall, angular person was Miss Jenny Clairmont, and there was small, barrel-shaped Mrs Lucy Higgins – were two sisters ever more different? – and pink-faced Emily, in her apron. On each of the 'warm-boxes' at either end of the fender, which held sticks and kindling, sat a blond child. They had remarkably similar strong-featured faces with full lips, large, straight noses and blue eyes. But one had his hair cut short back and sides, while the other's was bobbed in a no-nonsense way round her ears, parted at one side and with a pale-blue ribbon tied at the other. Among this sea of faces there was not one that was not smiling. Even the dog, which was now lying by the fender, was panting in a smiley way.

She must have looked such a pathetic thing, even in her new hand-me-downs from the vicarage, with her wonky eye, toes pointing in like a pigeon's, a finger stuck in her mouth.

Mrs Higgins came and knelt by her, reached for her hand and drew her close.

'Hello, my dear.' Margaret looked into kindly grey eyes. Mrs Higgins was wearing a cardigan of moss-coloured bobbly wool. 'Do you like to be called Margaret? Or should we call you Maggie?'

Margaret nodded. She liked being called 'Maggie'. Tommy had sometimes called her that. She also liked being given the choice.

'So, Maggie it is. Now, you must meet your new friends. This is John . . .' The blond boy got to his feet. 'And this is his twin sister, Patty.'

They came over and Margaret felt herself shrinking inside. Would they be horrible to her?

John had his hands pushed down into the pockets of his long shorts and one of his socks was riding at half-mast. He put his head on one side and said, 'Hello, Maggie' in a gruff, but amiable way.

Patty came straight up and took Margaret's hand like a little mother.

'C'mon, Maggie – come and sit on the warm-box. It's where we sit a lot 'cause it's nice in the cold. And Mrs Higgins says, as a special treat 'cause you've come, we can have buttered toast. Emily's going to make it.'

Patty delivered Margaret to the box, and Margaret could feel warmth coming from it, though it was nothing compared to the fierce heat of the fire on her face. She looked at the shiny brass handles of the fire-tongs and poker and felt the warmth start to tingle through her hands. For some reason Patty knelt behind her and thought it a good idea to rub Margaret's back.

She didn't mind. She found it comforting, as was the sound of John and Patty's Birmingham accents.

Soon Emily carried in a plateful of thick slices of bread, which she toasted with a fork on the fire and spread with butter. It was the most delicious thing Margaret had ever tasted.

Jenny Clairmont had worked for many years as an elementary-school teacher, so Orchard House had become an additional school for the evacuees. Much later, when more and more evacuees (including John and Patty) had trickled back home, the remaining few were fitted into the village school. At the beginning of 1940, though, this was where the evacuees gathered.

Those years merged now, were distilled into a collection of images. After the ride in the trap, past frozen furrows and icy trees, the bliss of that singed toast (with more butter than most of the rationed country could have, as they kept cows and could make their own), all Margaret could remember was kindness. And there was the excitement of living in the countryside, of tree climbs and birds' nests and the sight of lambs, chicks and ducklings in spring.

In the paddock, between the orchard and kitchen garden and the copse, the sisters kept two Guernsey cows, Poppy and Mildred, and the Shetland pony called Rags, which pulled the trap. There were chickens with less definite names, which were just called The Fowls. On Starveall Farm nearby there were also sheep.

Helped by a combination of good food, fresh air and kindness, Margaret thrived as never before. There were rides round the paddock on Rags while Sissons, or sometimes Patty, held the leading rein. They played endless games in the garden. A lot of the time it was just with Patty, who loved having a younger child to mother and boss.

'I'm going to be a teacher like my father when I grow up,' she would declare. 'So I'd better get into practice.'

But when John joined in there was often the best fun. They made a see-saw one summer day, with a plank balanced across a metal bucket. The plank kept slipping and John stood on it to counterbalance the unequal weight of the girls on each end, moving from foot to foot and yelling, 'See-saw Marjorie Daw . . . Bet you're going to fall off first!' Margaret could remember clinging to the jolting plank and laughing so much that she could hardly breathe.

Sometimes she allowed her mind to linger on the memories. There were so many riches. Sitting round the table with bread and butter, ham and cakes. Patty doing her hair, bending over her, her blue eyes stern with concentration: 'Sit *still*, Maggie. If you want plaits you have to be patient . . .' Learning to read and write and do sums. Miss Clairmont reading *A Christmas Carol* to them by the fire, or other stories under one of the pear trees in summer. Patty loved to read to Margaret too, sitting her on her lap, teaching her.

There were all the animals: the scuttling hens; Dotty stealing people's shoes and hiding them in the orchard; the grassy breath and slow stare of the two cows; and Rags the pony's mischievous ways. And the dray horses, with their big fringed hooves clopping along the village lanes, pulling carts that brought coal and salt and milk to the houses. She'd loved the passing seasons, the green buds and grass in spring, the vegetable garden bursting full in summer, the autumn's frisking leaves, then snow, seeming to seal them into the house and village, muffling everything in a magical white.

As Margaret grew and changed, blossoming under the kindness of the two sisters, she was only really aware of the war because of them talking about it: the ration books, their worries about John and Patty's parents in Sparkhill when the bombs were falling on Birmingham. And then – and hardly at any other time – she wondered about home, and how her mother was; about Tommy and her half-sister Elsie; and all of it seemed very far away.

One day Tommy came.

It was during that first summer of 1940, before the bombs began falling on the cities.

'It seems only right that you should see your brother,' Mrs Higgins said. 'He is some way away, but I could probably arrange for Sissons to collect him and have him here for an afternoon. Would you like that?'

Margaret beamed at her. 'Oh, yes please, Mrs Higgins!'

Tommy! It was an age since she'd seen him – in fact nearly nine months. Most of the time now she was so caught up in everything at Orchard House that she didn't think about her family. When she had first arrived, the sisters had asked her if she thought her parents intended to visit her. Margaret had just shrugged. Nothing happened, and the question was not raised again. But now the idea of Tommy coming here was so exciting.

The night before, Margaret lay in bed wide awake for ages, willing time to pass. The next day, after lessons were over, she, John and Patty waited by the gate for the trap to appear. It was a breezy day with racing clouds. Margaret had on a green pinafore dress and T-bar sandals, which the sisters had given her. Would Tommy like her new clothes, she wondered? Impatiently she scuffed at the road with her shoes. It seemed an age before they heard Rags' hooves and the trap came into view with someone perched up at the back.

John and Patty stared with great curiosity as Sissons halted Rags. Margaret looked hungrily up at the back of the trap and saw inside what to her appeared like a little man whom she could barely recognize. Tommy jumped down in one athletic leap and stood in front of her. He was eight now, but he had always been big for his age and he had grown and filled out. He seemed huge to her, with his broad shoulders. His dark hair was also longer than she'd ever seen it and quite unruly, and he was swarthy from being outdoors.

''Ello, Sis,' Tommy said.

''Ello, Tommy.' She wanted to put her arms round him, but when she went to do so he shook her off.

'None of that,' he said with a swagger.

He was wearing a very large pair of trousers cut down for him and belted in at the waist, and a brown shirt that also looked too big, so that he had enormous rolls of sleeve up each arm. On his feet were a pair of muddy black boots, and there were smears of muck and mud all over his trousers. Margaret was in awe of him, and a bit frightened.

'So, this is where you are.' He looked at the house with a direct gaze. 'Looks very nice.'

'It is,' Margaret said. 'And this is John and Patty.'

Though they were older than him, Tommy looked them up and down with a slight air of disdain. Margaret could see that he considered himself a man now, and all of them children.

'D'you want to have a look round?' John asked. He had been pleased there was another boy coming.

'All right,' Tommy said as if he was doing them a favour. His voice sounded loud and rough compared with John's.

They showed him round the orchard and garden, then the paddock. While they were walking down there, Margaret tried to keep close to Tommy. She wanted to be near him. 'Have you seen our mom?' she asked him.

Tommy turned in an irritated way. 'How d'you think I'd've seen 'er? She ain't gunna come out 'ere, is ' er?'

They showed him round everywhere, though of all things Tommy seemed most at home in the paddock with the cows. The sisters had arranged a nice tea, and he sat at the table with them and certainly ate his fill. He talked about the farm where he was billeted, about milking cows, and about barns and hay and straw and chickens. He talked about his hosts, Mr and Mrs Wilkins. Once Margaret heard him refer to them as Mom and Dad. Inside, she could smell his clothes too.

To give Sissons time to get back, they had to leave straight after tea.

'Bye then, Sis,' Tommy said, climbing up on the trap.

'Bye, Tommy. Will you write us a letter? I'll write you?'

Tommy made a gesture with his hand, which she could see meant that he wouldn't.

'See yer,' he said. 'Glad you're all right.' And he sprung up onto the trap and sat with his knees agape.

For a moment it felt unbearable that he was leaving, but then the feeling passed.

Margaret stood waving him off, with John and Patty, who were now far more like a brother and sister to her than her once-beloved Tommy. Now Tommy seemed like a stranger.

Eighteen

On 18th March 1944 the RAF dropped more than three thousand tons of bombs on the city of Hamburg.

In the scale of world disaster, compared with the devastation of this city or that, the grief of a little girl in a rural English village registers zero – below zero – as do the feelings of all children in wartime. But that same day, 18th March 1944, felt to Margaret like the end of her life.

She was nine years old by then – two months away from her tenth birthday. For more than six months now she had been the only child living in Orchard House. John's and Patty's parents, who had in any case visited them regularly, came to the conclusion that they would now be safe enough back in Sparkhill. They were missing their children too much to leave them in the country any longer – and there was always the option to come back.

'You will come and see us, when you get back to Birmingham, won't you, Margaret?' Patty said before they left. She had grown into a tall, graceful fourteen-year-old. John had also shot up and become rather gangly.

Margaret missed them both terribly. But she was made much of in Orchard House by the sisters, one of whom missed her own sons, while the other had never achieved her hope of having children of her own. And by now Margaret was also attending the village school. She had made other friends, learned to talk like them, be one of them. She was a village girl now, with a country accent, living in a house with educated, gentle people. She was learning at school, completely used to the routine and the teachers. Until someone mentioned it and reminded her, Margaret had almost forgotten she was an evacuee and had forgotten about Tommy, who had never come to see her again. These days she never gave Birmingham a thought.

She felt secure and loved, and she had learned to love back. There were so many creatures to love: the sisters of course, and Patty and John. But there was also her constant, tail-wagging companion Dotty, and the cows (Mildred had died and been replaced by another called Beryl, and Poppy was still going strong) and Rags. And there were the hens, whose warm eggs she was used to going and collecting before breakfast, and a favourite lamb every year on the farm ... And there were kindly Emily, and old Sissons, who let her help him around the garden and paddock, talking to her now and then through his pipe.

This was life, so far as she was concerned. It would just go on and on.

The sisters had not told her that they had received a note from Ted Winters, her father, that was so brusque and rude they hadn't known how to reply or what to do.

That Saturday midday they were finishing off making bread, with Margaret and the sisters and Emily the maid all round the big kitchen table, which was dusted with flour. The room was cosy and the windows steamed up. Margaret was standing on a stool. They had taught her how to knead the dough, which she was doing as hard as she could.

'That's it, Margaret – a nice lot of air in it,' Jenny Clairmont said. 'We'll soon have it in the oven.'

The knocking came at the back door. Margaret first saw a pair of scruffy boots on the step, and some faded black trousers. Above, a jacket swinging open, a stained green jersey and a rough, dark-eyed face, shadowy with stubble.

'May I help you?' Mrs Higgins asked. Margaret could hear that she was afraid of this stranger with his grim expression.

'Ar – yer can. I've come to fetch my wench. A right rigmarole I've 'ad getting 'ere an' all.' He nodded towards Margaret. 'That 'er then?'

Margaret's hands were clogged with dough. She just stood there as it dried on, encasing her fingers. Jenny Clairmont wiped her own hands and went to join her sister by the door.

'I'm sorry,' she said. As the taller of the two, she seemed to have more power in the situation. 'I'm afraid we have no way of knowing who you are.'

'I'm that wench's father,' Ted Winters said angrily. 'And I've come to tek 'er back 'ome with me. That's all yer need to know about me.'

'Maggie?' Jenny turned. 'Is this – do you know this man?'

Margaret's knees had gone weak. She shook her head. Dimly, very dimly she did remember him, but . . . But . . . Her head started to whirl inside. Her father? What did this mean?

'Course she does,' he said. ''Er always was a slow'un. Now, you pack up and come with me. You're needed at home – sharpish. Got to get back to Birnigum today.'

Margaret managed one word, which came out as a whimper. 'Mom?'

'Yer mother passed on years back. Now get yerself together. Don't keep me waiting.'

'I'll take her upstairs,' Jenny Clairmont said. 'Wash your hands, Maggie.'

She was in a state, Margaret could see. As soon as they were out of earshot Jenny took hold of her by the shoulders.

'Is that really your father? Are you sure?'

Margaret nodded. It was as if three thousand tons had gone off in her head. It was hard even to breathe.

She thought Jenny Clairmont was going to weep. 'We should so like you to have stayed here ... But you're his daughter. I can't—'

Margaret sucked in a gulp of air. 'I want to stay here with you. Don't make me go!'

There was nothing much the sisters could do. The child's father had come; they could hardly refuse to give her back to him. They hurried to give her everything they could: a holdall with her clothes and shoes, her teddy, sandwiches and fruit. They helped her put her coat on.

'Goodbye, dear ...'

'Oh, goodbye ...'

She kissed each of their soft cheeks, wet with tears, as were hers. She had a scream bigger than herself trapped inside.

'Let us have your address before you go, Mr Winters,'

Mrs Higgins asked, 'so that we can write to dear Maggie . . .'

'Two, back of sixteen, Upper Ridley Street,' Ted Winters called dismissively over his shoulder. Without another word of gratitude or civility for the women who had cared for his daughter all these years, he hustled Margaret out of the door, not caring that she was sobbing her heart out.

'We've got a long walk ahead of us, so yer can pack in yer blarting,' he said. 'Give us that bag and let's get on with it.'

The sisters had to shut Dotty in the house to stop her chasing after them. They came out to the road and stood waving and wiping their eyes as Margaret and her father began the eight-mile walk to Worcester, from where they would catch a train to Birmingham.

Margaret sat in her front room as the memories washed through her. It came to her as physical pain, the same aching sickness she had felt then, as this man who called himself her father tore her step by step away from everything she knew and loved.

She could see her feet as they had been then, in some brown, second-hand boots that she had been given once she had grown out of Tommy's, her blue wool skirt and little macintosh. Her father's feet marched ahead of her, his heels worn almost to nothing. She watched those heels with loathing. Everything about him was foreign to her. He was carrying the holdall, but after a while he said, 'Bugger this, I ain't carrying this all the way . . .' He threw it over the gate into a field.

Margaret stalled. Everything of hers was in there: her little life, her treasures. 'I want it,' she said.

'Why?' he turned, sneering. 'Is there summat we can sell in there?'

'My things . . .' She moved to go and fetch it, but he grabbed her by the arm.

'Goo on – get moving, yer silly little bint.'

Now, all these years later, Margaret closed her eyes and let herself remember that day when her real self, her glowing little soul that had been nourished by her life in Buckley, had sputtered and died. Her face creased with the agony of it, of all that it had meant. And back then, as a nine-year-old, she had not known what was waiting for her in Birmingham, of those desolate years ahead. All she knew was this tearing away by a man whom she already hated with all a child's hurt and passion.

Nineteen

Meena sat on a stool by the breakfast bar in the kitchen, a long cardigan over her nightclothes, cradling a mug of tea up close to her face. Its sweet, milky aroma filled her nostrils. Silently she watched her husband getting ready for work.

Khushwant was at the table with his back to her, munching toast and turning the pages of yesterday's *Evening Mail*. His hair needed cutting, she saw. Once a raven-black, vigorously sprouting head of hair, it was greying now and encroaching down over the collar of his black jacket. The collar also showed up scattered specks of dandruff. He finished the last of his hot chocolate, belched softly and pushed his chair back. Closing the newspaper, he tapped it with his finger, twisting round to remark, 'All this beating up of miners – sticks and truncheons! This country's getting like India.'

Meena smiled faintly. Her husband was a good man, she knew that now. At forty-five years, he was prematurely stooped as if a weight was bearing down on him, and his joints were already arthritic: the fruits of years of hard work and worry, and his love of fatty foods. He was a big, lumbering man these days, with a heavy stomach on him.

'You should become a *sannyasi* like the Hindus,' she would tease him sometimes, patting his blancmange of a stomach as they lay in bed. 'Go out begging for a handful of rice to fill your belly. Then you wouldn't be so fat.'

Khushwant would chuckle.

'Leave me alone, woman. I'm a prosperous business-man – what need have I to go begging? Anyway, how would it look if I was lean like a beggar? Everyone would think my business is failing.'

'Too much butter,' Meena would retort. Her own body stayed stubbornly wiry and thin. 'So much fat – I could light you up, like a candle!'

Laughter and teasing. It had not always been like that. It had taken years for them to grow into each other. These modern women, she thought, they would have left long ago.

'Is *she* going out today?' His heavy features lifted towards the ceiling. Both knew he meant Roopinder. Neither of them had warmed to their daughter-in-law or found her easy.

'To her mother's.'

Khushwant rolled his eyes.

'See you later.' He picked up his lunch box, which she had prepared, stuffed with his favourite things: cheese sandwiches with lime pickle, onion *pakoras*, KitKats, bananas, and his flask of sweet, milky tea. She heard the front door close and the car starting up. Even now it astonished her that they had not just one car, but three. Roopinder had a little one to run the children about in, and Raj had just bought another to get to work. In the evening the tarmac at the front was crowded with them. Meena could remember when a bicycle had seemed an unaffordable luxury.

She was jolted out of her reminiscences by Raj. He nodded sullenly at her. His appearance immediately made her anxious and she spoke sharply.

'You'll be late. You need to hurry up.'

Raj poured himself a bowl of cornflakes, clicked on the radio and sat glued to it as he ate. He was sideways on to Meena and she studied him, assailed by the usual, almost unbearable tension of emotions that both her older two children now brought out in her.

The crisis in Amritsar had resulted in the army storming the Golden Temple, causing terrible damage. Among the dead, they discovered in the aftermath, was Jarnail Singh Bhindranwale, the leader of the occupation, now being hailed by his followers as a hero and martyr. The Sikh uprising had been brutally crushed. Everyone was scandalized, grief-stricken, but Raj took it deeply personally. He had been full of grief and anger ever since.

Raj's blue turban was tied immaculately. Below it he wore a neat, black sports shirt over black trousers. She knew he had practised hard to get the turban right. Wearing it, even with his new growth of beard, made his face look rounder and more boyish, though she would never have aroused the wrath of a warrior for Khalistan by saying so. The sight of it twisted her inside, pride and concern all entangled.

When he was small she had left his hair uncut, tied it up in the traditional topknot worn by young Sikh boys. When they came to England, although there were other Sikh children (some with topknots, some without), Raj had become very embarrassed by it at school. He begged her to let him stop wearing it.

'They tease me, Mummy – they say I look like a girl.' She could see his anguished little face now, his eyes full of tears.

Khushwant had ceased wearing a turban and went clean-shaven. He said it was much easier to get a job in

England that way, to fit in and build a life in the country. Unlike some people, they had had no thought of going back to India to live. They had already been uprooted once, each of them in childhood, from what was now Pakistan. India had never felt quite like home. Khushwant's family had come to Delhi from Jhelum in western Punjab. Both families knew what it was to leave their livestock, their crops rotting in fields that their people had farmed for generations, to go to a place where you had no land. Leaving a second time was a little easier. They had cast their lot in the UK and it had to work.

So Meena had untied Raj's topknot and taken him for a haircut at the front-room barber's down the street in Smethwick, feeling as if God, the Gurus and every Sikh in the district was breathing down her neck.

And, now, Raj wanted to be a Sikh, to wear the turban and bangle and other marks of his religion with pride. And she was proud of him for it, tender towards him. But she knew that for him it was not just a matter of pride – it was rage and defiance and self-assertion of a kind that Raj had had brewing inside him for years, and this made her tremble for him. To be proud to be a Sikh was one thing; but what of the way Bhindranwale had done it? Blood leading to more blood. In those faces on the TV screen, in the eyes of those young men who followed him, she saw that fanatical hatred and bloodlust that awoke images she never wanted to remember. Things you could never talk about. Eyes she had seen in Amritsar, eyes that led to screams and blood and flames. And sometimes she saw Raj's eyes looking out that way.

The phone rang. Raj leapt up to answer it, clicking the radio off. A heated conversation followed: in Punjabi, so she could understand it. There were to be demonstrations, arrangements for Hyde Park. Raj was full of fighting talk. 'We've got to show those bastards . . . Fight to the death, if necessary . . .'

Meena watched him: Raj's whole frame was tensed with anger and self-importance. Now he had a focus for his anger. She sighed from the depths of her. Why couldn't Raj be like his father and just keep out of it all? But all he could seem to feel for his father was contempt.

'Won't you be late?' she said again, coldly, as he put the phone down.

'Yeah, yeah,' he said, dismissing her.

'Son . . .' Her voice was gentler now. She was fighting back tears. If she cried, he would despise her more. 'I am afraid of what will happen.'

He didn't even look at her. He pushed away the half-eaten cereal so hard that it nearly fell off the table. 'We'll handle it. It's our business. Nothing for you to worry about.'

'All this violence – it's no way to—'

'What do you know?' he roared, turning on her. 'They're going round the countryside in Punjab hunting out Sikhs, killing people – *our* people . . . Oh, you're just a woman. You don't know anything . . . Look, I've got to go.'

He slammed out. Everything was suddenly quiet. It was still only seven-fifteen and the others were in bed.

Meena slipped down from the stool. She went to the table and sat spooning up the remains of Raj's cereal. It would go to waste otherwise.

The time she had first told Raj they were going to England was on a warm September afternoon. They had been in Delhi for some time by then, having left Amritsar after the great fire took their house.

Khushwant had left for England in the summer of 1960, but Meena had remained behind with his brothers and acid-faced mother. Their humble family home in Delhi was not far from where her uncle Nirmal lived, which made Meena happy to be there, as she saw him often.

Mama-ji Nirmal was her mother's younger brother, who had left Gujranwala with them. With his gentle, humorous ways he had long been the most important person in her life. His proximity, with his wife Bhoji and their children, made life with Meena's mother-in-law much more bearable. Nirmal was doing well with his taxi business and he often came to see her, bringing treats, bangles and sweets or a little toy for Raj. Somewhere Nirmal had heard about Father Christmas in England and his 'Ho, ho, ho!', and that was often how he announced himself when he arrived.

'Ho, ho, ho!' they would hear at the door and Raj would run, giggling, to greet Nirmal, whose big teeth always gave him a look of smiling mischief. He would scoop Raj into his arms. A smile spread over Meena's face as she remembered. Nirmal was always the person who had brightened her day, made her feel safe. He had been the one it had made her heart ache to leave behind.

At the back of the house was a small piece of scrubby ground shaded by a *peepal* tree with its big, rustling leaves, and that afternoon she was sitting beneath it on the dry ground, her little son in her lap.

'We are going to see your *Pita-ji*,' she told Raj carefully. He had never met Khushwant, who had left for England two months before his son was born in September 1960.

Raj twisted round to look at her. His glossy hair was tied in a little white topknot. His huge, long-lashed eyes shone with excitement.

'*Pita-ji*? We are going to see *Pita-ji*?' Raj was convinced his father was the most exciting thing in the world. The reality had been a betrayal from which she believed he had never fully recovered.

They had been married for seven months when Khushwant left. She must have conceived Rajdev in the first week of marriage, bruised and desperate as she was.

For the first three nights he had set about her as soon as they were alone, slapping her face, knocking her to the ground. Khushwant had been a well-made man, even in those days, though he was not carrying surplus fat. He cut her lip one night and she hid her swollen face the next day. Two of her teeth came loose. All this was the prelude to sexual relations, a fast, thrusting event in the dark, which hurt her even more because of her bruises. For a time she bore it. Bear everything: he is your husband, he is as God ... On the fourth night a cry burst from her lips.

'Why are you doing this? What have I done that you punish me like this?'

Khushwant, who was drawing his hand back to strike her, stopped, looking in astonishment at the frail, pretty woman before him.

'You are my wife!'

'But why should you hit me? I have done nothing wrong.'

The room was almost dark. She could see the glint of his eyes in the candlelight.

'It is my place to hit you. It is what I must do.'

Meena's father had never hit her mother. Even after all that had happened, after the severest of provocation a man could endure: no violence. The two of them had suffered in silence.

'No,' she said quietly. 'It is not. Why do you think it is?'

Even now, looking back, she was amazed by her certainty and courage. It was almost the only time in her life that she had spoken out.

By the time he left for England the beatings had stopped. Sometimes he lashed out at her, when he was impatient in the way of a husband, but he did not make a session of it, as he had at first. She knew Khushwant was not naturally a violent person. He did not welcome physical exertion. His father and brother had led him to think this was the way to do things – to beat her into submission from the first day. She showed him that he had already succeeded. He did not need to beat her; she would meet his every need and command. There were no feelings – not then. All she hoped for was a life without being assaulted each night, to have a roof over her head, food in her belly . . . and to have a family. By the time Khushwant left she was carrying his child. If he was pleased, he didn't show it.

Despite all her fears of leaving India, and the wrench of leaving *Mama-ji* Nirmal, she had been ready to go. A woman on her own was useless, of no status, Meena felt, even though she had given birth to a son. She needed to be with her husband.

Lapping up the last spoonfuls of Raj's milk, she remembered an English saying that Sooky had once translated for her: *A woman needs a man like a fish needs a bicycle.*

At first she had stared blankly at her daughter. Then

she laughed until her sides ached. 'Hah! So I am a fish and he is a bicycle. That is marriage!'

She had been ready to come here, to the damp, shared terrace in Smethwick, a mile from the High Street, with its freezing rooms, its outside toilet and pale, incomprehensible neighbours. The friendliest had been Mrs Platt next door, with her hair curlers, jiggling false teeth and little zipped boots, who talked on and on at Meena, even though she could understand not a word the woman was saying. But she always made a fuss of Rajdev, chucking him under the chin and greeting him with, 'Oooooh, bab . . .' followed by a string of words that seemed kindly enough. Meena tried smiling and nodding her head, and that seemed to satisfy Mrs Platt, who soon scurried off into her own dishevelled house again.

'What did she say?' she'd ask Raj as he grew older and was speaking English. But even then he'd shrug, looking bemused.

'When are we going home?' he asked, all through that first winter, his face twisted with misery.

Never had Meena been colder or more lonely. The other four occupants of the house on the Oldbury Road were all single men, and Meena found it was her job to shop, cook and clean for them all. Khushwant came with her at first, to show her where to go, how to shop and use English money. He had learned some broken English by then. She found it hard to go out sometimes, as she didn't have the right clothes and her shoes were flimsy. All the white people seemed to be staring at her. One day Khushwant came home with a big pair of wellington boots for her, which at least kept the water out, though she didn't like to wear them. They made her feel like a man.

'Just be thankful you weren't here last winter,' he told her. The early months of 1963 had already become a legend of snowbound endurance. Meena thought the cold this time round was quite bad enough. The greyness and drizzling rain dragged her spirits down.

And though her husband was seldom violent towards her now, it felt as if they were strangers to one another. She had not known him well to begin with, and England had changed him. He and the other tenants were working long hours in a foundry. Khushwant was always under pressure, tired and mostly absent. He had never been a religious man and in those days seldom went to one of the *gurdwaras* that were being set up in Smethwick. At that time Meena did not like to go by herself. It was only later that she made some friends. The men's favourite way to unwind was over a pint in the local pub. Meena spent many hours alone, on a blanket laid on the linoleum, crouched up by the old gas fire. She never complained; and met troubles with silence.

Sometimes she dreamed of running away, of getting on a boat or a plane back to India. If she begged her uncle, would Nirmal take her in?

That winter the men had clubbed together and bought a second-hand television. Meena left the Test Card on for company when there were no programmes, its jaunty music streaming through the house. On its jumpy black-and-white news broadcast she saw the President of the United States of America being shot, the month after she arrived in England.

Even when Khushwant was home, they didn't have much to say to each other. Home was for food, sleep and sexual relief.

'Why doesn't Daddy come home?' Raj would ask, hurt.

Khushwant showed little interest in his son, who had arrived in England three years old and a stranger. He had not seen him grow up and had no idea how to handle a child. He seemed to have no feeling for Raj: the boy was Meena's business, so far as Khushwant was concerned. Raj was to be hustled off to bed as soon as he appeared.

'Tell him to stop making that noise,' he would say grumpily if Raj was playing. Now and then, at weekends, he would join in and come on a visit to the park. But Raj knew; he did not feel loved or wanted by his father. Not the way his younger siblings were wanted when they arrived. Nor did he feel in the least English. He was the one born in India, the one who was different. It had always marked him.

It was Sukhdeep whom Khushwant had wanted the most. The first child born in England, somehow she had made things better. Meena had been surprised by this. Sukhdeep was only a girl, after all. But she seemed to help Khushwant belong, to feel as if he was truly part of a family. And Sukhdeep had adored him from the start. They were in tune with each other in a way that he and Raj had never been.

A memory came to her of following Khushwant and Sukhdeep down the street when the little girl was about six, a wiry, bright-eyed little thing. She was clutching her father's hand and looking up at him, chattering and skip-skipping along. Khushwant turned and looked down at her with a smile, the sort of smile Meena had never seen truly directed at her, spontaneous and full of love. It was a glimpse of what was possible. *It's not her fault*, she had told herself as the blade of jealousy stabbed through her. *Not her fault if her father loves her . . .*

As Sooky had grown older, she had also grown closer to her mother. Meena loved having daughters. As well as enjoying their company, their duty was to fulfil the family's *izzat* – the honour of doing right in the community. Sooky had been a good student and a sweet, lively child. But then came her marriage.

Meena closed her eyes. As usual, any thought of her daughter filled her with rushing emotions, like two waves surging towards each other in opposing directions and colliding, causing her nothing but turmoil.

Twenty

Joanne pushed Amy's buggy into the church hall and looked round, surprised. It was already twenty past ten, no toys had been put out and the hall seemed deserted.

Tess appeared out of the kitchen in a pea-green vest and a green-and-blue patterned skirt. Even in the week that had passed she seemed to have grown much more heavily pregnant. Her frizzy hair was pulled into a high ponytail and she was fanning herself with a cardboard plate.

'Oh, hi!' she smiled in her usual warm way, but Joanne could sense her weariness. 'Well, today's the day. I'd planned to take us all off down to the park at some point, and it's so lovely out there . . .'

'Oh, right,' Joanne said. 'Amy, we're going to the park with your friends. That'll be nice, won't it?'

She knew Amy had been longing for the painting table. Her face was beginning to crumple.

'It'll be fun – and I expect Priya's coming.'

Tess squatted down, knees splayed round her bump. 'Hello, Amy. We're going to take some games outside, and have some races. Can you run fast?'

Amy loved Tess. She nodded, sucking on one of her fingers.

'Where's your lad?' Joanne looked round.

'Actually I left him with my mother today. I just felt

155

a bit grim this morning, and running this is so much easier if it's just me – at least at the moment!' She stood up with an effort. 'Oof,' she said. 'Lucky I do yoga!' There was a sheen of perspiration on her forehead.

'It must be really hard, doing all this,' Joanne said. 'When're you due?'

'Early August – about four more weeks. We've only got two more weeks in here anyway – we pack up over the summer.'

'Oh, I see.' Joanne felt her heart sink. Of course they would, but she hadn't thought about it. The toddler group felt like her lifeline.

The others started arriving, and Tess went off to greet them. Joanne hoped Sooky would be on time, though Tess said that she would leave a note on the door to tell anyone who arrived late where they had gone. In a few moments a wave of happiness passed through Joanne as she saw Sooky push Priya through the door. She was wearing pink today, Asian clothes, with a black cardigan over the top. As soon as she saw Joanne she waved and hurried over.

'Hello!' Her face was all smiles. Joanne thought how pretty she was. 'Hello, Amy. I got here on time for once! I hear we're going on an outing?'

The little girls were bouncing with pleasure in their buggies.

'I'm glad you got here. Yes, Tess has got it all organized. I think we'll all have to help her carry stuff, though.'

Soon they all set off, with various bags from Tess stashed under their buggies. The green of Handsworth Park opened out in front of them, the flowerbeds bright with colours, and Joanne felt her spirits lift.

'We'll go and let them feed the ducks first,' Tess

passed back the message. 'Then we'll spread out and do some games.'

Tess, ever prepared, had brought a couple of cheap loaves of bread, and soon all the children who were old enough were on the bank, hurling bits of the white pap at the ducks and Canada geese. Then they moved on to the flattest piece of grass they could find, as the park had a lot of slopes. Tess was announcing that the children should get into a line as they were going to do an egg-and-spoon race.

'Blimey, she's even brought real eggs,' Joanne laughed. 'There's going to be scrambled egg all over the park after this!'

'I think she hard-boiled them,' Sooky said. 'She's amazing. Our girls are too young for that, though.'

The children old enough to take part were just getting lined up when a voice called out, 'Hold on: one more!'

Kieran, the dad who sometimes came, was trotting towards them with the baby strapped to him in a sling and his little boy holding his hand. 'Go on, Billy – look. Get a spoon . . .'

Billy was very eager to join in and balanced his egg earnestly.

'Hi,' Kieran said, appearing beside Joanne and Sooky. 'I'm glad I made it. I went to the hall first – didn't realize you were all coming out here.'

'He seems happy enough,' Joanne said, looking at Charlie, the baby, who was fast asleep against his father's chest.

'Oh yes,' Kieran said, grinning. He had widely spaced teeth and this had a cheerful effect. 'He loves it in here.'

Tess produced a couple of balls and the children

took turns to kick them between goalposts made from their mother's jumpers. Amy and Priya were quite happy playing together in their own little world. After a few more games they all sat down for squash and biscuits, which Joanne had carried along on her buggy. They all sat, half in shade, half in sun.

'Ah, this is the life,' Kieran said, stretching out his legs, but still rocking gently to keep Charlie asleep.

'How's your wife?' Sooky said carefully.

'Well, some good days, some bad, you know. She's called Gerri by the way. Geraldine.'

'D'you think she's getting better?' Joanne asked. It made her think of her mom. You never quite knew how you'd find her.

Kieran's face was solemn, and for a moment the strain of it all showed through.

'God, I hope so. The hospital are talking about ECT . . .'

'What's that?' Joanne asked.

'Electroconvulsive therapy,' Kieran said. 'They sort of pass electricity through your head – it's supposed to help depression.'

'Whoa!' Sooky said. Her face was full of sympathy. 'That's a big thing.'

'Yeah,' Kieran shrugged. Joanne realized how haggard he looked when he wasn't putting on a cheerful face. 'I'm praying they don't do it. But you just wonder if you're ever again going to see the person you knew. It's like watching someone get lost – as if she can't find herself.' He looked over at Billy, who was sitting beside one of the other boys. 'Or us.'

'How's he dealing with it?' Joanne asked. She could see that Kieran was relieved to have someone to talk to.

'Well, we go and see her sometimes. It upsets her

a lot. I mean, this one's so young – she wanted to breastfeed him, but I've had to give him a bottle . . . I think Billy understands that Mummy isn't very well. But in the end he's only just four. It's very tough on him.'

'It's tough on all of you,' Sooky said.

Kieran gave a wonky smile. 'Yeah, you could say that.'

'I think you're very brave,' Joanne said.

He chuckled. 'No – not brave. You just have to keep on keeping on. Anyway, enough of all this. Let's talk about something else. And I need to give this one a bottle soon. And check whether Billy needs to pee . . .'

Kieran got up and went over to his son.

'Poor bloke,' Joanne said.

'Yeah.' Sooky was watching him. Joanne saw that her own expression was very sombre. Now that Kieran had moved away, Joanne realized her friend had something on her mind.

'Is everything okay?' she said. 'I mean, I hope you don't mind me asking?' She liked the way Sooky had spoken to Kieran so directly. 'Is your mom speaking to you again yet?'

Sooky turned to her, shaking her head. 'No, not really. I mean, she says things through Dad, or whoever else . . .'

'That's terrible – I mean having to live with that. Mind you, my mom's not the easiest of people . . .' Seeing the pain in Sooky's eyes, she stopped. 'What's up?'

'Oh, it's just that they want me to see someone. He's coming on Friday.'

'You mean a man?'

'Yes, someone who's come over from India. He's got relatives in Leicester.' She was looking down, her slim fingers plucking at the grass almost as if she was ashamed.

'But surely you can't even be divorced yet?'

'I'm not. But, you know, he's the same age as me, and all the other things . . .'

'What other things?'

'He's a Jat: that's our group, our caste . . . He wants to come and live here.' Sooky's picking at the grass became more forceful. 'I think the idea is that it will take time for me to get a divorce. I'd go to India and marry him, you see, and then he can apply to come to the UK as my husband.'

Joanne was filled with a sense of panic on Sooky's behalf. 'But what if you don't like him? Are you just getting married for your mom?'

'I probably won't like him,' Sooky said. 'He's grown up on a farm in India, he doesn't speak English, he's never lived in a city. It's like someone coming from Jupiter and asking me to marry him.'

'I thought that's what you wanted?' Joanne joked. 'Someone off the *Starship Enterprise*.'

That set them both off laughing.

'He might have green ears,' Sooky said.

'Or one big eye in the middle of his forehead!'

'The thing is,' she managed to say, still laughing, 'I'm supposed to be grateful for anyone wanting to marry me – I'm soiled goods. And he wants a visa!'

'Oh God,' Joanne groaned. 'But surely you can say no?'

'Yes, I can say no.' The laughter had faded from Sooky's eyes now. 'I want to apply to college. But how many more times is it going to take? Do I have to get married just to get my mom to speak to me again?'

As they cleared up, packing away the snacks and toys, Joanne felt suddenly that she could not bear to go home to her empty house. She wanted more company. Going up to Sooky and Kieran, she said, 'Look, I wondered if you'd both like to come back to mine. I live quite near the church – I could make a bit of dinner for the kids and they could carry on playing . . .'

She saw them both hesitate.

'Thing is,' Kieran said, 'I'd like that a lot, but I'm going to have to get home. I haven't got enough formula, and I'll have to put Charlie down.'

'Oh yes, sorry.' Joanne felt herself blush. 'Silly of me. Maybe another time?'

'No, I know what – you could come to ours. I'm really near: in Holly Road. I've got bread and fish fingers and stuff . . . and I could find something for us as well. Would that do?'

Joanne and Sooky looked at each other. Neither of them especially wanted to go home.

'Well, that's nice, if you're sure,' Sooky said.

'Course – it'd be great. I can get the paddling pool out.' Kieran was beaming and Joanne ended up feeling that she had done him a favour.

They all mucked in. Kieran took them to his home, a cosy terrace with comfy sofas, bookshelves, prints of modern painters on the wall and bright Mexican rugs covering the floorboards. While Kieran fed and changed

Charlie before putting him in his cot, he instructed Joanne and Sooky where to find everything to make food for Billy, Amy and Priya. Billy was a friendly little boy and showed the girls outside. Sooky went out with them, while Joanne grilled fish fingers and made bread and butter and slices of cucumber. She smiled at Billy's paintings, which were stuck to the fridge with magnets. As they came through the back room she had seen a gallery of photographs along one wall of Kieran and Gerri and Billy. Gerri had wide blue eyes and thick blonde hair, cut neatly at collar length, and a wide smile. The sight of her happy face seemed heartbreaking.

'There – back to sleep,' Kieran said, coming down again. 'He's a wonderful baby, thank goodness.'

'You're very good with him,' Joanne said. 'Right, food's ready for them.'

They supervised the children eating, while Kieran put some tepid water into a little inflatable paddling pool, then they sat and had their own sandwiches, watching the children splash and scream. Sunlight reflected off the water. Joanne felt herself relax and enjoy the day. She realized with a shock that she hadn't felt so at ease in weeks. The children were having a great time, and it was so nice to have other people to pass the time with.

They all found out a bit about each other. Sooky didn't mention the man coming on Friday. She said she was thinking of applying for a part-time degree in sociology at the Poly.

'Great!' Kieran said. 'That sounds really interesting.'

'I'd like to train as a social worker,' she said. 'Maybe one day, anyway.'

'What about you, Joanne?' Kieran asked. His freckly face was full of genuine interest.

'Oh, I never even finished my A-levels,' she said, with a pang. What a fool she'd been: it would only have been another year. No time at all!

'Well, you could, couldn't you? You can do them at evening classes and stuff now.'

'I suppose so – yes, I might.' Until then it had barely crossed her mind. She felt a flicker of excitement, of possibility opening up.

Kieran told them a bit about his teaching job. 'I s'pose I've always liked kids. I like their inner world and the way they think. And you can be the first person to teach a child to write their own name: that's pretty amazing. It's exhausting, but I can't imagine doing anything else. They've given me the last few weeks of term off – compassionate leave. Hopefully I'll be able to go back next term. We'll have to see.'

The sadness descended again for a moment. Joanne saw that he was relieved to have them there. Three people, all with reasons not to go home and be alone, she thought.

A moment later, Kieran cracked a joke and they were all laughing again.

Twenty-One

All afternoon the house was full of the smell of fried snacks, spicy and mouth-watering.

Sooky kept out of the kitchen. She had twice asked Mom if she wanted any help preparing for the visitors, only to be met by the usual blank silence. When she last peered through the door, Meena was standing at the cooker despatching a batch of spinach *pakoras* into the seething pan of oil, her back ramrod-straight, elbows sticking out. Sooky crept away again and stayed in her room with Priya.

Harpreet came home from school and went into the kitchen for something to eat, only to be chased swiftly out again. She'd managed to salvage a bag of crisps on the way and crept up to find Sooky, who was on her bed, doing a puzzle with Priya.

'What time are they coming?'

Priya bounced up and down with pleasure at the sight of her auntie.

'Six-thirty, I think,' Sooky said.

Harpreet frowned. Through a mouthful of cheese and onion she said, 'Will Dad be back by then?'

'He'll have to be, won't he? He made the arrangements.'

Mr Sohal, the young man's uncle, ran a pharmacy in Leicester. It had suited him to meet in the evening.

Harpreet kicked off her school shoes and curled up

on the bed beside Sooky, seeming stricken with anxiety. Priya slid to the floor and started trying on Harpreet's shoes, her feet like tiny islands inside them.

'God, Sooky, what d'you think he'll be like? I mean, that photo they sent was useless – it could be of anyone.' It was a passport photo, poorly exposed and more like a silhouette. Even so, it hadn't looked too promising.

Sooky shrugged. Somewhere inside her she had switched off and was not allowing herself to feel anything about it.

'His name's Kanvar,' she said, deadpan. The girls looked at each other, then erupted into giggles. Kanvar meant 'Young Prince'. They laughed until tears ran down their cheeks. Priya giggled at the sight of them, until Harpreet ended up coughing because of the crisps. She scrunched up the bag and threw it into the bin.

'Oh, I can't wait to see this,' she said, wiping her eyes. Then her face changed and her tears were sad ones. 'You might end up marrying him, Sooky ... I don't want you to. He'll probably be revolting; and I don't want you to leave me again. It's no fun here with just the boys – and *her*. Crow-face.' They were united in their dislike of Roopinder.

Sooky swallowed. She loved her sweet little sister. She didn't want to leave her either, but how could she just stay on and on here, the shadowy, disgraced one? For a moment she imagined having a little house of her own, for herself, Priya and Harpreet – and maybe Pav, if he wanted.

'You're going to come in this time, aren't you – and Pav?' Sooky said. 'I need a second opinion. And a third and fourth.'

'Yeah, Mom says we've got to. What about Raj?'

'He's out – some meeting.' Both of them rolled their eyes. 'It's a good job really. He'd start lecturing them about politics.'

Harpreet took Sooky's hand and lifted it to her cheek. Sooky felt the plump, damp warmth of her sister's skin against the back of her hand. They sat in silence for a moment. Then Priya climbed up and laid her hand on Sooky's other cheek, making her want to cry.

'Come on,' Sooky said, getting up. 'What're you going to wear?'

'That . . .' Harpreet pointed at a peach-coloured Punjabi suit that was just visible in the cupboard. 'Mom says.'

'That's pretty. Good choice.'

'Are you wearing that lovely red-and-green one?'

She nodded. Meena had chosen both their clothes, new for the occasion. Sooky felt a sad, sinking feeling. Mom had a funny way of showing she cared.

The house was immaculate. The first thing you saw walking through the front door, across the grey-and-black carpet, was the picture of Guru Nanak on the far wall. On the table underneath it, between two brass candlesticks, Meena had placed a vase of red-and-yellow chrysanths and another on the coffee table in the front room.

Sooky, dressed in her bright, flattering colours and wearing careful make-up, served drinks and snacks to the visitors while Mrs Sohal, the boy's aunt, watched her with an intent, but strange expression. As Sooky passed in and out of the room bringing plates of food,

166

she could feel her mother's stress emanating towards her as she willed her to do everything right. Sooky felt as if she had passed into a weird dream.

They were all positioned round the room on the comfortable fake-leather sofas: Pavan, forced into a suit and looking as if he had a rod up his back; Harpreet, homely in her peach outfit; Mom in a pale blue and gold with a touch of lipstick and her hair up, held back with matching blue plastic combs; and Dad in his best jacket.

Facing them were Mr and Mrs Sohal, who were both rather small, neat-looking people. He was about fifty, wearing a pale-blue turban and suit, and had a gentle expression. His wife, in a deep-green outfit, looked . . . what was it? Sooky puzzled as she handed her a cup of tea and received a nod in acknowledgement. Gradually it dawned on her that the woman was very, very embarrassed.

Seated between them was the Young Prince. Sooky had managed to sneak glances at him while she was waiting on everyone. First impressions had been bad enough, but once she was able to sit down, she could take a good look at him. She had been told that he was twenty-four, but he looked a lot older. He was small, dead-eyed, with a strange knobbly nose, as if some kind of fungus was growing on it, and the worst case of acne scarring she had ever seen. His mouth made her think of toads.

I thought they'd eradicated smallpox, was her first thought. She told herself not to be so cruel. After all he couldn't help it. Perhaps he had hidden depths.

In the meantime the families had been chatting in Punjabi about their respective lives and businesses. Then they moved on to their children.

'Pavan is a very good student,' Meena told Mrs Sohal. 'He is studying now for his A-levels in physics, maths and further maths: he is hoping to become an engineer. And our other daughter, Harpreet, she is doing her O-levels.'

'GCSEs,' Harpreet pointed out. 'They've just changed it.'

'Oh,' said Mrs Sohal, uncertainly.

Then they came to Sooky. They knew about her marriage, of course.

'Sukhdeep was also an excellent student,' Khushwant told them. Sooky was warmed by the real pride in his voice.

'And as you see, she is proficient in her domestic duties,' Meena went on.

Sooky sat, staring mainly down into her lap, partly to look like a good, modest Punjabi girl who had been shamed and chastened. But it was equally because she was afraid that if she met Harpreet's eye the hysteria that was building inside her would burst out in a fit of crazed cackling. Every so often she glanced up with a slight, modest upturn of her lips, careful to avoid looking anywhere near her sister.

Then it was Kanvar's turn to be discussed.

'Does he not speak *any* English?' Khushwant asked, switching to English himself for a moment.

'He has not had the opportunity to learn,' Mr Sohal said.

Mrs Sohal gave a desperate smile. 'I'm sure he would pick it up very quickly,' she said. 'He is quite an intelligent boy really.' She didn't sound entirely convinced about this.

Sooky took a quick peek round the room. Poor Pav was sweating uncomfortably in his suit and tapping his hand rhythmically on one knee, perhaps as a way of hypnotising himself into staying sane. Her father was munching snacks, throwing peanutty handfuls into his mouth. Her mother sat demurely. Sooky slid her eyes quickly over Harpreet to examine the Young Prince.

He was dressed in Western clothes: black trousers and a white shirt with a jacket that didn't quite match. His hair was plentiful, well-oiled and cut in a style faithful to the 1970s, a parting on the right and all flicked back towards the left side. Even though nearly all the conversation was conducted in Punjabi, he sat staring vacantly ahead of him. He did not once meet her eyes. For a moment Sooky found herself imagining that everyone in the room had animal heads on their shoulders. Kanvar would definitely be a toad. She almost heard a croak escape from him. Dad was a dog, one of those big gloomy ones with long ears; Mr Sohal a camel; Mom a nervous gazelle . . . She knew Harpreet would look like a scared rabbit . . . She dragged her gaze back to her lap.

The Sohals were raking around for any praises they could sing of Kanvar. He was hard-working, they were told. He had been his father's right-hand man on the farm in India, but he was the third brother in the family. There was not enough farm to go round. His ambition was to run a shop in this country. He was very keen to have a family and settle down; he just had to find the right girl . . . Mrs Sohal's eyes grew wider as she spoke. They reminded Sooky of Pinocchio's nose getting longer and longer. He was also a good religious boy. He said his devotions every morning and frequented the *gurdwara*.

After this conversation had gone on for what felt like several decades, a silence fell. Khushwant wondered,

'Perhaps it would be best if we let these two young people speak to each other alone – just for a few minutes?'

Mrs Sohal looked very unconvinced as to the wisdom of this, but suddenly Sooky found her mother prodding her thigh, urging her to get up. Two chairs had been placed in the little side room by the front door for herself and Kanvar, and everyone else retreated. As they walked side by side for a second, she realized how short he was. Sooky was five foot seven and he came up to about her ear.

They sat, and now she was alone with the toad. He leaned forward, rubbing his hands together (even his fingers looked a bit froggy), his head lowered. His smell, a rank combination of hair oil and sweat, made Sooky want to wrinkle her nose.

She waited for him to speak. Eventually he raised his eyes to her with an arrogant, contemptuous expression and, in his roughly spoken Punjabi, brought out the words, 'So, you left your husband? You are dirty – second-hand goods. And you have a child? A *girl?*' He almost spat out the word. 'You'd better be able to have a son next. You should be grateful for anyone even thinking about marrying you. Lucky for you I came along. I want a visa. Anything to get out of India. You'll do for me to get that. So long as you do everything I say.'

Sooky looked at him expressionlessly, at his ugly, pockmarked face. *Have you no idea just how revolting, how vile and repellent you are?* she wanted to say. Terror seized her. Supposing Mom and Dad thought he was all right – that she should just marry anyone who came along? Honour must be satisfied . . .

He sprawled back in the chair, as if drawing attention to his groin, and stared at her insolently. 'So, what have you got to say?'

Sooky rose slowly to her feet.

'Over my dead body,' she said. In English.

When the Sohals had gone, having been told that they would be hearing from the family, the Baidwans sat down in the front room. There was silence. The room stank of Kanvar's sweaty armpits.

Khushwant took another dip into the bowl of spicy *chevda* mix and sat munching frantically. Meena was crouched forward on the sofa, her elbows resting on her knees, hands supporting her chin, looking at the floor, her face unreadable. Pav and Harpreet didn't seem to know where to look.

After a few moments it occurred to Khushwant that he needed to take charge of the situation. He rubbed his hands together, then wiped them on his thighs to shift the salt and spices.

'Perhaps we could speak to Sukhdeep alone?' he suggested warily.

'Dad, you can't be serious!' Harpreet burst out, to Sooky's eternal gratitude. 'He's the most disgusting thing I've ever seen – he looks like some kind of mutant dwarf! And he reeks! You can't force Sooky to marry him.'

Sooky heard Pav suppress a chortle on the other side of the room.

'Harpreet!' Meena scolded. 'That is very rude and disrespectful.' But even she sounded half-hearted.

'No one is talking about forcing,' Khushwant said with dignity. 'Sukhdeep, *beteh*?'

Hearing this term of affection for the first time in as

long as she could remember, and seeing his serious but kindly expression, made Sooky's throat ache, as if a well of tears might pour out of her. It suddenly felt as if she was his little girl again.

'What do you think of marrying this man?'

'D'you really need to ask, Dad?' She spoke gently. 'I know I'm not a credit to you, that it's hard for you to find anyone, but please, please – not him. I'd rather stay single. In fact I'd rather die.'

Her tears did begin then, the tension of the evening releasing. She put her hands over her face as the sobs took over, and felt Harpreet's hand slide onto her lap, offering comfort.

Her father was quiet for a moment, then she heard him say, 'Very well. I will tell them.'

Tears streaming down her face, Sooky turned to Meena.

'Mom?' It came out as a wail. 'Say something, please. Just *please* talk to me – I can't bear it.'

As her mother looked up, Sooky saw that there were tears in her eyes too. She shook her head.

'He was not right for you. He was a rough peasant and very ill-mannered. It was obvious. There are other men.'

Her body shaking with sobs of relief, Sooky said, 'Thank you. I'm so sorry . . . Thank you . . .'

Twenty-Two

Meena stood in front of the mirror brushing her hair forward over her left shoulder. It hung darkly against her pale nightdress. Head on one side, she studied her reflection: a forty-one-year-old face, thin, with deep lines running from her nose to the corners of her mouth and furrowing her forehead. Once she had looked much like Sukhdeep, though not as pretty. Now her face looked old and a little severe.

'My hair is so sparse these days,' she remarked.

In the mirror she could see Khushwant behind her, already lying in bed, arms bent back under his head. His tummy made a mound under the bedclothes.

'One plait is now so thin. I used to be able to make two like this.'

That had been the fashion among the women when she first came to Smethwick. She had worn two thick, glossy plaits down her back. For a moment she is back inside her younger self, muffled up in a second-hand C&A coat – brown and cream checks – walking down the Oldbury Road to the shops, the cold wind biting through her thin *salwar*-trousers. Now she would be wise enough to put on tights or long-johns underneath. She is holding Raj's hand, the plaits swinging along her back. Walking beside her is her friend Tavleen, with her poor little handicapped girl in the pushchair . . . Sweet, gentle Tavleen, whom she was unable to save,

173

who threw herself in front of a train two days before her twenty-fourth birthday.

Meena forced the memory from her mind. Speedily fastening her hair into one braid again, she stepped out of her slippers, pulled back the bedclothes and climbed in. Khushwant, who by now would usually have been snoring, was wide awake and looking round at her. She met his troubled gaze.

'You are thinking about that Sohal boy?'

'*Boy?* You couldn't call him a boy. He looked about thirty-five years of age!'

There came a wheezing sound and Khushwant's body was shaking suddenly. A guffaw of laughter finally escaped from him, his fleshy face all creased up.

'My God – they really are sending us the scrapings from the bottom of the barrel. I've seen a dead dog with more life in it!' He lay wobbling with laughter. 'And much more handsome too!'

Meena watched him. What was so funny? she thought sniffily. As ever she was the serious one, the one who took everything heavily. The very sight of Kanvar had made her heart sink so low that she could hardly bear to look at him. Enraged as she was by her daughter's situation, the thought of shackling Sukhdeep to that ignorant, stinking *reptile* of a man made her feel like vomiting.

'That poor Mr Sohal – they've got properly saddled with him!' Khushwant was still laughing. 'They'll spend the rest of their lives hunting for a bride. A woman with very bad eyesight will be required.'

'I wouldn't be so sure; there are plenty of desperate girls,' Meena said. 'He is a clod – but the Sohals are nice people. They seem decent.'

'Yes,' Khushwant agreed. 'Nice enough. Poor

things.' He looked round at her, serious suddenly. 'You are going to stop now – this not talking to Sukhdeep? It is creating a very bad atmosphere in the house. It is not good for the others, either. And what will it achieve? It is over; we have to think of her future.'

Meena looked ahead of her towards the mirror, the long green curtains. She felt her mouth tighten, as if clinging to her silence. She knew Khushwant shied away from trouble – of any kind.

'Wife, you have punished her enough. It is hardly her fault if her husband had perverted habits. This she could not be responsible for.'

Meena lowered her head. In a very small voice she said, 'I am afraid. I don't know what to do. Everything is changing.'

Khushwant was snoring now, the fulsome, intermittent snores of a fat man. Meena lay beside him, staring upwards. There was a crack of light round the door. Raj must have come in and was still up. Roopinder, thankfully, had kept out of the way all evening.

As Khushwant fell asleep, she had almost turned to him and spoken. *I am not punishing her*, she wanted to say. *You've got it wrong*. Something had fallen into place like a coin fitting into a slot. Yes, she was angry about Sukhdeep's failed marriage. But, in truth, it was not Sukhdeep she was angry with: it had not been her fault. It was that filthy dog Jagdesh who was to blame.

Instead, the helpless, conflicted rage that seethed within her was aimed towards life itself: at the blows it dealt, at the way she had no control over anything, could do nothing about any of it, and never had been able to. Her silence had been the only way she could contain her feelings. She could find no words for what happened to her mother, to her ravaged country; for Uncle Gurbir; for those cold, desolate beginnings in Smethwick; for Tavleen and others . . . It was all locked inside, eating at her. The English were always talking about things – she heard this from Sukhdeep, and from her friends. Talking, talking. But who was she supposed to talk to? Who had there ever been who wanted to hear her voice? What is the voice of a child when a country is being torn apart? Or the voice of a child with a man's thrusting weight on top of her?

She squeezed her eyes shut. She must not think, must not remember. Kanvar's face swam into her mind, so gross, cruel and ignorant. The moment she had seen him she had known Sukhdeep would refuse him. It was an ugly prospect: that her beautiful, clever daughter could ever be shackled to that filthy village oaf. The thought filled her with anguish.

She had not met Khushwant before their wedding. They were living in Delhi by then, so the full ceremonies usually observed back in the village had been diluted. She did not have to sit out all day in the heat being walked round, examined and commented on by all the relatives, as if she were a stone statue. Of course they all voiced loud opinions anyway. But the main thing she remembered was the moment when she and Khushwant first sat side by side. She had glimpsed him through the red weave of her wedding sari. Beside her he seemed solid, as big as a bear, though he had not been fat then. He seemed both fearsome and reassuring. When she saw him face-to-face, she liked his eyes and thought they looked kind.

When the beatings began, his strength became terrifying to her, his attempts to act out what he had been told was rightful and male. But then he was gone, and when she came to England, he still had no idea about women and children, or how to be a husband. He had no sisters and he had taken a long time to learn.

He even sent someone else to meet them from Heathrow on that grey October day.

'Is that my *Pita-ji?*' Raj had asked, seeing the gangling young man whom Khushwant had sent with a car.

On the journey to the Midlands, Meena had sat huddled in her flimsy clothing, still reeling with amazement at the toilets in the airport and the strangeness of it all. She stared out at a sky the colour of an iron pot, wondering if England was always like this. Khushwant had not thought to warn her about the cold. In more than three years he had only written home once a year – to his mother. He had told them hardly anything. On departure she had said goodbye to his family and to her own. It was her uncle Nirmal who had shown most emotion when she left, and Bhoji his wife. Her own mother went through the motions with no sign of feeling. Jasleen was like a woman in a tomb. Meena felt certain she would never see her again, and she was right. Jasleen had died in 1978 and Meena had never returned home.

But on that car journey, though cold and afraid, she was also excited. She was joining her husband! She was in a new country as a married woman. To marry and to reach England were seen as huge fulfilments.

They moved through streets of smoke-blackened terraces. The house had a thin, dark hallway. As the door opened, she stared at Khushwant's face and, to her relief, recognized it. If anything he looked thinner. Her one shock was his short hair, a fringe falling in a wave across his forehead.

'*Sat Sri Akal*,' he said solemnly. 'Welcome, Wife.'

He paid the young man and Meena took her first step into the house. She remembered him leading her and Rajdev into the back room, where there was a battered sofa covered in a shaggy grey fabric. He told her to sit while he made a cup of tea. She always remembered that cup of tea. His making it for her had felt kind, had warmed her, and it had been strange drinking from the mug he handed her, which was pale brown, with ears of wheat painted on it in dark blue. Of what they had said to each other she had no memory at all. That night, on a creaking metal bedstead, he was almost romantic, falling on her like a man starved, sobbing with pleasure as he throbbed inside her.

Weeks went by in which she hardly felt she saw him at all. The foundry where he worked was not far away, in Spon Lane. But with overtime he was working a fifty-hour week. After work he spent the remainder of most evenings at the Waggon and Horses, quenching the thirst brought about by the hottest and filthiest job of them all: working with molten iron. There a group of them could gather and speak Punjabi together. It was their one indulgence. Most of the men whom she saw lived very frugally – saving, always saving to send money home, to return home themselves or to bring wives over, as Khushwant had done.

The other men in the house, also foundry workers, would be out too, and Meena was left alone. Even anyone who was friendly, like Mrs Platt next door, she could not communicate with as she had no English. She was afraid to go out into the grey streets and gritty air, hated being stared at and the rude comments, even if she could not understand them. As she did not understand English, she was spared the signs in the windows advertising rooms to let: NO COLOUREDS – NO IRISH – NO DOGS.

In the house the other men had their own rooms. She and Khushwant had the biggest, upstairs at the front. Inside, on the brown lino, stood their bed, one chest of drawers and one wooden chair. The walls were covered in ancient, flowery paper with strips torn off and there was a small fireplace with a gas fire. Apart from the tiny kitchen with its stove, sink and drainer there was nowhere else to go downstairs, as all the other rooms were slept in.

'We have combined our funds to buy this house,' Khushwant told her when she complained at being so crowded. 'You are lucky. Before, we were sharing: fifteen, sixteen in a house. This way we can buy. One day we will have our own house. You should stop complaining.'

In his busy working life he could not understand the isolation of hers, or the sad disillusion of their son who was desperate for his attention.

That winter she attended to the household tasks of cooking and washing. She would hum to herself, her voice bouncing off the damp walls. There was a thin garden at the back where she hung out washing, which the smoke from the foundries soon turned grey. Sometimes it all froze solid on the line. The outside lavatory had been a challenge too. The cold seat made her want to scream, and she was worried about snakes out there at first, until Khushwant told her there were none.

She spent almost all the rest of the time in their bedroom, only going out when she was forced to buy food or take Raj for some fresh air. Often she got into bed to keep warm. It was very hard to occupy her little son, cooped up in the room. She watched him turn pale and silent. Khushwant had obtained a couple of toy cars for him and Raj resorted to playing endless games with them.

When she was so cold she could not bear it, Meena would take a match to the gas fire, seeing the pale honeycomb strips flare orange, and sit with a cup of tea, in all the woollens she had, and her coat too, huddled close to it. She tried to make her mind a blank, or to think only of what she must cook for dinner that night: *dal*, rice, some meat once a week . . . For what was the use of dreaming? Home was nothing to dream of, except for the warmth of the sun. And in England? She had no idea what sort of future she might dream of. Her duty was to follow her husband and do his bidding.

As the winter closed in, she would sit for hours, staring at nothing. Later, when they bought the television and rigged it up in one of the downstairs rooms, she sat on the edge of a bed and stared at that instead.

Now, looking back on all those years, she felt grief at the smallness of her dreams.

'You should go to the *gurdwara*,' Khushwant kept telling her. 'That way you will meet others.'

She had walked past the Guru Nanak Gurdwara on the High Street a number of times, but in her depressed state did not have the courage to go in anywhere that she was not forced to by necessity. When Khushwant and the other men went, she stayed alone in the house.

Khushwant told her that the *gurdwara* had first been set up in a school further away in Brasshouse Lane.

'They hired a room, a few of them – and they made arrangements for the Guru Granth Sahib to be transported here from India. Now they have funded the purchase of that church building on the High Street.'

Meena listened to him solemnly. She was awed by these bold arrangements. The idea of making such changes, of asking for the things that were needed – bringing the holy book on an aeroplane all the way from India! – seemed extraordinary to her. It was almost beyond her imagination.

Though not an especially religious man himself, Khushwant seemed to grow taller with pride speaking about it.

'It is the first *gurdwara* outside London,' he said.

When she agreed to go at last, feeling also that Raj should go, she realized that other men were beginning to bring their wives to England. Gradually her world expanded. She met Tavleen and Banita, who became her closest friends and in turn introduced her to others.

As the summer came, they started taking their children to the park together. And Meena realized she was expecting another child.

Slowly, life began to get better.

Twenty-Three

Of the friends she made back in the 1960s, the one Meena was still most in touch with was Banita, whose family also came to live in Handsworth.

Handsworth, like Smethwick, had grown into a 'little India'. So much more was set up now: *gurdwara*s, shops and banks, places where you could watch Punjabi films and networks for everything you could need.

Banita had always given Meena courage. She was several years older and, when they met, already had three children. Tall and thickset with flashing eyes and wide hips, she favoured pinks and oranges for her clothes and invariably decorated her fulsome lips with bright *surkhi* powder. Her husband, despite being officially in charge because he was male, was more than slightly afraid of her. She was loud, forceful and hard-working. In the terms of the community, Banita never put a foot wrong. She bore healthy children – four out of six of them sons – she was devout, saying her morning devotions and attending the *gurdwara*. She was a pillar of the *langar*, the big canteen in the *gurdwara* where the communal meals were prepared. In the hot, steamy atmosphere she could always be found cooking up vats of *dal* and rice pudding. In her rough, country way she was also very kind.

Now, twenty years on, Banita had a nice big house, six grown-up children, a wide, self-satisfied girth and a deep belly laugh. She also appeared to have a contented husband.

Meena was always happy to see her, even though she felt like a skinny little twig in the shadow of Banita's fulsome looks. Banita, a true friend, was one of the ones who had been kind about Sukhdeep's failed marriage.

'Sukhdeep is a good girl,' she said. 'She would not do such a thing to harm anyone on purpose. That husband of hers was a bad lot, a pervert. Best for the child to be out of there. Divorce is not good, but sometimes it has to happen. Times change, you know.'

For this largeness – while others, judging and spiteful, were whispering behind their hands – Meena loved her.

Mostly they didn't mention Tavleen. A lot of time and many other joys and tragedies had passed since then, but once in a while, if they happened to meet around the anniversary of *that day*, they spoke of her.

That day was 24th November 1965, a grey, ordinary Wednesday morning. Tavleen had got up early and, leaving her arrogant, sadistic husband and two-year-old twin girls asleep, had taken four-and-a-half-year-old Jasvinder in her arms and carried her out of the house.

Jasvinder had been born with multiple handicaps. For one thing, she was not a boy, which her father regarded in itself as almost amounting to a crime. She had very little sight and could not walk or speak. The arrival of twin girls two years after her had given Tavleen's husband even more sense of entitlement to beat and bully his wife. To tell her she was a failure. Where was the son he had planned on?

As well as receiving many beatings, her body bore tight, shiny scars where he had thrown a kettle of boiling water over her. A few days before Tavleen carried her daughter through the dawn to Smethwick Rolfe Street station, where she put an end to their suffering forever, she had heard that her beloved sister had died in India, of tuberculosis. Her hopes of one day being reunited with her were snatched away.

'We did not know how bad things were,' Meena and the other women had said to each other in the stunned weeks afterwards. They had known about some of the violence. Tavleen had not been able to hide everything. But she had suffered courageously and mostly in silence. In any case, what could they have done?

To Meena she had been the sweetest of companions. Tavleen was much more softly spoken and shy than Banita. The women got into the habit of congregating together. None of them worked, except a few who did bits of piece-work with a sewing machine at home. Meena had done piece-work for a while, when Khushwant was getting his factory going. She had sewn dresses for a Smethwick firm called Sunshine Fashions.

The women were all looking after children, and it was seen as a lowering of status for a wife to leave the house to work. They would meet in Victoria Park when the weather was fine, or in each other's houses. But it was never Tavleen's house where they met.

The other women all liked Tavleen, with her ready smile. Her two top middle teeth crossed over one another in the middle and the effect was attractive. When they met to chatter or do *gidha*, traditional dancing, she always brought sweets or cakes. And she was kind to everyone's children. Rajdev adored her.

'Is Auntie-*ji* going to be there?' he would ask of any outing. As soon as he saw Tavleen pushing Jasvinder's buggy, he would run to her and she would always halt the buggy and bend down to hug him and give him a special sweet. Looking back, Meena thought she had sensed a kind of loneliness in Raj that echoed her own. This thought pained her as much as any other.

After she died, Raj cried inconsolably. He was quiet for weeks. And Meena saw Tavleen everywhere. At times it was as if she was walking at her side, as she had so often done, and she would find her lips moving, talking to her. She would see her friend buying groceries in a shop and rush in without thinking, to find it was someone else. The sight of a bright-coloured Punjabi suit disappearing round a corner could have her speeding up, to check, just in case . . . Could it all have been a dream, a mistake? Sometimes she heard Tavleen's soft voice when she was alone in the house and would whirl round. At times she feared for her own sanity. Grief, she realized, did strange things to you.

And always there was the sense of guilt. Should Tavleen have been able to talk to her more? If she had known more, couldn't something have been done? But there was always this silence – a silence of fear and of loyalty to tradition. Sometimes a silence that went on until it was all too late.

Tavleen's husband sent the twins back to India to be cared for and disappeared from the community. Soon it was rumoured that he had been seen in Yorkshire.

Tavleen's death changed things for Meena. Until then her own marriage had been functional, nothing more. She expected nothing much from it other than to bear children, to cook and clean and be her husband's servant.

Meena started to look more closely at Khushwant.

What she saw was a man who began to touch her emotions. Khushwant was not a leader or a thinker. He liked to keep his head down and be told what to do. He had begun their marriage by beating her because he believed that was what was expected. But he had learned and changed.

That year, as her belly bulged outwards with the growth of Sukhdeep inside her, among the men Khushwant worked and drank with there was a growing discontent. Pubs like the Waggon and Horses operated an unofficial colour bar.

'They are saying,' Khushwant explained to her, 'that the pub gaffa tells us we can drink in this room, but not in that. That room is for whites only. Whites can drink anywhere, but we have to keep to one or two rooms only. Some people are getting angry about it. A lot of pubs are doing the same thing.'

There was also anger that the black immigrants always got the lowest-paid, hardest work, with no chance to develop to something more skilled.

'Always a "mate" to the white worker, you see,' Khushwant explained. 'They get all the skilled jobs, when we could learn to do the job – easy – and get better pay.'

Meena could see how unfair this was, but when there was talk of forming a union to get things changed, Khushwant slid away from it.

'I don't want to get involved in all that,' he would say wearily. 'I've got enough on my plate. Let others do it, if they want.'

She realized he was afraid. He was not one to stick his head above any parapet, or be political. He did not like change or disturbance. Seeing this, she realized it had taken him a particular kind of courage to leave his homeland, to make this great transition to England and build a future for their family. She admired him afresh for it.

Four months after Sukhdeep was born, in June 1964, there had been a General Election, which affected Smethwick in a particularly ugly way. The Labour candidate, who had held the seat for the previous four General Elections, was expected to win comfortably. However, he was ousted. Smethwick, which had chosen Oswald Mosley as its MP in the late 1920s, voted in a Tory called Peter Griffiths on the slogan, 'IF YOU WANT A NIGGER FOR A NEIGHBOUR, VOTE LABOUR.'

Meena was, as usual, protected from the raw impact of all this by her lack of English. She still rarely spoke to anyone who was not a Punjabi like herself. But everyone was talking about it. Cradling Sukhdeep in her arms, she felt a deep sense of belonging with her new daughter, with her people and with her husband who had to confront such problems and hostility every day.

It was all because of his hard work, she saw, that they were about to move into their own terraced house in Smethwick. For the first time they would have hot water: an Ascot heater in the kitchen. Later there were more moves. To the first house in Handsworth, a bigger terrace with a bathroom. This was after Khushwant and his friend Sachman had got together to set up the leather-goods factory. In the end, Khushwant had bought Sachman out. He had enabled growth upon growth in their fortunes by his dogged hard work.

After Sukhdeep was born it felt as if they were more united. Khushwant truly seemed to feel he had a family now, and he doted on his little girl. Raj observed this and sometimes played up. Pavan and Harpreet followed. In 1978 they moved to Handsworth Wood.

One evening when they were still living in the first, smaller Handsworth house and Harpreet was roughly twelve months old, Meena had gone through all the day's usual routines. She had fed the older children, who now clamoured for fish fingers and baked beans instead of rice or *dal*. ('Why don't you learn English?' Sukhdeep asked her sometimes. 'There are classes you can go to.' Meena never felt the need. It seemed too late, after all these years.)

That evening Khushwant was, as ever, working late at the factory. She had cooked him Indian food: *dal* and rice and potato and cauliflower curry. The children were all in bed.

At about nine o'clock she heard Khushwant's key in the lock and stood up to greet him. Going through to the front room, she saw him for a moment with his back to her, his hand still on the Yale lock, fastening the door. His clothes had the sagging look of cheap garments that had been much sat in. He was not so fat in those days: the business sapped his energy. It was a heavy, anxious struggle for an already anxious man. Every line of him – the droop of his shoulders, his lank hair and slow manner – spoke of exhaustion.

In that moment Meena knew for the first time that she loved her husband. The feeling swelled and glowed inside her.

He turned, his smile growing uncertainly to meet hers.

'Come,' was all she said. 'I have food ready.'

This growth of love was a certainty she had clung to through the years. It was right: God-given. It made sense of everything about the system in which she lived.

The English criticize us for arranged marriages, she thought. But this is how it is. We marry a stranger, we create a family, struggle together through thick and thin. We make a life and, with God's help, we grow into love for each other. She saw this in Banita also. She could dismiss Tavleen's husband: Tavleen had been married off to a man who was evil and godless from the start. In her mind she placed him in a different category. Though it was Tavleen's death that had bequeathed her the gift of looking at her husband and starting to see the good she had.

Now she clung to the certainty that her religion, her culture was right. If two good people came together with their families' help and God's blessing, they would learn their way into a marriage. The belief made her feel steady and safe. It helped to heal things about her past, the rupture that had happened in her parents' lives. This was the wisdom of God, unchanging and benign, and it was wise to surrender to it. It was the way to be a woman: it made sense of everything in life.

Or it did until the end of Sukhdeep's marriage.

Twenty-Four

Birmingham, 8th May 1945

Margaret sat on the edge of her bed in the darkening room, the blue envelope in her lap.

She could hear the buzz of celebration from outside. There were tables all along Upper Ridley Street, with adults and children alike crammed along them. Strings of bunting rippled over their heads and the children waved paper Union Jacks and wore party hats. Everyone had pooled meagre rations and done their best to make it into party food, laying out plates of sandwiches, dry cake and jelly, and here and there a precious bottle that had been saved up for a celebration.

UNCONDITIONAL SURRENDER BY GERMANY!

So far as Europe was concerned, the war was over! It was Victory in Europe Day and a public holiday.

Mrs Jennings from next door had done her best to involve Margaret in everything, although she was rushed off her feet herself and was scatty at the best of times. Out of loyalty to Alice Winters, and fondness for the little Margaret she remembered from before the war, she looked out for her, trying to bring some care into the misery of her life. Dora Jennings' four children were older than Margaret, but she was kind enough to let Margaret tag along.

The morning had been full of busyness. The men who were at home gathered anything they could find in the way of tables; the women were preparing food. There was an atmosphere of wild excitement, and those who were full of grief instead of celebration tended to keep to themselves. One woman in the back court where they lived had lost her son at Monte Cassino. Another's husband was a prisoner of war. Even Ron, Mrs Jennings' husband, who was usually a chirpy soul, was attacked by a fit of gloom.

'It's all very well,' he said through a cigarette stub, rifling around in the scullery, 'but will there be any jobs now it's all over?' (Rattle, clatter.) 'It's all right when there's a war on, but the dole queues'll be back again.' (Bang!)

'What *are* you looking for, Ron?' Mrs Jennings called out. She, Margaret and Sally Jennings, who was sixteen, were spreading bread with fishpaste and jam. Dora Jennings had her dark hair up in a scarf. Her handsome face turned, exasperated, towards the scullery.

'I'm trying to find the hammer,' Ron said. 'There's a nail sticking right out of that table – could do someone a nasty injury. I know we had a hammer . . .'

'It's in the bedroom,' Dora said, going back to spreading the bread.

'What the hell's it doing up there?'

'I don't know, Ron.' (Spread, spread.) 'You most probably must of left it there . . .'

Margaret's spirits lifted a little as she carried food out to the tables and felt the party atmosphere. Odd bits of song kept bursting through, and the colourful bunting made it look really cheerful.

It was a beautiful, warm day and everyone sat out, eating and enjoying themselves, still hardly able to believe it was all really over.

'Your pa not around, then?' Sally Jennings asked Margaret, in between eating Madeira cake and joining in the cheering. The air was full of the smells of food and cigarette smoke.

'No.' Margaret shrugged. What difference would it have made if he was? Ted Winters showed no fatherly feeling towards her. She might as well not exist, except as a skivvy.

Later on in the afternoon, as the other kids played around the tables and there was well-oiled singing, she could not bear it any longer and slipped away. She knew no one would miss her. They'd just think she'd gone to the lav.

Slipping inside the house, she went up to her room. She sat staring at nothing for some time. Then, as she so often did, she reached under her pillow for the letter.

Orchard House,
Buckley,
Worcestershire
15th December 1944

Dear Maggie,

We do hope this letter reaches you all right. Lucy and I have not written to you sooner, partly because it took us quite some time and difficulty to obtain your full address, and also because we thought it wise to let you have some months to settle back into your home life. We hope very much that you have now done so and are feeling well adjusted and happy in your family home.

Your leaving of us was so sudden that I must confess I found it most upsetting and it has taken us quite some time to get over it. Dotty was lost without you, and I'm quite sure Rags and 'the girls' in the paddock missed your visits as well. All of them are well. Since your departure, and quite recently, Dotty, though far from being youthful herself, has mysteriously managed to find herself a suitor and is, as I write, expecting pups! That will mean a certain amount of disruption in the house, I'm sure, but we are now of course rather excited at the prospect.

Lucy and I are most interested to know how you are getting on, and we both hope very much that you will write us a few lines to tell us your news. We hope you are still progressing well in your lessons. You are a clever little girl, dear, and could go far. John and Patty are getting along well at school now they are back in Birmingham – I'm sure they would also be delighted to see you, Maggie dear, as would we, if a visit could ever be arranged. Their address is as follows. [There was an address in Sparkhill, and then the letter signed off with another entreaty for Margaret to write with her news.]

Yours affectionately,
Jenny Clairmont

Margaret had read the letter hundreds of times, and knew every sentence in it off by heart. She sat holding it, comforted by the good quality of the paper, which contrasted with the cheap, lined sheets she had to write on – when she could find any at all. Paper was in very short supply.

Still holding the letter, she stared down at her feet,

which were clad in a pair of old black lace-ups, which Mrs Jennings had got for her from the rag market. They were a size too big, 'But you'll grow into them, bab,' Mrs Jennings had said. She had then had the task of extracting the money for them from Ted Winters, who claimed to have no idea that children grew and had to be clothed and shod.

'Why should I pay to dress your daughter?' Dora demanded of him. 'You do bugger-all else for her – the least you can do is keep her in shoe leather.'

Margaret thought of the nice pair of brown T-bar shoes that the sisters had bought for her when she was in Buckley, which had fitted her feet like soft gloves. They had been in the holdall that Ted Winters hurled over the gate that March morning. The morning he had thrown her life away.

This was supposedly her real life, but she felt like an outsider. The life she yearned for from the depths of her heart, and the place where she belonged – all this was in Buckley, where she was a real person. A girl called Maggie.

That freezing night when she and her father, Ted Winters, finally reached Birmingham and trudged the last mile from the railway station, the smells of the city rushed in to meet her. She had forgotten it. In more than four years she had become a country girl, breathing air flavoured with leaf mulch and wood smoke in winter, blossom and wheat in the warmer months. Stumbling along these murky, blacked-out streets, all the smells were of a manufacturing smokiness that was bitter and acrid.

On the main roads, by the dim lights of blacked-out

buses, she caught glimpses of the bulky outline of her father. He had walked all day in silence, except to curse her and tell her to 'Get on!' Already she loathed him. At last, after a day that had seemed several eternities, they turned down the slimy entry in Upper Ridley Street, groping along in the darkness.

The house was as cold as a tomb. When Ted Winters struck a match and lit the gas mantle, Margaret giddily seized the back of a chair. She was already weak from hunger and exhaustion, but the sight of the room stunned her. She knew it so well, knew it the way a dream comes back to you in the morning. Was this real? Is this where she had come from? And of course she knew, with dread certainty, that it was. That last morning came rushing back into her mind: her mother coming round the door; the smell of the newly baked loaf . . .

'Mom?' she murmured. 'Where's my mom?'

Ted Winters was riddling the range, hoping to stir some last life into it. He barely turned his head.

'I told yer – your mother passed on, years back. You won't be seeing 'er again. You're the one who's gunna keep the 'ouse now.'

He did at least brew a cup of tea and gave Margaret some in a jam jar. There was just one cup in the house. She sank onto the rickety chair and found her feet could touch the ground. Last time she had sat on it, Tommy had lifted her up there.

'Tommy?' she said. Her forgotten family seemed to rush back to her. 'Is Tommy coming back too?'

Ted Winters was crouched over the table, holding his cup up close to his stubbly chin.

'Yer brother? Nah. Gone for good, 'e has. Yer won't be seeing that one again. Good riddance. And you're only 'ere 'cause yer've got a job to do. I'm not looking for another mouth to feed.' He cocked his head towards the stairs. 'Go on now – get up to bed. You can sleep in the attic.'

Sitting on the bed, as the victory celebrations went on outside, Margaret pressed the letter against her body, as she had done so many times, trying to find comfort in it. She knew she would not reply. She would never see the sisters again or go back to that life. It had been like a miraculous land at the parting of the sea, over which the waters had closed again, leaving her with a knowledge and a hunger that she would not otherwise have had. She was Margaret Winters, the boss-eyed daughter of a man called Ted Winters, a girl who skivvied and slaved without a word of thanks, who barely had a rag to call her own and whose father didn't care if she lived or died, so long as she did his bidding. But that letter reminded her that, inside Margaret, there was a girl who knew how to speak differently, who had read and played in the fresh air, done sewing that wasn't just darning the old man's socks, ridden a pony and played with Dotty the dog. Inside was a girl called Maggie who knew how good life could be.

But now, that Maggie was dead and buried.

Twenty-Five

The morning after Ted Winters brought Margaret back to Birmingham, she woke up to hear him bawling up the stairs.

'Wench! Get yerself down 'ere! You're no sodding good to me lying around in bed.'

Margaret leapt up from sleep and sat hugging her knees, shivering with cold and gazing, bewildered, round the attic room. The floor was bare, rough boards, and the only furniture was a narrow cupboard and the iron bedstead on which she had slept. She had covered herself with one thin, yellowish blanket, which had an odd, brown stain up the middle. The dark cupboard had one of its hinges missing, so that its door hung drunkenly to one side. Margaret could see daylight through cracks around the window frame.

'Where are yer?' His voice hectored. 'Get yerself down 'ere!'

Margaret badly needed to relieve herself and there was no sign of a chamber pot. She dimly remembered that the lavatories were up at the other end of the yard. She was still dressed in her clothes from yesterday, so she pushed her feet into her shoes and crept down the stairs. The Old Man was standing with his back to her in a singlet, shaving at the scullery sink, over which hung a small, rectangular mirror.

''Bout time. I dain't bring you all the way back 'ere

197

just to lie a-bed. You can get the fire going – and get some tea on,' he ordered.

'I need the lavatory,' she said. That's what they called it in Buckley.

'Ew!' He mocked. '*Lavatory!* Well, cowing well hurry up! It's the lav round 'ere – and you need the key. Don't you know anything?'

Hugging herself to try and keep warm, she stepped out into a yard paved with blue bricks, some of which had heaved up with all the damp, making it necessary to watch where you walked. In the middle of the yard was a lamp and, on the far wall, a tap. The dwellings around, which backed on to others opening onto the street, looked cramped and grimy after the beautiful house she had been used to.

Margaret had the strangest feeling walking across the yard. Everything about it – the walls and doors, the patterns of the bricks – felt almost as familiar as her own body, while at the same time it all felt strange and dirty and alien. Beyond the brewhouse, the communal wash house, were the lavatories.

She hesitated outside, nose wrinkling at the stench. She thought of the spotless privy at Orchard House. But she was so desperate, she knew she would have to go into the dark, cobwebby place. She did her business as fast as she could, not looking round in case there were spiders or roaches crawling towards her down the rough bricks, then fled back out into the yard.

It was quiet and she realized it was Sunday morning. The only person about was a boy close to her age in a long, stained shirt and seemingly not much else, who gawped at her with his mouth open. The next thing it occurred to him to do was to make a sneering grimace, then stick his tongue out as far as it would go. Margaret turned away. Her chest ached with the need to cry, but she could see already that she'd get no sympathy from any quarter here. She swallowed her tears and went indoors.

Ted Winters had gone to all the trouble of fetching Margaret home to number two, back of sixteen Upper Ridley Street, because he was short of a housekeeper. If it wasn't for Dora Jennings next door, he wouldn't have even let Margaret go to school.

'She's got to go, Ted,' Dora insisted. 'It's the law – and if they don't find out for themselves that you're keeping her back, I'll set them on you. It's not fair on her, making her do all your dirty work.'

Dora was the one person who seemed pleased to see Margaret and bothered with her. Over the next days, though hard-pressed herself, she helped Margaret by teaching her how to do things in the house: getting the range lit, black-leading it, cleaning and cooking. And, as they worked, she talked to Margaret about her family and what had happened to them.

'Your mother only lasted a couple of days after you and Tommy went away,' she said as they swept the neglected floor of a sneeze-making accumulation of dust and soot. 'Oh, it broke her heart, poor lamb, seeing you both off. But she was so ill already, she could never've looked after you – you remember that, don't you, bab?'

Margaret nodded. She was full of an ache, all the time, her whole body hurting. Now she was back here, she was remembering her mother and grieving for her.

She had been a gentle, put-upon woman who had done her best for her children in often desperate circumstances.

'Poor soul,' Dora went on. 'Both your brothers – half-brothers I should say, Edwin and Cyril – joined up as soon as they could, so they were gone. No one's heard from them; we don't know where they are. Anyroad – that's it, bab, we'll scoop it up into that bucket and take it down the bottom of the yard ... Now Elsie – your half-sister – you remember her, don't you?'

Margaret nodded, hopefully. Of her half-siblings, Elsie had been the nicest.

'Course yer do. Well, she's married: living over Digbeth way, and she's got her hands full with two babbies. But we'll go and see her one day, shall we? Anyway, about yer dad, the thing about him is, he can spruce up and he's got the gift of the gab. He can charm the birds out of the trees when he's of a mind to, and of course he's not bad-looking, with a bit of help from a razor and a lick of soap. That's how he hooked up with your poor mother, desperate as she was, on her own with three babbies. He soon found another hopeless case to come and keep house for him. Gladys her name was. He never even married her, neither. A poor thing she was – not much to 'er. But even she took off, only a month ago. And what with the war, he's had to shift hisself and do a bit of work – they caught up with him, packed him off into munitions. Even then he drank all his wages away. That Gladys found out in the end what an idle, boozing sod he is ... Sorry for coming out with it like that, Margaret, but we all know what 'e's like, don't we?'

Margaret was certainly finding out. He never had a

word for her except to grunt orders, and he was always out, asleep or in a drunken stupor. She had quickly realized that for him she was not a person. She was an object, a slave to do his bidding.

Buying food was very hard for Margaret, because if she left it until after school there was nothing left in the shops, and there were the ration books to contend with. Dora helped as much as she could, and took Margaret to get a new ration book for herself. But Margaret often had to skip school days, or was caned for being late. The rest of her time was spent cleaning and cooking, and she never was very good at either.

She dreaded the moment he came home after work. She was expected to have a meal ready. He would loom dark in the doorway.

'Where's my tea then?' As often as not it was some sort of stew, the tiny meat ration eked out with vegetables.

'What d'you call this slop? I'm a working man: d'you expect me to eat this?'

Once or twice he threw the plate at her, smashing it on the range. The first time Margaret burst into tears at the sight of the concoction, which she had been anxiously stirring in the old saucepan, seeping down the front of the range to the floor.

'No more than pigswill!' he was bawling. 'What bloody good are you to anyone, yer stupid wench! At least your mother could cook.'

Dora, hearing the crash and the shouting, ran in from next door to find Margaret cowering by the range, hands over her face.

'What's going on in 'ere?' She was barely five foot, but her energy and flashing eyes made her fearsome. 'What're you doing, Ted Winters? Oh, I see – so you've thrown yer plate over, have yer? Well, what're you going to eat now then, eh? You've got to give her a chance to learn, Ted. She's only young! And while we're about it, she's only got the clothes she's standing up in, thanks to you throwing everything away.'

'Well, what am I s'posed to do about it?' Ted retorted. 'I don't know about anything like that.'

'No, you don't know anything about much 'cept pouring it down yer gullet, do yer? You give me the money and I'll sort her out, poor little wench.'

Ted snatched up his cap again. 'Stop nagging on, woman. Christ! I'm off down the pub.'

'That's it: go and get kalied – *again.*' Dora was screeching with anger this time. 'That'll solve all yer problems, won't it? You're an idle sod, Ted Winters, idle and a coward, that's what you are!'

But Ted was already off along the entry.

'Here, bab, don't cry. Look, I'll help you clear up the mess,' Dora said, going out to fill a pail of water. 'It ain't no good expecting anything off of him, bab, 'cause you ain't going to get it. It's a hard thing to say, but he hasn't got a decent bone in his body, that man, and the sooner you get that into your head, the better.'

It took Margaret a long time to settle in school. Having been away for more than four years, she spoke differently from everyone else and felt like a foreigner. She tried to get her Birmingham accent back so that she could fit in, but with her wonky eye and lack of confidence she was already fair game. She stood at the edge of the playground when they had the dinner break, wishing she was invisible. There were a few other children in the school who had been evacuated and had returned, but none of them had been away for anything like as long. One had run away, and the others had been fetched back by their parents before Christmas 1939, long before the bombing had even started.

'Our mom said we'd all stick together,' a girl called Nance told her proudly. 'She said if we were gunna die, we'd all do it in our own home.'

Nance had been sent to Wales for a few weeks and she was the first person who Margaret thought of as a kind of friend. But that first winter home was full of lonely misery. She didn't have time to play out in the yard with the other children, so she didn't make friends with them, and the boys taunted her and called her names. If the younger Jennings kids were around, they stood up for her, but they were already out at work and not there much. Margaret shrugged it off. A deadness took over inside her. She didn't let herself feel anything. Feelings were too unbearable.

The other person who showed her a bit of kindness was her half-sister Elsie. One Sunday, Dora and Margaret walked over to see her. It was very cold, the streets full of grey Sunday stillness. Margaret traipsed along beside Dora. The buildings they walked between looked very high, the chimneys breathing out swirls of smoke. There was nothing nice to look at, except for a black horse pulling a cart along, but it made Margaret think of Rags, and then she had to stop thinking about it so that she didn't cry.

They stopped at the door of a house that opened straight onto the pavement. Elsie came to open it. Margaret saw a young woman who was taller and thinner than she remembered, but she did recognize her face and her lank brown hair. She had a look of their mother, which tore at Margaret's heart.

'Hello, Elsie,' Dora said. 'Look, this is little Margaret, your sister.'

By this time Elsie's two little girls had come to peer out from behind her. They were both very small and dark-haired, with sharp faces like their mother.

'Margaret – oh my, is that really our little Margaret!' Elsie cried, amazed. 'Ooh, it is: I can see by your eyes. Where've yer been then all this time? Oh, look, you'd better come in, it's cold.'

They sat round the table in the cramped room. The place was not much different from the Upper Ridley Street house, except that there was a lot more sign of home-making. On a shelf was propped a wedding picture of Elsie and her husband, and there were little knick-knacks on the mantel and a cheery red-and-white checked cloth on the table. By the fire there was a rag rug in bright colours. Elsie briskly made a pot of tea while the two little girls stood staring.

'My, you've grown, Margaret,' Elsie said when they were all drinking the weak brew. 'I can't get over it. I mean you were – it was at the beginning of the war, just before our mom . . .' Her eyes filled and she trailed off. 'You were only about . . . ?'

'Five,' Dora Jennings told her. 'Five and a bit. And now you're just turned eleven, aren't you, bab? That's it, Elsie – she's been away all that time. And now she's back with the Old Man . . .'

Elsie's face tightened. 'That rotten old—' She didn't let herself finish. 'Well, that can't be much of a life for you, Margaret. Now, look – ooh, silly me, I haven't even told you their names. Come 'ere, you two: this is

Susan and this is little Heather … Now, you two, this is your Auntie Margaret. She's been stopping away for a bit away from the bombs, but she's come back now.'

The two little girls, four and two, stared at Margaret, who looked back uncertainly at them. After a moment the oldest, Susan, smiled shyly and moved a bit closer. Margaret's heart leapt and she smiled back. Heather put her hand over her mouth and giggled, and this made Margaret smile even more.

'Hello,' she said, remembering how kind Patty had been and wanting to be like her.

The little girls squirmed and smiled.

'Say hello then!' Elsie urged, though they were overcome with shyness. But they had made Margaret's day. Oh, maybe, just maybe, the little ones would like her! She could play with them, the way Patty had played with her.

'You must come and see us sometimes,' Elsie said. 'I don't go and call on the Old Man – what's the use?' Her voice was bitter. After all, he wasn't even her real father. 'I don't have time to go gadding about. But if you want to come and see us, Margaret, you can.'

Margaret nodded gladly. But on the walk home she realized what a long way it was.

'That was nice, wasn't it?' Dora said as they headed back along Digbeth. 'Are you pleased we went?'

Margaret nodded in a vague way. Just for once her heart was singing, but she didn't know what to say.

'Well, you're a funny one,' Dora laughed. Then her face fell again, looking down at the sad child beside her. 'Poor little sod,' she muttered.

Twenty-Six

The summer the war ended, Ted Winters started bringing another woman home. The first time Margaret saw her, she had been out to the huckster's shop down on the corner for a box of matches. Crossing the yard, she could see someone through the open door, the rear view of a voluminous pale-pink dress, a pair of thick calves and feet in white heels planted heavily on the floor.

Ted Winters was pouring them a drink.

'Ah, 'ere she is – me daughter.' Ted pointed towards Margaret the cup into which he had been pouring.

Margaret had her first sight of Peggy Loach's mean, fleshy face and peroxide hair, which was rolled back into various elaborate coils at the side of her face, and one in a knot on top. Her lips were painted bright red and her cheeks were thick with powder. Margaret could see that her skin was rough and pockmarked underneath all the war paint.

She stared hard at Margaret, her piggy eyes hard and calculating.

'So, this is the only one of your brats living here with you then, Ted?' She had a rough voice and a thick Irish accent.

'Oh, ar . . . Don't you worry, Peggy. I've got this'un 'ere to keep 'ouse. 'Er's no trouble – I've got 'er trained. ''Ere you are, Peggy: bottoms up!'

Peggy turned to take the cup off him and drank, leaving a 'tache of froth on her lip. She stank of sweat and a heady smell of cheap perfume. Margaret could see that her father was in wooing mood – shaved and spruced up, belly tucked more thoroughly than usual into his trousers. He was a stocky, swarthy man with brown eyes, which gave him a spaniel charm. He let out a flattering laugh at anything Peggy said.

'How old're you then?' Peggy nodded in Margaret's direction.

'Eleven.' Margaret had been trying to slide away towards the stairs to get away from them.

'Oi, where d'yer think you're off to?' Ted demanded.

'Nowhere.' She linked her hands together at the front and stood awkwardly.

'I should think not – us'll be wanting our tea. There'll be an extra one tonight. Peggy will be dining with us.'

Margaret did as she was told. As school was out, she had already made a pot of stew, and now she stood at the table peeling potatoes while Ted and Peggy sat at the other end, drinking. Peggy laughed a lot, her belly wobbling, and saying, 'Ooh, Ted . . .'

'You can take yours upstairs with yer,' Ted said once the spuds were cooked. 'Leave me and Peggy in peace.'

Margaret sat up in the gloom, eating her stringy stew and potatoes, glad to be away from them. Peggy's booming laugh came up through the house. Later she heard a lot more giggling from the bedroom next door, the bedsprings squeaking and some grunting noises. She lay in bed with her hands over her ears.

*

Peggy Loach spent more and more time at number two, back of sixteen Upper Ridley Street, and within a couple of weeks she had moved into the house.

'Ooh, I don't like the look of that one at all,' Dora said. 'Looks like a prize fighter – hard-faced with it. You let me know if you have any trouble with her, Margaret. I hope she'll take on some of the work now.'

This, however, was quite the opposite to what Peggy Loach had in mind. She had left an upbringing of acute poverty in Ireland. The prospect of a man to keep her and a girl doing all the drudgery was like a gift from heaven. The first time they were alone in the house, Peggy turned on Margaret. She came round the table to where Margaret was standing by the range.

'Any trouble from you . . .' She loomed huge and pugnacious. Close up, her skin was mottled and scarred. Margaret cowered away from the woman, wrinkling her nose at the stink of her, which enraged Peggy.

'What're you making that face for, you little bitch? Now, you listen. I'm living 'ere now, wit your father. So far as anyone else needs to know, I'm his missis. Any trouble from you, and you'll be feeling the back of my hand just to start wit – got it?'

All Margaret could do was nod. The thought of a belting from Peggy Loach was really frightening.

As it turned out, whether Margaret 'watched it' or not, Peggy took any chance she could to deal out a cuff or a slap. Margaret, in her usual numb way, took it, not knowing what else to do.

One Saturday that winter she set out to get coal from the wharf. It was a freezing day, the air biting into her cheeks, her breath making clouds of white. Margaret pulled her sleeves down over her hands to push the old pram that Dora Jennings always lent her to fetch the coal in. There were a few others about on the street, some obviously heading in the same direction. Margaret kept her head down. Going to the wharf always reminded her of Tommy, and how they used to go together. She wondered where he was, and whether he ever thought about her.

She had just gone round the corner when she realized that someone who had been following her had almost caught up. A wooden crate bodged onto a couple of pram wheels appeared beside her, followed by a tall, gangling boy. He was pushing the makeshift handle of the cart with one hand and trying to hold his jacket closed with the other. She saw this was because he had nothing on underneath it.

He nodded shyly at her, then turned his head away as if he expected her to reject or insult him. He was extremely thin, a drooping, shambling figure. She realized that she had seen him before, but couldn't think where.

'You going up the wharf?' he asked after a few seconds.

'Yes,' Margaret said in a small voice. She mainly avoided speaking to people, not expecting anything much good from anyone these days. But she could hear him trying to control his shivering and she felt sorry for him. His jacket didn't seem to have any buttons.

The boy glanced at her, seeming grateful for being spoken to.

'Perishing, isn't it?'

'Yes,' she said again. She didn't want to look directly at him because then he'd see her funny eye.

'Still, once we've got the coal we can make a fire.'

He seemed encouraged by her. 'Does your dad do the fire or your mom?'

Margaret didn't want to have to explain that she did more or less everything, so she said, 'My dad.'

'I ain't got one,' the boy said. 'Our dad was killed in the war.'

'Oh,' Margaret said. 'I ain't got a mom. She died in the war too.'

'Did you get bombed out?'

'No – she just died.'

They reached the back of the queue and waited. The boy was quivering all over.

'Haven't you got a shirt?' Margaret asked. She wondered how old he was.

'It's soaking wet – our mom washed it. T'ain't dried 'cause the fire's gone out: it's froze solid.'

She couldn't avoid him looking at her now that they'd stopped walking, but he didn't seem to see anything amiss. She looked up into a long, gentle face with big grey eyes. His lips were cracked and sore-looking and he was hugging himself to try and keep warm. She thought he looked sad.

'Where d'you live?' he asked. 'I think I've seen you about before.'

When she told him, he said, 'Oh, that's not far. I live in Washington Street – behind the leather works.' Now he had started talking, a stream of information came out. He was thirteen, had a sister who was nine and a brother of seven. His father had been a rear gunner in the RAF and had died in North Africa. His mom was trying to cope on her own.

By the time they had fetched the coal and parted, pushing heavy loads, at the corner of Upper Ridley Street, he had asked if he could call in and see her.

'I'll meet you on the corner,' Margaret said. She didn't want Peggy Loach anywhere near this fragile friendship.

The boy told her his name was Fred Tolley.

August–September 1984

Twenty-Seven

At the last toddler group before they broke up for the summer, Joanne and the others had a little party, to say thanks to Tess and the other helpers.

Everyone had brought along a few bits and pieces – sandwiches, cheesy biscuits, Twiglets and crisps – and laid them out on the kitchen table.

Tess was wearing an orange sundress. Her face was a little swollen and she was obviously very tired and heavy, but remained as good-natured as ever.

'I'll miss you all,' she said, 'but I hope to see you all again in the autumn. I should be up and running by then, if all goes well. But Mavis here . . .' Mavis stood smiling modestly. 'Mavis has been great, hasn't she? And she's off to college next term to start her training as a children's nurse. So let's all wish her luck!'

There were murmurs of 'good luck' to Mavis. Joanne went over to her afterwards. She had grown to respect Mavis a lot.

'I just wanted to wish you all the best,' she said, smiling. 'You'll be really good.'

'Oh!' Mavis looked delighted. 'Well, thank you. And I'll come back and see you all – when I can!'

Joanne was just turning to go and sort Amy out when someone tapped her arm. She jumped violently.

'Hey, calm down, it's only me!' Sooky was smiling.

But she looked concerned as well. 'You scare easily. Are you okay?'

'Yeah. Course. I'm fine.' Joanne laughed it off, but her heart was pounding horribly hard. It was like this all the time now. Things had got worse. The mood Dave had been in the last few days meant that she was living constantly on her nerves. All his sorrow and contrition had disappeared. He kept giving her cold looks, which held a threat. She knew that if she had challenged him, he would have told her she was imagining things. But there was so much tension in the house that she felt slightly sick all the time and was finding it hard to eat or sleep properly. She fought giving in to it. The easiest thing would be just to do everything he wanted. But she could see that was crazy. Why on earth should he stop her going out or being with other people?

'You going to that group again?' he'd asked that morning.

'Yes,' Joanne said, trying to ignore his sneering tone. 'But it's the last one – it stops for the summer.'

'Good,' he said. 'About time. You can stop at home then, like a proper wife.'

'A proper wife?' Joanne was really riled by this. 'You seem to think you're the only one who knows what that is, these days.'

Dave had stared at her, a hard, dangerous look in his eyes. It's no good, Joanne thought, I can't let him get to me. She tried to outstare him, but in the end lowered her gaze, feeling her cheeks flush pink. Of course he got to her. He was trying to control every aspect of her life, wasn't he? Sometimes she started to wonder if it was all inside her head. But she knew how frightened she was of him, and she was having to fight against that fear with all her strength.

'Are we still going to the park?' Sooky asked.

'I think so – we can take the remains of the food with us. The kids won't want much dinner after all that, will they?'

'No,' Sooky smiled. 'They'll be far too busy anyway!'

Over the past few weeks, when there was a chance, they had stayed on together after the toddler group finished. It was so good for everyone – both children and adults – to have the company. It was a way of getting through the day. They'd been back to Kieran's house a couple of times. Billy and the girls got on very well. Today they had agreed to go to the park.

They sat on the grass, looking down towards the boating lake: Joanne and Amy, Sooky and Priya, and Kieran and his boys. They had each brought a few toys along and a soft ball for them to kick around. Kieran fed baby Charlie his bottle while Billy played with the girls.

'How's it going, Kieran?' Sooky asked.

Kieran always tried to be cheerful, even when things looked really bleak, but he seemed genuinely hopeful today.

'It's going okay, thanks.' He looked up from feeding Charlie, a smile spreading across his freckly face. 'Good news: Gerri's coming home this weekend – just for a couple of days to begin with.'

'Oh, that's great!' Joanne and Sooky said together. Joanne felt herself lifted out of her own troubles. Poor Kieran, he had really had a plateful. Gradually she was beginning to relax. Being out of the house was such a relief.

'How d'you think she'll manage?' Sooky was asking. Joanne admired her, the way she was so open and interested in other people and not afraid to ask.

'Well, I hope she'll be okay.' Kieran's face became serious again. 'It's quite a lot for her – you know, home and the kids and everything all at once. What's terrible is seeing how frightened of everything she's become. Still, it's all relative. A few weeks ago she couldn't even manage to make a cup of tea. Now she's managing things like that, doing her hair . . .'

It made a sad picture. Joanne thought about her mom. She'd said she'd been low after having Karen. Is that what she'd been like? She hadn't been in hospital, or not as far as they knew. She felt like asking her dad – but would she get an answer? Most likely not. Had he even noticed at the time that his wife was depressed?

'Well, I hope it goes really well,' Sooky was saying.

'Thanks,' Kieran said. 'It's one step at a time. I'm not expecting miracles . . .'

Joanne thought was a nice guy he was. For a moment she had a pang of longing. If only she was with someone as nice as Kieran! Then she felt disloyal. She loved Dave, she *did*. But she loved the old Dave, as he had been, not the frightening stranger he had become. That wasn't him, not really, was it?

In that moment, a terrible realization came to her. *If I don't do something, we'll lose each other forever. Look at Mom and Dad: they've been strangers for years. I've got to . . .* But what? Despair came over her. Dave was so angry and forbidding these days. So hard even to like. It felt impossible to try and begin a conversation.

'Joanne? Hello?' Sooky had evidently been trying to get her attention for some time. 'You really are on another planet today! I said, shall we put the rest of the food out?'

'Oh, yeah! Course, sorry.' She shook herself out of her thoughts. She should make the best of being here, with friends. A warm feeling filled her. Yes, she had friends. As they laid out the rest of the little picnic there were a rare few minutes without interruption, so she took the chance to say, 'How're things with you, Sooky?'

'Oh, they're fine,' Sooky said. 'No, Priya – wait till I've finished ... Better, actually. My mom's started talking to me again now.'

'Really, that's great!' Joanne said, with a sudden rush of longing for hers to do the same. 'What brought that on?'

Sooky put her head on one side. 'I'm not really sure. But after they had that man over – you know, the marriage meeting ...' Her face twitched as if she wasn't sure whether to laugh or cry. The laughter won. 'Well, he wasn't very nice. In fact he was a disaster. And somehow Mom – I don't know ... But she's been different ever since.'

'You didn't say you'd marry him, did you?'

Sooky shook her head. 'I'd rather be abducted by aliens. In fact,' she added seriously, 'I'd quite *like* to be abducted by aliens. Now that could be really interesting – don't you think?'

'No!' Kieran laughed. 'It sounds nightmarish.'

'Sooky's got a thing about sci-fi,' Joanne said.

'Yes, but that's taking things a bit far,' Kieran said. 'I mean, as a way of getting out of marriage!'

They were all laughing. The children giggled too as they gathered round, drinking squash and eating pieces of banana that Sooky had brought along.

'We'll go and see the ducks and geese after, shall we?' Kieran was saying. 'Give them our crusts?'

They looked down towards the boating lake, from where there were sounds of splashing and laughter. Some teenagers who had finished their exams had come to take boats out and were having a riotous time. The sun glanced off the water. Two women in bright blue-and-orange *salwar-kameez* glittered past, chatting together on the near side. Beyond the water were a few dog walkers, a man standing, looking . . .

Joanne's eyes focused on him, the one without a dog, standing still, hands thrust into the pockets of his jeans, staring across at them. Her insides turned to ice.

'Oh, my God!' she murmured.

It was his stillness that was menacing, the way he had so obviously come to spy on her. But how did Dave know where she was? Had she mentioned that they were going to the park?

'What's up?' Sooky asked, following her gaze.

'Nothing.' Joanne spoke abruptly, looking down quickly. The shock had stolen her breath and she was almost panting. Had he seen her notice him? She desperately didn't want Amy to see that he was there.

'Hey, you look really upset,' Sooky said. Joanne could feel both her and Kieran looking at her. She hadn't breathed a word to anyone about what was happening at home. It was a private nightmare that she tried to forget when she was out. But these were friends. They shared their own problems with her. Could she say something? Dare she?

'It's just . . .' Her blood was thumping through her.

She could hear it in her ears like a drum. She looked up. 'I'll tell you in a minute – not with the kids here . . .'

The children were soon absorbed again, and Joanne dared to look across the boating lake. The teenagers had quietened down, probably after warnings. He had gone. There was no one the other side. Had she imagined it? Was she really going funny in the head?

'You okay?' Sooky asked again.

'Yeah.' It seemed daft to tell them now that there was nothing to see. 'Just having a few problems at home at the moment. Nothing to worry about. I expect it'll sort itself out.'

Twenty-Eight

Joanne felt very uneasy for the rest of the time they were together. When they all parted to go home, she was queasy with dread. Amy was fractious about parting from her friends, and Joanne had some tense moments with her before she finally drooped sleepily in the buggy.

At the front gate she stopped, her pulse pounding once more. What if he was at home, waiting? Should she go for a walk instead, spend the afternoon wandering round Handsworth – because she was afraid to go into her own house? Even in her worked-up state the craziness of this was obvious. But there was a prickling sensation at the back of her neck and her hands were cold and clammy, even in the heat of the day.

She saw her neighbour Mrs Coles approaching along the street with her rocking walk, bags of shopping swinging on either side. She was a barrel-shaped lady, wearing a dress patterned with swirls of blue and purple and little flat navy shoes, which her bunioned feet had pushed out of shape. Her hair was escaping from the rough bun she wore it in and she was perspiring mightily in the heat.

'All right, Joanne?' she greeted her huskily from a distance. 'Been out, have yer? How's little'un?'

Joanne snapped back into herself, praying that Mrs Coles wouldn't wake Amy. Mary Coles was the kindest of souls and Amy adored her, but Joanne just needed some peace for a while.

'We've just been to the toddler group. She's fast asleep – worn out!'

'Aah, God bless her.' Mrs Coles leaned over Amy. A gold crucifix leaned with her, swinging out of the front of her dress. 'Look at her, little angel!'

'Have you been shopping?' Joanne asked, though she obviously had.

'Just picking up me bits and pieces: bit of liver for Jim – he likes his liver and onions of a Tuesday . . . I'm going to have a nice sit-down now.' She drifted to her own gate. 'See yer, bab.'

'Bye,' Joanne said. 'Enjoy your rest.'

'Oh, I will,' Mrs Coles chuckled. 'Cup of tea and a couple of Penguins by the telly, that'll see me right . . .'

Joanne watched her fondly. She pulled herself together and went up to the house. Pushing open the front door, she wheeled Amy's buggy inside, leaving her in the hall. Inside felt quiet and unoccupied, but just to be sure she walked from room to room, even upstairs. There was no one there.

Back in the kitchen, she put the kettle on. Maybe a cup of tea and a couple of Penguins would sort me out too, she thought. She saw that her hands were shaking.

It was a hot, languorous afternoon. There was no need for lunch after the snacks in the park, and Amy was deeply asleep. Joanne hung out the washing, but it felt too hot to do any serious housework and she found herself at a loose end.

She wandered around the silent house, into their bedroom where she pulled the covers up and tidied the bed, then she folded away Amy's clothes. She went back into her own and Dave's room and sat on the edge of the bed. From where she was sitting she could just see the rooftops of the houses beyond. Why was she in here? She felt unable to think clearly.

Realizing she had still not made the tea, she went back down. Despite the heat, it was still the comfort of hot tea that she wanted. Carrying her mug, she went to the shelves in the front room, took down their photo albums, one dark blue, one white, and went and sat at the table. It was too glaringly hot to be outside.

She wanted to think about her husband. To try and straighten out her mind.

The first album was made up of a motley collection of old snaps of both their families. They'd used those camera films that you used to send away in the post, and the colour had leached out of them already, making the past look faded and longer ago than it really was.

The cellophane-covered pages showed a few pictures of her and Dave as children: he blond, gap-toothed, always grinning; she skinny, with bonny pink cheeks, pretty curls of hair around her face and already obviously long legs. At school she had sometimes been called 'Storky'.

There were fewer of the middle years: one or two small school portraits, then Dave in his football kit. There was a full-page picture of him after he was selected for the Juniors at Aston Villa. He was twelve years old, standing proud, grass all around him, one foot on the ball. 1973: the Villa coming out of a downer, back up to the Second Division. It was the year the new manager was appointed: Ron Saunders. By 1977 the Villa was back up to the First Division and in European competitions. There were pictures of Dave, taller, broader each time, scattered across that period and always playing football. In 1977 they let him go. *You're good, lad, but not quite good enough.* He'd taken some getting over that: maybe he'd never got over it.

She peered more closely at a picture taken the next year. It was a family group: Brian and Wendy, Dave's mom and dad, Wendy's sister Clare and herself and Dave – all sitting round a white plastic table at the back of Dave's parents' house. It was when barbecues started becoming popular, and Wendy, liking to think she had a gypsy nature, was all for it.

'I love eating outside,' she'd enthused. 'It's so much more natural.'

There she was with her long honey-coloured hair, a big daisy clipped in on one side, and cut-off denim shorts, looking like a Flower Power teenager in her early forties. And Brian, in what now looked like a custard-coloured shirt (Joanne remembered it had been bright yellow at the time), with his cheerful smile, very like Dave, but smaller and stockier.

Joanne's eyes slid over everyone, stopping at Dave and herself. Dave had been seventeen, she sixteen. Even though he was no longer training, he still had his clean-cut footballer looks, a royal-blue shirt with a collar. She was grinning broadly, in a cream sundress (hadn't it been cheesecloth?), her hair flicked away on each side.

She moved the album up close, homing in on Dave's face. He was smiling too. Did he look older suddenly than in the months before? Harder, sadder? After it happened, he hadn't told her, not for a fortnight. He'd disappeared, wouldn't even come to the door. It was Wendy who told her what was wrong. She came out and spoke to Joanne a couple of times.

'He says he'll phone you,' she told her. Once, Joanne could see she'd been crying. She was holding a dish-cloth and twisting it tight. 'It's not you, love. The bottom's dropped out of his world. He won't say a word . . .' She moved back, closing the door. 'Just give him a bit of time, love. '

She remembered the agony of waiting, of feeling shut out, wanting to throw her arms round Dave, tell him she didn't mind if he wasn't a great footballer, she loved him anyway and always would. She was cut up for him, knowing what it had meant. She prepared herself to give comfort. She expected tears, sulks, oper-atic emotions. When he did finally get back to her, he shrugged it off.

'Oh, well, that's how it goes in football,' he said. 'I gave it my best and it wasn't good enough. But at least I did give it my best.'

He said it in a stiff way, as if it was something he'd read somewhere.

There were a few more family groups, then nothing. In the summer of 1979 Brian Marshall had died sud-denly at the garage, of a heart attack. He didn't even make it to the hospital. By then Dave was working with him, though he wasn't there when it happened. Joanne knew Dave had adored his dad, and how proud Brian had been of his son's football achievements. But he'd been sensible about it. Brian had been able to offer him something else to do. *Never mind, son, you know you can come and work with me – you've always been good with your hands . . .*

But when Brian died, Dave hadn't reacted much, either. He stood dry-eyed at the funeral, shrugged off her attempts to mother him. Wendy was the one who sucked in everyone's sympathy. Dave kept it all inside.

Frowning, she closed the blue album and opened the white one: their wedding pictures, taken at Birmingham Registry Office less than two years ago on a balmy September day. The colours of these pictures were bright and distinct. She had been five months pregnant with Amy, holding her bunch of roses and pinks over her stomach, even though the pregnancy was no secret. The dress was another cream one, short and stylish. She hadn't wanted a long, fancy thing with lace and veils. As usual she was smiling. She was good at that, at looking the way she was supposed to.

Dave, in his suit, was as smart and neat as ever.

There was Dad, skinny and somehow dishevelled, even when he was doing his best to scrub up; and Mom in a suit the colour of raspberry yoghurt, hair tightly permed. Mom stared back at the camera with what passed for a smile, but now Joanne could see the effort, the blank, closed look. Karen had worn a pink summer suit, which clashed horribly with Wendy's full red-and-orange garb with paisley patterns and silver thread running through it. She was not long back from three months in India, and everything she wore then seemed to gleam and jangle. Her wrists were loaded with bangles. Looking at it, Joanne could hear the tinkly sounds: there had even been little bells at the ends of the cords tied at her neck.

But it was Dave's face she pored over, tutting in frustration. Photographs told you so much, yet so little. There he was, staring at the camera, smart, handsome. Did she imagine that he looked ill at ease, that the smile was forced? But it was he who had most wanted to get married. Joanne hadn't been too fussed, but he had almost steam-rollered her into it.

'We've got a babby on the way. We can't go on

playing at it,' he'd insisted. 'It's time we did it right – a proper wedding and a home of our own.'

There were a few more pictures: Amy, newborn, her tiny form swathed in soft white wool; Joanne looking hollow-eyed, but smiling as ever; and Dave's enigmatic stare. She looked for a long time at the last one. He had suggested that they go and have a studio picture taken of the three of them.

'First proper family photo,' he said.

The background was all soft-focus. Joanne, in a pink dress, had been arranged on a backless chair with Amy in her arms, Dave behind, leaning over in a solicitous way, both of them looking up into the lens. It made them appear eager and very young. She felt a pang looking at it. She stroked her finger over Dave's cheek, suddenly full of tenderness.

'What's the matter?' she whispered. 'What's happened to you?'

Even though she was full of memories of the Dave she knew he really was, she was still anxious about him coming home. She cooked a meal she knew he especially liked – chicken in a mushroom sauce – and made sure the house was tidy and Amy bathed and ready for bed.

When she heard his key she jumped violently, but went to greet him with a smile. He turned from shutting the door and for a split second stared blankly at her, almost as if he had never seen her before. Then, as if deciding something, he smiled back, but even in her relief she could see that it was a stiff, strange smile that did not light his eyes.

'All right?' she said, finding herself gabbling. 'It

must've been really hot at work. I've got tea ready – I thought maybe we could have it outside, once I've got Amy settled?'

'All right,' he said.

He went to wash. Joanne put Amy to bed, taking her to say goodnight to him first.

'G'night, babby.' He kissed the top of her head and she giggled.

So far so good. He did not seem obviously angry. They talked about the day as they ate. She made a point of telling him about the picnic in the park to show she wasn't keeping secrets. Dave made no comment. He listened carefully as she talked. Almost too carefully. She couldn't put her finger on it, but although everything seemed fine, she became even more uneasy. Something about his quiet calm felt ominous, as if underneath it something else was lurking. She told herself she was imagining it.

As they got into bed she leaned over to kiss him and he kissed her back woodenly.

'Dave? Is everything all right?'

He stared hard at her. 'Yeah, why?'

'I don't know – you just seem a bit ... sort of distant.'

He gave her an odd, intense look. 'You tell me,' he said.

He just kept looking at her until she was thoroughly unnerved, her heartbeat picking up again as if she was racked with guilt, when she had nothing to be guilty about. She tried to laugh, to break the tension, though she was now completely unsettled. 'I don't get you,' she said. 'Nothing's up.'

'Good,' he said abruptly, turning on his side. 'That's all right then.'

Twenty-Nine

Joanne slept very badly and woke next morning with a knot of tension in her stomach. Miraculously Amy was not yet awake, but Dave was in the bathroom. She heard the sound of the toilet flushing, his electric razor, the splash of water.

She lay pretending to doze as he came back in to get dressed. After a few moments she thought she heard him move stealthily round to her side of the bed. The room went very quiet, but she could sense his breathing nearby. Confused, she opened her eyes and her whole body jolted. He was very close, leaning over her. Her body went limp, as if her bones had been replaced with liquid.

'What're you *doing*?'

She tried to sound calm, but her voice spun up high. He must have heard her fear. He stood, staring down in a weird, intense way, before finally straightening up. He had on a pair of navy pyjama trousers and a white T-shirt. As ever he looked spruce, even in his night things, almost like a soldier.

'Dave?' She lifted herself up on one elbow, trying to laugh it off.

'D'you want a cuppa tea?'

'Tea? Well, yeah. Thanks.' She found herself talking in that light, almost cajoling, nothing's wrong voice. 'Amy seems to be giving me a lie-in today.'

He went downstairs and Joanne lay back, letting out a gush of breath. *What the hell is he playing at?* She was trembling. But she didn't want to think any further.

Dave came back with two mugs, set one down beside her, then sat on the edge of the bed.

'Aren't you having breakfast?' she asked. 'You're not even dressed – you'll be late.

'In a bit.'

She sat up, one arm round her bent knees, the other holding the mug. The tea was sweet and she was glad of it, feeling she needed something to give her strength.

'So – you won't be going out today, will you?'

It felt like an order. Joanne pretended to consider this. 'Er, not much. I'll have to go up the shops, pick up a few things. But apart from that, no, I don't think so.'

One of these days, she thought, I must invite Sooky round. She realized with a pang that she didn't even have her friend's phone number. How could she have been so stupid as to forget to ask?

'Just the shops then.'

'Yes, but I don't think I've got any money. Have you got any?'

Dave looked back at her and an odd, mocking expression came over his face. 'You gonna beg me?'

'What d'you mean?' she said, irritation overcoming her uneasiness.

'Nothing. Only, I'm the one earning the money. So you ought to ask me . . .'

'Well, I am asking you. That's exactly what I was doing. But if it's a bother, I'll go to the bank . . .'

'What?' His look was insolent now. 'And get out *my* money?'

It was her turn to stare. 'What d'you mean?'

'Well, I don't notice *you* earning any money. It's my wages in the bank. So you're living off *my* money.'

Furiously Joanne pushed herself upright.

'What d'you want, Dave? Me to go out to work again? What – go back to W.H. Smith, and you stop at home and mind Amy? We've got a child now, in case you hadn't noticed. And you're the one who said you didn't want me working. To be honest, much as I love Amy, some days I'd quite *like* to be at work. Some days it'd be a lot easier than looking after her, and not so lonely. You can't have it both ways: you said you wanted to be the one to earn the money.'

He stared down at the duvet, pale blue with flowers on.

'And anyway . . .' She'd got going now and out it came. 'I've been thinking. I left school without even finishing my A-levels. One of these days I want to go back and do them – maybe do more: college even. I could get a much better-paid job then.'

'Don't be stupid!'

He laughed in a sneering way. Getting up, he went round the bed and pulled off his pyjamas, stretching his strong, naked body as if to show it off, thrusting his hips forward in a way that also implied a threat. Then he quickly began to dress.

'You – at college! You're too old! And anyway you've been at home too long. I'm not having you going off, tiring yourself out.' He looked across at her as he buttoned his shirt. 'You wouldn't have anything left for Amy – and what about if we have another babby, eh? What then?' All this was said in a mocking, I-know-what's-best-for-you tone.

Before she could reply he left the room and came back a moment later holding a ten-pound note.

'Here, for the shopping.'

Joanne was boiling inside. *Don't tell me what I can and can't do!* she wanted to shriek at him. God, just like Mom! Whatever she'd done, however hard she worked at school, Margaret had greeted any new idea with a blank, unimpressed 'What d'you want to do that for?' *Because I don't want to spend my life staring at the bloody wall, like you, like a zombie* ... The number of times she'd wanted to say that, or something like it. And Dad wasn't much better; he just said, 'All right, bab,' whatever you suggested. But that wasn't the same as taking an interest. That was what Dave had offered her when they were young: energy, vitality, zip.

She was still seething with anger by the time he left. He put his head round the door.

'I'm off.' The intense look was back again, as if he was trying to nail her down with his eyes. 'I might pop in later, we'll see. Amy's awake, by the way.'

'Right,' she said coldly. 'Bye.'

But she didn't move straight away. She thought back to when she and Dave were first together. For him, the meaning of life had been football. He had left school at sixteen.

'What d'you want to stay on for?' he'd said, as if she was mad. 'There's the real world out here. You don't want to be stuck in the classroom. Tell 'em to stuff it.'

And she'd been so besotted with him, so young and stupid, as she now saw it. She'd trotted after him like a little dog, thinking he was right about everything, that he had the world to win for both of them.

Amy was chattering to herself in the other room. It wouldn't be long before she cried out.

'I'll bloody show you – all of you,' Joanne said,

climbing out of bed. 'I'll go back to college, I'll make something of myself . . .'

Then she sat, despondent. How did she think she was going to do that? All the voices dragged her down. 'A-levels? What the hell for?' And there was Amy. She was her life now. And Dave. It was all right for Sooky. She was divorced and had a ready-made babysitter, living with her mom. Her spirits sank. Not much chance for her.

She knew she was going to spend the day catching up. It wasn't as hot as yesterday, but fine enough for another lot of washing. Once she and Amy had had breakfast, she put her in the buggy.

'Come with Mommy up to the shops? We'll get some bananas – you like those, don't you?'

They wandered up the Soho Road. Joanne was glad to be out of the house. Dave's threatening moods and her own anger and frustration made the walls seem to close in. The thought frightened her. A year ago – less, such a short time ago – she had been so happy. She had her lovely daughter, a home they could rent, everything had felt promising. How had things shifted so fast? It all felt out of control and she didn't know what to do.

She went to her favourite Asian shop. The lady behind the counter was friendly to Amy again and slipped her a chocolate frog. Amy's hands and mouth were soon covered in chocolate, but she was quite happy.

'Look at the state of you!' Joanne said, but her mood had lightened. 'You were s'posed to be having a nice banana, not sweets.'

'Sweets!' Amy echoed happily, with a brown grin.

As Joanne walked into the house the phone was ringing and she ran to answer it, leaving Amy out in the patch of garden at the front.

'Jo?' Dave sounded very put out.

'Yes, what's the matter?' She had almost recovered her temper from the morning and wondered if something was wrong.

'Nothing. Just calling. Only I phoned before and you didn't answer.'

'Well, no. I was out.'

'Out – where?'

'I told you, up the shops. We've just got back. I haven't even got Amy in yet. She's out the front. Look, I've got to go.' Putting the phone down, she said, 'For goodness' sake,' and rushed to fetch Amy.

He phoned again while they were watching *Sesame Street*, and again sometime after three o'clock. Just to say hello, he told her. Both times he was quite friendly, asking after Amy. The second time she said, 'Dave, why d'you keep phoning?'

'Just – you know, keeping in touch. I miss you.' His voice sounded almost tender this time and it disarmed her. She could picture him in the tiny office next to the workshop, tyres piled outside; phoning when he knew Al and Stuart wouldn't be able to hear.

'Well, that's nice. But we'll see you in a few hours.'

'Love you.' It was a hoarse whisper.

'That's nice,' she said again. 'Love you too.'

After Amy's nap, Joanne put a bowl of water out the back with some plastic toys for her to play with. She brought the phone book outside and sat next to her. She had a rough idea where Sooky lived; maybe she could find the phone number. But then she was at a loss. What was Sooky's surname? She had no idea where to start. How *stupid* that she hadn't asked! They were always so distracted with the children around that things like that got forgotten.

'Duck wet!' Amy giggled. She was wearing only pants and a pink T-shirt and was bending over a fat rubber duck, which was bobbing in the red washing-up bowl. 'Amy in.' She pointed.

'All right, you can paddle,' Joanne said. 'Mommy'll lift you in.'

If Amy had been a bit older, she might have known Priya's surname. She remembered from school that Sikh men were Singhs and women were Kaurs, but there was always a family name as well.

Amy stood in the bowl, laughing in delight. Her legs were white and frail-looking. They're quite long, Joanne noticed afresh, like mine.

The telephone clamoured in the house again. Joanne tutted. 'Not again! You just come with me a minute, Amy.'

She picked her up and rushed to the phone. Amy struggled in her arms, screeching with annoyance. Surely to goodness he wasn't phoning again, checking up on her? Because she knew that was what he was doing.

'*Yes?*'

'God, you sound in a good mood.' It was Karen.

'Oh, hi. Sorry, it's just . . .' She didn't try to explain, and Amy's cross roaring seemed enough reason. Joanne put her down, and Amy wandered back towards the garden.

'I can hear you can't talk for long,' Karen said. 'Only – are you going to be over this weekend?'

'Why? Is anything wrong? How's Mom?'

'Oh, you know. I think they've got the dose down a bit. She's a bit all over the place really. I just wanted to talk to you about something – getting her some help. I was talking to someone at the Poly . . . I'll explain when I see you.' Karen said this in her important way. 'And it'd be nice to have some support.'

Joanne smiled at the phrases Karen came out with these days. *Have some support*. It was these people she mixed with at work.

'Yes, we'll come over on Saturday. But if you need to talk without Mom around . . .'

'Oh, only for a minute or two. I'm just finding it all a bit stressful.'

Joanne felt contrite. Yes, it would be. Mom and Dad always had been *stressful* somehow. They'd just never known the word for it before.

'Don't worry – I'll be over. I'll bake a cake.'

Thirty

'The thing is,' Karen announced as they stood in Mom and Dad's back kitchen while everyone else was outside, 'I've been talking to Jill at work – she's one of the tutors. We ended up having a coffee together, a couple of weeks back when I was upset about Mom.' Karen's eyes filled.

'Oh dear,' Joanne said.

Karen waved her sympathy away, but Joanne could see that her sister, still living at home, was carrying far more of this than she was. But it was bringing out the best in Karen, showing her softer, less business-like side. She was even dressed more casually today, in a pair of loose, cerise cotton trousers and a black T-shirt. Joanne, as usual, was in jeans, a vest top and flip-flops, though she had rolled the jeans up.

'She's such a nice lady – she just asked one or two questions and it all came pouring out ... Anyway, she said, "Look, Karen, it sounds to me as if your mother really needs help. Have you thought of asking her if she'd like some counselling?"'

'Counselling? What: talking to someone? A stranger?'

Karen nodded, putting teabags in the pot. Everything Karen did was with neat, economical movements. Joanne's wonky Victoria sponge was on a plate nearby, jam oozing over one edge. Thank goodness Dave had wanted to come too, and she hadn't had to manage Amy and a cake tin on two different buses.

'She keeps having odd moods – crying. I've gone up a couple of times when I've got in from work, and she's been in bed in floods of tears. But she'll never say what's wrong. I just don't know what to do, and of course Dad's hopeless. I've asked him whether it's something about her past, but he doesn't seem to have a clue. I said to him, "Didn't you notice anything, Dad?" And he just said he thought that was just the way she was. How can you live with someone all this time and not know *anything* about them? It just seems incredible.'

She banged the kettle down angrily after pouring in the water.

'I mean, I know you don't necessarily go on talking about everything after – what? – they married in nineteen-sixty, right? So that's twenty-four years of marriage. Twenty-four! But you'd think they'd have talked about something *sometime*, wouldn't you? He barely seems to know who she is.'

Joanne felt she had more than an inkling of how your wife or husband could become a total stranger. How they could start to behave in odd and frightening ways. The phone calls had continued all week. But she didn't say anything and pushed the thought away. She did know a lot about Dave's past, though. She had shared most of it.

'We'd better go out,' Joanne said. 'I'll bring the tray.'

'What about it: the counselling?'

'I can't for the life of me see her doing that – can you, seriously?'

Karen sighed, looking deflated. 'No. Not really. I just thought it might do her good.'

'It probably would,' Joanne said, picking up the tea tray. 'I s'pose we could ask her. But I don't think she's very keen on things that would do her good.'

Outside they found Margaret sitting on a folding chair, beside her pots of geraniums, which looked as if they were gasping for water. The patio was still bathed in sunlight and Margaret was wearing a pale-green shirt-waister dress that she'd had for years, which was a bit tight on her and made her look washed out. Joanne recognized it with a pang. Why didn't Mom go and buy herself something new and nice?

Dave was with Fred, halfway down the garden, bent over the lawnmower. Amy had toddled over to watch.

'Ah, look at Amy!' Karen said. 'She always has to know what's going on, doesn't she? What're they doing?'

'There's summat wrong with it,' Margaret said. 'Fred's been complaining all week that he couldn't get it started. I said to him: you want to get Dave over to look at it.' Margaret turned her wonky-eyed stare to the table. 'Cake looks nice, Jo.'

Joanne felt surprisingly flattered by this rare compliment. There were shortbread fingers as well. Mom liked those: she thought they were posh. She pulled open the other folding chairs and set them down with a metallic clatter.

'You'd think Dad'd know about things like that,' Karen said, pouring tea.

'He only drives the buses,' Margaret said. 'He doesn't stick his head in the engine.'

'Dad, Dave – tea!' Karen called. 'Amy, love, d'you want a piece of cake?'

'Nice cake, bab,' Fred said as they sat round.

'Ta, Dad.' Not much baking went on in that house. Joanne looked at her dad's skinny frame, his saggy, melancholy face, and wondered about him. I don't know much about him, either, she thought. She did know that his background had been very poor. Lots of people had grown up in the back-to-backs. Slums, they were called by others. The cheapjack, cramped houses one room deep, backing onto another the same behind, had been built to cram in as many workers as possible close to the factories. Most of them had gone now, cleared after the war. The inhabitants had been scattered to tower blocks or far-flung estates. It wasn't unusual. But Dad's father had been killed in the war, and his Mom had never got over it and died not long after. The little she had heard about it had given Joanne the impression of a cold, underfed upbringing, flavoured with grief.

'He was a poor thing really,' Mom had said once. They didn't talk about anything from the past much, either of them. They just got on with it, as they would say. But Joanne felt tender towards her father. He was clueless in so many ways, but he'd always been kindly and gentle with them. Mom did her best too, but she was the one who had a temper.

'Business going all right, Dave?' Fred asked, as he always did. He was tucking into the cake.

'Yeah, not bad, thanks,' Dave said, as he always did. He was more relaxed here. He knew his parents-in-law liked him and always had. They'd been a bit in awe of him when he was young, with his good looks and his football. But he'd never been slow to help them.

'Nice cake, eh, Amy?' Margaret said. Amy was leaning against Joanne's knee completely absorbed in sponge and jam. There was a dust of icing sugar over her lips. They all laughed and Amy looked round, then giggled at all this attention.

'More tea anyone?' Karen said.

But the men were keen to get back to the lawn-mower. Amy toddled after them.

'She's growing up fast,' Margaret said. She gave Joanne a direct look. ''Bout time you gave her a brother or sister, isn't it?'

Joanne prickled inwardly with annoyance. She knew Mom was right, in a way, but something in her resisted. It was the way things felt so inevitable. You have one baby and so, as night follows day, you have another.

'I might,' she said.

'You don't want her growing up an only child, do you?' Margaret said. 'That wouldn't be much fun for her.'

'I don't s'pose it'd be the end of the world,' Joanne retorted. 'She's got lots of little friends . . .'

'Anyway,' Karen slipped in, 'you did, didn't you, Mom?' There had been talk of her half-sister Elsie, but otherwise Mom's childhood had come across as solitary. 'Didn't do you any harm, did it?'

'I wasn't an only child, was I?' Margaret said as if it was obvious. 'I mean, I had Tommy – well, at least, until . . .' She stopped, looking down.

Joanne and Karen looked at each other. Mom was looking tense and angry now, as if she hadn't meant to speak.

'Who's Tommy, Mom?' Karen asked, carefully.

'My brother.' She blurted it, angrily. 'My older brother, if you must know. Two years older.'

The girls exchanged looks again, at a loss. They'd never even heard of Tommy before, let alone met him. Mom's mood was becoming suddenly dangerous.

'You've never told us about Tommy,' Joanne said. She could feel such strong emotions coming off her mother that it made her nervous. But it all seemed so silly not to be able to ask. 'Where is he – I mean, is he still alive?'

'How the hell would I know?' Margaret said. 'He never wanted to come back, so he didn't. The last I saw of him . . .' She stopped as if a memory had assaulted her. The girls saw her thinking, collecting herself. 'He was evacuated with me. He went to a farm, and he liked it there, so he never came back when the war was over. He wanted to be a farmhand. So he stayed.'

This was hard to take in.

'So you mean . . .' Karen stumbled into speech. 'We have an Uncle Tommy – somewhere? Well, where?'

'Worcester way. Back then, anyway. He could be in Timbuktu by now, I don't know. He certainly never bothered to tell me where he was going.'

There was something in the way she was talking that made Joanne realize her mother was struggling on the verge of tears. She thought they'd better stop talking about Tommy, at least for the moment.

'Where did you go to, Mom, when they evacuated you?' she asked gently.

Her mother took a while to answer, but after a moment she looked up and Joanne could see a change in her, the usual flatness coming back over her as she took control.

'I was near Worcester as well – I told you. We were sent away together. It's a nice part, over there. I was sent to one lady, and then on to another place with two sisters.' She spoke impersonally, as if talking about someone else now.

'Well, when?' Karen asked.

'Oh, well, they evacuated a lot of children right at the start. We went at the beginning of September 1939, Tommy and me. And I came back in 1944 – March.'

'But you must have been ever so little!' Karen exclaimed.

Margaret nodded. There was an odd feeling coming off her, as if she was both glad to speak and resentful about being asked anything.

'I was five.'

'But why did they send you – couldn't your mother have gone with you? Our ... Our grandmother?' As Karen spoke, Joanne saw the realization break over her that they knew nothing about that grandmother, either. They didn't seem to know anything.

'No, my mother was ill. Died soon after, by all accounts.' This was said with no emotion. 'I never saw her again.'

A hundred questions ran through Joanne's mind, but she could see that her mother was on the point of shutting down.

'So, what was it like?' she asked, desperate to keep her talking.

'Oh,' Margaret said dismissively. 'It was all right, you know – most of the time.'

Inside, washing up together, the two of them were silent for a time. Then Joanne said, 'I feel sort of *ashamed* – that we don't know anything. That we've never asked.'

Karen swished water round in the teapot. She seemed angry.

'I don't feel ashamed. I feel quite put out actually, Jo. I mean, if we ever asked about our nanna and granddad, we were just told they were all dead – and that was that. I mean, what's the big secret? I think we have a right to know things like that.'

Joanne dried up a cup, slowly rotating it. 'Well, maybe we will now, in the end. It's funny, isn't it – it's as if this Valium thing has opened the lid on everything.'

'Well, she opens it for a second, then slams it shut again.' Karen banged the pot down on the side. 'You never know where you are with her.'

Margaret sat on outside as the others tinkered with the lawnmower, glad for the girls to do the washing-up. She sat so still that from a distance she seemed to have fallen into a doze. However, her mind was anything but quiet. Things were rushing to the surface.

That hadn't been the last time she had seen Tommy, that visit he made to the house in Buckley, as a tanned farm boy who had found a new life.

Not long before she left her father's house, left him to it with that vicious harridan Peggy Loach, she had seen Tommy again. It was a Sunday afternoon, sometime in the summer of 1946. She remembered it being very warm – the doors open all round the yard.

Her father and Peggy were upstairs in bed, sleeping it off, and she went out to fetch a bowl of water from the tap. A few bits of washing were hanging on the lines outside in the sun and, as she stood waiting for the bowl to fill, she glanced across the yard.

Between the drying clothes she caught sight of someone standing just at the end of the entry: a tall, strong lad with an unmistakable face. He was staring intently along the yard towards their house. She dropped the bowl with a clatter, water splashing her feet. He looked across and, seeming afraid, turned away.

'Tommy!' The tap was still running, but she tore after him, saw him leaving the entry. She ran into the street, just as he started to run as well. 'Tommy – stop! *Stop!*'

Her desperate shriek forced him to stop and turn round, slowly, as if he could hardly bear to look. He was so big now, a fourteen-year-old man, towering above her in a white shirt and waistcoat of rough black serge, trousers, boots.

'Tommy?'

He stared down at her. She saw the same frank look, the cheeky turn to his lips. His face was a weathered, healthy colour. They just stood there, gazing at each other, trying to take in what was in front of them.

'Are you coming home?' She could hardly bring out the words, her throat was so full and aching.

Tommy shook his head and started to step away. 'No, Sis – no. I can't. This ain't home. Not any more. No, never. But I just had to come and . . . Is Mom . . . ?'

'She's gone. She passed away soon after we left. You know she has.'

Tommy swallowed. 'Yes. I knew it really. I just had to come and see – just the once. But I'm off now. I can't stay, Maggie . . .'

He hurried away. There was nothing she could do. She knew he couldn't stay, could see that he had belonged to another life for a long time now.

She stood in the street, watching him through the tears, which came then, until he turned the corner and was gone.

Thirty-One

Harpreet had slipped into the house that warm afternoon, home from visiting a friend. The hall was full of delicious cooking smells. She stopped and listened.

Voices were coming from the kitchen, her mother and big sister chatting together, over the sizzle of onions and spices. Harpreet's round face broke into a smile. Stepping towards the portrait of Guru Nanak, she said, 'Thank you, *Guru-ji* – that's *so* much better.'

Later, upstairs, she flung her arms round Sooky.

'Hey, Mom's talking to you again, isn't she? I'm so-o-o happy!'

It was only a few days after the visit from Kanvar, the 'Young Prince'.

'Yeah,' Sooky said, giving her a squeeze. 'Me too.'

Harpreet's face creased with anxiety for a moment. 'They have told the Sohals you're not going to marry him, haven't they?'

'Yes, Dad told them.'

Harpreet sank down on the bed with exaggerated relief. 'Phew! Fate worse than death! Does this mean things'll go back to normal now? Are they okay with it?'

'I don't know about normal,' Sooky said, laughing. 'What's normal round here anyway? But it's much better. I think they've realized that marrying me off to just anyone might not be the answer now.'

She had cooked dinner with Mom, this time not in

the brittle silence that had persisted for the past months. Only now that things were beginning to heal could she look back and take in just how much pain and loneliness her mother's silent distancing of herself from Sooky had caused.

Harpreet was staring indignantly at her. 'I should think not!'

'Hey . . .' Sooky pulled Harpreet down on the bed beside her. 'Look, it's not really just Mom and Dad's fault. They've had to put up with a lot over this as well – you know, people bitching, the gossip.'

'But that's just it!' Harpreet exploded. 'They get all these horrible things said about them – and you. And you get the blame for all of it when it was all Jaz's fault! It's not fair, it's just *ridiculous*. I don't get why you've just accepted all that, said you'd had an affair with someone else to get a divorce, when you know you hadn't done anything . . .' Harpreet was almost in tears.

Sooky sighed, stroking her sister's hand. 'I know it's not fair. It's *absolutely* not fair. At the time I just wanted to get out of it so badly that I was prepared to take the blame. I feel like a coward now: I should have stood up to Jaz, told someone about his . . . problems. What really gets me is wondering who else Jaz might start on.' She looked at Harpreet. 'We're bound to hear if he gets married again – and I'll warn her. I honestly will. I don't know what else I can do now.'

'But what about you: *you're* the one who looks bad! And people remember all this stuff forever and ever.'

Sooky stared ahead of her. 'It's the whole family honour thing – *izzat* . . . Daughters keeping up the tradition. Mom and Dad are just caught up in that; we all are.'

Harpreet fumed beside her. '*I* don't want to be. I'll run away. I don't ever want to get married!'

Sooky squeezed her hand. 'But then what? You lose your family – you're all on your own. Oh, I don't know. It's all stupid and unfair, and some of it needs to change. But the thing is, I still wish things had been different . . .' Her eyes filled. 'That I could have made Mom and Dad proud, the way they wanted me to.'

'Oh, Sooks.' Harpreet put her arms round Sooky again and they sat hugging for a minute, both tearful.

'The main thing is,' Sooky said over Harpreet's shoulder, 'that at least Mom's talking to me.'

Until all this happened she had never experienced that simple longing for her mother's presence. She wanted everyday things: for them to cook together, do the chores, look after Priya and chat, the way they had done before. This felt like a sacred part of life. Now she had lost it and regained it, she knew how precious it was.

At first communication was stiff, like an unused wheel cranking into action. Both Meena and Sooky had been polite, but wary of each other. They had to take time to relate to each other on a new footing.

The schools broke up and the weather was hot. Pav spent a lot of the time out with his friends, mostly quiet, studious boys who gave no cause for worry. Harpreet had just finished her GCSEs and was relaxing and socializing too.

Roopinder, who was now six months pregnant, insisted that she needed to rest and seemed to find it hard to tolerate the company of the children she had already. She seemed quite down in herself, sleeping a lot and snapping at everyone. So for much of the time

Meena and Sooky were looking after Amardeep and Jasmeet as well as Priya, sometimes with Harpreet there to help.

As the days passed, Sooky became more and more aware of her mother's own need to talk.

At first Meena confided her worries about Raj. Sooky felt very distant from her brother these days. He was so angry, so vile to her, that it was hard for her to find any sympathy for him. But she knew he was suffering too. He had been a sweet, sensitive boy once and they had got along well. As a teenager he had become sullen and troubled, never sure how he fitted in. And now he was so fired up and self-important, it was almost impossible to have a normal conversation with him.

'I am so worried,' Meena said one day as they walked the children to the park. 'I am frightened that he is getting himself into something too extreme. Everyone is so angry, talking about fighting. What will happen? I don't know who he is seeing, who he is talking to – look, there, see what I mean?'

On the grass near the park gate a group of Sikh men was sitting in a circle under the trees, their turbaned heads close together. Sooky had seen them before, but Meena did not walk out to the park very often. She could see her mother straining to make out whether Raj was among them, even though he was supposed to be at work. But he wasn't in the group, and Meena relaxed a bit.

'You see?' She nodded at them. 'They are always talking about Khalistan – nothing but Khalistan. But we should not be thinking of this, breaking up the country even more. If we do, it will cause more fighting; like before, when they made Pakistan. We need to remain calm – enough of all this hating. Otherwise there will be nothing but more bloodshed.'

As they settled on the grass with the children, Sooky glanced over at the little knot of men. For a moment she saw them through other eyes: white eyes. How did they look to other people, to non-Sikhs? She had a flash of memory of two boys in her class at school, Patrick Hanlon and Mark Steel. She'd kept out of the way of those two whenever possible. They'd both been poor specimens, without much of a home life behind them. Both had been bullies – Mark especially. He was the one who had sullied her name, creeping up behind her, hissing suggestive, nasty things about it. From then on she had made sure everyone called her Sooky.

The thing she recalled most strongly about the boys was that they had both stunk of stale fat. This constant aroma of the chip pan made sitting anywhere near them especially unpleasant. They had seemed so alien, with their pink-and-white blotchy skin, their rank smell and lack of manners ... They had taunted all the Asian kids: 'Ughh, you smell funny! Eerrgh, your food stinks!' Had anyone ever found the nerve to tell them they stank too? That they were not necessarily the standard of 'normal', from which everyone else was a deviation? There had always been that divide: different skin colours, food, smells; so many little things on a daily basis that you hardly noticed that you were always having to face differences and choose whether to make an issue of them or overcome them.

At first Meena began talking about her childhood home. She did not raise the subject, but if Sooky asked her something, it would set off a rush of memories.

'What was it like in India when you were young?' Sooky asked one day, when, once again, they were in the park. 'Weren't the British still there? Can you remember that?'

'No, not really.' Meena sat down with a little grunt, arranging her clothes comfortably. Jasmeet was sitting next to her on the grass. 'Your grandfather called them the "pink-faced monkeys!" They both laughed. 'But where we lived, we never really saw them. It was only a small, small place. The life of the village went on. I don't remember anything about it. Amardeep, stop that – you let her play with you!'

Amardeep, being older and more agile, was running about with a ball, and Priya was wailing, struggling to keep up. Reluctantly he kicked it to her, too hard, so that she had to run a long way to fetch it, squeaking with indignation.

'Can you remember the village?' Sooky asked. She didn't want Meena to stop. She needed her mother to talk and talk.

A smile spread across Meena's face. She took the lid off Jasmeet's bottle of milk and sat feeding her as she talked.

'It was very beautiful,' she said. 'All the fields around: green or gold with ripe wheat. And flowers – such lovely blossoms, pink and red ... And we had buffalo. I remember washing them in the water of the tank nearby, and we drank their milk. Life in the village is very hard work – oh, here it is so different! In the village there is nothing: no supermarket ... My mother, she was working from sunrise until sunset, cooking over the fire, grinding the spices and flour, kneading the bread, baking. So many tasks all day, it never stopped. No machines for washing clothes and grinding

252

and sweeping; and the oven was made of mud – and the house also!' She laughed. 'All day the men worked in the fields, planting, ploughing: there was an ox ... And the women stayed in the house, always working. Only sometimes late in the evening there was time to sit and rest, and to talk, once the sun had gone down.'

There were often snippets like this, of her earliest memories. Sometimes in the evening, Meena said, as they sat in the dusk, moths fluttering round the lamp, her mother would massage her father's feet. Sometimes there was singing. She talked about the games with the other children, remembering the firelight fading to a glow in the darkness, the vast night sky. And about her favourite uncle, Nirmal, her mother's younger brother, who was only eleven years older than her and had always played with her.

Sooky had only once met *Mama-ji* Nirmal, when he came on his only visit to the UK in the early Seventies, when they were living in the first Handsworth house. She remembered a slender, haggard-looking man whose face would light up in radiant smiles. He was full of laughter and jokes. And she had heard his warm, teasing voice on the telephone many times from Delhi. He always booked a call to them around the time of *Vaisakhi*, the new year, and *Diwali*. But Nirmal was not enchanted by England.

'I don't know how you managed to make the switch, *beteh*,' he said to Meena. He belonged in India.

Soon after his visit, he and Bhoji moved the family to a new settlement in Delhi, called Trilokpuri, east of the river.

'One day, we will all visit,' Meena would say. 'Now the business is doing so well.'

While she was talking about these things Sooky

understood that she was happy, remembering all that had been lost, in the Garden of Eden before Partition.

But it seemed so much more difficult to ask about what had happened after that. Sooky understood that her mother's feelings were torn by conflict. But she didn't understand fully what the root of this conflict was, or why her response to things was often so confusing.

Thirty-Two

One afternoon Meena started talking, across a table strewn with vegetables and tomatoes and half-chopped onions.

She was moving back and forth across the kitchen, between stirring lamb in a pan and finishing mixing flour and water for *roti*. Sooky was sitting on one side of the table dealing with the onions and garlic, her eyes and nose running. Harpreet, opposite her, was running her hands through a pan of *dal* to check for bad bits and stones. On a chair by the sink Priya stood floating toys in a bowl of water and chattering.

Sooky and Harpreet had been talking about the episode of *Brookside* they had watched last night, and then a silence fell into which Meena, hands in the dough beside them, abruptly announced, 'What I have never told you is that the night we came away from our village, travelling in the darkness, my mother was taken away. It was more than three years before we saw her face again.'

After delivering this bombshell, Meena picked up the blue plastic bowl of dough, set it on the side with a tea-towel draped over it and went to the sink to wash the sticky remnants of it from her hands.

Sooky and Harpreet both froze, Harpreet with her right hand buried in the pan of *dal*. Sooky badly needed to blow her nose, but sat absolutely still. Their eyes were wide with shock. Was there going to be more? Should they ask any of the questions that herded into their minds like panicked cattle? *When was this exactly? What do you mean 'taken away'? Is that why we've never heard much about her? More than three years – what do you mean?*

Meena stirred the pan of simmering lamb. Its spicy, delicious smell became entangled with the silence, which grew longer, seething with emotion. Sooky watched her mother, her apron straps crossed over at the back of her primrose-yellow *kameez* and tied round at the front as she was so thin. Her elbow, moving the wooden spoon, looked sharp and frail. Sooky thought about how different, how strange, her mother's life seemed. For a moment an image of her came to mind: a bony scrap of a girl, running at the edge of a Punjabi wheat field, happy, innocent, with no thought that this would not always be her home. It brought tears to her eyes.

It was a struggle to realize that her mother needed help and that she herself had to find a way of giving it.

'Mom?' She got up with a glance at Harpreet, whose face was a study in dismay. 'I'll make us a cup of tea. Why don't you come and sit down?'

'But there is food to prepare . . .' Meena half-turned.

'We can do the vegetables and *dal* together. Come on, *Ma-ji*.'

Seeing them all settling at the table, Priya wanted to be included, and she climbed down from the sink. While Sooky heated a pan of tea, Harpreet went to the bowl and scooped out a handful of dough. She sat Priya on her lap and started to teach her how to make *roti*.

Sooky brought mugs of tea to the table, sweet and

frothy, and sat down between her mother and sister and daughter.

'Tell us – will you, Mom?'

Meena took the pan of dry *dal* from Harpreet. She sat running the little green pulses through her fingers in the way they had seen her do countless times before, avoiding looking at the girls.

'At first we were in Amritsar,' she began. 'We left our village quite early – in the March or April – and were able to catch a train and survive the journey. People say how lucky we were. Later on, round the time of Partition – in August – thousands left their homes, never to see them again. Very many walked in the *kafilas* from each side of the border, long snakes of people, carrying everything they could.

'We Sikhs and Hindus were travelling east, while the Muslims were passing the other way, west out of India. It was very dangerous: everyone was afraid. There were many killings on both sides; people seeing those going the other way, knowing that they would take the homes they had just left: the farms, even the animals. Trains arrived each side of the border – in Amritsar, in Lahore – on which there was hardly a soul still left alive. The corridors and *bogies* ran with blood. Many stayed in camps near the border; they had nowhere to go . . .'

Meena talked fluently, matter-of-factly, gesturing with her free hand as if, all these years, she had been waiting just to say it all. Priya seemed aware that something special was happening and sat quietly, squeezing dough with her fingers and looking solemnly round at them all.

'My father had a friend in Amritsar and somehow we found a place to live: in the Muslim quarter, where many people had left. *Mama-ji* Nirmal wanted to go to Delhi – he had the idea that he could make a good living. He loved cars and wanted to go into business, but for the time being my father said no, Amritsar was nearer to home and we would stay there. My uncle, *Thaya* Gurbir, was a cripple, so he could only do certain kinds of work and they had to find him something. But he was lazy. Only some days he went out, dragging his leg. He preferred just to sit. I stayed with my *Thayi-ji* Amarpreet.

'My mother had been taken away. That night when we left, she went out into the field to relieve herself and was abducted by men whom we never saw. Many mothers, sisters, daughters were taken away by the Mussalmen, wanting to rape them, to make them convert to their religion. She went into the darkness. We didn't see her after that. I was my mother's oldest child, born when she was nearly fourteen years old. I had a sister, Parveen, who was two at that time. My mother carried Parveen with her in her arms and I never saw her again. Even later, when my mother came back, I never once saw my sister.'

Sooky glanced at Harpreet, who was holding on tight to Priya. Her face wore the same appalled expression that Sooky knew was on her own.

'We were in Amritsar for only a short time – maybe three months – and then the bazaar nearby where we were living was set alight. All the houses were burning. It was dark; night-time. My father was not there – I don't know why. I think he had gone to see someone about some work and was late back. *Thayi-ji* Amarpreet had just given birth to her baby son a few weeks ago, and she and Gurbir were asleep upstairs and so was I. There was one room up, one down. Nirmal came in, shouting, shouting at everyone to get out – he picked me up and carried me into the street. Everywhere was full of smoke, of the sound of screaming, everything burning . . .

'My grandparents, *Dhada-ji* and *Dhadi-ji*, slept downstairs; they were able to move outside, and I stood holding my grandmother's hand. There was nothing we could do. The flames were crackling and devouring. We felt their terrible heat on our faces . . . Nirmal went to rouse the others, but they were slow and, as he went back to the house, the roof collapsed.' She motioned with her hand. 'Everything fell. He could not go inside. Nothing was left.'

'What about your uncle and aunt – and the baby?' Harpreet broke in.

'All died.' Meena paused for a minute. Still without meeting their eyes, she slowly shook her head. Again Sooky and Harpreet looked at each other, out of their depth.

'In Delhi things were better. My father found work in a flour mill, a Sikh business, and after a time Nirmal got a job as a taxi driver.' Meena smiled. 'This was his dream. They were able to keep us and buy food for us. We found a humble place to live. I stayed with *Dhadi-ji* in the daytime – there was no one else. Eventually I started to go to school.'

Pushing the chair back suddenly, she took the *dal* to the sink to wash it, wringing the stuff in her hands to shift the dust. She added them to the fried onions and spices, filled the pan with water and set it on the gas. Wiping her hands on her apron, she came back to the table. They all suddenly remembered to drink their cooling tea, stirring away the skin that had formed on top.

'I was missing my mother and sister. I was sad and lost, in a strange place. Only *Mama-ji* Nirmal was my comfort – and *Dhadi-ji*. I began to understand that my mother was not the only woman who had disappeared at that time. People were talking, and I would hear. But I didn't know even then that there were so many. Volunteers from each side crossed the border to look for them, these abducted women. They would go from village to village, questioning, listening to rumour and gossip, following talk of any small sighting. There were some exchanges of such women between India and Pakistan. Your abducted wives and sisters for our abducted ones ... My father asked them to find her. Over and over he said her name: Jasleen, Jasleen, as if it could make her appear, like snapping his fingers. It took such a very long time, but he never gave up. He was very lonely. I do not know if he despaired. Always he seemed to have hope – he never asked them to stop looking.'

Sooky listened, an ache filling her body. Harpreet wiped her eyes, trying not to show Priya that she was crying.

Meena picked up a knife and began slicing off the stalks at the end of the pieces of okra.

'Then, one day, they brought her back. Some men came. My father wept when he saw her, walking between them, being held by her arms. She was wearing turquoise clothing when she came to our door, I shall always remember it.' Meena paused in her work, but still didn't look up. 'When I saw her face I could hardly remember it. My grandmother had died by then and I was left with *Dhada-ji*, who was an old man. I was eight years old, and for half my life I had not seen my mother.'

What did she say? Sooky was bursting to ask. *What was she like?* But she didn't want to interrupt.

But Harpreet, who was openly weeping now, cried, 'Oh, that's amazing – all that time! She must have been so happy to be back!'

Meena moved her head in a harsh way that contradicted this.

'No, she was not glad. She was a stranger to us, and we to her. Later, when at last she started to speak, we found out that she had given birth to two children in Pakistan. She was already carrying a child when she was taken away, and had since given birth to another – both boys. Those two boys and Parveen, my sister, she had had to leave behind in Pakistan, with their family. The only family they knew. We had become dead to her in that time – and then they came to force her to go back.'

The full impact of the situation began to sink in.

'But . . .' Harpreet protested. 'Didn't anyone ask her whether she *wanted* to go back?'

Meena directed a look of scorn at her.

'She was the property of her husband. Why would anyone ask her? No one asks a woman anything. And anyway, there were agreements – legal arrangements for exchanging such women. She came back to my father, but she was in a foreign country now, a city where she had never been before. She had no choice but to get used to it. My father was a good man and he loved my mother. He wanted her back with his heart – not just because she was his. But she had no feeling for him. I think she had given her heart to another. And she had left her children . . . She had lost not once, but twice. Her own heart was broken right down the middle.'

'What about you?' Sooky said. 'You were her daughter too.'

Meena raised her head and spoke, looking past Sooky, across the kitchen. Her eyes went dull, her voice very flat.

'I suppose she remembered me. Of course she must have done. But I was not the baby of her heart any more – she had lost her two boys. It took her a long time. She was not cruel, not hitting or shouting. Something worse. She was just . . .' Meena looked down then, fighting her own emotions.

'She never spoke – not for a long time: a year, perhaps more. She was there, but not there. My poor father . . . But then her belly grew big with another baby and she began to speak at last.'

She looked up again and took up her vegetable knife.

'Until that time though, she said nothing. There was only silence and suffering.'

Thirty-Three

Meena laid her paring knife down then, covered her face with her hands and began to weep. Sooky and Harpreet, seeing her heaving shoulders and hearing the long-withheld, heartbroken sounds, went and stood each side of her, their arms round her shoulders. They were both crying as well. And Priya, catching all the grief in the room, clung to Sooky and soaked her leg with tears.

When they were all calmer, Sooky fetched the box of tissues from the other side of the kitchen and handed Meena some.

'Oh, Mom,' she said. 'It's all *so* sad.'

'Why didn't you tell us anything before?' Harpreet asked, tears still running down her cheeks.

Meena looked up at her. She seemed dazed and tired, but, reaching out, she took Harpreet's hand and pulled her soft, sweet daughter towards her. She stroked her arm.

'Don't be upset. No one wants to talk of these things. It was the same for everyone. For some, much worse things happened – whole families killed. But we were the lucky ones because my mother came back in the end. It was her *kismet*, her fate. Whatever is your *kismet* you cannot prevent. You can never argue with it.'

*

'Do you believe in *kismet*?' Harpreet asked.

It was later on that night and Sooky and Harpreet were up in their room. The house had gone quiet, but the girls were still trying to take in what had happened that afternoon. They were sitting on their beds opposite each other, each leaning exhausted against the wall.

Sooky considered the question. 'What, you mean like Mom does?'

'Yeah. Like everything's laid down. Whatever you do, it's all going to happen like that, and you can't do anything about it.'

Sooky stretched her legs out in front of her. 'I wonder if she thinks it was really my *kismet* to stay with Jaz.'

'She probably does. But then in a way she doesn't – that's the problem, isn't it? She can't work it out. She's pulled in every direction.'

'So what happens if you break your *kismet*? You defy fate?'

Harpreet looked uneasy. 'I dunno what to think. It's what we're brought up with . . .'

'The idea that you can't decide anything for yourself?'

'Yeah. I get it in one way, but it just seems . . .'

'Claustrophobic?'

'*Yes*,' Harpreet said intensely. She leaned forward. 'And where does it end? I mean, if I go downstairs tomorrow and I decide to eat, say, Crunchy Nut Cornflakes for breakfast instead of Rice Krispies – I mean, is that fate? Or doesn't it apply to breakfast cereals?' She was laughing now. It was a relief.

'You could try asking Mom,' Sooky giggled. 'No, I suppose it's just big things. The grand sweep-of-life things . . .' She considered it seriously again. 'But no, really, I don't think I do believe in it. Not the way Mom does.'

'But do you believe that out there somewhere there's the perfect man for you?' Harpreet drew her feet up and sat cross-legged, looking keenly interested in the reply.

'Well, maybe. But whether Mom and Dad would recognize him is another matter! I don't know, Sis – there are actions and consequences and personalities, and all of them interrelate. I don't think there's anything "out there" called fate, though. Or at least I don't think I do . . .'

'It just seems so sad,' Harpreet said, her face solemn again. 'What happened to Mom and to our grandparents, and all the killing and everything. Why did it have to be like that? They were all suffering when Partition happened, so why did they have to hate each other so much and kill so many people? As if everyone had gone crazy. And whatever happens, no one ever seems to think anything can ever be any different.'

Sooky shrugged, shaking her head. They sat silently for a moment.

'What're you going to do, Sukh?' Harpreet appealed to her. Sooky could feel how desperate she was to know what to think about her life, and to be led by someone. It stiffened Sooky's determination.

'I think what I'm going to do,' she said slowly, 'is ask about applying for that part-time degree.'

Harpreet looked worried. 'What if they find you a husband – soon?'

With more confidence than she felt, Sooky said, 'It could take ages. And anyway, do I really have to spend my whole life waiting for a husband who'll take me on, soiled goods that I am, and never do anything else?'

'No, but . . .'

'It's a bit late in the year – the Poly might not take me anyway. But I think I'll give it a try. My A-levels should be good enough.'

'What if you don't get in?'

'Well, little Sis,' Sooky smiled. 'Maybe that's down to *kismet*.'

At first Meena was resistant to it, as she always was to new ideas.

'What will your father say?' she asked, when Sooky found a moment to ask her about it the next day. They were sitting in the living room with the TV on in the background. Roopinder had at last gone out, after drifting round complaining for most of the morning.

Sooky smiled. Her mother always liked to portray her husband as a towering figure of paternal authority, when what Khushwant usually said about anything in the family was, 'Ask your mother.'

'If you're okay with it, he probably will be too.'

Meena sat staring at the TV. Sooky felt herself tense up. She could see another lecture coming on about her disgrace, the need for her to marry, to redeem herself and the family's *izzat*. God, she thought, can't they change the record?

'Mom?'

'You have always been a good student, Sukhdeep,' Meena said. She turned her head at last, and Sooky could see another tortured inner tussle going on within her mother.

'I just thought, as I'm here and not doing anything much, I might as well achieve something. That's if you'd be prepared to look after Priya while I'm at the Poly – if they'll have me?'

'What do you want? You want to get a job?'

Yes, Sooky thought.

'I don't know. I want to do social sciences of some sort. Maybe become a social worker – be able to help people.'

Meena seemed to look at her with new eyes – eyes that were full of a clashing mix of admiration and panic.

'Help people? But what about getting another husband? Children?'

'Well, there's no one on the cards at the moment, is there? Can't we just give it a chance? Maybe I could even do both? Some people do, you know, Mom.'

Meena turned back to the TV. Sooky sat with her heart thumping.

'You are a kind girl, wanting to help people. There are many people needing help. But is it really a job for a woman? Such rough people you would be dealing with . . .'

'I wouldn't be getting a job yet,' Sooky reassured her. 'It could be years before I got a job – I might be married again before then. But this would just be to find out. Maybe at least get another qualification.' She knew Meena liked certificates, with their thick, classy paper and look of official grandeur. 'It might even increase my marriage chances. Can I at least give it a try?'

Meena hesitated, then slowly gave a slight inclination of her head.

Thirty-Four

Margaret waited, all that week, for the shivering, skin-and-bone boy she had met at the wharf to call in as he had said he would, but he never did. She realized she recognized him from school, where she had seen him standing to one side of the yard, looking cold and lonely. He was in the form above hers, and she didn't dare go up and speak to him and he didn't speak to her, either. He seemed to be as much of an outsider as she was.

By the Thursday she had given up looking out while she was working in the house, to see whose boots they were that she could hear crossing the yard. Her small tentacle of hope, which had just begun to peep out, curled itself back in again. Of course he hadn't come. He was only saying it; he hadn't meant it. Why would anyone want to come and see her?

Next Saturday she set off for the wharf, expecting nothing. She stood shivering in the queue, the scraping sounds of coal being shovelled growing gradually closer. A mucky mist hung over the cut. She waited, hunched up with her hands in her pockets, one hand stroking a bruise on her left thigh where Peggy Loach had landed a kick at her last night. 'Get out of my way you useless little brat!'

Margaret was numb – beyond even hating Peggy. There seemed no way out of any of it, and she tried not to feel anything. The only bright spot in her life was going to Elsie's house and seeing Susan and Heather, her little nieces, who were always pleased when she came. But she only got over there once a month, if that.

She was already trudging home, pushing the pram-load of coal, head down, so that she didn't even see him until he loomed close to her.

'Margaret, ain't it?'

As she looked up she saw him flinch, as if he expected her to reject him. She remembered the gentle, timid face. This time he was wearing a shirt and didn't seem quite so paralysed with cold.

'You got yours already,' he said, nodding at the pram.

'Yes. I'm going home.' Too late, she decided she ought to smile.

There was an awkward silence, then Fred said, 'I've had a lot of jobs on this week – for Mom. She ain't been too well.'

'Oh,' Margaret said. 'Poor thing.'

'She's a bit better now . . .'

More silence. Both of them were hopeless, had no idea what to say.

'I've seen you at school, haven't I?' Fred said eventually.

Margaret nodded. 'You might've done.'

He nodded too, and looked away down the street. Finally he said, 'I'd better get along. Our mom wants to get the fire lit.'

'T'ra then,' Margaret said, leaning against the handle of the pram to get it going.

'See yer around.'

She did see him around. Now and then she saw him at school, but sensed that he didn't want to be seen talking to a girl – especially one in a lower form. He seemed afraid. And soon the school term ended for Christmas, and she met him at the wharf and in the streets a couple of times. Margaret was so unsure of herself that she might not have stopped when she saw him, but Fred, though having a cringing sort of shyness, never pretended not to see her, or passed her by when they were outside school. He always came up and spoke.

'You all right?' he asked, running into her one dark Friday afternoon.

'Yes, ta,' she said, looking up at him, hoping her wonky eye didn't show up in the gloom.

'Only I thought you looked a bit . . . I dunno. Poorly or summat.'

'I've got a bit of a cold, that's all,' Margaret said.

Fred looked up at the tin-grey sky. 'Looks as if it'll snow.'

The clouds seemed full to bursting.

'You going to the wharf tomorra?'

Margaret nodded.

'Can I walk with yer?'

Her heart beat faster, just as it had when Elsie's girls had showed they wanted her. The little hope-tentacle popped out again.

'All right then.'

It was nice having someone to go to the wharf with.

It was like when she used to go with Tommy. Fred was nothing like Tommy, who had been bold and strong, but it warmed her to think he would be waiting for her.

When she got up that morning there was no sign of her father or Peggy. They'd be sleeping it off for hours yet. The house stank of stale booze tinged with urine from the bedside po's. The range would be cold, so there was no prospect of a warm drink, and there was nothing left but a handful of slack. Margaret dressed, pulled on her old boots and hurried outside, collecting the pram from the brewhouse where Dora Jennings kept it stowed.

She pushed the pram down the entry, careful not to slip on the icy bricks. Would he be there somewhere? All the time she was telling herself not to expect anything. As she turned into Washington Street, though, she saw him waiting for her near the corner, with his makeshift cart.

He was looking out for her and, as she drew closer, a smile lifted his woebegone face.

'All right, Margaret?'

'Yes, ta.'

They went along to the wharf and, as they waited, Fred pulled from his pocket a dog-eared collection of cards, held together with a rubber band.

'D'you wanna see my collection? My uncle give me them – they're from before the war.'

'All right,' Margaret said.

Soon they were going through the well-worn collection of cigarette cards: there were ships and sportsmen, beautiful actresses and views of foreign cities Margaret had barely heard of. She could see why Fred liked to have them; it was like carrying a picture book in your pocket. It made her think of the books of fairytales they had read in Buckley, and this brightened her day.

'Come on, you two – get a move on, if yer going,' the woman behind said to them. 'Some of us ain't got all morning, yer know.'

Once they'd got their coal and were on their way back, Fred stopped her for a moment.

'I was thinking,' he said, 'as it's nearly Christmas . . . whether you'd come round to ours: meet our mom and the others?'

'What, now?' Margaret said.

'Well, no – not now. What about Monday: it's Christmas Eve? You know, just for a bit. For tea?'

Margaret could feel her cheeks turning red. 'Won't your mom mind?'

'No, she'll be pleased. We don't have much company.'

'Yes, all right then.' And she dared to smile properly at him for the first time.

'Oh, good!' Fred seemed really pleased. He told her his address in Washington Street. 'See you then – in the afternoon?'

Thirty-Five

It was already dark when Margaret went round to the Tolleys' house. It was a back house off a yard off Washington Street, very like her own, but that didn't make her any less nervous. Her hand was clammy as she raised it to knock on the door.

Fred opened it almost at once, and in the dim light she could see his grin. At home, he seemed less edgy and there was an excitement about him.

''Ello – come in! We're all 'ere.'

Behind him a woman and two children were peering round trying to see the visitor, standing near the table, which to her seemed stacked with food. An anxious pang passed through her. The cooking at home! She had peeled a pan of spuds for Peggy to boil and there was leftover stew. Just for once Peggy Loach would have to do something for herself.

'Bring her in, Fred,' Mrs Tolley instructed. 'Don't leave the poor wench on the doorstep – you're letting the heat out.'

And Margaret stepped into the cosiest room she had seen in a long time.

'Mom, this is Margaret,' Fred said shyly. 'This is our mom – and this is our Jean, and Bobby.'

'Nice to meet you, dear,' Mrs Tolley said. She had a light, gentle voice and Margaret could see immediately that Fred must have favoured his father, as he looked nothing like her. Mrs Tolley was small and frail as a bird, with black curly hair, brown eyes and sallow skin. Bobby, who was seven, took after her in looks, but Fred and Jean were skinny, long-legged and hollow-eyed, with pale-brown hair. Much, much later, Margaret would see those looks reproduced in her daughter Joanne.

'Come and sit down and we'll have our tea,' Mrs Tolley said. 'The kettle's on the boil.'

She seemed desperately keen to please and to make the evening into a little party.

'Here y'are . . .' Fred pulled out a chair for her and Margaret said, 'Ta', as the others scrambled eagerly to the table and the plates of bread and butter, pot of jam and a fruitcake, everything laid out nicely on willow-patterned china. They seemed excited over the Christmas celebration as well.

Jean put her hand to her mouth and hissed from behind it, 'There's jelly for afters, as well!' Margaret liked Jean, who had plaits and big gappy teeth and seemed to be a chatterbox.

She gazed round the room, amazed. Her father's house was so neglected and dismal. Her mother's old crocks were mostly broken now and the rooms were bare of anything but the few essentials. Their living-room table was covered by a stained oilcloth and there was nothing about the room to make it homely. But the Tolleys' downstairs room was warm and cosy that evening, with lots of things to look at, and the table was spread with a white cloth.

The range was alight, heating a big kettle from which Mrs Tolley was brewing tea in a big brown pot. The walls were painted pale blue and there was a picture of a ship on one wall. She saw the shadowy shapes where

274

there had been other pictures and wondered where they had gone. Only much later did she realize that Mrs Tolley must have pawned them.

On one end of the mantelpiece was what must have been a wedding photograph, slipped in alongside ornaments and candlesticks and jugs, and in the middle stood a brass carriage clock. In pride of place at the other end a framed portrait looked down on them of a thin, hollow-eyed man, smart and upstanding in his RAF uniform, and Margaret knew she was seeing Fred's dead father. The floor was softened by two colourful rugs, and brightening the backs of the two armchairs were strips of crimson cloth serving as antimacassars. Draped from the corners of the room were paper streamers crossing in the middle and someone had pinned a star, cut from yellow paper, at the point where they crossed.

Most fascinating of all to Margaret, though, was the small table close to the window with its crimson curtains, on which sat a cage containing two green budgerigars, which kept making cheerful chattering noises.

'Go and see 'em if yer want,' Jean said, noticing Margaret's fascination. 'That's Wally and Flo.'

'Save it for after your tea,' Mrs Tolley said, bringing the pot to the table. 'It'll be cold else.'

All her life long, Margaret could never get over the contradiction between that charmed evening and all that followed. It was almost as painful for her as it had been for Fred, because during those hours, in that little house, she felt that she had stepped again into a kind of paradise that she had lost on her dismal return to Birmingham.

They all sat round the table, as a family – something she had not done since leaving Buckley. Mrs Tolley was at the head, presiding over the tea in the chair that had once been her husband's. As she poured the tea, Margaret noticed that her hand shook badly and she thought it was because the pot was heavy. She didn't notice the amazed, grateful looks that passed between the Tolley children that night. She thought their excitement was just about Christmas. All she saw was family life, and all the warmth and comfort for which she yearned.

Mrs Tolley mostly sat quiet as the children chattered, especially Jean. Fred kept smiling, his pinched face soppily happy. As she sat beside him, Margaret saw that the sleeve of his blue school jumper that he was wearing was coming unravelled. She noticed how thin his wrists were as he carried the bread and jam to his mouth, eating ravenously.

They toasted with tea: 'Happy Christmas, everyone!'

Afterwards Mrs Tolley seemed to have exhausted her energy, and the children cleared the table and sat round to play games. There was a cheap pack of cards for Happy Families, and they played Noughts and Crosses and Hangman. Margaret found herself laughing as she hadn't in months. One of Bobby's favourite things was making terrible faces, like a gargoyle, and Jean was full of jokes. Bobby got cross when he didn't win the games, though. Jean crowed over him, but Fred was always kind and appeasing.

'Go on, Bobby,' he'd say. 'You have another go. You'll win this time.'

Mrs Tolley sat in a chair near the fire. When she noticed Fred glancing at her from time to time she would smile, at least with her mouth. Margaret just saw it as a smile.

When the clock chimed nine o'clock, Mrs Tolley roused herself and said, 'Had you better be getting back now, Margaret? Your family'll be missing you.'

Fat chance of that, Margaret thought. Dread filled her. It was like waking from a dream. Did she really have to go back, away from this charmed place?

'Fred, you walk her home,' Mrs Tolley insisted.

Margaret shyly thanked Fred's mom, her words seeming wholly inadequate to express the bliss of that evening. Then she and Fred set off along the freezing street. When they reached her entry, Fred stopped by the lamp. Shyly, he handed her something from out of his pocket.

'Here – I got yer this, but I didn't want to give it yer in front of the others . . .'

Margaret could almost hear his blush sizzling on the cold air.

'Oh!' she gasped, mortified. 'You got me a present! I never got you one!'

'Never mind – here, take it. I hope you like it, that's all.'

He thrust something papery into her hand. It felt like a piece of an exercise book, but there was something wrapped inside.

'Open it when I've gone.' He was backing away. 'T'ra, I'll see yer . . .'

'Thanks – for tea and everything!'

'S'all right,' she heard, as his long, skinny form retreated.

Despite the cold she didn't want to go inside. Full of curiosity, she moved closer to the lamp and unfolded the piece of paper. Out of it slid a ring, a light, cheap thing. When she held it up to the lamp, the stone in it gave off a deep-red glow.

Entranced, she slipped the ring onto the third finger of her right hand and it fitted perfectly. Margaret hugged herself. A ring! He had given her a ring!

Glowing with happiness, she stepped into the dark entry.

'Where the hell've you been, yer little brat?'

Peggy's barrel-like, red-eyed figure came at her the minute she stepped through the door. The room reeked of beer and spirits and of the sweat of two large, lazy people. Far from being out of it or away at the pub, as Margaret had hoped, they were here, large as life and twice as ugly.

Ted was sitting by the range, his eyes also bloodshot. He barely looked capable of standing up, let alone coming for her, but Peggy was spitting mad and spoiling for a fight. Drink always made her pugnacious. She had a police record for brawling in the street.

For a second Margaret thought of retreating back through the door, but Peggy read the idea in her face and grabbed her by the shoulder.

'You get in here, ye little vormin!'

Margaret managed to wrench herself away from Peggy and get the other side of the table.

Peggy was swaying slightly. Her dyed hair had a greasy, mustardy look and her face was covered by a sheen of perspiration, her cheeks red and puffy. She was obviously finding it hard to focus.

'Where the **** d'yer think you've been? Going off without cooking our dinner . . .'

'I did the spuds,' Margaret said. 'All you had to do was boil them . . .'

'Bile 'em?' Peggy roared. 'Let me tell ye – I don't

bile anything round here: that's your job. And what's this mess?' She leaned over and lifted the lid on the remaining stew. 'Not fit for the pigs, that it's not . . . Not for a grown man like your father.'

'Sorry,' Margaret said, eyeing Ted to see if he was going to move, but he slumped back in his chair.

'Sorry! You'll be sorry all right!' Peggy roared. She went to lunge round the table, but had to steady herself at the corner. 'You ever do that again without my say-so and I'll beat the ****ing life out of ye, d'you hear?'

'Yes.' Avoiding Peggy's eye, Margaret shifted closer to the stairs. She could see Peggy was in no condition for any sudden moves.

Peggy frowned, struggling to focus. She pointed, unsteadily.

'What's that on your finger?'

'Nothing.' Margaret shoved her hand into her coat pocket.

'That wasn't nothing! You've got somethin' on your finger, and I want to see it! Come here . . .' She began lumbering round towards Margaret. 'Where did you go getting a ring from? You give that to me, or I'll—'

Margaret bolted and fled up the stairs to her room. With all her strength she dragged the metal bed frame across against the door and sat on the edge panting, her heart booming in her chest.

From below she could hear Peggy cursing and carrying on at her father. There was a smashing sound, but Peggy didn't come up the stairs. She wouldn't have been able to exert herself that much.

'Fat bitch! Go to hell, you fat, stinking bitch!' Margaret stuck her tongue out as far as it would go, as if Peggy was in front of her. 'I *hate* you.'

But she was safe for the moment. She lay on the bed,

waiting for things to quieten down. They'd soon be sleeping it off. There was no light in the room to look at her ring, but she turned it round and round on her finger, hugging her hand to her chest.

'He gave me a ring! For me! Specially for me!'

She lay smiling into the darkness.

She saw Fred Tolley just once more after that.

There had been no Christmas to speak of in their house. Ted and Peggy spent most of the day sleeping off the excesses of the night before. Now the war was over, Ted no longer troubled himself with work and there was barely any money. He didn't give Margaret anything extra for Christmas food, so she ate the last scrapings of stew and stale bread and spent most of the day on her own, cleaning up the house.

But even in this cheerless activity she was not downhearted. As she scrubbed and mopped, her spirits were kept high by the sight of the ring on her finger, the stone giving off its warm red glow. She was making a friend, and his mom kept a cosy house and he had a brother and sister. If she was allowed to go round there and visit once in a while, it would make all the difference to her life. She had something to hold on to.

A couple of days after Christmas she was on her way to Howlett's in Cregoe Street to fetch some groceries with a few coppers that, in desperation, she had stolen from her father's jacket.

On her way she suddenly saw Fred tearing along the road, his face pale and tense. He didn't seem to see her. As he ran past, his jacket flying behind him, she said shyly, 'All right, Fred?'

He didn't even turn, just ran on.

Margaret was hurt, but she could see that he was in a hurry for some reason, so she didn't think much more about it.

During the last days of the school holidays she kept looking out for him. She didn't dare call round at the house, and there was no sign of him anywhere. Her high spirits began to seep away. Fred didn't want to see her again, that was what it was. He'd obviously decided she was no good and he didn't want to know her. She wrapped the ring he had given her in a scrap of cloth and hid it at the back of the attic cupboard.

The school term started and there was no sign of him there. When she hadn't seen him at school for a couple of days, she wondered if he was sick and whether she should pluck up the courage to call at his house and find out. Mrs Tolley might be pleased that someone was concerned about him.

So after school one afternoon she walked nervously round to Washington Street. It was a heavy, grey afternoon with more snow threatening, but as soon as she walked into the Tolleys' yard she knew there was something more than the weather weighing the place down. It was strangely quiet. There was a woman mangling clothes at the end of the yard, who turned and stared.

Margaret walked up to Fred's house. The windows were dark and it had a silent feel, with no sign of life. She was just reaching out to knock when the mangling woman shouted, 'No good calling there, bab. There's no one about and there won't be, neither. Who've yer come to see?'

Margaret jumped, her nerves were so on edge. The woman, who was big and wearing a calf-length black skirt, was coming over to her, grim-faced.

'I've come to see Fred,' Margaret said.

The woman regarded her for a moment as if unsure what to say.

'You a pal of his?' she asked eventually.

Margaret nodded. She hoped so anyway.

The woman's face softened a fraction. 'You've not 'eard, 'ave yer? Those children ain't living 'ere any more. The Corporation or someone came and took 'em away after . . . They couldn't just leave 'em 'ere to fend for themselves.'

Margaret felt a deadly chill start to spread inside her. She knew something terrible had happened, but she couldn't make any sense of what it was. She could only echo, 'Took them away?' in hardly more than a whisper.

'To the orphanage, I s'pose. Look, bab.' She spoke gently. 'I'll tell yer, as yer don't know. Mrs Tolley took 'er own life. Hanged herself. 'Er'd always 'ad troubles since Mr Tolley was killed. It all got on top of 'er in the end. So they ain't 'ere – none of 'em. I dunno where they've gone, bab, or I'd tell yer.'

The cold spread through Margaret, like the numbness of holding your hands in icy water.

'Oh,' she said to the woman. 'Thank you.'

She left the yard and stood in the darkening street. A cart clopped past and the driver called out, 'Penny for 'em, wench!' She didn't want to go home. She didn't know what to do. . . . *Took her own life . . . Hanged herself . . .*

All she could think of was that evening they'd had – that wonderful, happy evening, with Mrs Tolley being a mom and tea round the table, when it had all looked so perfect. And she couldn't put the two things together at all.

Thirty-Six

Margaret stood by the kitchen sink in Institute Road, holding a glass from which she had just drunk a long draught of water.

The window faced over the back garden. Outside the sky was cloudless, but hazy, promising to burn into another very hot day. Fred and Karen were long gone out to work.

She looked at the glass as if she had forgotten she was holding it, then slowly rinsed it out and stood it upside down on the plastic drainer.

I must water those plants, she thought, noticing the gasping geraniums on the patio.

But she just stood. That odd, swimmy feeling came over her, as it did a lot of the time, as if she wasn't quite present in her own life. When she walked about, even that didn't feel right, as if the floor was padded with cushions. Her body was full of sensations. Were these feelings normal? She could no longer decide.

With a shaky hand she reached for her ciggies and lit up, then stood staring out. The lawnmower (still not fixed) was grounded by the old clapboard fence.

'Where were you going, that day I saw you?' she had asked Fred, years later when they had met again. 'You were running down Cregoe Street – you looked in a terrible state. Was that the day she . . . ?'

'No,' Fred had said. 'That wouldn't have been that

day. It was just before. I was running for the doctor. That afternoon I came into the house and Mom was out cold on the floor, in front of Bobby an' all. He was crying like a babby – he dain't know what to do. I never knew what she'd taken, but I went for Dr Greaves. It was after that – a few days later – when she . . . yer know.'

Thoughts thudded through her head. She couldn't seem to stop them. She recalled standing in the street that day for who knew how long. She had no idea where Fred and the others would have gone or any hope of ever seeing them again. This was how life went. People were taken from you, and that was that.

What she could remember now was somehow walking back to Upper Ridley Street, to the house that contained her unloving father and the vile, slovenly Peggy Loach. She stopped in the darkening yard, looking across at the mean, cold house and something in her gave way, like a rock fall.

Her sister Elsie stood facing her, her pale hair straggling out of its pins after a chaotic morning of toil with a maiding tub, dolly and mangle while minding two tiny children. She was wearing a stained, damp pinner and had her hands on her hips in an attempt at resistance.

'*Please*,' Margaret insisted. 'I'll do anything for you. I'll cook and clean – I know how. And I can help with these two . . .'

Susan and Heather were leaping about the room, excited as baby goats at Margaret's arrival.

Elsie's face wore a frown, but Margaret could see she was on the point of caving in. The offer of help was too tempting, even if it did mean another mouth to feed. And Elsie had always had a kind heart.

'But what about school?' she protested. 'You can't get to school from all the way over there. And you can't just stop – I'm not having the wag man pestering me. You have to stay on now, till you're fifteen, they say.'

'I'll go to another school, over here,' Margaret said. 'I'll do anything you say, but don't make me live with the Old Man any more. You wouldn't want to, would you?'

Elsie's face darkened. 'That I wouldn't, especially not now that scheming Irish trollop's moved in on him an' all.'

'She hits me,' Margaret admitted miserably. 'And all they ever do is drink.'

She didn't cry because she almost never did, but Elsie could see all the troubles laid out.

'Well, when would you come?' she asked.

'Now.' Margaret had with her a small bundle containing her few bits of clothing and Fred's ring. 'I haven't left anything over there.'

Elsie pulled a chair out from the table and sat down rather abruptly. She laughed suddenly.

'Well, I'll say summat for you – you know when your mind's made up, don't yer? What in heaven's name is Jack gunna say?'

As Margaret was to find out, Elsie frequently wondered what her husband Jack was going to say about this or that, when the fact was that Jack Trinder left major statements of opinion to Elsie. Jack was cheerful and sandy-haired, with a smile that crinkled his face into mischievous lines. He was truly a family man and hard-working. He had stayed in Birmingham throughout the war in a reserved occupation working in munitions. Though a bit out of it among the forces lads, there were plenty like him in the city, and he had his mates around him and had not suffered the problems of a disrupted marriage. He and Elsie rubbed along happily; she was in charge, though she pretended he was, and they had two sweet, happy little girls.

Margaret soon realized she had landed on her feet. She bunked up with Susan and Heather in one room, while Elsie and Jack had the other. They didn't discover for some time how Ted and Peggy had taken her bailing out on them. More energetic people might have come looking for her, but they were either too drunk or too lazy to bother, and after a week or two Margaret started to relax. School was all right, certainly no worse than the last, and now she had the enjoyment of being with her two little nieces.

She stayed with Elsie and Jack for the rest of her single life – most of thirteen years, until she married Fred in 1960. Once she left school she picked up work in factories nearby. She was always a help to Elsie and a companion to the girls, especially Susan, to whom she was closest. News came from Dora Jennings that Peggy Loach had decamped from Upper Ridley Street not long after Margaret. With her skivvy gone, she thought herself too good for the place. Ted replaced her with another woman, then another. By 1951 he was dead of a liver complaint. Elsie and Margaret went to his funeral, but they had never seen him alive again.

When Elsie and Jack moved out to a little semi in Yardley in 1954, there was no thought but that Margaret would go with them. They were amiable, settled years, in which she felt safe, was obliging and grateful and expected very little for herself.

'Why don't you go out and enjoy yourself?' Elsie would say sometimes. 'Find a nice boy?'

Once or twice there was someone, but it never seemed to last. Margaret was already shy about her appearance and was never sure what to say to anyone. Boys found her closed and dull, and moved on to someone else. And Margaret never expected life to be especially good; she was just glad to keep it from being very bad. Safe and humdrum suited her. Once sweet-rationing was over, she took to sucking bull's eyes and barley sugars, a comfort that had done her teeth no good. She also, enthusiastically, took up smoking.

After the move to Yardley, where for the first time she had her own room, she got fed up of having to take the bus into Birmingham to a factory every day. Instead she found herself jobs more locally, first in a grocer's shop in Stoney Lane and later in a cafe nearby. She liked that job. It was sociable in a way that was not very demanding, but stopped her feeling isolated. She liked wearing an apron and feeling slightly official in it. She enjoyed the warm smells of toast and buns and tea, the repetitive actions of wiping tables and refilling sugar bowls.

One day as she was working her way round, wiping away cigarette ash and grains of sugar, she looked up into the face of a customer at the next table and their eyes fixed on each other's. His face was thin, hollow-eyed, sad-looking. He paused, holding up a cup of tea.

'Margaret?' he said.

*

She came back to the present, still standing by the sink. It felt as if hours had passed. Turning to the clock, she saw that it had been seven minutes. Time seemed endless, slow as the flow of tar. The hours of the day alone in the house became huge and baggy. All she could hear was the tick of the living-room clock and a distant vibration of television from the house next door.

Fred Tolley. Her smile had met his that day. A man she had not seen for more than twelve years and whom she had barely known even then, when they were children. Yet they felt destined for each other.

'Why did I marry Fred?' Her lips moved, but there was no sound.

Answers came that she had never let herself think of before. Because he was the only one who ever wanted me, and I was grateful. Because he seemed kind. Because I wanted him to be Tommy, to take his place, like he did at the wharf all those years before. Because I had had tea at his house and thought he would offer me heaven. And because I had no idea what else to do . . .

Fred was a good man in his way. They had a life, a family. But his own past had taken its toll. He was timid, cowed by life, never seemed to feel much about anything, though she knew with shame that he felt more for her than she ever had for him. That he loved her, or at least needed her, and in some way she felt contempt for him for doing so. She had never felt she could tell him who she was – the real Maggie, and all it had meant. He would have stared blankly at her and shrugged. The dread of that was worse than him not knowing anything at all.

A terrible sensation rose in her, like nausea, a swelling sensation that filled her with panic. She was finding it hard to breathe. For a moment she put her hands over her face as if to cry, but the tears wouldn't come. It was like something that had happened after Karen was born – as if there was something inside struggling to get out. She hadn't been able to bear it. The doctor had given her the pills.

Unsteadily she went to the back door and stepped out. The heat was building up and she stayed in the shade of the patio. She clutched a fist to her lips, biting into it to stop herself screaming out, howling like a wolf across the back gardens of Kings Heath. Managing to control it, she leaned against the wall by the kitchen window and took deep, shuddering breaths until it passed.

Thirty-Seven

As the summer went by, Joanne could no longer pretend to herself that things at home were in any way all right. In fact she could barely remember what 'all right' meant.

The phone calls continued, Dave checking up on her two, three or more times a day. She had given up asking him not to. Even though she rolled her eyes every time the phone rang, she tried to sound relaxed and appeasing, though her nerves were often at screaming pitch. If she ignored it, he just kept ringing again. And if she was out, had warned him she was going to the shops or the park with Amy, he would always call an extra time later in the day.

In the evening, once he came home, they never saw anyone else any more or socialized together. It had been harder since Amy anyway, but Dave's mate Pete used to ask him out, and Michelle would come round once in a while. Now it had all fizzled out and they had lost contact with people. When she heard the engine of his car fall silent outside the house and his key in the lock, she felt a surge of claustrophobic panic. From then on they were shut in together.

That was when her efforts truly began. She would be waiting now, often reading Amy a story, tensed as a wire, even though she tried to pretend to Amy that nothing in the world was wrong. Even before he came home, her heart would start to pound.

'Here's Daddy!' she'd say brightly, despite her sledge-hammering pulse. She'd pick Amy up and go through to meet him, a smile pinned across her face.

'Hello, love – all right?'

'Yeah, all right,' he usually replied, stiffly kissing first her cheek, then Amy's. 'Just gunna change.' He would go upstairs.

And she would be left in the hall in the whiff of resentment that came off him like aftershave. There was always an atmosphere, a tense-making undertow of angry feelings, no matter how hard she tried to be the perfect wife. She always had the tea ready. And she spent every evening working to dispel his suspicion, to make sure he was in a safe mood.

Once Amy was tucked up she served him dinner, watched TV, sometimes holding hands, while he drank cans of lager. Then bed. He wanted sex almost every night now. It was not lovemaking, not anything that took account of what she might like or need. He would lie up close to her until he was aroused enough to begin, when, without speaking, he would pull on her to roll her over, or push into her from behind. She never refused. She had tried at first to see it as desire, hoping it might bring them closer in a way they couldn't manage with words. Now she knew it was nothing like desire. His quick, hard thrusts and the way he pushed her down, were a way of dominating her, and left her feeling sad and invaded. But she did what he wanted, to avoid trouble.

There had been no major scene, not for weeks. He hadn't hit her, or even lost his temper, thanks to her efforts. It was like shadow-boxing, always something there under the surface to fend off. But at least there was a kind of peace. Nothing had happened.

He didn't like any changes. One day Karen phoned and asked Joanne if she'd like to go out for a drink. Joanne was really pleased that Karen had asked, but didn't feel she could go.

'Sorry, Sis – I'd really like to, but you know it's not a very good time of day for me. There's Amy to get to bed and Dave's tea . . .'

'Well, why can't Dave get Amy to bed?' Karen asked. 'He can look after her sometimes, surely?'

'Yes, I know, but it's just the stage she's at. It disrupts her routine and then she won't sleep. We'll get through it in the end. Maybe we could do it some other time?'

'God, you've really turned into a proper little house-wife, haven't you?' Karen didn't speak unkindly, she just sounded puzzled. When they were younger, Joanne had seemed by far the least domestic of the two. 'Look, tell you what: maybe I could pop over and have a cuppa with you instead, and see Amy?'

Joanne hesitated. She could see how ridiculous this was, how scared she was to disrupt the delicate balance of things.

'Well, yeah,' she said slowly, knowing she sounded unwelcoming. 'Would you be able to come quite early?' *And be gone before Dave gets home?* She couldn't say that. *He doesn't like me seeing anyone.*

'Okay, I'll come Wednesday,' Karen said. 'I get off a bit earlier.'

She came wearing a pink-and-mauve flowery dress that showed off her curves and brought a bag of marshmallows for Amy. They had a cup of tea outside in the late-afternoon sunshine. Karen chatted about work, but then suddenly said, 'Are you okay, Joanne?' She squinted keenly at her. 'You seem a bit . . .'

'A bit what?' Joanne fought to seem relaxed.

Karen put her head on one side. 'I dunno. Nervy? You're ever so dark under the eyes. And *skinny*. Have you lost weight?'

'Nah – well, if I have, it's just running round after madam here.' Amy was at their feet on a paving slab with paper and wax crayons. 'I'm fine. Anyway, how's Mom?'

Karen shrugged as if she was a bit sick of the subject.

'Hard to tell. You know what she's like. About the same. Not very nice to Dad at the moment, but then she goes through her moods. She has reduced the dose a bit, though, I know that.'

'That's good.'

As Karen left she looked hard into Joanne's face, wearing a puzzled expression. She kissed Amy, then touched Joanne's upper arm. They weren't huggers, not in their family.

'Take care of yourself.'

Joanne stood with Amy in her arms, watching Karen go back to her car. Karen turned and waved at them briefly. Her sister was getting nicer, Joanne thought. For a moment she was full of a warm feeling. Then the sick dread returned. Dave would soon be home.

Some days, she rebelled angrily.

'You can't just keep me in the house like a prisoner. I'm not your possession, like some toy you've bought from a shop.'

Her ranting was always to herself, while she was pegging out washing or wiping down the kitchen. Sometimes she wanted to explode with frustration and self-pity at the loneliness of it all. But she never said anything to Dave's face. She was far too frightened, too desperate to keep the lid on it all.

'Damn you,' she'd mutter sometimes, yanking the buggy into the hall. 'I'm bloody well going out, whether you like it or not.'

There was always something to buy from the shops anyway. One morning, a while ago, she had run into Tess in the Soho Road, still heavily pregnant. She felt shy of saying hello, but Tess, who was outside a shop with her little boy, Joe, holding her hand, spotted her straight away.

'Hi, Joanne!' she said, smiling. She looked different, her face swollen, hair scraped back, but she was cheerful.

'Hello,' Joanne said. She leaned down to Amy in the buggy. 'Look who it is. It's your friend Tess! And little Joe.'

'Hello, Amy.' Tess smiled.

'You've not had it, then? I thought you were due ages ago.'

'So did I,' Tess grimaced. 'I was supposed to be due a week ago. It feels as if I'll be pregnant forever now! They're going to induce me in a day or two, if nothing happens.'

Joanne wished her luck and parted from Tess, uplifted at seeing a friendly face.

About a fortnight later she set out shopping again and ran into Tess once more, pushing an old-fashioned pram, with Joe holding on at the side. In the pram she saw a round, contented face. Tess told her that she had had another boy and they had called him Christopher.

She looked thinner, but still had the misshapen look of the weeks following a birth. They discussed labours and weights and sleep patterns for a few minutes. Tess looked as if she was managing very well, which was what you would expect with Tess, Joanne thought.

'See you when the term starts,' Tess said. 'You're coming back to the group, aren't you?'

'Oh yes – I hope so!' Joanne said.

There was a pause. Tess looked intently at her. 'Are you okay, Joanne? You look really tired.'

'Oh yes, I'm fine.' She made up something about Amy not sleeping well and got away as fast as she could.

As she walked home, it was with a sinking worry inside. She longed to get out to the toddler group, but it would be another cause of tension and suspicion. For a moment Joanne found herself wishing desperately that she was not married. It was hard being a single parent, but nowadays she felt like a single parent anyway, only with a moody, oppressive man to deal with as well. She knew her attitude to Dave had changed. She could hardly find any positive feeling for him these days. He was someone she looked at objectively, as another difficult task in her day. And, increasingly, she was frightened.

Rebelliously she thought, I've had enough of this. Why the hell shouldn't I go out and see people?

She didn't know where Sooky lived, but at least she knew Kieran's house and it was quite close. She hesitated. Maybe Gerri would be home from hospital by now? In which case she didn't want to turn up and make things awkward. She'd never met the woman and didn't know what state she might be in.

But her desire for company made her decide to

chance it. When they got to Kieran's house, she saw his red car was outside with the seats for Billy and Charlie. The house felt occupied and she thought she heard voices, perhaps the TV.

To her relief, Kieran opened the door. He seemed both taller and thinner than she remembered. After registering who she was, he smiled broadly.

'I was passing . . .' Joanne started to say.

'Great, that's great! And you managed to make the bell work – it can be a bit dodgy. Come in, have you got time for a drink?'

'Oh yes, I've got time!'

Kieran laughed. 'Acres of it, I expect.'

'Only I didn't want to disturb you – not if Gerri was home . . .'

Kieran led her through and put the kettle on. 'No, not yet; we're starting with weekends. She's doing okay – a few setbacks. It's just quite a slow process. Coffee?'

'Tea, if that's okay.'

Amy had fallen asleep on the walk, so Joanne left her in the buggy and she and Kieran went outside with Billy. The baby, Charlie, was also asleep. The two of them sat out at the back while Billy played on the grass.

'Have you seen Sooky?' Kieran asked.

'No, have you?'

Kieran, swallowing a mouthful of coffee, shook his head.

'I forgot to ask where she lives,' Joanne said. I know it's in Handsworth Wood – Selbourne Road, I think she said. But I haven't got a number or anything. She's really nice, isn't she?'

'Yes, lovely person,' Kieran agreed. 'Oh well, I expect she'll come back to the toddler group when it starts. Not that long now, is it?'

Joanne reported that she'd met Tess, and Kieran said he'd seen her as well. They talked about kids for a bit: broken nights and feeding, and how Kieran's boys were adjusting to their mother coming and going. Kieran got Billy to show Joanne the wormery he'd made in a big glass far. She admired it, though the jar was so big that there were no worms to be seen, as they seemed to have taken refuge deep in the middle somewhere.

Once her drink was finished, Joanne thought with a jolt of the phone ringing at home, of Dave waiting for her to answer.

'I'd better be off,' she said, 'or Amy'll be awake and then I'll never get away.'

Kieran smiled again. She thought what a boyish, innocent kind of face he had. It was such a relief to be with someone other than Dave. 'Well, we wouldn't mind the company. Pop round again if you get time.'

'Thanks, I expect we will.' She felt unwelcoming not saying the same in return: *Come to ours: Amy would love it.* But ridiculous as it was, it didn't feel safe having him in the house, even if Dave was out.

Kieran and Billy waved her along the road and she walked home, feeling, at least for a while, that life was something approaching normal.

Thirty-Eight

Dave decided to take the last week in August off.

'We could have a few days out,' he said. 'Even if we can't afford a holiday.'

Joanne had mixed feelings. It would be good not to have to get through each day with Amy on her own. If Dave was at home, maybe he'd relax and not feel he had to keep checking on her. But the thought of him being there all day was also unsettling. Was she ever going to be able to relax for a moment herself? These days she often felt she was struggling for air.

Over the weekend Dave caught up with some jobs in the garden, mowing the grass and replacing a rotted fence panel at the end of the garden. It was a relief that he was busy. His mood had not lifted. On the Saturday morning Joanne stood hand-washing a few of Amy's clothes at the sink. She could see Dave at the end of the garden, his strong figure bending and straightening as he worked. His blond hair was short and neat as usual, and his face and neck were turning pink in the sun.

Joanne stood with her hands in the soapy water. Last night he had pulled her over onto her back, when she had been curled up hoping for sleep. He stared down aggressively into her face.

'What's the matter? Don't you want me any more then? You too good for me, are you?'

He was always doing that: throwing ridiculous questions at her, so that whether she answered 'yes' or 'no' she was caught out.

'Don't be silly – course I want you,' she lied. 'I'm just a bit tired, that's all.'

'Tired.' He looked scornful. 'What've you got to be tired about?'

She felt sore after his treatment of her last night. Watching his unhappy, forbidding figure, that stranger the other side of the glass, she thought, *I hate you, Dave Marshall.*

They went over to see Dave's mom, Wendy, that afternoon, and to Kings Heath to see Joanne's on the Sunday, so the weekend was more or less taken care of. Dave suggested they take Amy out to Brueton Park one day, have a picnic. Maybe even go out Tamworth way to Drayton Manor Park on another.

It was Sunday night and she was cooking tea.

'Brueton Park'd be nice,' she called through to the back room. She was at the stove, mashing the spuds. 'I think Amy's a bit young for Drayton Manor – some of the rides there are really big.'

Dave appeared at the kitchen door.

'So?' The aggression was so instant, so out of proportion that it jarred her, making her heart race. His arms were folded, face full of rage, his eyes boring into her.

'Well . . .' She could hear her voice trembling and fought to keep it under control. 'It's just – as she's so little, it might be a waste of money. We could go when she's a bit bigger.'

Dave nodded his head in a nasty, mocking way. 'Oh yeah, waste of money, is it now? And whose money is it, eh? Who earns every penny of the money around here? Those clothes you're wearing – that food – who bought all that, eh?'

She knew this was not the moment to point out that Karen had given her the shirt she was wearing for her birthday.

'Well, you do, but . . .'

'I do. Me.' He came up very close, speaking right into her face. 'So who decides whether or not I can take my own daughter out for the day, if I want to? You?' The sneering tone increased, the eyes boring into her. 'And what do you bring into this house, by the way, if anything?'

'Dave!' She tried to back away.

'No, I'm serious.' He was forcing her into the corner of the kitchen and Joanne started to feel her knees go weak. Her hand was gripping the potato masher. It was a tinny thing, not much of a weapon for self-defence.

'Look, I know you earn the money . . .' She was beginning to panic, feeling trapped in the kitchen. She turned and pulled open the cutlery drawer, trying to break the mood. 'Could you go and lay the table for us – please?'

Again he stared hard at her, taking his time, then turned away. She followed him out to the back room, anger coiled within her. He was round the other side of the table now, the way clear if she wanted to run out of the house.

'Since you ask,' she said, 'if you had to pay a childminder to look after Amy all day, you'd soon find your precious wages disappearing, I can tell you.'

His head shot up. She saw fear in his face for a split second, before the hard, controlling eyes were back, trying to pin her down, body and soul.

'Why would I need to do that?'

'You don't – that's the point I'm making. I'm just saying my days are worth something, that's all. You're not the only one.'

For a second she thought she had pushed him too far, that he would lash out, but to her relief he seemed to subside and go off the boil. As she served the food Joanne realized that standing up to him might be the best thing. It just took so much energy and felt so risky and frightening.

'Look,' she said as they ate their meal, 'I don't mind if you want to go to Drayton Manor Park – we'll go, if that's what you want.'

'Oh, *thank you*,' he said with heavy sarcasm, as if he had just been granted an enormous favour. And he stared her out again. The battle of the eyes. She found it hard to swallow her pie and left half of it.

It was later that he hit her, unannounced, from behind.

They were undressing in their room and she was standing by the bed, her shirt off, in the process of unfastening her bra. He was suddenly behind her, punching her hard, between the shoulder blades. The pain was extreme and she fell forward onto the bed, gasping. Eyes closed, absorbed in the blackness, all she could think of was the pain, the need to get her breath. She heard her own shuddering sobs, once she could suck the air in and out. There was nothing to say. She had gone to a dark place in herself, like an animal surviving.

He was standing over her. As she surfaced she became aware of the denim-covered legs near her by the bed, alien as something from outer space. Without a word to him she got up, not looking at him, blanking him out.

'Jo?' He put a hand on her shoulder.

'Don't touch me!' she snarled, shying away.

She was too hurt and upset to think about whether he would hit her again. All she could think of was getting out of that room, away from him, from a man who could just hit you, out of the blue, for nothing – a man who was supposed to love you.

Trembling with shock, jolting sobs shaking her, she went to the pillow on her side of the bed and pulled out her nightdress. She didn't look at him. She was like a machine.

'What're you doing?' he said. He didn't sound angry, just bewildered.

'I'm going to sleep in with Amy.' She marched to the door. She felt electric, full of sparks that might burst out any moment in the form of screams that would never stop.

'No, Jo, don't . . .' He had started to sound wretched. 'I'm sorry.'

'I said don't touch me! I don't care how *sorry* you are! What good is *sorry*? Get away from me . . .'

'Don't walk out on me – just come to bed and it'll be all right.'

But she was already across the landing, into Amy's room, frantically moving the chest of drawers against the door to keep him out. She never wanted to see him again, ever.

Stiff and in pain, she crawled into bed with Amy and took comfort in the warmth and yeasty smell of her little daughter. She held her, kissing her cheek.

'Oh God, babby, my babby . . . My little girl . . .' Then her words were lost as her body shook with tears.

Thirty-Nine

Somehow, the next morning, they managed to act as if nothing had happened, for Amy's sake. And for their own, because neither of them knew what else to do.

Joanne woke early when Amy stirred and carried her downstairs, thinking that Dave would be asleep. It was only six forty-five, but she saw him outside, painting wood treatment onto the new fence.

'Dada!' Amy pointed, squirming with pleasure.

'Yes,' Joanne said flatly. 'Dada.' Each time she took a breath it hurt.

Dave seemed calm when he came in. Joanne avoided his gaze. She felt cold and closed in on herself and did not speak to him except for a few abrupt replies. He could pretend nothing had happened, when she felt the result of it in every move she made. It was hidden from him, though – not like a black eye, something that would make him see what he had done.

There was a lull. They managed to avoid each other for most of the morning. He stayed outside as the morning warmed up, then went out for a while, to buy things at some DIY place. Joanne took no notice. She did some chores, entertained Amy, ironed some clothes, numb and mechanical. It felt the same to her if he didn't come back at all.

That morning, though, it came to her with full force just how far down he could push her; how far down she was already, like a prisoner in her own house with little will of her own.

It wasn't until later in the morning that she realized they needed bread and other food.

Cursing herself for not noticing earlier, she flew into a panic. If only she could get Amy ready and get out to the shops before Dave came back! She felt a desperate need to get out of the house on her own, to walk the streets, to see people and be warmed by the pulse of other lives.

Every move of getting Amy into the buggy seemed to take an eternity, clipping the straps into place, finding her purse, then her keys.

'Right, Mommy's ready!' she said, opening the front door.

Dave was coming up the path with his shopping. He looked startled to see her coming out. They regarded each other. Joanne's mouth went dry as she saw the suspicion gather on his face.

'Where're you off to then?' he asked, pretending to be casual.

'We've not got much bread – or milk. And we need a few other bits and pieces.'

'All right. Let me put these down. I'm coming with you.'

'There's no need,' she said breezily. God how she wanted to be away from him!

'Oh, I think there is.' He pushed past her and left the bags in the hall. 'That's what this week is for, isn't it? Us being together.' He locked the front door. 'See, Amy? Daddy's coming shopping as well.'

Amy smiled and jiggled excitedly, which made Joanne feel betrayed. Daddy was exciting.

They made their way down to the shops in silence,

Dave having to keep walking behind to let people past. It didn't improve his mood.

'I hate crowds of people,' he said grumpily.

Well, don't bloody come with me then, she thought. *I don't want you here.* But she said, 'It's not as bad as Saturdays.'

They went to a couple of shops and bought groceries, Dave staying outside with the buggy. With every move, lifting and carrying, Joanne could feel the pain in her back and chest. Soon they had bread, milk, biscuits, tins of corned beef and fruit loaded on to the tray at the bottom of the buggy and were heading home.

She couldn't have avoided the situation; it was too late by the time she realized. They were both walking up to one of the Asian greengrocer's with an awning outside and, just as they reached it, someone else pushing a buggy emerged from the shop, almost blocking the path. They were face-to-face. Kieran. He gave his usual friendly smile.

'Oh – hi, Joanne!' he said. 'Sorry, didn't mean to ram this into the path like that – only it's mayhem in there. I was just escaping!'

Joanne forced a smile.

'Hello,' she said. 'Look, Amy, there's Billy and Charlie!'

Dave was at her right shoulder. She could feel him there like a boulder about to fall on her. She turned and saw the suspicious, unfriendly look on his face, which he didn't take the trouble to hide.

'Kieran, this is Dave – my husband. This is Kieran – Amy and Billy play together sometimes.' She didn't feel she could say *we're friends*. Dave had seen them in the park that day; surely he must recognize Kieran, with his ginger hair?

'Hi, nice to meet you, Dave,' Kieran said, holding out his hand.

Dave ignored it, gave a stiff nod and said something that might have been 'Hello', but it was muttered ungraciously. Kieran lowered his hand, too good-natured to show he was offended.

'Yes, the toddler group's a godsend,' he said. 'Helps you get through the day. It's been quite tough not having it there to go to over the summer. Still, it'll be starting up again soon, won't it?'

Dave just stared at him as if he hadn't spoken.

'Yes, it's great,' Joanne enthused. 'We'll see you there, I expect. Better get along now – get Amy's dinner!'

They parted with cheery goodbyes. There was a long silence until they'd turned off into their road. Then, in a loaded tone, Dave said, 'So who was that, Joanne?'

'Kieran – I told you. He looks after his kids because his wife's in hospital, depressed. She's only at home at weekends at the moment. That's why he started coming to the toddler group.'

'You said it was only mothers.' His voice was very quiet, menacing.

'Well, it was – until he started coming.'

'What is he, some kind of poof, or summat?'

She kept her fury at this under control. 'He's just a nice bloke – that's all.'

Without comment Dave fished in his pocket for the keys to the house. Joanne lifted the carrier bags of shopping from the bottom of the buggy. He took them, without looking at her.

It was one of those summer days when the contrast between sun and shade is extreme. She was standing in the sun, beyond the shadow of the house; he seemed to disappear into darkness, going into the hall and out again. She stood watching. Despite the heat, her senses were alert in an exaggerated way, as if she might be able to hear ants marching in the flowerbed. She could not avoid the feeling that something was coming towards her, slow and silent as a tidal wave.

Dave lifted Amy's buggy into the narrow hall with her still in it, putting it down beyond the carrier bags. Amy was hungry and grumpy in the heat and was starting to whinge. Joanne closed the front door and they were sealed away from the glare outside.

As she bent over to pick up the bags of food, he swung at her with the flat of his hand, catching the left side of her face so that her head jerked back, jarring her neck.

'Bitch!' The pent-up rage poured out. 'You twisted, cheating slag!'

As she was still reeling, he slapped the back of his hand across her other cheek, catching the side of her mouth. She fell, tasting blood, banging the back of her head against the side of the stairs. Her foot landed on something in one of the bags and she slipped, ending up on the floor, her back against the side wall of the staircase.

Her yelps of pain, and Dave's frightening tone, set Amy off crying, even though she was facing the other way. 'Mama! Mama!' Her voice rose in terror.

Dave was bent over Joanne. His face was red and looked puffy, as if it might burst open. He took her by the throat.

'You slag – you've been with him, haven't you? All this pretending: "Oh,"' he mocked her tone nastily, '"I'm just taking Amy to the *toddler group*, with the other *mothers*." When all the time . . . I've seen you with him in the park, cosying up to him, that weedy little ginger prat – never knew I'd seen you, did yer? Not such a fool as you think, eh?'

Joanne was terrified. Her face throbbed and he was pressing her throat so that she could only just breathe.

'No,' she tried to say. She was shaking her head, while a dribble of blood ran down the side of her chin. 'No – I've never. You've got it all wrong . . .'

'You think you can make a fool of me, you bitch . . .'

She grabbed his hands, trying to pull them away from her throat.

'Get off me – you're hurting.' Panic seized her. 'I can't breathe—'

'*Mama!*' Amy was screaming, the sound filling the hall.

Something in Dave seemed to give way.

'Shut up!' he roared at the top of his voice. 'Stop that bloody racket!' Releasing Joanne, he went round the buggy and yelled right into Amy's face. 'Shut up your noise! She's not your mother – she's a whore, that's what she is! Who knows if you're even my daughter? *Stop that*, you little brat . . .'

Amy's cries spiralled up into complete hysteria. Joanne was on her feet.

'Get away from her!' she screamed, launching herself at him, but he was so much stronger and heavier that it only set him back a little. He came at her, shoving her hard so that she lost her balance and fell again, banging her shoulder on something in one of the plastic bags. She groaned with pain.

Dave was unstrapping Amy from the buggy.

'Come here, you whining little bugger . . .'

Amy's cries were going through Joanne like knives, shredding all her nerves to pieces. She fought to get up, her feet sliding on oranges, onions. For a moment it seemed impossible to get off the floor.

Dave yanked Amy out of the buggy and held her in front of him, under her arms, away from him as if she was wet or dirty. Kneeing Joanne out of the way as she struggled to get up, he hurried up the stairs.

The whole of Joanne's mind was full of Amy's screams. It left space for nothing else. She found herself whimpering, 'Amy, babby – my little babby . . .'

What the hell might he do?'

A tiger's rage filled her. She scrambled to her feet and, as she did so, her hand pushed against the hard thing in the plastic bag onto which she had fallen. Rummaging frantically, she pulled it out – a tin of corned beef. In a second she was following Dave up the stairs.

'Shut up!' she could hear him yelling, from Amy's room. He sounded desperate, full of rage, but also as if he was on the verge of tears. 'Just bloody shut up screaming! Amy – Amy, stop it! STOP IT! Stop it, or I'll slap yer – I will . . .'

From the back she could see him holding Amy over the bed, gripping her and shaking her so hard that he was making her head flop back and forth. Amy was in such a state that her screams were becoming gagging sobs of distress.

Joanne didn't hesitate. Holding the narrower top of the tin, she slammed the other end as hard as she could into the side of Dave's head. She saw blood immediately, from his ear. He yelled in pain and within seconds she had done it again, even harder.

'Put her down!' Her own screams were completely hysterical now. 'Put her down, you bastard!

He was dropping Amy already, on the bed, clutching

at his ear. Before he had any time to recover, Joanne raised her leg and shoved him in the belly, forcing him away. She seized Amy, hugging her close, and ran from the room, slamming the door.

All she could think of was getting out of the dark of that house, into the light, away from him. She took nothing with her, just yanked the front door open. Thoughts stampeded across her mind. Where could she go? She had no money, nothing. If she took off down the street, he'd catch her up in minutes.

Holding the sobbing Amy against her, tightly, she did the only thing she could immediately think of doing, which was to run into the next garden and bang urgently on the Coles' front door.

Forty

At any moment Dave might erupt out of the house. Clutching Amy, rigid with distress on her hip, Joanne desperately imagined Mrs Coles out in her garden, and the time it might take her to get to the front door. But seconds later the door swung open. Mrs Coles stared at her.

'Can we come in?'

'Ooh, bab,' Mrs Coles said. 'Oh, dear.'

Without questioning her, she held the door open and Joanne was swallowed into safety, the door closing behind them.

'Who is it, Mary?' Jim Coles called from the living room. When Amy paused for breath, Joanne could hear the telly, some kind of sport.

'It's young Joanne from next door,' Mary Coles said. 'She's just popped in. No need to worry, love – I'll take 'er through to the kitchen.'

But before they could move there was a furious banging on the front door. Joanne jumped, her blood lunging round her body.

'Don't let him in!' she begged.

Jim Coles erupted from the front room.

'What in the name of God is going on?'

His blue eyes took in the sight of her. Only then did Joanne remember she was bleeding. She licked her lips, tasting blood.

Jim Coles was a burly Irishman, overweight now with a belly on him, but once a builder and fit as a flea. He had a ring of grey hair round a bald patch, a bacon-coloured complexion and a strong, dignified manner.

'Did he do that to you?'

All Joanne could do was nod.

'Now, Jim . . .' Mary began.

But he was already heading to the door.

'Get through to the back, love.' Mary seized Joanne's arm. 'You don't want him seeing yer.'

Joanne heard the door open.

'What's all this?' Jim Coles was saying. 'No – no, that's enough of that now, Dave. You get away from my door until you can handle yourself . . .'

She was terrified that Dave would hit him and force his way in. But though they heard a further brief altercation on the doorstep, soon it went quiet. The door closed again.

'He's gone,' Jim called through the kitchen door. 'I told the fella not to come bothering you.'

'All right, love – that's good.' Mary called.

She turned back to Joanne, who was shaking, struggling not to cry. Amy was still sobbing, though more quietly.

'Oh, now, look at the pair of yer.' She came over and stroked Amy's back. 'The poor little angel – look, you sit down at the table and I'll get the kettle on. I've got our Patrick's little drinking cup here. I can give her a drop of milk, and I'll make us a nice cup of tea.'

Joanne sat down, stunned and grateful. Amy had been in such a state that she was now beginning to shut down and go to sleep. Joanne held her, rocking her.

Mary Coles set a mug of tea down beside her and drew up a chair. Joanne knew she owed her an explanation: details of what had happened. But she felt very embarrassed, ashamed to be talking about it. Like Amy, she just felt like dozing off to sleep, now that the immediate danger had gone.

For a few minutes Mary sipped her tea, her lined face wearing no expression. Joanne realized, though, that she was thinking. Mary put her mug down and looked across at Joanne.

'I've had all this with our Angela,' she said. 'D'you remember when she was stopping here for a bit with little Patrick?'

'Oh,' Joanne said. 'Yes.' She'd had no idea why, though.

Mary Coles rolled her eyes. 'Does he get like that very often?'

'No!' She stroked Amy's back for comfort. 'Well . . . not often. But just lately . . .'

Mary nodded, as if this was something she'd seen before. Joanne felt a surge of gratitude towards the kindly woman. Mary had worked as a nursing auxiliary at Dudley Road Hospital for many years. She was no stranger to human traffic.

'I've seen you a few times lately and I've wondered,' Mary said. 'D'you know what set him off?'

'To begin with? Not really – a few ideas, but . . . It might just be having Amy. Maybe he's not getting enough attention.'

Mary nodded without comment.

'You're going to have to decide what to do,' she said after a moment. 'You can stay here for a while, of course, and welcome, but you can't hide out in here forever.' She hesitated. 'Strictly speaking, you could call the police. He's assaulted you.'

Joanne was already shaking her head. 'No. I can't

do that.' It seemed an enormous thing: unreal and extreme. One minute they were in the hall, a family; the next, blue lights and social workers, and who knew what else . . . That was not the way she was going to do things.

'What about your mother?' Mary asked.

'What about her?' Joanne said bitterly.

'Could you go and stay for a while maybe?'

'Not really. Mom's not too well herself. And she'd never believe me anyway – not about Dave.'

Suddenly there came noises from the front of the house, the letterbox clattering.

'Joanne? Come out, for God's sake! I won't hurt you – I promise! Just come out here . . .'

Her pulse, which had just been slowing at last, took off again and her limbs turned to jelly.

They heard Jim Coles begin a conversation through the slit in the front door. Jim was calm, as if talking to a wild horse. Dave sounded wretched, begging. 'Just tell her I'm sorry – I just want to see her.'

'Look, love,' Mary said. 'You don't have to go out there. But if you want to, in the long run you're going to have to do something about it. Once they start, they don't stop, unless you stop them. I've seen it all before.'

Joanne hadn't told Mrs Coles about what he'd done to Amy. He had shaken Amy like a rag doll, hurt and frightened her. In those seconds he had drawn a steel line across her heart. She knew already what she was going to do.

'I'll go now,' she said, standing up. 'We'll sort it out. He's calmed down now, so it'll be all right.'

Mrs Coles eyed her doubtfully, but Joanne thanked both the Coles and went to the hall.

Jim opened the door. Dave was outside, looking distraught and pathetic.

'Any more trouble from you, young man, and I'll be reporting you, make no mistake,' Jim Coles told him, wagging a finger. 'And, Joanne, you know where to come. You don't want to be standing for that.'

'Thank you,' she said again, stepping out into the day, one that already seemed to have gone on forever. 'Thank you so much.'

There were the usual tears, the sobbing apologies and vows not to do it again. Dave needed to be forgiven and endlessly reassured.

Later that day, while Amy was asleep again, worn out, Dave led Joanne up to their bedroom and insisted on making love in the warm afternoon, with the window open and a balmy breeze lifting the edge of the curtain. For the moment she let him do what he needed to do, the hard release he required. As he climaxed in her he began to sob again, releasing his weight down onto her, his head half-buried in the pillow beside hers.

'Oh God, I'm sorry. I'm so, so sorry, Jo. I'm a monster. I don't know what made me do it . . .'

Joanne went through the motions of comfort. They lay pressed together, sticky with sweat, and she stroked his back, feeling the familiar strong line of his spine under her fingertips. She felt utterly distant from him.

He pushed up on his hands again and looked down at her, his face pink and wet with tears. She stared back up at him. There were grains of pity in her, but now mostly she felt as icy as metal.

'I love you, girl,' he insisted. 'Oh God, I love you, and I need you so much. I don't know why I do it. It's like being taken over – like being someone else. I can't help it . . .'

'Maybe you should get some help,' she suggested, knowing he would never agree to it.

'Help? What – *me*?' He removed himself from on top of her and lay on his back beside her. She could feel him withdrawing from her at this suggestion, almost mocking it. It felt like a test, his one last chance: *If you say you need help, you know there's really something wrong.* But all Dave wanted was for her to forgive him, wipe the slate and say it was okay. But she wasn't going to say it. It very definitely wasn't okay.

'Nah,' he said. He sounded relaxed again, relieved and reassured by the sex, by her coming home and seeming compliant and forgiving. 'That's not for me. I'm not some kind of nutter. I've just got a bit of a temper.' He turned to her. 'We'll be all right, won't we, Jo: you and me?'

Joanne carried on staring up towards the ceiling. Her cut lip was throbbing.

'Yes, I expect we will,' she said.

As he had taken the week off, she knew Dave would be highly suspicious of any attempts on her part to get him to go back to work.

That week he couldn't do enough for her and Amy. They went to Brueton Park, as planned, and Amy loved their picnic in the green space. They let her play and play, and bought ice creams. Dave was the solicitous father all day, telling Joanne to sit down and have a rest.

'I could do with one like that,' another woman said

to Joanne exhaustedly, when Dave headed off to give Amy yet another swing. 'Mine's useless – he just watches the football all the time. I dunno why he wanted kids.'

Joanne smiled and said nothing. Coldly she watched Dave, her handsome, well-dressed husband, pushing his little girl on the swing. Amy was shrieking with laughter. He was trying to make it up to them, money in the bank of 'All I've done for you . . .' But today she was seeing his better self. She knew it wouldn't last. Pangs of heartbreaking emotion rose in her at the thought of what was to come. But her resolve was strong.

Dave took her advice against going to Drayton Manor Park. Instead they took other little trips, to the Science Museum and Cannon Hill Park. Joanne was polite and civil and did everything he wanted. She kept the peace, feeling that she was seeing their life from a distance. On Sunday they went to see her mom and dad in Kings Heath, and Dave finally got Fred's lawn-mower working again.

'You all right?' Karen asked. She seemed to have become very sharp these days.

Joanne was startled. By now her lip had healed, the mark on it barely visible. 'Yeah, why?'

'You just seem a bit out of it, that's all.'

'Oh, I'm okay.' In truth she had been making lists in her head to add to the enquiries she had been making. Phone numbers, information. 'Just got a few things on my mind, that's all.'

'Back to work again tomorrow then, son?' Fred asked Dave.

'Yeah, but it's been a good week, hasn't it, Jo?'

Joanne nodded. Like a robot, she thought. *I'm getting like Mom.*

He went off to work on Monday morning, back to the usual routine. It was a cooler, cloudy day too, which felt right. But everything was unreal. The day should go on, as it always did: washing and tidying, cleaning the house, bathroom and loo, pegging out and ironing . . . Their little house. Home. Routine. But how long before he hit her again? Or shook the life out of Amy?

Soon after he had left, she was packing bags: things for her and Amy. One under the buggy on the tray – some toys, bottles, Amy's favourite blanket. Other bags hanging from the handles. Money. Keys. Milk. Phone numbers. She mustn't stop. Mustn't waver.

'Come on now, love,' she said, lifting Amy into the buggy. 'We're going on a little outing.'

Forty-One

'Here we are.'

Megan, the social worker, steered her car into the parking area of a big, shabby-looking house. There was a bay window, shrouded by net curtains. The front of the house had long ago been coated in cream paint, which was now stained and dirty.

Joanne was too stressed and disorientated to take in exactly where they were: the other side of Birmingham somewhere, off the Hagley Road. It was an ordinary, anonymous street, with small houses one end, getting bigger as they moved along it. It could be anywhere. She felt pulled inside out with nerves. Before this journey there had been a wait of several hours in the Social Services offices, when she tried to keep things calm and normal for Amy. But she was anything but calm – especially after what they told her. When she arrived there, all she would seem to do was cry. Even after she managed to stop, the fear and worry had upset her stomach and she kept having to ask to use the toilet.

First she had gone to her Health Visitor, who had speedily referred Joanne and Amy to Social Services. Megan, a neat, well-dressed woman in her forties, with a broad smile and a hint of a Welsh accent, had made tea and sat and listened to her.

'You do believe me, don't you?' Joanne had pleaded, after pouring out what had happened.

'Of course I do,' Megan said kindly. 'No one wrenches themselves away from home like this unless they have to. It's a very big decision.'

'Only . . .' Joanne had still been crying at this point. 'Sometimes I think it's me – that I'm going crazy. Or *making* him do it somehow. But I'm not, I don't think . . . And it's been a few days since anything's happened, but I'm frightened he'll just keep doing it again. He's just changed so much. And I'm so worried about Amy . . .' She relapsed into sobs.

Megan gently told her that Amy would need to be looked at by one of their medical officers. She started talking about case conferences, child-protection procedures, the police.

'No!' Joanne had protested, horrified. 'No, we don't need all that! Amy and I just need to go away for a bit. To be somewhere safe.'

'And then what?' Megan said. 'I'm afraid, Joanne, it's not as simple as that. If this was just between you and your husband – well, it would be up to you whether you pressed an assault charge. But with a child involved – and in possible danger – it's very different. I'm afraid, now that you've brought this to our attention, we are obliged to act to protect her.'

Joanne stared at her. It was hard to take anything in.

'No . . .' she started to say, shaking her head. Megan kept looking at her, firmly but kindly. 'You mean the police . . . Dave?'

'Quite possibly, yes.'

'And social workers?'

'I'm a social worker,' Megan pointed out. She stood up. 'Look, try not to worry. I'll get you a cup of tea. Just sit and think about it all for a bit. We are here to help you, you know – not to make things worse.' She leaned reassuringly towards Joanne. 'From what you've said, your daughter is in danger. You've done the right thing.'

Joanne sat, cuddling Amy, her head full of panic and confusion. She had just left home, that was all. That's all it had felt like at the time. Why had she done it? To get away and find help and refuge. She didn't realize she was crossing this line, into a place where so many other people could take over and have a say . . . She felt very frightened. I'm not that kind of person, she thought. Oh God, what have I done? She sat weeping quietly, wishing she could turn back time to this morning and be at home again. Would she have done the same thing? She no longer knew.

The waiting began. Megan phoned round in search of somewhere for her and Amy to go. They found a few toys to keep Amy happy, as they sat in a back room with old filing cabinets and a table and chair. A doctor examined Amy, but so many days had passed that there was not much to see, except a few tiny remaining bruises. Someone brought Joanne yet another cup of tea and asked if she had food for Amy, which she had. Time passed, somehow.

'Joanne,' Megan said with firm gentleness, seeing her woebegone face. 'It's okay. It's not your fault. You're doing the right thing. You've done something about it, before it got any worse. A lot of women don't. That makes you very brave, in my book.' This made Joanne cry all over again.

It was well on into the afternoon when she came to

Joanne and said calmly, 'We've found you a place in a refuge on the south side of the city – well away from home.'

Joanne felt anything but calm as they got out of the car. She looked the place up and down, full of dread. The parking area at the front was covered in potholed tarmac and a drift of crisp and sweet packets had blown in and caught on one side against the garden wall. The clouds had thickened as the day wore on. Her idea of a women's refuge was a place full of rough, frightening women with black eyes.

'It's all right,' Megan said, seeing her expression. They were getting a sleepy Amy and her few possessions out of Megan's old green car, which had a child seat in the back. 'It's much nicer than it looks – honestly. Some of the rooms are quite cosy.'

She pushed the buggy with Joanne's things loaded onto it, and Joanne carried Amy. A ring on the bell, which was discreetly placed to one side of the door, with its spy-hole in the centre, resulted in an almost instant sound of unlocking. Two faces appeared, one white, one black.

'Oh,' Megan said, sounding surprised. 'Are you still here, Sue?'

The white woman, the younger of the two, with curly auburn hair, baggy, colourful clothes and long, spiralling earrings, seemed pleased to see Megan.

'Marcia and I were doing the changeover; I'll be off in a minute. Thought I'd stop and say hello. I've got a few days off from tomorrow – Jackie'll be in.' Her smile took in all three of them.

Marcia, a much plumper woman in tight black leggings and a big mauve T-shirt, also smiled broadly.

'This must be Joanne and Amy?'

'Hello,' Joanne said, relieved at the kind welcome, even if everything felt a bit unreal. It was reassuring that they already knew her name, as if they were welcoming a friend.

'Let's get you all inside,' Marcia said, with a cautious glance towards the street behind them.

Joanne found herself ushered inside with Amy and Megan, and the door thudded shut. The light in the hall was rather dim, but Joanne could see a worn-looking black-and-white chequered floor and a staircase carpeted in dark red. To one side was a large noticeboard covered in lists and charts. From upstairs, Joanne heard a child having a tantrum and a woman's voice trying to be heard over it. The other women glanced at each other on hearing the noise, but said nothing.

'I'll just say hello,' Sue said. 'I've got to be off, but I might see you, if you're still here . . . So this is Amy?' She smiled into Amy's face, but Amy was looking sleepy and bewildered. 'Nice to meet you, Joanne.'

Her pink-and-green trousers shimmered out of the door.

'Come into the office a minute,' Marcia said. 'Then I'll show you your room and we'll have a look round.'

As they followed Marcia through the door into the downstairs front room, Megan gave Joanne's arm a squeeze and smiled reassuringly at her, as if to say, *You'll be all right with Marcia.*

*

When she was finally alone, Joanne lay down on the bed with Amy, cuddling her daughter close to her, on the cheap, flowery duvet cover, letting the tears come again. She felt queasy and exhausted and would dearly have loved to sleep for hours and block everything out. But Amy was awake now and was upset by her mother's emotion.

'Mama?' She pushed her face right up close to Joanne's and tried to wipe away her tears.

'Okay, pet – it's all right.' Joanne wiped her face.

It was such a relief to be inside, to feel safe and away from the constant tension of living with Dave. Yet at the same time she had never felt more lost or lonely than in this dingy old house, cut off from everything and everyone she knew. If she hadn't had Amy to be strong for, she didn't think she could have coped at all.

Amy slid down from the bed and went to explore. Joanne lay feeling completely limp, as if all her fight had gone from her. From the other two rooms on the middle floor she could hear voices and bangs. A child cried and cried. The sound made her feel even more tense and sad. Who were the women in these other rooms so close to her?

She looked round the room. It faced out over the front and the windows were covered by more thick net curtains. There was a shaggy, mustard-coloured carpet and the walls were covered in woodchip paper, painted pale peach. Beside the bed where Joanne lay there was a set of bunkbeds and other basic furniture: a chest of drawers, a small cupboard and a wooden chair. In one corner there was also a cot.

She dragged herself groggily into a sitting position, trying to remember the things Marcia had told her as she showed her round.

'It's all right – I know you won't take it all in now,' Marcia had said kindly, over a mug of tea and some squash for Amy. 'I expect we'll go over it again. But there are certain things I have to say now.'

She had impressed upon Joanne that she could stay securely here while they made a plan for her future and tried to get her sorted out. There had been strict warnings about security, and about not disclosing the address of the refuge to anyone outside. Marcia outlined the question of the rent she would need to pay, and the benefits she could claim, until Joanne's head was spinning.

'But don't worry about that tonight. I'm sure you'll have had enough for today. And your social worker will be in to see you. There are a few things you do need today, though. Like food. Have you got any cash on you?'

'Yes,' Joanne said. 'Some.' She'd made sure of that.

'Good, there are shops at the bottom of the road – you can walk down there. Now, a few house rules . . . And I'll take you round and show you the ropes!'

She led Joanne into the communal sitting room, where a large TV blared to an invisible audience. Marcia turned it off. Then to a little playroom where there were child-sized tables and toys. Amy perked up and looked interested at this. At the back was the kitchen. Marcia talked more about sharing the kitchen and other rooms, about the time at which everyone had to be quiet at night, about use of the TV and the pay phone. Joanne immediately, automatically, thought about phoning Dave, then realized, with a stab of agony, that nothing was as it had been even twenty-four hours ago.

Just as they were about to come upstairs, Joanne

caught her first glimpse of one of the other inmates. A small, slight figure appeared at the top of the stairs, her head covered by a black scarf. She came speeding down the staircase, head lowered, not making eye contact with anyone, a closed, terrified expression on her face. The girl looked as if she wished she was invisible. Joanne thought she seemed very young.

'Hello, Mariam,' Marcia said. But the girl unfastened the front door and was gone, without even turning.

'She lives up at the top,' Marcia said, looking sad and concerned. 'She either can't or won't speak English. She's Bangladeshi – we have to keep getting an interpreter in. If you can get her to say a word to you, all the better.'

Amy wandered over to the bed. 'Bikkik?' she said hopefully.

What was the time, Joanne wondered? It must be getting on for five o'clock.

'Here you are, darlin'. Here's a biscuit – then we'll go out and buy some tea for Amy and Mommy.'

Everything felt alien. Home seemed so much closer to her still, so much more real than this place. In about an hour Dave would get home, would discover that they'd gone . . . She felt a flash of triumph, then an ache filled her. What had she done? Was this the end of it all – her marriage to the man she had known since she was so young? The enormity of it washed over her. And he had been so nice last week. Much more like the Dave she had known in the past. She thought with anguish of the bright, hopeful lad she had known at the beginning. Perhaps he had really changed again, back to his real self. Maybe it had just been a bad phase he was going through, and she had now run off and hurt him, not giving him a chance. She'd destroyed everything.

He wasn't all bad, that was for sure. How could she have done this to him?

Then the memory of seeing him shaking Amy came back to her, the shrieking pain in her scalp as he had dragged her, the taste of blood, his face full of rage and aggression ... But it was because of Amy that she had left. She could just about cope with him when he hurt her, but not Amy. Because if he could go that far with her, what else might he do?

Forty-Two

Joanne did not sleep well.

She had put Amy down on the bottom bunk, but she had woken crying and Joanne took her into her bed. It was comforting, but sleeping in a single bed with a child meant that she kept waking, and stayed awake in the small hours with her thoughts churning, full of remorse and horror at what she had done.

Now she was away from home, she felt a fool. Dave had always been a good guy. Had it really been so bad? Hadn't she overreacted and done something far too extreme, instead of staying and trying to sort it out? It's not as if he had hit her very often, and there was obviously something wrong with him. Shouldn't she be trying to support him and help him get better? Now it sounded as if the police would be turning up on his doorstep! That wasn't what she had intended – she longed somehow to explain it all to him.

And what on earth had happened that evening when he had found her gone? Had he called the police himself? She knew the Coles would have been able to give him some idea of what was going on, even though they could say, hands on hearts, that they didn't know where she was. He'd have phoned Mom and Dad, and they'd be worried. She almost got up at four in the morning to phone them, or *him*, to let them know she was okay, so that they wouldn't worry. But she didn't feel up to wandering about in this strange house at night. She also knew she didn't have the right change for the phone. The night crawled past and gave her no rest. She lay feeling desolate and exhausted, cuddling up to Amy and longing just to go home.

I'll go and see Marcia in the morning, she thought, and tell her it's all a mistake. I need to go back and work it out with Dave. It's as much my fault as his. He's not a bad man – he's just got himself in a state over nothing.

Before she had even left her room to go down to the kitchen, though, she heard a terrible racket break out, raised voices, over which a child's wild screaming and shouting roared. Joanne opened the door and listened. The sound was so savage it turned her stomach. A moment later the door opposite hers opened and a round face peered out, with sandy-brown hair cropped at chin length, blue eyes and very pink cheeks.

The woman stared at Joanne.

'You'll be the new one then,' she said. She sounded Irish. Opening the door more fully, she came over and nodded contemptuously towards the stairs.

'That'll be the boy from there.' Another nod of the head towards the third door on their floor. 'He's a wild one – you can hear. My girls are terrified of him.' Seeing Amy peeping out from behind Joanne's legs, she went on, 'You've just got the one? Well, you'll want to be keeping her away from that lot, I can tell you. You'd never think it to look at them, but they're like animals, those boys.'

She disappeared back into her room with a self-righteous air and closed the door. From downstairs the cries escalated, and Joanne could hear the struggle moving from the kitchen into the hall. Marcia's voice was raised over the yelling and fighting.

'Now, Jason – no, no ... We're just going to stop that. Stop, no, you've got to calm down ... Calm, easy now ...'

Joanne decided to stay in her room until things had quietened down. Eventually the noise died out, so she picked Amy up and crept downstairs. Entering the kitchen, she came face-to-face with another inmate of the house. For a moment she thought the woman was one of the children, she looked so slight and young, sitting by the table at the side of the kitchen opposite a little boy who was eating toast. She was very pretty, blue-eyed, with long, wavy blonde hair taken up in a thick bunch at the back. The boy, who looked about three, was also blond and obviously resembled his mother.

'All right?' The girl gave a brief smile, though she seemed preoccupied.

'All right,' Joanne replied, standing hesitantly by the door.

'You the new arrival? You can come in – I won't bite, not like my boys.' She laughed at this with real mirth, though Joanne couldn't think what was funny about it. 'Get some breakfast. Have you got any food?'

'Yes ...' Joanne went to her cupboard to fetch the sliced bread she'd bought from the corner shop last night. She and Amy had had beans on toast. As she was doing everything one-handed, she went to sit Amy at the table, beside the little boy.

'Oh no, I wouldn't sit her there.' The young mother got up and moved round to sit next to him, freeing the chair opposite. Joanne noticed she was hobbling badly. 'Only he's a bit – you know, he might not be very nice to her.'

To Joanne's horror, as she moved close to him, the

face of the angelic-looking boy had taken on a hateful expression of aggression and he clenched his fists. Cautiously Joanne sat Amy opposite him, out of reach.

'This is Michael,' the young woman said. She seemed intelligent and chatty. 'I'm Gina, by the way. And my other boy you'll have heard earlier – Jason – he's with Marcia at the moment. She's quite good with him. The pair of them have had so many beltings they don't know what else to do.'

'Oh dear,' Joanne said, shocked by the openness of this admission. 'Your husband?'

Gina looked squarely back at her. 'Yeah. And me. We're both bad like that. But he drinks and he goes for me. His heart's in the right place and he's a good dad in many ways – but when he drinks he turns into a complete fucking nutter. This time he's gone and broke my toes.' She held out her feet, dressed in huge, fake sheepskin slippers, which obviously covered dressings. 'Got his hammer out, he did. I just have to get out of there for a bit sometimes.'

God almighty, Joanne thought. *What have I come into?* She realized she was staring in frank amazement and didn't know what to say next. Things that she found almost impossible to talk about, things she'd never even *imagined*, to this woman seemed quite natural. Gina handed Michael another finger of toast. She was scowling now.

'They want to take my kids off me – I know they do. I keep telling them: they don't understand. Thing is, me and him, we have our problems, right? But that's just it – they never do anything to help. I say to Marcia, "Look, me and Benny, we need help. What're you going to do about it?" But all they go on about is the kids this, the kids that. They say I've gone back on my

331

promises, but the thing is – it's not that easy. Once me and Benny get together, well, we're lovers, right? We're really into each other. But we're a bit different from other people, the way we are together. They don't understand, that's the thing. It's all one size fits all, with the Social. Their way's the only way – it makes me sick ... Eat up, babby. What's your name then? You got problems with your old man?'

'I'm Joanne.' She fed slices of bread into the toaster and clicked it down. She didn't know what to say. 'Yes, things haven't been too good.'

'Does he drink then, does he?'

'Not – well, a bit. But he doesn't get drunk as such ...'

'What's up with him then?' Gina asked.

Joanne was struggling to find an answer to this – *he's sort of lost himself* – when Marcia's head popped round the door.

'I've put him in the basement for a bit,' she said to Gina. 'He's calming down. But he needs some cool-off time.'

'All right then, ta, Marcia,' Gina said. She seemed unconcerned, despite the murderous sounds that had been going on earlier.

But Marcia was not going to let her get away with this. She was wearing the black leggings again, but this time with a long, emerald-green blouse. She folded her arms. 'We need to talk, Gina.'

'All right then,' Gina said nonchalantly, not meeting her eye.

'Hello, Joanne,' Marcia smiled. 'You two have met then. Got everything for the moment?'

'Yes, thanks,' Joanne said.

'And how's little Amy this morning?' She came over and made a fuss of her. 'How did you both sleep?'

'Not very well,' Joanne admitted. She felt tearful again and swallowed it back. What the hell was she doing here, in this dismal house with these crazy people?

'Oh, I don't think anyone does the first night,' Marcia told her. 'You'll settle in, don't worry. Now you've met Gina and, well, you saw Mariam, didn't you?' She turned to Gina. 'Any progress there, drawing her out?'

'What – that Paki girl? Nah . . .'

'Gina . . .' Marcia said in a warning tone.

'Sorry, Marcia – but she's not going to talk to someone like me, is she?'

'I don't see why not; you're friendly and outgoing . . .'

'Nah.' Gina denied any positive praise. 'She'll just think I'm a scumbag . . . She's one of them religious ones, isn't she?'

Marcia sighed, hand on her hip. 'All I'm asking is that you try a bit. Is that too much to ask?'

'I do try! I do!' Gina protested with an exaggerated shrug. Joanne could see that, though she was in her twenties, she was still somehow a child.

'Now who else is there . . . ?' Marcia said.

'I met someone upstairs: an Irish lady . . .'

'Ah yes, Maeve – she's got two little girls with her. In fact the youngest, Siobhan, is only a bit older than Amy. They might play together all right. The older one, Roisin, is young for her age too. They're both very quiet, withdrawn . . .'

'Not like my lot,' Gina put in, almost proudly.

'No,' Marcia said in a dry tone. 'Not at all like your two. Anyway, the other woman here is Doreen – up in the attic with Mariam. She's quite a quiet lady, a bit older than all of you.'

'Fucking punchbag that one,' Gina said.

'Gina!'

'I mean, poor woman, that's all . . .' Gina put on a wheedling tone, which immediately made Joanne feel even more wary of her.

'She's here with her youngest son, Danny – he's seven? Isn't he?'

'Yeah, not that you'd know it,' Gina said.

'I'm going to check on Jason,' Marcia said firmly. Joanne was impressed by her air of authority. 'When you've finished breakfast you'll need to go down to him, Gina, right? Jackie's coming in today, so she'll come and do some stuff with them. And, Joanne, we'd better have a chat later, talk over a few things – when you've finished in here, okay?'

Joanne nodded and attempted a smile. Her face had trouble with that and, instead, tears rushed into her eyes. 'Okay,' she said.

'How're you feeling about things?'

They were sitting in Marcia's office. Jackie, the other residential worker, had put her head round the door. She was a dark-haired, big-boned woman in her thirties.

'Catch you later,' she said. 'Don't want to interrupt.'

Marcia had put a few toys out for Amy and she was playing with a big articulated crocodile at Joanne's feet. From her chair Joanne could just see cars passing on the road, behind all the netting. The world outside seemed very distant, as if she had already been removed from it for weeks. Tears ran down her cheeks.

'I feel really bad. I don't think I should be here. I mean, I'm sure everyone else is in a far worse situation. I shouldn't have come – I should have stayed and worked at it with him. I've been so stupid. He's not a bad man . . . I just think I ought to go back . . .'

Marcia leaned forward, her face full of concern.

'But you *did* come here, didn't you?' Her voice was calm and gentle. She paused for a moment, then went on, 'No one does that lightly. You took a very big step, in leaving – a very brave step. You must have had your reasons. Would you like to tell me a bit about it?'

Joanne hesitated, then it all came spilling out, about how Dave had changed, how it had all built up so that she was afraid of him. The phone calls; the way he had punched her and tried to control her.

'It wasn't all the time – I don't want you to think that. Some of the time he was perfectly all right. Only lately it had got worse; he was always on at me – wouldn't trust me. He kept on at me: you know, in bed as well. He thought I was having affairs with other men – even if I just talked to someone. And I wasn't, I'm not like that. But I could manage . . .'

She patted her pockets, looking for something to blow her nose on. Marcia reached over and offered her a box of tissues. She looked solemnly into Joanne's eyes.

'Are you saying he raped you?'

Joanne felt a shock go through her. 'Raped me? No!' She thought for a moment. 'No. Not that. I mean, I never said no or anything – it wasn't like that. I s'pose I just did what he wanted, but I wouldn't call it rape.'

Marcia nodded, listening.

'Then last week, he started on me – but then he took Amy upstairs. He was already in a temper and he'd hit me, thrown me across the hall . . .'

Marcia held up a hand. 'Stop a minute. Can you hear what you just said?'

Joanne thought about it. She looked down into her lap. 'Sounds bad, doesn't it?'

'It's not normal behaviour.'

'No. But then the thing was, he lost it with Amy. She was crying because she could hear us and she was frightened. He grabbed her out of her buggy and took her upstairs. I was scared to death of what he'd do . . .' She began weeping again, remembering. 'I ran up after her and he was in the bedroom, shaking her, hard. Her little head was shaking back and forward . . . I was afraid he'd break her neck.'

'So what did you do, Joanne?'

'I hit him. I had a . . . I had a . . .'

A wave of hysteria passed over her at the memory and she started laughing helplessly, the tears still flowing.

'It's not funny – I know. But there was this tin of corned beef in my shopping. I took it upstairs and I whacked him with it: on the head, twice. He was bleeding and he let go. Corned beef . . . !' The uncontrollable laughter surged up in her, then dipped into more tears.

Marcia watched her, quietly. 'Do you want to go back to this man?'

Slowly Joanne raised her head. '*Yes*. No. Oh God, he's my husband, he's Amy's dad . . . I don't know at the moment.'

'In the end,' Marcia said, 'the decision's always yours

about whether you go or stay here. But why not give yourself a bit of time to think? I know it must feel really difficult, miles from home in a new place. But you've done it now. Look.' She stood up for a second to click on the kettle that was resting on top of the filing cabinet, then perched on the chair again. 'I'll fill you in on what'll happen, to begin with. Megan will be round later today and there'll be a case conference – I'm guessing tomorrow . . .'

'Will I have to go?' Joanne said, horrified.

Marcia nodded, smiling gently. 'Well, of course – you don't want people discussing you *without* you being there, do you?'

'Well, no . . .' It sounded terrifying, as if she was the one on trial.

'Look,' Marcia seemed to read her mind, 'they're there for you. Not to tell you off or be against you. It's all to help you decide what to do. And to be honest, from what you've told me, you've been very strong and done the right thing. It takes some people years to do what you've done.'

Forty-Three

That first day seemed endless to Joanne.

It was grey and overcast outside, and in any case she did not want to go out. It didn't feel safe. She wanted to wrap the house round her like a cocoon, even though it was dark and gloomy and foreign to her.

Megan came to see her, late in the morning, and once again they sat in Marcia's office and talked about the case conference, which only increased Joanne's worries.

'The police will almost certainly interview your husband,' Megan told her.

Joanne's nerves were in such a state that all day she found it impossible to relax. The stress of all that had happened, of being in this strange place with other people whose reactions she was uncertain of, filled her with tension. Smells of other people's food came from the kitchen. Her stomach was queasy and she found it difficult to eat anything, or to settle to do anything. Apart from seeing Megan, she stayed in her room trying to keep Amy occupied.

All she could think about was the telephone. She knew Dave's work number off by heart. Perhaps if she just gave him a quick call? She felt as if a thick piece of elastic, attached to him, was pulled tight inside her. As if she needed to explain to him, for him to understand. *This is why I've done this to you. Can't you see?* Marcia had told her it would be very unwise to contact Dave at this stage. Perhaps she should call Mom and Dad? But no, what could she say? The only person she could talk to would be Karen, and she wouldn't be home until later. Maybe she should call Dave first . . . ? The thoughts spun in her head, giving her no peace.

Eventually, Amy's bored restlessness drove her downstairs. She went to make a mug of tea. Thinking the kitchen empty, she walked in, her guard down. But there was someone there after all and she jumped, her pulse racing: Mariam. The girl's head whipped round when she heard someone come in. She too was intensely on edge. But immediately she looked away again. Joanne examined her, a tiny, frail figure in a dark-blue Asian suit and a black scarf. She only looked about sixteen, but it was hard to tell. Joanne felt very sorry for her. Suppose she didn't speak any English? She must feel so alone here without any of her own people.

She struggled to remember what she had been taught to say by some of the girls at school. Softly, experimentally, she said, '*Salaam* . . . ?'

There was a pause, then a tiny mutter came from by the cooker. '*Salaam aleikum.*'

But Mariam didn't turn round. A moment later she poured hot milk into a mug and walked past with it, with only a flicker of a glance in Joanne's direction. However, she looked a fraction less severe and frightened than she had the last time. She disappeared and Joanne heard no footsteps receding. The girl moved like a feather drifting over the ground.

Joanne thought about Sooky. An ache filled her. If only she'd just walk in here now. It would be so good to see her familiar face and friendly smile.

*

After her tea and some milk for Amy, she went to the playroom. The house was surprisingly quiet after the comings and goings of the morning. There had seemed to be a constant stream of people in and out: social workers, advisors about benefits and housing. To her relief there was no sign of Gina or her boys. She heard Marcia's voice from behind the office door, talking fluently as if on the phone.

In the playroom she found the Irish woman with her two girls, who both jumped visibly when she opened the door and looked round with terrified expressions. With her was another woman with a young boy. Joanne realized the woman must be Doreen.

Hesitating at the door, she said, 'All right if I come in?'

'Course it's all right,' the Irish woman said. 'But shut the door behind you, will you?'

The other woman merely nodded, sitting hunched on a chair beside one of the child-sized tables. She was horrifyingly thin and wrung-out-looking. Her hair, almost grey with a few streaks of remaining brown, straggled round an emaciated face, the skin loose and prematurely aged, out of which stared blue, watery eyes that seemed to hold an infinite sadness. Her son, also skinny, with a very pale face and cropped, mousy hair, had also leapt to his feet when Joanne came in. After looking at her, he subsided warily back to the floor, where he was playing with some cars.

Amy toddled over to the other girls as if drawn by a magnet and stood watching them chalking on a little blackboard. They were guarded at first, and then the oldest, Roisin, quietly got up, took Amy's hand and pulled her to sit down with them. The little one, Siobhan, reached up and touched Amy's pale hair.

'That's it,' their mother said. 'You play nicely now.' She looked at Joanne. 'What's her name?'

'Amy,' Joanne said.

The woman said her name was Maeve. She seemed to take charge. 'That's Doreen,' she added, nodding across the room. 'And Danny.'

Doreen gave the faintest nod.

Joanne tried to smile at her. 'I'm Joanne,' she said.

The three of them sat there for a few moments, not knowing what to say.

'Have you been here long?' Joanne asked Maeve eventually.

'Ah, no, just a few days. We'll not be here long.' She spoke in a way that suggested she wasn't really here at all and was above all this. 'Just a bit of a misunderstanding,' she added.

Joanne looked at Doreen, who was rocking gently on the chair. There was something vacant about her, as if her spirit had long ago left her body. Joanne wasn't sure whether to talk to her, but it seemed unkind not to.

'What about you?' she asked gently.

Doreen seemed to come to herself as if from another world.

'Oh – me?' She spoke with a soft Brummie accent. 'I don't know. I think . . . I mean . . . No . . .' Instead of rocking, she began to move her head repeatedly from side to side. These somehow childish movements and her beaten, shocked look made Joanne feel great tenderness towards her. 'No – not now. No, I won't be going back . . . Can't, not now. No . . .'

*

Amy's needs helped to give the day some sort of shape. It was a relief to cling to this: getting her some lunch, then tea. Making sure she played and slept.

All Joanne could think about was home, the telephone, what was happening. All evening she was on tenterhooks. First of all Gina monopolized the phone for ages, talking loudly, quarrelling with whoever was on the other end. Even though the phone was down at the bottom of the back corridor, her voice carried all over the house.

'I've told him – I don't trust him, and I don't love him. He's a ****ing bastard to me, and he doesn't deserve to have kids . . . I know, he's a ****ing nutter, he ought to be locked up and the key thrown away, but in the end he is their father . . .' On and on she went. Joanne's nerves were stretched taut.

She couldn't phone Mom and Dad's house too early. She knew Karen nearly always stayed up watching TV. She needed to wait till ten or so, to be sure she'd answer. Was she even allowed to use the phone that late? She thought about phoning Michelle, but it was so long since they'd spoken, and Meesh might be sympathetic, but in the end she'd just say, 'Told you so.'

By the time ten o'clock came, she was shaking with the need to do something. Gina had at last shut up and hobbled off upstairs.

She dialled and inserted the money, her blood banging. The phone connected: Karen. Thank God!

'Hello?' Karen's voice sounded very cautious, as if expecting trouble.

'Karen?' she spoke quietly as if the house were all listening. 'It's me.'

'Jo!' Karen's voiced lifted in relief, then erupted into anger. 'For God's sake, where are you? We've all been worried sick!'

'I had to leave . . .' She broke down. Hearing her sister's voice signalled her real world coming back to her in this foreign place. 'Has Dave been round?'

'Has he been round? What do you think? Of course he has! He's been beside himself. What on earth're you playing at, just disappearing without telling anyone? Where are you?'

'Is he angry?' She was snivelling down the phone.

'What do you think? Yes! Well, no. He was at first. He was wild. Now he's all over the place. What're you playing at – everyone's in a right state. You've caused no end of trouble, Joanne. Who're you with?'

For a second she didn't understand the question. 'Who . . . ? You mean . . . ? I'm not with anyone!' Her voice rose in indignation. 'Is that what you all think: that I've run off with someone? For Christ's sake, I'm in a home – a refuge. I couldn't stand it any more. He'd been hitting me, for months. I never said, but then he started on Amy, and that was when I knew I had to go . . .'

She was weeping now, hardly able to get the words out.

'How could you think . . . ? You got to believe me, Karen. I don't know what's up with Dave, but he's not the person he used to be. He gets angry and lashes out. I'm frightened of him. And now the police might be onto him . . .' She trailed off into sobs.

There was a silence down the other end of the phone, which seemed to go on forever.

At last Karen said very solemnly, 'Is this true?'

'Of course it's true – what d'you think I am?' Joanne

343

wailed. 'But don't tell him! For God's sake, don't mention the police to him! I mean, they might not even . . . I don't know. Just don't say anything . . .'

'I won't.' Karen sounded dazed.

'*Promise* me.'

'I won't, I told you. I thought . . .' Pieces of a puzzle were coming together in Karen's head. 'Last time I came over. There was something not right – I could see, but I never thought. Oh, Sis, I'd never've thought Dave . . . Is it really true? That's not like him.'

More quietly now Joanne said, 'I know. But it's true. I don't know what to do. I think he needs help. I'd come back, but my social worker says . . . I've got a case conference tomorrow.'

'Case conference? You've got a social worker?' Karen sounded very sober now.

'Yes. I didn't have any choice once I'd . . . It's weird, Karen, everything just gets taken over.'

Slowly Karen said, 'Look, I'll have to tell Mom and Dad what's happened. Try and get them to take it in. Where are you?'

'I'm not s'posed to say.'

'No, I suppose not. Mom and Dad aren't going to find this easy. I'll just tell them you're okay – they're worried sick.'

'What've they said?'

'Mom's furious. More angry than I've ever seen her. She thinks it's terrible. You know: Dave can do no wrong. Make your bed and lie on it – all that. Thinks you've gone mad. Dad's been tutting, but it's hard to know what he thinks.'

'Well, yeah.' They both laughed, faintly.

'Stay where you are. I'm going to talk to someone at work, tomorrow if I can – get some advice. Look, are you okay? And Amy? It's nowhere near your house, is it?'

'No, it's okay. He wouldn't find us. And we're all right for now. It's not very nice – some of the other kids are terrible. But there's a nice woman in charge.'

She wanted to break down and sob for her sister to come to her, but knew it would be unfair. She swallowed and kept control of herself.

'That's good. Now, look, phone me tomorrow – same time.'

'I will.' Joanne felt a surge of warmth and relief. Karen was all right really. She was more than all right, in fact.

'Give Amy a kiss from me.' Karen paused. 'It *is* true, isn't it? About Dave?'

'It's true,' Joanne said miserably. 'I wish to God it wasn't.'

Forty-Four

The next night she spoke to Karen, quite late, once the house had at last gone quiet. Or, rather, Karen spoke to her. Joanne could hardly get a word in edgeways at first. Karen had consulted Hilary, her counsellor friend. She had also spoken to Dave.

'The thing is,' she spoke carefully, but Joanne could hear her enjoyment of a certain kind of authority in the situation, 'Dave's blaming you for everything – and, at the moment, Mom agrees with him. You know what their generation are like about marriages breaking up. You don't do it. Must be the woman's fault, she's supposed to be the centre of the marriage and the household, blah, blah, and all that.'

Karen sighed, heavily.

'To tell you the truth, I'm quite surprised what it's brought out: the way Mom's been on about it. I thought she might have been a bit more understanding. She won't hear a word against Dave – she thinks you ought to come back and get on with it. Knuckle down, sort of thing.'

'What, even if he's violent to us?' Her hurt and anger made Joanne's voice shrill. 'Even if he hurts Amy?'

'The thing is, she doesn't believe he's capable of it.'

'Why's she taking his side? She's my mom, not his!' Joanne was trying to swallow down tears. 'And what about Wendy?'

'Well, you know what she's like – in a world of her own half the time. Won't hear a word against him, either.'

'Was she nasty about me?' Joanne wasn't sure why she asked this, but she seemed to need to know if everyone in her life had turned against her.

'No – she wasn't actually. I just don't think any of it's really sunk in. Anyway, what I was going to say was, I had a conversation with Hilary, the counsellor woman at work. She talked to someone else, who she said had worked with a lot of battered women . . .'

Battered women? Joanne thought. She remembered Doreen, and the state of Gina's toes. God, she'd become a label! She'd had enough of this.

'Look, it doesn't matter what she thinks. We had the case conference today. The police are going to interview Dave. It's a first offence, and there wasn't much evidence. Amy had some bruises, but they'd almost gone by the time we got here. He might just get a caution . . . If I go back, we might end up with a supervision order, I think they call it.'

'Oh, I see.' Karen was silenced for a moment. 'Well, I s'pose they have to . . . The thing is, if Dave's blaming everything on you, no one's really got anywhere and you're safer staying out of his way. You need to give yourself some time to think, away from his influence – and with all this going on.'

'I know,' Joanne said, but her spirits sank, dismally. What she wanted to hear was someone saying: Go home – you can forget about this nightmare. She just wanted everything to be all right again.

'No one's really talked to Dave, I don't think. Not properly,' Karen said. 'They're all just saying, "Oh, poor Dave, his wife's run off with their kid." So he's not really looking at himself. Maybe I should . . .'

'Maybe you should be a counsellor,' Joanne suggested wearily.

'Umm,' Karen said, sounding pleased. 'Perhaps I should. But maybe the police had better talk to him first.'

September weather was setting in. The trees drooped, leaves turning rusty at the edges. Joanne ventured out with Amy. From the house they had access to Edgbaston Reservoir and Summerfield Park. The weather was changeable, but as often as possible she took Amy out, happy to get away from the house and all the misery and aggravation it contained. At first she felt vulnerable stepping outside. Everyone was obsessed with security and wary about the house being watched. Although she knew Dave had no idea where she was, she, like the other women, felt as if they stood out a mile as soon as they left the house. Doreen never went out at all.

Dave, she had heard, had been formally cautioned by the police. Although the pressure was always on in the refuge to make a plan, to sort yourself out, and Megan was in and out talking to her, Joanne knew she needed some days of quiet, to think.

She walked for miles with Amy in those gusty, early autumn days, sometimes stopping to feed the ducks. She would find herself standing for heaven knew how long, gazing out over the grey water, then coming to and wondering how long she had been there. Sometimes sobs rose up from her thoughts and she would weep uncontrollably, in the middle of the park. Her emotion was often brought on by thinking about her early years with Dave, how full of hope he had been: he had been special, chosen, brimming with confidence. She had almost worshipped him. She wept for all that had been lost, for both of them. Now he was full of rage with her and a sense of betrayal – according to Karen.

Thinking about the future seemed impossible now. It was as if she was in limbo in this place, this house of alien smells and people, which was neither a home of the past nor the future, but a holding pen from which her life must somehow go on.

She had great respect for the women who ran the refuge – especially Marcia, to whom she found she could talk easily, and she admired the way she handled a lot of difficult situations. But in Jackie she also saw someone who had special gifts, especially with the children. What they really needed, Jackie told Joanne one day, was a man to work there, to show the children that not all men are violent abusers. But such men were hard to find.

However, Jackie was one of the few people who could get any response out of Gina's boys, who despite their angelic looks and winning ways were devious, angry and violent. Their blond sweetness would alter in seconds to show furious, snarling faces, boys who bit and kicked at any sign of attention and who went out of their way to trip up and bait other children. Maeve kept her cowering girls well out of their way, but there were endless problems involving the boys.

As the week passed, Joanne gradually learned more about the other women in the house. Gina, the prettiest and closest to her age, was always the most forthcoming. If they met in the kitchen she was always full of chat, but Joanne soon learned not to trust her.

'Gina's been in and out of here,' Marcia warned her. 'I wouldn't believe everything she says. To be honest with you, we're in the last stages of having those boys taken into care. Gina looks sunny, but her own background was a nightmare – and the dad's more of the same. The trouble is she has no idea what normal behaviour is, bless her.'

Gina would relate with relish some of the injuries that Benny, her husband, ten years her senior, had inflicted on her.

'The first time I come here – that was when he blacked both my eyes – you should've seen me; like summat out of the *Black and White Minstrels*! That's 'cos my nose was broke as well; and I had a broken rib or two, but you couldn't see that. Then there was the time he broke my jaw – see here, I've got wire in here, but they made a lovely job of it. I had Jase as a baby then, and Benny couldn't stand him crying ... This was before he got systematic about it – I mean, this time, with the claw hammer: he just worked his way along ...'

All this told while frying bacon. Benny was a big softie really, she assured everyone. It was only she who understood him. Gina completely horrified Joanne, and she found herself avoiding conversation with her.

She never really worked Maeve out, and in any case she was gone within a few days. Devoutly Catholic, she managed to give off an air of self-righteousness while also blaming herself for all that had happened. Her daughters looked cowed and terrified, but Joanne never worked out where the truth lay there. She was replaced by an older lady called Linda, who seemed very depressed and just said she couldn't stand any more. Her children were grown-up. She'd had enough.

Of the other two, it was Doreen for whom her heart bled. Joanne gradually learned, both from Marcia and from Doreen herself when she occasionally stopped and spoke, that the woman was forty-five and had seven sons. Her husband had been violent all through their marriage, but at any backchat from her or attempts to leave him he had immediately got her pregnant again, so that she didn't feel she could desert the family. Now the boys had grown up, and after their education in violence from their father, the older ones had started setting about their mother as well. Doreen had at last acted on repeated advice from social workers and health visitors to get out of there and try to save Danny, the youngest, from going the same way. Now she lived in terror of her husband finding her. Joanne could hardly take in the pain, fear and heartbreak that this gently-spoken woman had suffered.

As for Mariam, she really did not speak English. She had been brought over as a bride from Bangladesh by a man who had already twice tried to kill her by throttling her. She was fifteen years old.

Joanne found she longed to be out, to do something normal.

One afternoon she decided to try getting on the bus into town. She asked Marcia's permission, and Marcia told her it was absolutely up to her, to assess her own risks. Where could be the harm? Joanne reasoned. Dave was the one person she really couldn't risk running into, and he would not be in town on a workday afternoon.

All the same, sitting on the bus as it crawled along the Hagley Road, she was surprised at how nervous and strange she felt. It reminded her of when she first had Amy, coming out of the hospital as if to a world that had changed. Whereas of course it was she who had changed. It felt today as if everyone was staring at her.

She still had most of the money she had brought with her. Her faded old jeans, which she lived in, were all in holes, and Amy needed one or two things. Joanne had only been able to bring a small amount from home.

'We'll go and have a look in Mothercare,' she whispered to Amy, calming her own nerves by her chatter. 'And we'll go to the Bull Ring, and then Mommy and Amy might go and get a drink – would you like that?'

Amy nodded, solemnly. Since they had left home she was not talking as much as she had been and she seldom smiled. This tore at Joanne's heart. One thing she noticed, though, was that Amy never asked after Dave. She seemed to accept that wherever Joanne was, was home.

Once they were off the bus she unfolded Amy's buggy and pushed her round the shops. It was overcast, but thankfully not raining. They went into Mothercare and she let Amy choose some little trousers and a top to go with them. She also needed some underwear for Amy and for herself, which she decided to see if she could get in the Rag Market, and also look for a cheap pair of jeans. She was just pushing Amy down the ramp by St Martin's Church when someone gently squeezed her arm. Joanne started violently.

'Sorry, I didn't mean to make you jump – only I said hello twice!'

It was Sooky, also pushing a buggy with Priya in it. Amy was squeaking with excitement, showing more animation than she had in days. She and Priya reached out their hands to each other.

'Oh!' Joanne laid a hand on her pounding chest. 'Sorry, I was miles away.' She took in Sooky's smiling, friendly face. 'It's *really* nice to see you. Only, I meant to take your number – when the playgroup ended – and I never got it.'

'But I was looking for you this week,' Sooky said. 'You never came.'

'Has it started again already? Yes, I s'pose it would've done.'

Having stopped on the ramp with two buggies, they were clearly irritating people, provoking some forthright comments about standing right in the way, so they moved in against the wall of the church.

'Were you away?' Sooky said. 'We were looking forward to seeing you.'

'I . . .' Joanne hesitated. 'Look, I've had to leave home for a bit.' To her annoyance, tears filled her eyes. What must Sooky think of her? Still, at least she'd left a marriage herself. 'We had a bit of trouble.'

'Oh dear.' Sooky looked really concerned. 'Are you all right?'

'Yeah – yeah, I'm okay.' She wiped her eyes, trying to pull herself together.

'Tell you what,' Sooky said. 'How about a coffee? Then we could have a proper chat. If you've got time, that is.'

'Oh, I've got plenty of time.' Joanne looked up and managed a watery smile. 'That would be really nice.'

Forty-Five

They went to a bakery with a cafe and settled down with their drinks and squash and currant buns for Amy and Priya. The little girls faced each other, beaming in delight.

Joanne also felt a rush of pleasure. How nice it was, this simple thing, meeting a friend for a chat. Apart from that one snatched coffee with Kieran, she could not remember the last time she'd done something like this. It came home to her again how isolated she had become. Only now could she see the extent to which Dave had controlled her every move. How had she let things get like that? It was as if she had been in a trance. She sat up straight for a moment and took a deep breath, as if throwing off a burden.

'You look nice,' she said to Sooky, who was in jeans today, with a black blouse and black jacket. She had a lovely slim figure.

Sooky glanced down at herself, then back at Joanne, smiling in surprise. 'Oh, thanks!'

'How d'you decide what to wear every day?' Joanne asked.

'What, you mean – oh, whether I wear a Punjabi suit?' Sooky shrugged. 'It's nice and comfortable wearing them round the house. If I'm going out, well, it depends what mood I'm in. That's all: no big mystery!' She smiled again.

'Mind you, when I was younger, Mom always wanted me to wear Indian clothes. If I ever bought anything else, like a denim skirt, she'd be going, "Oh, *Hai Rabbai*" – that's like, "Oh my God, what is *that* you're wearing?" Every time she says *Hai Rabbai* she does this.' Sooky banged her forehead with the heel of her hand. 'She had a pink mark on her head for a long time, with me around, wanting to wear the latest fashions! But she got used to it in the end. She's okay with it now.'

Joanne laughed. 'You're good at taking people off.'

'Am I? Well, with Mom I've seen that enough times!'

Priya was nudging for Sooky's attention and for a moment they helped the girls tear open their buns. Priya began painstakingly picking out the currants and eating them first, and Amy copied her.

Sooky turned to Joanne and said gently, 'So d'you want to talk about it?'

Joanne sipped her milky, comforting hot chocolate. It was easy to talk in here, with all the burble of other people around, the selling of cakes and clinking of cups on saucers. And Sooky's face was so kind and understanding.

'I keep trying to work it out,' she said. 'What's happened to him – to us. We've been together a long while now, Dave and me, and before he'd never've raised a finger. He just wasn't like that. It started after I'd had Amy. I don't know, maybe I was too wrapped up in her and didn't give him enough attention.'

She stared ahead of her for a moment.

'It was all right at first. But he's got more and more, well, angry and *weird* – always checking up on me. You know, that day in the park, when we had the little party, Dave was there. I saw him suddenly, across the other side, just staring at us.'

'Oh yes, I remember!' Sooky said. 'I saw him too, but obviously I didn't know who he was. Is he blond – short hair?'

Joanne nodded, swallowing. 'Yeah. Once he'd seen me notice him, he went off. Then he kept phoning. At first it was once or twice – then he'd be phoning about once every hour to check what I was doing.'

'Ooh,' Sooky looked dismayed. 'Creepy.'

Joanne nodded. 'It *is* creepy. He didn't like me seeing anyone. Even with my family it's a bit difficult, but at least he will come and see them, and he's nice as pie to them. He wants them to think well of him, and they all think the sun shines out of him. But anyone else ... It was as if I'd committed a crime if I spoke to anyone. God!' She rolled her eyes, remembering. 'What finally set him was off was that we ran into Kieran – just out shopping. I couldn't pretend I didn't know him, so we had a chat, but when we got home ... he went mad. He accused me of having an affair with Kieran. He thought I was covering up the fact that there was a man at the toddler group.'

'Does he hit you?' Sooky asked.

Joanne nodded, looking down, blushing in shame. She was glad to be asked in a matter-of-fact way, but it was a hard thing to admit.

'More and more. But I would've put up with that if ...' She looked into Sooky's eyes, needing some kind of assurance. 'It was when I saw him start on Amy. I was scared he was really going to hurt her.'

Her eyes filled then and she couldn't go on for a minute. Then she told Sooky what had happened.

'Oh, my goodness,' Sooky exclaimed, her dark eyes full of concern. 'Oh, you did the right thing. It was the same for me. I found Jaz with Priya, and I knew things weren't right. It was sex with him – he never hit her or anything. You can put up with things for yourself, even though that's not right either, is it? But . . .'

She turned, looking upset, and stroked Priya's glossy head. The little girls were making faces at each other and giggling.

Sooky went on, 'Even my mom, who's the most traditional person ever about marriage, supported me over that. But then Jaz and I hardly knew each other. What about you?'

Sooky let Joanne talk and talk. She told Sooky all about the refuge and the other women there, and about how she and Dave met as teenagers.

'I suppose life hasn't turned out for him how he wanted,' she said. 'He had high hopes – he was going to be a famous footballer.'

'That's a big thing to have snatched away from you,' Sooky said.

'Yes, but he seemed to get over it quickly. He's always had work with his dad's little firm and has done well. It's his business now, basically, even though some of the blokes there are much older than him. He's got a good life: a wife and child . . .' She sighed. 'I don't know. Anyway, I'm talking your hind leg off. And I'm fed up of thinking about it all! Tell me more about your marriage?'

Sooky told her briefly what had happened with Jaz.

'That sounds awful,' Joanne said. 'And what with your mom, and everything. But I don't really get that: you just said she supported you?'

'I know, I don't really get it, either.' Sooky fiddled with her teaspoon, turning it round in the cup. 'I think she's just got so many things pulling her in different directions – our religion, and what people will say in the community because divorce is so shameful. The thing is, she knew it was wrong – what Jaz did – absolutely wrong, but somehow she wishes it hadn't ended the marriage . . . Maybe she thinks I should have been able to stop it, I don't know. She hasn't got much confidence; she doesn't speak English and she hasn't ever really learned to read much even in our language. She comes from a village in India where things change a lot more slowly, and she's trying to adapt to everything being different from how she expected. She thought everything would be so much better for all of us – and of course in lots of ways it is. But bad things still happen. And I think she does understand in a way; she's quite kind-hearted really, my mom, she's just a bit confused and stuck in her ways.'

'Oh, tell me about it. You should meet mine! That's if she ever speaks to *me* again.'

Their eyes met and suddenly they were laughing at the sheer awful complicatedness of everything. They couldn't seem to stop.

'The thing about my mom is,' Joanne managed to say at last, 'we've only just discovered she's been addicted to Valium for the past twenty years and nobody knew!'

'But,' Sooky's expression sobered quickly, 'that's awful – what about your dad?'

'He didn't notice.'

Sooky considered this. 'I don't think my dad would've noticed, either.'

At this, they both burst into laughter again. Amy and Priya stared at their mothers, put their heads back and giggled gleefully, even though they didn't know what the joke was.

'That's not funny!' Joanne managed to splutter, tears running down her cheeks.

'I know.' Sooky agreed between outbursts of laughter.

Every time they looked at each other, they set each other off again. Joanne felt as if weeks of tension were draining out of her in this laughter about things that realistically weren't in the least funny. At last they managed to control themselves and wiped their eyes.

'Oh,' Joanne said, feeling suddenly limp, 'I feel better for that. Shall we have another drink?'

While Joanne went to the counter, Sooky reached into her bag and found a spiral-bound notebook, a pen and a pencil. She gave some sheets to the girls to doodle on.

'Great!' Joanne said when she came back. 'That'll keep them quiet for a bit. I've got nothing with me at all.'

'I'd thought I might go to the Central Library,' Sooky said. 'Make a few notes – although I'm not sure what about. Did I tell you, I'm going to start a degree at the Poly next term?'

'No – that's fantastic! You said you were thinking about it. What about getting married, though? Are your mom and dad okay with it?'

'Yeah, Mom's okay with it, for now anyway. She'll look after Priya while I'm there – it's part-time, you see. If anyone comes along for marriage – well, we'll see. They're not pushing it too hard at the moment, not after the last one.'

Joanne was surprised by the stab of envy she felt, at the thought of those possibilities opening out, of a bigger life. 'That's so good. I wish I could do something like that.'

'Maybe you could?'

'I haven't even got A-levels. And my mom certainly wouldn't help, not like yours. She doesn't see the point of all that. And she can hardly look after herself at the moment.'

'No, I know I'm lucky like that.' Sooky put her head on one side. 'What will you do, d'you think? Will you go back to him?'

Joanne knew she had been avoiding this question. So far it had been easier to remain in limbo, waiting – as if fate or God or a social worker would sort it out for her. In her heart of hearts she knew she had never seriously considered anything else. In the end she would go back; somehow things would get better, and she and Dave would go on much as they had before. That was what she had always assumed, and she couldn't imagine much else.

But there were other things, other lives she might have: A-levels, work. She could be a single parent – other people managed. It felt exciting and very frightening, all at once. Amy's piece of paper drifted down by her feet and she bent to pick it up, then looked up at Sooky.

'I really don't know,' she said.

By the time they parted Joanne felt cheered and heartened.

'It's been so nice to get out for a bit,' she said, as she and Sooky headed along New Street. She hadn't done all her shopping, but this had been much better.

'I can imagine,' Sooky said. 'It must be really hard in there.'

'The noise is the worst thing,' Joanne said.

'Look,' Sooky said shyly, 'I know you can't come to

the toddler group at the moment. I won't be able to, either, with my course starting. Most of the classes are on a Tuesday. But d'you want to meet up again?'

'Oh yes, I'd love to,' Joanne smiled. 'It's been really nice.'

'What shall I tell them: Tess and Kieran and everyone, if I see them?'

'Oh, I don't know – tell them I've had to go away for a bit. That my mom's ill or something.' She hesitated. 'No, that's silly. You might as well tell them the truth.'

They stopped, needing to part for different buses.

'See you next week?' Sooky said. 'Same time, same place?'

Joanne smiled as she watched her friend walking away along the crowded street.

Forty-Six

'Well, when exactly *does* she think she's coming home?'

Margaret stood by the table in the back room, doling out the food: chicken-and-mushroom pies with oven chips and peas. She saw Karen looking down her nose at the meal.

'What's up with you, miss? Not good enough for yer?'

'No, it's just – now and then Mom, it'd be better for us if we had some fresher food, that's all. Instead of ready-made stuff. All the vitamins get lost in the processing . . .' Karen trailed off, silenced by the look in her mother's eye.

Margaret stared at her, holding the spatula she was using to lift the pies. She felt like slapping Karen with it. Little Miss Know-It-All. And of course Fred wouldn't say anything – he'd just sit there, gormless as ever.

'Anyway,' Karen said hurriedly, keen to keep the peace, 'when Joanne rang last night she said – well, like I told you – Amy's fine and she's going to stop there a bit longer and give Dave time to cool down. She wants to think things through.'

'Well, that seems—' Fred started to say, but Margaret interrupted.

'I should think she *does* want to think things through

– and the quicker, the better. Going off, leaving her husband; it's an absolute disgrace . . .'

She set off on the explosive diatribe that Fred and Karen had heard many times since Joanne's first phone call two weeks ago. Even when she'd sat down, her rage seemed to billow, bigger than her, around the table.

'In my day, you made your bed and you lay on it – none of this fooling about.' She sat down and sprinkled Sarson's vinegar on her chips. 'There's that lad struggling on his own, and not being able to see his daughter . . .'

'Well, surely he can look after himself for a bit?' Karen said, trying to quell her impatience. 'He's not completely helpless.'

'That's not the point,' Margaret said, knifing her pie so that steam came swirling out of it. They couldn't seem to see it – none of them. Joanne had done wrong; you just didn't leave home like that. Didn't call attention to yourself.

'Mom,' Karen said sharply, 'Dave's been violent to her: knocking her about – God, how many more times? And he had a go at Amy. That's what made her leave . . . She was protecting her child – *your grandchild.*'

'He shouldn't be doing that,' Fred said mildly.

'You don't think I believe that for a moment, do you?' Margaret said. 'Not Dave. I mean, he's a good lad – always has been. Why would he start suddenly doing that, out of the blue? She must've provoked him. That's the trouble with you girls nowadays; you want too much, never satisfied.'

Karen sighed, delving into the pastry to salvage its contents. She slid the soggy pie-case to the side of the plate.

'People change, Mom,' she said, but without much hope of getting through to her. 'Something's happened to him, even if you can't see it. And if you can't give support to your own daughter, instead of someone else's son – well, I'd say that's pretty sad.'

Margaret went up to bed by half-past nine. She never seemed to feel well, one way or another, and at the moment could hardly stand being with any of them. She could barely cope with herself, on her own.

'I'll wait up and see if Jo phones,' Karen called to her father. He was in the front room watching telly, something about detectives, and for a minute Karen didn't think he'd heard her. But he lurched forward and turned the TV off.

'She'll be phoning soon, will 'er?'

'It depends . . .' She went into the front room, stepping over the torn bit of carpet. It was a shaggy thing in brown, black and orange squares. All the chairs faced the TV. 'The house is quite noisy – kids playing up and everything. She tends to wait till things have settled down a bit. It could be a while.' She hesitated. 'Did you want to speak to her?'

Fred seemed to shrink into the chair as if under interrogation. 'Well, I thought I might.'

Karen sat down on the chair closest to him. 'I'm sure she'd be really pleased. She's missing everyone. She feels as if everyone's turned against her.'

'Well, they haven't, have they? You haven't, for a start.'

'No, I know – but Mom, and . . . it's just I suppose she's not having an easy time. It's easy to get upset over anything and everything.'

Fred nodded. Karen watched her father's thin, saggy face with a mixture of affection and exasperation. He'd always been a kindly dad, if a bit ineffectual. She wished he'd stand up more to Mom and her moods.

'You believe her, don't you, Dad?'

He rubbed a hand over his face. The effort of speaking about such things was almost physical.

'I can't see why the wench'd make it up. Not after all this time. Anyway, 'er's not like that.'

'I'm sure she'd like to hear from you.'

Fred nodded, with the air of a man facing the gallows. Then he said, 'Your mother's not had an easy life.'

Karen got ready to seize an opportunity. 'The war, you mean?'

'Oh no, I don't know much about the war. I mean her home life: I saw her a bit when we was kids. The Old Man – well, he wasn't very nice. And he had this woman in tow . . . Thing is, I only saw them about the place a bit. I never knew them proper, like.'

'Why not?' Karen said, puzzled.

'Well, as soon as I got to know Margaret a bit, we had to move on and I never saw 'er till years later.'

'I never knew that: that you'd known each other when you were children!'

'Well, hardly – I mean, not for long . . .'

'So, why did you move? Where to?'

Fred seemed to shrink into himself. 'Well, there was just us kids, yer see. My father was killed in the war. And then Mom . . .' He shook his head as if he couldn't find the words, and for a second Karen thought he was going to give up, but the spasm passed.

'Well, our mom, she tried her best, but she couldn't cope with it all – like, all of us on her own, and Dad gone. And I came home that day and—' He looked up, indicated something hanging. 'There she was . . .'

Karen sat, stunned.

'So there was nothing for it – we was taken to the Home.'

'Oh, Dad, why've you never said before?' Tearful, she went to reach out to him, take his skinny, scrawny arm, but he withdrew and got up out of the chair.

'Sad times,' he said, looking away. 'But you have to get through them. Put it be'ind yer. It was all a long time ago now.'

They watched TV together, the *News at Ten*. Karen made cups of tea and brought them through, treating her father tenderly. The phone rang just after the break. Karen rushed to answer.

'Hello? Jo? How are you? How's Amy? Oh, you've been into town again – that's good.'

Nothing much had changed. Joanne always wanted to know about Dave: had he been round? (He hadn't, not for a while now.) What was happening? Saying that she'd leave it one more week, but she couldn't stand the refuge much longer. Some of the women were okay, but there were kids there who were a nightmare.

'Joanne, Dad's here – he'd like a word.'

Karen beckoned Fred over. He took the receiver as if it was something burning hot and held it close to his ear in a wary fashion.

'Hello? Love?'

Karen heard the Pinky-and-Perky scramble of Joanne's words coming through the phone. She sounded upset.

'Yes, I know, love, I know. It's all right. No – of

course I don't, no. Well, yes, I s'pose you will have to sometime . . . No, no, I won't. Oh, I don't know about that. No – you look after yourself, love. Bye-bye then. Tara.'

'What about Mom?' Joanne said tearfully, when Karen was back on.

'She's still finding it all a bit difficult,' Karen said.

Margaret lay in bed, turning her head from side to side, trying to get comfortable.

She was still brimming with fury over Joanne, but Karen's words that evening had got through to her and shamed her: *And if you can't give support to your own daughter, instead of someone else's son* . . . Lifting herself on one elbow, she tilted the shade of the bedside light so that it wasn't shining in her eyes and took a sip of water. Once she was settled down again on her back, staring up at the walls, she tried to sift through the unfocused rage inside her and work out what she felt about things. Thoughts came to her like yells of protest in a debate.

Promises are meant to be kept!

Dave's a good boy – what's he ever done that's so terrible?

Nobody knows the meaning of sticking at things these days! *I've* stuck at it, God knows . . .

Some things must last – surely there must be something good that lasts?

Karen kept going on about Joanne making a choice. *She had to make a choice, Mom.* This, above all, made Margaret clench her fists with explosive rage.

You weren't supposed to have a choice!

'Why should she have a choice? When did *I* ever

have any choice?' she said out loud, her tone curdled with childish resentment. 'Choice? Since when has there ever been a choice – about anything. Tell me that, eh?'

Forty-Seven

Joanne was finding life in the refuge more and more difficult.

She saw Sooky again, and it was the best thing that happened all week. Each day there were the comings and goings of social workers. Megan had visited a number of times. They talked about Dave's caution from the police. Megan steered Joanne into thinking about her future. If she went back home, they would very likely be looking at a supervision order, a social worker visiting regularly for a time. Alternately, if she was going to leave him, they could offer help with finding accommodation.

Joanne felt paralysed and unable to decide anything.

'Just give me a few more days,' she pleaded. She knew they didn't want people lingering too long in the hostels. They were a refuge, but they were not to become home – too many others were waiting.

The difficulty lay partly in the days hanging so heavily, and all the uncertainty of her own future. But also in the stress and misery of living with some of the other women. Over the fortnight she had been there, she had got to know Doreen better than any of the others. Doreen was a cowed, depressed woman with a drink problem, but in her passive way she was pleasant, and she and Joanne sometimes sat and talked. Her son Danny also seemed to have a sweet nature, though he was fearful and changeable. Doreen told Joanne she had done the right thing, getting out before things got even worse.

'I should have left him years back,' she said, rocking back and forth as she did almost all the time. 'I blame myself. I never had the spirit for it – and I didn't feel I could leave the boys, not with him.'

Mariam, also, had begun to meet their eye. Every so often she was called into the office for conversations through interpreters, which left her frightened and weeping. Her case presented all sort of problems, Marcia said, the more so because of her age. At fifteen she could not be legally married in Britain. She was frightened of being deported and equally terrified of being sent back to her husband. But at least, Joanne found, they could exchange looks of sympathy now – she, Mariam and Doreen. Linda was locked in her own world, and psychiatric social workers were calling now. There was talk of her being taken into hospital.

It was Gina who caused all the trouble. In any case, all her emotional life flowed near the surface and was acted out in public. Now, in addition, the big toe of her left foot had gone septic. Since Gina caused a huge ruckus about everything she did, everyone soon knew about it. The pain this was causing her, and her resulting bad temper, brought on a crisis.

Late one afternoon Joanne was on her way downstairs to the kitchen to give Amy her tea. She stopped on the stairs, the rising sounds from the kitchen making her heart pound, as it did so easily these days: raised voices – Gina in full cry, shrill and out of control.

'We'll go back up and wait till they've finished, shall we, babby?' she murmured to Amy, who was in her arms. Amy looked at her, wide-eyed at the noises from below, and clung to her more tightly. 'Yes, it's not very nice, is it? It's just those naughty boys, don't you worry, pet.'

There was a smash of glass and then the sounds escalated, building into a piercing scream. Joanne's stomach turned over. A second later Mariam came tearing from the kitchen and across the hall to hammer on the office door, just as Jackie, hearing the noise, opened it. Mariam, who appeared terrified, beckoned to her urgently.

The screams from the kitchen were like those of a pig being killed. Doreen silently joined Joanne on the stairs, holding Danny by the hand. Danny hid his face in his mother's waist.

'It's Gina,' Joanne said. As if she needed to.

Jackie's muscular form rushed back across the hall to the office. They heard her phoning. A few moments later she crossed the hall again and returned leading a limping, loudly sobbing Gina and the boys, the younger of them shrieking and sobbing, clutching a blood-soaked cloth to his face, which was contorted in pain.

'Oh my God!' Doreen breathed, sinking down on the stairs.

'What the hell has she done?' Joanne said. The sight chilled her right through. Amy started to cry.

'The boys won't be coming back,' Jackie said, when Gina and her sons had been taken in the ambulance. Her sallow skin had gone pale and she was visibly shaking. Joanne, Doreen and Mariam were standing in the office.

'Her social worker is on her way to the hospital –

Jason and Michael will be going into care.' Jackie seemed to need to recite events, as if to make sure she had done everything necessary. The line between staff and inmates suddenly felt very thin. 'I've had to call the police as well. God, she really has reached the end of the line.'

'What exactly happened?' Doreen asked.

Jackie looked at Mariam, who was wide-eyed with shock and obviously close to tears.

'Mariam was the only one in there. One of the interpreters is on her way: we need to get the details straight . . . But Gina obviously lost it with them – well, with Michael, it seems. She smashed a glass and just went for him . . . slashed right across his cheek.'

Michael, the one with the face of an angel.

'Marcia says she's got form – with adults as well. It's not just her old man who's violent.'

They all tried to comfort Mariam, and their kindness needed no translation. Doreen stroked her back gently as the tears ran down her face. Soon the interpreter came, Mrs Akhtar, a motherly middle-aged lady who took charge of the girl.

Joanne fed Amy, her thoughts racing. The incident had shaken her deeply. I've got to get out of here, she thought. After all this, even Dave suddenly felt comfortingly familiar, when contrasted with the world of Gina and the other women, the cycles of violence and depression in which they existed. Surely Dave must have had time to see sense now, at least enough for them to talk? She just had to go home and try and sort things out.

The house was quieter that night without Gina's

boys. Joanne decided to phone earlier than usual. She'd been touched by Dad speaking to her the other day – and he'd had a little chat with her again just the other night. He never had much to say at the best of times, but at least he was trying. Mom was unlikely to answer the phone anyway. Once she'd got Amy down to sleep, she got some change out of her purse and called them, determined to announce that she was going to come back and give it a try.

Karen answered the phone, her 'Hello?' sounding guarded and anxious. 'Oh!'' she cried when Joanne announced herself. 'Thank God, I've been doing my nut!' She drew in a deep breath. 'Look, something's happened. It's Dave . . . You're going to have to come – straight away.'

October–December 1984

Forty-Eight

Sooky buttoned her mac and bent to pick up her bag while Meena stood watching, with Priya in her arms.

Guru Nanak also observed the proceedings with a benign expression from the wall behind them, his hand raised in a blessing, which Sooky truly needed and appreciated. She felt very vulnerable this week, a new student and leaving Priya behind.

'So, you have everything – money, food, all your books for study?'

Mom was fussing around the way she did when Sooky was a little girl going to school, and Sooky was touched by it.

'Yes, I'm fine *Mata-ji*. I've got all I need.'

Meena looked her up and down: her Sukhdeep, a modern young woman, today in jeans and her black blouse, the smart, tan-coloured raincoat over the top, the belt tied tightly at the waist, hair back in a pony-tail.

'You look nice,' she said, suddenly shy. '*Chic*. See, some English words I know.'

Sooky grinned. 'Actually I think that's French, but never mind.'

'Mommy go?' Priya said, reaching for her. But Sooky could see she was all right – she was already used to staying with her grandmother.

'See you later . . .' Sooky kissed her daughter and

mother and slipped out into the drizzle to catch the first of her two buses across town to Perry Barr.

It wasn't a very nice day, and when she stepped off the first bus in town into the drizzle, she wished she'd brought an umbrella. Walking among the crowds in Corporation Street, all on their way to work, or students like herself, Sooky felt a surge of happiness amid her nerves.

She glanced up at the high, elegant buildings, loving being anonymous in a crowd where it was unlikely there would be anyone who knew Mom and Dad from the neighbourhood, the *gurdwara* or any of the other Sikh networks that seemed to loop like vine tendrils round the city, their eyes wide-open for gossip. It wasn't as if she wanted to spend her whole time obsessing about being a Sikh, the way Raj did. She just longed to get on with her life! Out here, this morning, she felt younger again, and strangely naked not pushing a buggy. Just her on her own – a student. She was going to do a degree, achieve something! It felt like a miracle.

Reaching her next bus stop, she stood behind a skinny Asian lad in jeans and black Puma trainers. He kept circling his shoulders as if they were stiff, and she realized he was very tense. For a moment she was curious, then dismissed it. There were dozens of things he might be tense about. Such was life. But something about the way he was standing reminded her of Jaz.

It set her thinking about Jaz, how she might still be there, in Derby; he in his flash suits, she ministering to his scowling presence. Now and then they'd shared a joke together, at the beginning. Then for evermore it was two magnets, repelling each other. Shame washed through her for a moment, especially when she thought of her parents and of his. Part of the fault lay with her: she should never have agreed to marry him so quickly.

The bus swung into view and she pushed these painful thoughts from her mind. Here she was, with pens and files and pads of A4 paper waiting to be filled. She couldn't wait to get stuck into her studies. She had been in just once before to fill in forms and meet her study group. Most of them seemed nice, and as they were part-timers, most – like her – were older than normal student age. One or two looked as if they might want to be friends. Life was looking up. And as well as all this, she had Joanne and Amy.

'I'll be at the Poly on Tuesdays now,' she had told Joanne last time they met. 'So maybe we could meet up some other day – in the afternoon?'

Joanne had looked pleased and grateful to be asked.

The bus swung away. Sooky was in a window seat, and for once the window was quite clean. She looked out eagerly, as if rediscovering life. It was so good just to be out and about! Office blocks slid past, the bus leaned its way round roundabouts.

She thought about her mom. She would never have dreamed of doing anything like this – it was beyond any of her expectations. But Sooky knew that, despite everything that had happened, Meena was proud of her, and that meant everything to her. Life felt so much better now that Mom was talking to her again. She didn't want the talking to stop. It was like a thread that bound them all together, sharing words and feelings after the cruel desert of silence. Whenever the moment seemed right, Sooky kept asking her things. More and more came out: sadnesses, struggles – about India and Smethwick, and how it had been coming to England.

One day Meena had told her about her friend Tavleen and what had happened to her. Sooky felt very tender to her mom, now she had opened up a bit more. And Meena seemed more relaxed too; she was smiling, laughing more.

Sooky thought about her grandmother's life in the Indian sector of Punjab, of her being first abducted, then forcibly returned – having no say of her own. Then of Mom, making this huge step of coming to England, following her husband. No wonder Mom had clung desperately to the ways she knew from home. And now of herself, a student – probably the first in generations of women in her family ever to be able to read and write properly, let alone in English. And the next generation after that?

She saw Priya's little face in her mind's eye and smiled.

Forty-Nine

Meena went to the window and watched as Sooky disappeared along the street, muttering a blessing of her own. Pride swelled within her, not unmixed with other feelings.

The morning of Sukhdeep's first visit to the Poly for registration, Khushwant had kissed his daughter's forehead before she left.

'So, the student begins on her studies. Soon, *beteh*, you will be Prime Minister – like Mrs Thatcher.'

'God, I hope not!' Sooky said.

But there were tears in her eyes at receiving all this support and approval. Meena knew that the question of marriage had been shelved – for the moment. But it would not go away. What else could they do? Should Sukhdeep live at home, shamed, forever?

She *was* proud, all the same. Two children studying in university! Pav had got two As and a B in his A-levels and had just begun on a degree at Aston in electrical engineering.

Meena took Priya into the kitchen, then put her down. 'I don't know why I'm carrying you, lazy girl! You aren't a baby any more. You want a drink?' She spoke in Punjabi – she wanted Priya to know the language.

She sat Priya at the table, enjoying the lull before Roopinder came down with her two, her face sulky, belly jutting out. Roopinder loathed being pregnant and made everyone else suffer as a consequence. She expected to be waited on like a queen.

Priya sipped orange juice, suddenly still and quiet.

'Mummy has gone to college,' Meena told her, bringing her tea over to the table, a couple of Rich Tea biscuits lodged in the saucer. She sat down, straightening her *chunni* – yellow today – round her neck.

'Granny go college!' Priya said, pointing with an impish grin.

'Ah, no, no, no,' Meena laughed. 'Old ladies do not go to college!'

She felt no envy of Sooky being a student. Not that. It was too far from her, she who had had barely even a basic education in India. Things had been too disrupted – and she was a girl. She had learned the rudiments of reading and writing in Punjabi. But she had never expected much. It had never occurred to her to have big dreams. Her hope had been for marriage and children, a home of her own, for things to work out right. Having Priya to look after now gave her a sense of purpose.

But there *was* something she envied. She sat, enjoying the few minutes' peace, cradling her teacup, thinking about it. What was that something?

Picturing Sukhdeep walking away from her to the bus stop, she realized it was the way her daughter seemed to feel at home. This was Britain, the country where she was born. She stepped out of the door in her jeans, a smart leather bag from the factory over her shoulder, seeing only the city where she had grown up. Of course she understood that her parents had come from elsewhere. But she did not spend her life mentally looking over her shoulder at another country, as her mother did; and, Meena knew sadly, as Raj did too. A place that was once home, but could be no more, because they had moved too far from it in every way. Those who went back to visit said things were changing – even in the villages, though they were the last to hear the flutes of time beckoning them into new ways. Many of them had electric lights now, and televisions. Sometimes Nirmal told her things about modern India: women working in shiny office blocks, divorcing even, through their own choice! Of course Nirmal lived in the big city – in Delhi. But Meena still found it hard to believe. In her mind, India was eternal and unchanging, the way she had tried to be herself.

'Priya go college!' the little girl cried irrepressibly, holding up her cup as if toasting life.

Meena laughed and reached across to chuck her cheek.

'Cheeky girl! Yes, maybe you will. But that is a long time away.'

Even Khushwant had noticed that Meena seemed happier in herself. He thought it was because of Pav's A-level results and Harpreet's GCSEs (six As, three Bs, one C – the last in mathematics, which she loathed with a passion). All very satisfactory. And Meena was more proud and happy about that than she could say.

But it was the talking as well – the talk of women. She had sat with her daughters and told them things that had been locked in her heart for decades. It had begun to ease her.

That afternoon she took Priya out in her buggy, a blanket tucked round her knees and the rainhood clipped on. She knew that if she pushed Priya along the road, it was the one way to get the lively little girl to sleep at last. It was only spitting a little now and she put on her coat, securing her *chunni* tightly, and took an umbrella. It was October, and already cold enough to have tights on under her *salwar* trousers. She cursed this cool, mizzling weather. Why could it not just rain wholeheartedly – or not rain, instead of hanging somewhere in between for days on end? The endless greyness leached the colour out of everything.

On a whim, Meena did something she had never done before: she pushed a sleepy Priya along Hampstead Road and turned into the cemetery of the big red church, the other side of the railings from the park. She knew it was all right to walk in here because she had seen people in there before, strolling up and down, gazing at the gravestones.

There was no one else there today, though. Half-afraid, she pushed Priya ahead of her along paths that had been reclaimed from the overgrown green chaos, shrouded on each side by trees, so that it was like walking through a tunnel. Bramble thorns scraped at her clothes, and gravestones poked up out of the tall grass as if they were holding their heads above water. An obelisk loomed suddenly in front of her, topped with a hat of ivy.

Some of the graves had graffiti scrawled on them. She saw glue-sniffer havens, reeking plastic bags strewn among the bushes. The thought of all that might go on in here made her shudder. But she did wish she could make sense of the writing on the gravestones and read the names, as a mark of respect. Her lack of English still held her at a distance from this place, which had had to become home.

Reaching a clearer patch, she looked down through

the railings to the lake in the park, thinking of her children, her daughters in particular.

It was true that she had talked to them – but there were some things she would never tell them. Things that held too much shame and horror.

Thaya Gurbir, her father's elder brother, who had left the town with them that night, was one of those things. He had taken everything from her except her actual virginity. On those stifling afternoons in Amritsar, her aunt, *Thayi-ji* Amarpreet, slept on the floor upstairs, lying on her side to ease the weight of her pregnant belly. Her grandparents would be sleeping too, and Meena would pretend to be dozing beside Amarpreet, all the time with her heart thudding, ears pricked for his every move. He would lean over and shake her, placing a finger to his lips. Sometimes he would even begin to interfere with her beside his sleeping wife, his breath catching in excited gasps. Meena wondered now: could Amarpreet really have been asleep all the time? Did she just turn away, knowing what was going on?

Often he would seize her hand and pull her to the only place in the little dwelling not occupied by others: the stairs. They were brick steps, their hard edges digging into her back, her neck. The harsh, concentrated look on his face stopped her from crying out, whatever her pain.

Amarpreet never left the house. She was afraid in this new neighbourhood so far from home, where violence and fear were woven into every day. Nirmal and *Dhada-ji*, her father's father, were the ones who went out to buy food. Gurbir whined his uselessness.

'I'm no good for this. My foot . . .' It was twisted and deformed.

So, during those months in that crowded house, every chance he could find, he had molested her again and again. Once, just once, while Amarpreet was cooking, he managed to get her upstairs, his weight pinning her to the floor, one hand over her mouth, stifling her as he jerked against her, her clothes sticky when at last he rolled off; she knew this should not be happening, but could find no words or anyone to say them to. And in those seconds after Sukhdeep told her what Jaz was doing to Priya, her instant thought was: *get that little girl away from him.* And nothing else had mattered. And afterwards, the clash of anger and shame and sorrow had silenced her.

But there was worse shame even than Gurbir's disgusting molestation. When he died – oh, how she had rejoiced! She had dreamed of his death, longed for it, so that in some infant part of herself she thought she had caused it. Such wicked thoughts had boiled in her head: *I hate you, I hate you . . . ! I'm glad you are dead!* Had the flashing loathing in her eyes tindered a spark that started the flames?

She was not glad about Amarpreet or the baby. Her mourning for them was genuine. The terror, the smells and sounds of the fire still came back to her in her dreams. But Gurbir . . . It meant that afterwards she lived just with her beloved Nirmal and her grandparents in Delhi, which had been heaven in comparison. Sometimes she thought that what had happened had been Gurbir's punishment. The fire saved her.

She walked on, knowing that if she stayed still too long, Priya would wake. The rain was holding off, though there was a strong breeze. But she was restless and turned into the park to walk round the boating lake. Mallards and Canada geese glided close to her hopefully, then retreated again when no food was forthcoming.

It was too cold for sitting. Meena kept walking slowly, round and round. Her thoughts were dark and relentless.

Mother, daughter, granddaughter . . .

Mother, mother, mother . . .

She could still hear her father's tormented calling into the dense Punjab night: 'Jasleen! Wife . . . *Jasleen!*'

His cries were met only by silence. Yet even after Jasleen was returned to them from Pakistan, the brutal silence continued.

It was June, just a few weeks after her mother had come back, to that scrubby part of Delhi where they perched to make a new life. Not like the new, Seventies-built development where Nirmal lived now. He had done well, her uncle, with his beloved taxi.

It was the height of summer: the sun was beating down and Meena had fallen sick. At midday the heat was almost unbearable. Meena's grandmother was no longer alive, but *Dhada-ji*, a frail old man now, was lying on a string bed across the room, his stick-legs slack, mouth lolling open. Meena heard flies droning round the room. A truck started up somewhere in the road beyond. Sounds bulged close, then far away in her feverish state.

Jasleen came to her and lifted her swimming head, made her sip water. Her mother's eyes looked down at her, intent, but detached. As usual, she spoke not a word. Meena felt practical duty coming from her, but not love. Her feet padded into the back room where she did the cooking, the light chink-chink of anklets tracing her every move. The rooms were divided by a threadbare sheet of muslin that hung in the doorway. Sometimes they poured water over it to cool the house, and it helped keep the flies at bay.

Meena lay in a daze, penetrated now and then by tiny sounds from the other room. There were repeated splashes of water, the clink of a brass pot, a light swish of material. Sometime later, out of the silence, after sensing rather than hearing more movements, she heard a gossamer thread of sound, only a fraction louder than the hum of the flies, but it jolted her eyes open, made her heart drum in terror . . .

'Allahu Akbar . . . Subhana rabbiyal adheem . . . Sam'i Allahu liman hamidah, Rabbana wa lakal hamd . . . Allahu Akbar . . . Allahu Akbar . . .'

Now, so many years later, pushing her granddaughter round this English park, Meena could feel afresh the gut horror that had possessed her when she heard the secret whispering of these Muslim prayers threading through the air of their Sikh household.

My mother is . . . My mother is one of those . . . Those from whom they had fled, who had murdered their people, abducted their women, who were to be hated and feared . . .

Shrouded in fever, she had told herself it was a nightmare. Never again in the years she lived with her mother was she aware of this happening, and her father certainly never caught Jasleen praying as a Muslim. Did he ever know? Jasleen submitted to his ways, went with him to the *gurdwara* as she had done before. Her husband was a Sikh. She was a Sikh. Meena chose to forget.

My mother . . . All the deaths, the killing of sisters, mothers, daughters, the upheaval of thousands upon thousands to prevent this: conversion, desecration and shame ... *Her mother whispering Mussalman prayers* ... Meena felt the same revulsion rising in her fresh and primitive: it was all they had left home to escape, fleeing to the new India so as not to live in Muslim Pakistan. It was the greatest, unspeakable shame, something she knew she could never reveal, not to her daughters, not to anyone.

What had befallen Jasleen in almost four missing years? Had it been a forced, fearful conversion for the sake of survival? Or had it been love and the turning of her heart to the religion in which she would have had to bring up her two sons?

Meena's chest ached with the unshed tears of all those years ago, rising fresh in her now. Her mother had been snatched from her in every way. Even years later, though she never once spoke of her feelings, Jasleen seemed only ever to be in Delhi on sufferance. She too must have spent her life looking over her shoulder, at that other country that in her heart was home, but could be home no more.

Meena stopped at the side of the water and put one hand over her face. She felt a few drops of rain start to fall.

And what was Raj doing? Her son's intense face came into her mind. Wasn't he spending his life dreaming of a country that did not even exist, a Sikh homeland in which to cradle his needs?

She blamed herself – for the example she had set. How had she not taught him to *be here*, now, in the place where he really was, where he had to learn to belong, instead of living a dream?

Fifty

Joanne stood in the corridor outside the ward at Dudley Road Hospital.

The doors kept opening and closing with a suck of air as people passed in and out. Most of them held one door open and looked enquiringly at her, but she kept shaking her head and staying put by the wall, trying to compose herself.

At last a young nurse, on her way back in, spoke to her kindly. 'Are you here to see someone?'

Joanne nodded, and then they were inside the door and she was walking past the bays of beds towards him.

What had she expected? It wasn't a question of blood, of injury or disfigurement. In a way, what she saw was worse. Dave was propped up in bed, looking fixedly across the room towards the window, not doing anything. Just staring.

Joanne couldn't help feeling suspicious: was this just another way of trying to control her, a self-pitying dramatic act to blackmail her into coming home?

She crept forward into his eyeline, feeling the other patients looking at her. He focused on her, she was sure of it, but gave no reaction that she could see.

Eventually she managed to say, 'Dave?'

*

Al and Stuart, the two mechanics at the garage, had found him outside. They had thought nothing of it when Dave went out to the yard, as they all came and went throughout the day. It was some time before they noticed that he hadn't come back.

'Al thought he'd gone off home,' Karen had told Joanne on the phone. 'They couldn't see him at first, because he'd gone and sat himself round by the wall over at the side. It really upset Al – he said he'd never seen anything like it. Dave was just sitting there on the ground with his head against the wall, staring up at the sky. He couldn't seem to move – could hardly even speak – and he was a funny colour ... Al said they could see there was something really wrong. Course they tried to get him up, but Dave wasn't having it. That's why they called an ambulance in the end.'

'Well, what's the matter with him?' Joanne had asked.

'They don't really know. Some sort of breakdown. He's not said a word except that he wants you.'

Would he lash out at her? Surely not, in here, with all these people watching? But she was still afraid. It had become a habit. Cautiously, she sat down on the chair next to the bed.

Dave didn't speak, but she could feel emotion coming from him. His breathing deepened and became louder, alarming her because she couldn't work out what was going on.

'How are you?' she asked matter-of-factly.

There was no reply, but when she dared turn and look at him, he was shaking his head, tears welling in his eyes. In silence he let them roll down his cheeks, but though she waited, he still couldn't seem to speak. With a growing sense of compassion, she began to realize what a state he was in. He looked different: the sharp-edged, spruce Dave had slackened into someone who looked winded and defenceless.

She wanted to say, 'I'm sorry. I'm sorry for leaving you . . .' But she was still too hurt. She needed to hear his apology too, not just see his self-pity.

When she had sat for some time, he wiped his face with the back of his hand. She stood up to pass him some tissues.

'I'd best be off – Mom's got Amy.' She'd spent the morning trekking back and forth on buses to drop Amy off. 'But I'll come tomorrow. Maybe I'll bring her.'

Dave moved his head as if to say something, but she was turning away. He'd had plenty of chance to speak.

'See you then,' she said.

On the way out, one of the staff nurses intercepted her. She was a petite blonde woman about Joanne's age. Joanne felt rather awed by her, as well as wondering how on earth someone so small could manage to lift some of the big men on the ward.

'Are you Mrs Marshall?'

Joanne felt on the defensive immediately. *You caused this. You left him* – wasn't that what everyone would be thinking?

'Yeah,' she said, more aggressively than she intended.

'It's all right, I just wanted a quick word.' She drew Joanne close to the wall near the doors. 'Mr Marshall's mother has been in and has said that he could be discharged to her house. We're getting a psychiatric assessment done on him, but physically there's nothing

wrong with him, so we can't keep him in here for long
– d'you understand?'

Does she think I'm thick? Joanne thought, even
though she could see the nurse was being quite kind.

'Well, yeah.'

'I just wanted to ask your opinion – about the
discharge. Mr Marshall has not stated any preference
himself, but . . .' She spoke as tactfully as she could.
'Mrs Marshall – his mother, I mean – did mention that
you are not living at home at the moment. So are you
happy with him being discharged to her house?'

Joanne's mind raced. It was hard to think straight
about any of this. 'Yes – well, I think so. That might be
the best thing.'

'Right,' the nurse said, looking relieved. 'That's all
right then. I just wanted to check with you.'

On the stairs she met Wendy, who seemed to be
dressed today in the guise of a fortune-teller. She had
on a very full, calf-length black skirt with a red band
running round it about six inches from the bottom; a
black lacy blouse with a fringed black shawl over it;
and her hair, which was now dyed a dark, coppery
brown, was piled exotically on her head and held with
pins and combs. She was thickly made up, her lips a
glossy scarlet.

'Oh, Joanne! You've come back to him – oh, love,
I'm so glad!'

Joanne found herself enveloped in lace and scent as
both of them teetered on the same step of the stairs.

'Well, I've come to see him,' she said.

'D'you know,' Wendy confided, her mascaraed

lashes fluttering earnestly, 'I'm going to take him home – they've told you, haven't they?'

'Yes – listen, thanks, Wendy . . .'

'My poor boy. I know exactly what's wrong: his *ch'i* has got completely out of balance. I have a friend who can help . . . And I've got a room ready for him with exactly the right *flow* in it. I've got rid of those awful curtains – the new ones are a bamboo colour . . . Now—' She put her head on one side, stopping herself in full flow and smiled.

Joanne couldn't help smiling back. Wendy was a good sort, despite her crazes. Other people passed up and down the stairs around them as if they were a traffic island.

'I don't know what's been going on between you two, exactly. I've heard things I'd rather *never* have heard about my own son, and I'm not going to call you a liar because I've never known you to be one, Joanne. He's admitted a certain amount to me anyway – and there were the police . . . Oh, Joanne.' She laid a hand over her heart. 'I never thought I'd see my boy taken in by the police. Not for that.'

Joanne found herself feeling almost as if she ought to apologize, but she said nothing.

'Anyhow,' Wendy rallied herself. 'Dave'll come home with me and we'll take it from there, shall we?'

Joanne nodded gratefully.

'He needs to see his daughter. Don't keep her from him, love?'

'Okay,' Joanne said. 'I'll bring her in.'

Wendy moved her head back to look carefully at Joanne. 'Are you going to move back home? Don't you think it's time?'

Tears slid into Joanne's eyes and she looked away,

shrugging. 'I don't know.' After a moment she turned back to Wendy. 'If I did, he'd better not come back – not yet.'

They parted with a hug and Joanne realized she was lucky. Some mothers-in-law would have taken sides with a vengeance, no matter what their sons had done.

As she walked out to the traffic-clogged Dudley Road, she felt drained and exhausted. Nothing could go back to being just as it was. She saw that now, even if she had not seen it before. It wasn't just that she had left home: everything had changed. It was like rebuilding a house after an earthquake – if anything *could* be rebuilt. She and Dave would have to start from a quite new place.

Mom had not been quite as snotty with her as she expected, when she'd gone to drop Amy off late that morning, before the hospital visit.

'You'd better come in,' was all she said when Joanne arrived. Her tone was ominous and Joanne expected a diatribe, but it never came. She'd been away from home nearly three weeks – maybe they'd all got past the explosive stage and come to terms with it a bit. And Wendy would have talked to Margaret, as well as Karen.

Margaret had greeted Amy in her usual way, and Amy looked at first dazed, and then delighted to be back with Nanna in a familiar place at last.

'You're going to the hospital then?' Margaret said, going to the ashtray on the TV to stub out her cigarette. 'What's actually up with him?'

'I don't know really.'

'Karen says he's had a breakdown – but you know

what she's like,' Margaret said, as if she doubted anyone did ever really have a breakdown and considered such a thing to be some sort of myth. She often seemed annoyed with other people for having emotions.

'Anyroad, go and do what you need to do,' she said gruffly. 'There's no need to come carting over here all again later – your father can drop her back.'

'I'll have to meet him in town,' Joanne said. 'I'm not allowed to tell him where the refuge is.'

Now that she had seen Dave, and knew she could move back home without him being there, Joanne couldn't get there fast enough. Suddenly the prospect of another night in the refuge was unthinkable.

She hurried to the nearest callbox.

'Mom?' She felt excited. 'I'm going home. I've got to get my stuff, so tell Dad he can drop Amy off at home. I should be there after five o'clock!'

Fifty-One

Joanne spent her first half-hour at home wandering from room to room. Every inch of it was so familiar, but it felt as if she had been away for years.

It was upstairs that made her emotional: the sight of Amy's little bed with her bears and other toys rowed up on it, and their bed – hers and Dave's. She had pulled the duvet up over it before leaving, and it seemed just as she had left it. It was remembering how things had been when they were good that hurt the most. *I want my man back* . . . Thinking of all the nights they had lain there together, she was almost overwhelmed with sadness and longing and made herself go back downstairs.

She was restless waiting for Amy to arrive. Instead of sitting fidgeting, she hurried out to buy milk, called in to see the Coles next door, then unpacked while drinking tea. At six she turned on the TV, realizing that she had heard no news in weeks. Horrifying images met her eyes: faces honed razor-sharp by starvation, clusters of flies round their eyes and mouths – the worst famine in recorded history in Ethiopia. Unable to bear the thin wails of anguish, she turned it off again.

'Thanks for everything,' she'd said to Marcia, who had hugged her goodbye and wished her luck, saying, in the nicest possible way, that they didn't want to see her back again. Megan would be round to see them both very soon. Marcia offered advice and caution.

'Be strong, girl – he's got to know he can't get away with it again. I've got faith in you.' She'd held Joanne's shoulders and looked deep into her eyes.

'Thanks, Marcia,' Joanne had said tearfully. 'Thanks for everything.'

Sue hadn't been there, but Joanne parted with Jackie as well. She was sad at the thought she would probably never see Marcia again. Doreen's doleful face had lifted into some sort of smile as they said goodbye and wished each other luck. Mariam, to Joanne's surprise, held out her arms and they hugged. By this time Gina had left (noisily and emotionally) to resume her life with the man Joanne thought of as 'psycho Benny' – without their children. Gina's life was too awful to think about: the refuge would almost certainly see her again.

The letterbox rattled and she leapt to her feet. Fred was at the door with Amy, and Karen as well.

'Welcome back, love,' he said awkwardly. But there was affection in his voice and sadness, not judgement.

'Thanks, Dad,' Joanne said, tears coming on again. 'You coming in for a cup of tea?'

Amy was running round, squeaking excitedly as she recognized toys she had not seen in weeks.

'How's Dave?' Karen asked as Joanne put the kettle on. The sisters stood in the kitchen, and Fred stayed with Amy.

'I don't know. Not too good,' Joanne said. 'He wouldn't really speak. It's . . . it's like he's in shock or something. Like someone who's been in an explosion. I even wondered at first,' she confided, 'whether he was putting it on, sort of thing.'

Karen had on her listening face. 'I think it's gone too far for that.'

'Well, I know – now I've seen him.'

As they drank their tea in the back room, they talked a bit about her visiting Dave at Wendy's in Northfield.

'It's a bit of a jaunt for yer,' Fred said.

'Maybe it's a good thing he's not too close,' Karen said. 'And his car's still at work, isn't it? So he's not going to turn up too easily.'

Joanne didn't feel like talking about it much. She needed time to think about what she was going to do.

'Mom seemed all right yesterday,' she said cautiously. 'How d'you think she's doing?'

'Oh, not too bad,' Fred said.

Realizing he would have said much the same if she had just contracted bubonic plague, Joanne looked at Karen.

'She's going along,' Karen said. 'I think she's coming round a bit. Yesterday she did say she thought she'd been a bit hard on you.'

'Did she?' Joanne said, feeling relieved.

Karen leaned forward. 'I think she needs to get out a bit, so she's not so sunk into herself. Actually, I had this idea about something she might like. The library are putting on this thing – it's called a reminiscence group – and they're going to be talking about the war first of all: people of Mom and Dad's age and older. They're saying people ought to record their memories before it's too late. She never talks about it, but I thought it might be a good way of, you know, sort of getting her going on things. Maybe even make some friends . . .'

'Can't see her going to that,' Fred said gloomily.

'To be honest, nor can I,' Joanne said. As usual, she saw, they were all tiptoeing round Mom as if she was a ticking bomb. 'Have you asked her?'

'Well, I did show her the leaflet,' Karen said. 'It's on a Thursday morning. She didn't say no straight away.'

'But she didn't say yes, either?'

'What she actually said was, "What's all this rubbish?" You know what she's like. But she did pick the leaflet up again.'

'What – to put it in the bin?' Joanne suggested.

'No! That was the thing. She put it down by the phone. Anyway, I did say to her I'd take the day off and go with her the first time, if she decided to go. I thought it might be interesting. But we're quite busy at work. Now you're back, I wondered if maybe you could go?'

'You mean if she suddenly decides to go?'

'Well, yeah.'

'But she won't, will she?'

Once they had gone and she had Amy tucked up in bed, Joanne began to feel very stressed and uneasy. The nights were drawing in and it was soon dark. Several times she went to the front door to make sure it was locked and that the chain was fastened. Then she checked the back. She realized she still had a split image of Dave in her mind. There was the helpless, seemingly broken man lying prone in a hospital bed. She recalled his tears, his desperate silence. Surely no one could put that on? But the controlling, scheming, violent Dave still haunted her mind. Did he know she was home? What if he discharged himself and came back? What might he do then?

Mrs Coles had told her to call in any time she was worried or wanted anything. But Joanne didn't feel like sitting with the Coles, kind as they were. And she couldn't keep phoning Karen. Instead, she searched her bag and found the scrap of paper on which Sooky had written her number, saying it was fine to call her.

'Are you sure?' Joanne had said. 'It wouldn't get you into trouble?'

'No, of course not! You can phone any time. Why not?'

She felt nervous dialling the number, unsure what to expect, and once it was ringing she almost chickened out and put the receiver down. But she was in need of a friend.

A male voice answered, nasal and not all that old. One of her brothers, Joanne thought, not her father. 'Yeah? Hello?'

'Hello, can I speak to Sooky please?'

'Sooky? Yeah, hang on ... Sukhdeep – phone!' The yell switched into Punjabi. There was an uncomfortable pause, then she heard Sooky's gentle voice say, 'Hello?'

When Joanne told her who it was, she sounded pleased. 'You phoned! Oh, it's really nice to hear from you! How are you?'

'I'm back home,' Joanne said, feeling her composure slipping. She wanted Sooky to say that she'd come round now – keep her company.

'Are you? That's great. I mean, is it? What about ... ?'

Joanne explained and Sooky was full of sympathy. 'Look, I'm just starting on my first assignment tonight, but why don't you come over with Amy one afternoon this week? Priya would love to see her. It'd be fun.'

They agreed on an afternoon. She would fit visiting Dave around it somehow. When she'd put the phone down, Joanne sat for a long time, hugging her knees, rocking gently back and forth.

The next afternoon she took Amy to visit Dave. She was glad he was still in the hospital, a public, neutral place. Wendy would be along at some point as well. She felt very grateful to her mother-in-law, who despite her ditzy ways could be suddenly practical.

Amy caught sight of him along the ward and cried, 'Dadda! Dadda!', squirming to be put down.

Hearing Amy's voice, Dave turned his head and Joanne saw a smile appear on his lips. She put Amy down and the little girl ran to her father. Dave managed to reach down and lift her up onto his body, cuddling her tightly. His chest began to heave. He was holding her too tightly, and as Joanne reached the bed she saw his face contort and Amy was pulling away, panicking, crying out, 'No! Don't like it!'

'Sorry – sorry, bab,' he said releasing her. 'I never meant . . .'

Amy was sliding off the bed with a tight, terrified look. She ran to Joanne and clung to her leg, bursting into tears.

'Oh, Amy, it's all right!' Joanne said, upset. She could see the terrible hurt on Dave's face, knew he had not meant to frighten his daughter. But she could feel all Amy's distress and shock in this strange place, after all the changes of the past weeks.

'Oh dear, what's the matter?' One of the nurses was down their end of the bay and came over to them.

'It's me,' Dave choked. 'I can't even get that right.'

'It's okay,' Joanne said, heaving Amy up into her

arms. She felt like crying herself. 'She's had a lot of changes and she's not used to seeing her dad like this.'

'No – it's a funny old place, hospital, isn't it?' The nurse was middle-aged and sweet, and jollied Amy along, though Joanne just wished she'd go away. 'You can come and talk to your daddy, can't you? He's just a bit poorly, but he's going to get better.'

She went off, a clipboard in her hand, but her last remarks were cheering.

Joanne sat down. To her surprise, Dave talked this time, at least about himself. That was all right. She knew they couldn't start on all the big things – not in here.

'They're sending me home tomorrow – to Mom's, I mean.'

'That's good,' Joanne said cautiously.

'Someone came to see me yesterday: some sort of psycho person . . .'

'Psychiatrist you mean?'

'I dunno, maybe. She said she thought I had a kind of breakdown – nervous exhaustion she said. Summat like that. She asked a few things and said a few other things, but I couldn't tell you what they were now. Summat about stuff I've buried needing to come out.'

'So – you need rest, that sort of thing?'

'Yeah.' He sighed, looking up at the ceiling. He wasn't propped up so high today, was almost lying down. 'I've got pills of some sort.' Awkwardly he added, 'And she said about counselling – summat like that.'

Joanne was amazed at his acceptance of this.

'D'you think that might be a good idea?' she asked cautiously.

He turned to her, seeming to need her approval. 'Well, I need summat, don't I? I can't go on the way I was.'

'Yeah, I s'pose,' she agreed.

There was a silence. He looked at Amy. 'I'm sorry, pet – I never meant to scare yer.'

Amy looked at him still with solemn reproach.

'Friends?' He held out his hand.

Amy hesitated. Then she nodded, and began to smile.

Fifty-Two

That Friday morning Margaret found she had done all her housework. She didn't even need any groceries. So she did something she hadn't done in years. Pulling on an extra cardi, she set off up the road to the park, on a walk for its own sake.

What would Karen say? Mom, boring old Mom, doing something different! The thought made her feel rather pleased with herself, as if she had a special secret all of her own.

It was only ten in the morning, sun and cloud alternating. The park was quiet, except for a couple of mothers pushing buggies and a scruffy man on a bench, who clearly had nowhere else to go.

She walked fast at first, glad to have a physical outlet for the feelings that kept surging through her. More than anything she felt cheated of the life she might have had, right from the word go. If only Mom had not been sick, if the war had not ruined everything, giving her a taste of something so much better than she had ever had before or since – a paradise snatched away. And then all these years she'd spent in thrall to Valium, a half-life, spent with a man who was only half a person.

The rage began to boil in her again, but she knew that, as much as anything, it was rage against herself. They had had serious words at home a few days ago. It was over Joanne again, of course. She had been furious with Joanne playing fast and loose, as she saw it, but now the truth was coming out about Dave: blue lights outside the house, social workers called in. Margaret was having to eat humble pie. She'd been wrong, assuming that Joanne was making it up. She'd had to swallow her pride and admit that, at least to herself. So she had said something harsher than she really meant to.

'When's running away from things ever done any good?' This was at the tea table.

And Fred – *Fred* had looked up at her and said, 'You're being too hard on the wench, Margaret. She's been a brave 'un, she has. You're her mother; you could show her a bit of kindness.'

Kindness. Margaret had been struck dumb at this, and Fred had got up with his tea and taken it into the front room by the telly.

But Karen was still there and she was brewing up some choice remarks. She'd sat there with that pert, clever-clever look she had these days and said, 'The thing you don't seem to get, Mom, is that sometimes things need to change, and someone has to do something about it. And I think the reason you're so down on Joanne is that she's had the courage to get up and fight against what's been happening to her. Well, maybe that's what you should've done years ago, Mom. And maybe you're just jealous because you never had the guts.'

Then she was off, tea in hand as well, and Margaret was left at the table, outraged at their attack on her and even more so because it was beginning to dawn on her that they were right. That maybe the fixed ideas that she had clung to had been more of a hindrance than a help.

She had reached the part of the park with the birdcages and sat down on a bench, her heart banging frighteningly hard. The emotions this outburst had caused had gushed through her like a tidal wave. She knew deep down that her gut reaction to Joanne taking off had been to envy and therefore condemn it. Just walking out – just like that! How *dare* she? Even at that moment, the other night, she'd followed the others into the front room and, over the voices of *Coronation Street*, announced, 'All right – I admit it. I've been too hard on her.'

Karen leaned forward and turned down the sound, looking round warily at her mother.

'Well, that's all I've got to say. I just never would've thought it of Dave, that's all. But I know Joanne's a good girl, and I should've seen it more from her point of view.'

They both stared at her.

'Well, good – that's good,' Karen said.

Since then Margaret had thought a lot about Joanne, trying to open herself up to her daughter and how she must feel, instead of putting rules in the way like walls. All her life Joanne had been a sweet-natured girl. Margaret felt quietly ashamed. It was true; what sort of a mom was she, carrying on like that, blaming her? Being in that refuge – it must have been horrible, frightening, for her and Amy, and all she'd done at the time was criticize. And what did it matter about anyone else and what they might think – even Dave? It was her daughter she should be putting first!

A young woman with blonde hair approached,

pushing a buggy in which sat a baby, about a year old. She smiled vaguely at Margaret as she wheeled the buggy close to the cages to show the little boy the budgies and canaries, the mynah bird that said, 'Hello Rocky!' if you waited patiently. She seemed a calm, patient mother.

Margaret watched, shuddering at the memory of that stage of her life. It hadn't been too bad with Joanne, those first years. She'd been a placid baby and it had still been early days in the marriage. It was after Karen that everything went wrong. Karen was more fractious, it was true, but it had not just been that. It was *her own fault*, the way she had sunk into a dark cavern of numbness and despair that she could not climb out of. She could not cope, was unable to make anyone hear her, even though in that numb silence she felt she was screaming and tearing at the walls.

One evening in particular burned corrosively in her memory. By now she had realized what Fred was like, the hollow man she had married. But this day, when Karen was about two months old and Joanne was approaching her third birthday, she had spent yet another day seeing no one but the two of them.

It was March, wet and blustery. Karen wouldn't settle. Margaret hadn't got on with breastfeeding either time, but the formula didn't seem to suit Karen, either. She squirmed and screamed endlessly. There was no way to get out of the house; the rain was too heavy. The hours crawled by. Margaret sat, feeling crushed by the weight of the house, her marriage and the demands of the two children. She could hardly breathe or move, let alone manage the simplest thing. She wanted to run into the street screaming crazily for someone – just anyone – to come and rescue her.

The day passed somehow. She managed to cook sausages for Fred's tea, with Karen held wailing against her shoulder. By the time he came in, the children were asleep for the moment. He ate, head down, saying very little. He barely looked at her. Margaret's inner being was shrieking, *Help me, for God's sake just help me!* But she had no idea how to ask, or what she really needed.

Fred finished his sausage and beans and looked up at her.

'I'm just off to the pub then. Back in a bit.'

And he was gone. And in that moment, which to her felt like a total betrayal, when she knew she was completely alone and always would be, however much she might be married, any feeling for him that still touched her heart was gone too.

Soon afterwards she went to the doctor and was drugged out of feeling anything much for the best part of twenty years.

The young woman moved away, leaving Margaret alone with the birds. The sun peeped round a cloud. She closed her eyes in the warmth and took deep breaths. There was a fruity smell of dying leaves.

I'm not used to all these feelings, she thought. That's my trouble. Karen was forever on about feelings, as if she was some sort of expert. On the other hand, it was Karen who, when not being bossy, said things that made her heart swell and gave her hope.

'Look, Mom,' she'd said yesterday. 'I know it must be hard, but you've got the chance of a new life. We're grown-up now – you don't have to stop in for us. You can do new things, have a life of your own. You don't have to just stay the same.'

She'd brought that leaflet about the thing at the

library. Of course Margaret's first reaction had been to dismiss it – a load of old folks rambling on. Stupid waste of time! But she kept seeing the leaflet there by the phone, and it needled her. She had to admit, she was curious. And she knew they all thought she'd never do anything, would just stay stuck in her ways.

Now that the rage had passed through her she caught a glimpse of excitement. Her head felt clearer. A new life? It was a queer thought. Frightening. But she'd seen the way they looked at her sometimes. The thing that had come home to her was that they'd respect her more for making changes than for staying in the same old rut.

I'll show them, she thought. I can do better than this, surely I can? And I'm only fifty – not quite over the hill yet. I've got life in me! I *can* be different.

Getting up, she strolled back between the grass and flowerbeds. For one thing, she'd come here, to the park, more often. It was soothing and gave you a chance to think. It would be part of her new start.

How did she want to be, she mused, now that she could begin to look at herself? What might she be like, the new Margaret Tolley? Calmer, for a start. More adventurous perhaps? Thinking back to the people in her life who had meant the most – the sisters in Buckley, Dora Jennings, her daughters, even Fred at times, who wasn't all bad – she saw that they had one thing in common. That's what I'd like to find most of all, she thought. Kindness. Above all, I'd like to be a bit kinder.

Fifty-Three

Sooky had said that it would be better if Joanne called round in the week, but she phoned on Saturday morning and said things were going to be unexpectedly quiet that afternoon – would Joanne like to bring Amy over then?

Joanne hesitated. Wendy was collecting Dave from the hospital and she did not know at what time. But he would need time to settle in – maybe it would be better if she didn't go over there today.

'That's really nice of you,' she told Sooky. 'I'd love to.'

Almost as soon as she'd put the phone down, it rang again. Karen.

'You'll never guess what!'

'No, I probably won't,' Joanne said wearily, hoping that whatever she was supposed not to be able to guess was not bad news.

'She's said she'll go. To the group. With you.'

'What?' Joanne's mind was so full of other things that she had no idea was Karen was on about.

'Mom – the thing at the library.'

'Oh!'

'You can go, can't you?'

'Thursday morning? I s'pose, yeah.' She didn't like to say she felt a bit resentful about it.

'Great!' Karen enthused. 'I could really do with being at work. That's really good!'

Joanne put the phone down. Great! Taking Mom out to some weird meeting. Was that great?

Sooky's house seemed big and imposing, a tall Edwardian semi with bay windows and mock-beams decorating the top storey. Joanne was relieved when it was Sooky who answered the door. She was dressed in a pink Punjabi suit, her hair loosely fastened, and was relaxed and smiling.

'Hi, come in! You found us all right then? Hello, Amy!'

Even though it had been quite a walk getting there, Amy hadn't fallen asleep. She had been excited about seeing her friend. Wheeling the buggy into the spacious hall, Joanne saw a black-and-grey carpet and religious pictures on the walls opposite. The house smelled different from what she was used to, with a spicy, perfumed atmosphere, but she couldn't have said what the smell was. Priya came running to them from the back, giggling.

'Come on in,' Sooky said.

In the front room there were leather sofas, a big TV set, on at low volume, and toys scattered across the floor. Joanne saw a woman sitting on one of the sofas with her legs drawn up under her, in a turquoise suit. As they came in, she drew her scarf up from where it was lying round her neck, to cover her head. She was middle-aged, a thin woman, with a sweet, kindly face, though it wore a closed, shy look.

'This is my mom,' Sooky said. 'She doesn't speak English really – not much.'

She said something to her mother and Joanne heard

her name, then Amy's. Joanne and Sooky's mother nodded solemnly at each other, and Joanne suddenly felt like a foreigner and wondered what Sooky's mom thought of her. But she saw a slight smile play round the woman's lips.

'Would you like a cup of tea?' Sooky asked.

'That'd be nice,' Joanne said. 'Thanks.'

'There's some ready,' Sooky said. 'I won't be long.'

Amy and Priya had already settled themselves in with the toys. Joanne felt awkward sitting there in silence with Sooky's mom, but she was watching TV and only glanced at Joanne now and then and gave a slight smile. After a few moments a girl appeared, plump and jolly-looking. with a round face and big, smiling eyes.

'Hello, I'm Harpreet.' She had jeans on and a jumper, and plonked herself on the sofa. 'I'm Sooky's sister. You must be Joanne?'

She chatted away saying that their dad was out, 'working as usual', and their big brother Raj and his wife had taken their children out shopping. 'Thank God!' She rolled her eyes, but didn't elaborate.

'And then there's my brother Pav – he's probably still asleep! He's a student; doing science is *so exhausting*!' She grinned, giving a satirical shrug. Joanne liked her immediately.

Sooky came back with tea and biscuits on a tray and served everyone.

'I made you English tea,' she said. 'I hope that's all right.'

'Fine,' Joanne said. 'Thanks.' She wasn't sure how else you might make tea.

They passed a lovely couple of hours. Joanne relaxed

as the two sisters chatted to her. Sooky told her about the Poly, and Harpreet about her A-levels: biology, chemistry and geography.

'That sounds hard,' Joanne said, feeling a bit inadequate. They all seemed to be very clever! 'What d'you want to do after?'

Harpreet shrugged. 'Dunno, really. Maybe pharmacy? The only thing is, I'm not very good at maths.'

As they talked, every so often their mother would ask something and they answered and translated, and she was kept half in the conversation. Then she turned a video on low and watched that part of the time, still joining in. Amy and Priya were in heaven, and the time flew by.

'Are you going back to the toddler group?' Sooky asked as Joanne got up to leave, realizing it was nearly dinner time.

'Oh – yes, I expect so. I hadn't thought.'

'I'm really sorry I'll be missing it. Tuesdays are full up for me.'

Joanne wished she could offer to take Priya, but it was just too far to come and bring her back.

'Maybe your mom could take her?' she asked.

'*Mata-ji*?' Sooky said. Joanne heard her suggesting this idea in her language.

Sooky's mom smiled shyly, but shook her head, motioning a negative with her hand as well.

'No, I thought not,' Sooky said. 'She's shy – and she can't really talk to anyone ... Never mind. Can we meet up again?'

'I'd love to,' Joanne said. She hesitated. 'I think I'll be on my own at home next week – d'you want to come to mine?'

She walked home pushing Amy and glowing with the warmth of friendship.

In the middle of the afternoon the phone rang again. It was Wendy, sounding upset.

'Joanne? It's all right – I've got him home. But I think you're going to have to come, love. I thought we'd just have a quiet day, you know, settling him in. But he wants you. That's the only thing he'll say.'

Joanne felt her stomach knot up. There was a long pause as she considered the business of getting to Northfield. It was after three already.

'Look, call for a taxi – I'll pay for it, love,' Wendy implored her. Joanne was touched. Wendy was not exactly flush for money. 'But please come, Joanne – I don't think I can cope with him if you don't.'

It started to rain as the taxi drove them across Birmingham, looping round the city, down through underpasses and out along the Bristol Road. Joanne kept her arm round Amy on the seat beside her. The trees were turning, the summer long gone, and the roads looked grey and anonymous. She felt sad and old suddenly. Her emotions were a ragbag of sorrow and longing, of hurt and anger. She thought about Gina, who seemed to consider being beaten as normal. Her mom, she'd said once, had flayed all her kids from pillar to post.

But it's not normal for me, Joanne thought, rage rising in her again at the memory of how much of it she had allowed, how far she had let Dave oppress her. She knew she had been pushed too far, and hurt too much, to spring lightly back into 'Let's just try again.' Not just like that. Something had been broken – the guarantee that they would always be together. After being in the refuge, everything looked different. She had made the break and distanced herself from him. She had discovered that she was capable of acting in her best interests and to protect Amy.

And yet . . . There was the Dave she knew the best of, the man she loved. There was all their past and what they'd shared, their growing up together. There was Amy . . . By the time the taxi drew up outside Wendy's little house (the Wendy House, as they all called it) she felt more confused than ever.

Wendy came out, not dolled up today. She did have her make-up on, but was wearing grey tracksuit trousers and a pink jumper, which clashed with her coppery hair, but made her look more motherly. She paid the driver, then touched Joanne's shoulder.

'Just go up to him, love,' she urged. 'I'll look after Amy. I don't see enough of her as it is, bless her. I'll bring you up some tea. Don't worry about anything else. Just go and talk to him – *please*.'

The house stank of smoke and air freshener. Joanne knew where to find Dave. There were only two bedrooms. She climbed the pink-carpeted stairs and stood outside the door, her heart pounding. In the end, she knocked and went in.

Dave was sitting on the edge of the bed, dressed in jeans and a navy jumper. It seemed odd to see him dressed. He was leaning forward, arms resting on his thighs, and he looked up at her.

'Jo . . .' He sat up, naturally polite, but was then at a loss. His face crumpled and he clasped his hands over it. His shoulders started to heave with sobs. The sound wrenched her inside.

Unsure what to do, she closed the door and sat beside him on the bed, feeling both tender and guarded. He wept loudly for a few moments and she did not touch him. Gulping, he removed his hands and tried to speak.

'I can't seem to stop bloody crying. I don't know what's wrong with me . . .'

She noticed that he didn't seem to be blaming her, that things had gone beyond that, and somehow that was a help.

'Don't you know?' she asked. 'Don't you have any idea?'

His face wet, he shook his head. After a pause he said, 'Maybe, if I'm really honest . . .' A little calmer now, he turned to her. 'God, Jo – I don't know. When the police came . . . I mean, I felt like a criminal. *Me*, a wife-beater. And Amy . . . The way they looked at me.'

Again, his hands went to his face and he broke down, shaking his head as if to chase the memory of it away. It was some time before he looked up at her again, his expression humble and begging.

'Look, will you give us a cuddle? Lie here with me a bit? It's been so long.' He saw her hesitate. 'I shan't hurt you. I'll never hurt you again.'

'You've said *that* before.' Her own hurt spilled out.

'I know.' He was still weeping and she relented, her tenderness winning.

'Come here,' she said, slipping her trainers off to climb on the bed behind him. She drew him into her arms and then they were both crying. She wept and wept, her head held against his chest, and for the first time in a long time things started to feel a little bit right.

'Thing is,' he said, when they were calmer, tissues scattered round the bed. 'I s'pose I've never been any good at facing up to things. You know, really obvious stuff like Dad dying suddenly, the way he did. That lady in the hospital – she only asked me a few things, really basic like, about Mom and Dad and whether I was married and all sorts, but she seemed to be able to see things I couldn't even see about myself. And she told me the best thing is to be really honest with yourself, if you can, and own up to what you really feel . . .'

'Like what?' Joanne asked. She didn't want him to stop talking.

'Well, it came out about the football – and Dad. I mean, I can't think about it all at once, but . . .' She felt him start to dissolve into tears again. 'It was like . . . my world ended,' he sobbed. 'My whole bloody world. With both – but I never . . . didn't let myself . . .' He let out a long, shuddering breath. 'It didn't seem right to, you know, make a fuss. And I don't think I'd've known how. It's like – well, now, as if it's all coming out at once. And look what I've done! I'm so scared, Jo. I don't want you to leave me . . . And what if they come and take Amy away?'

Joanne stroked him, held him as he cried.

'They won't. We'll have to make sure they don't.' She knew Megan would be round to see them, though. She stroked his shoulders and said sadly, 'I suppose it had to come out somehow. I just wish it hadn't been like this.'

She could see it all, had wondered sometimes. But how were you to be sure about someone else's feelings? She felt so sad for him, but for herself there was still a part of her that was wary and standing back from him.

When he'd cried for a while and more tissues were scattered, she said, 'What about us? What happened to us, Dave?'

'I think . . .' He hesitated. 'I dunno. I s'pose I didn't realize how small I felt inside – after the Villa and everything. Like I'd failed and wasn't good for much. But I s'pose I felt I had you, and back then it was more like – well, you sort of looked up to me . . .' In a moment of humour he added, 'Maybe I was just imagining that!'

'No, I did. You were older, for a start. And I'd've gone anywhere with you. I was mad about you – you know that.'

'Yeah,' he said sadly. 'I s'pose. It's just, after we had Amy, everything felt different. I mean, don't get me wrong, I'd never be without her. I love her to bits. But somehow . . .'

'She got all the attention?'

'No – well, yes, maybe a bit. But that wasn't really it. I think it was you: you seemed to grow up a lot all of a sudden. You were a mom – you're *good* at it. You knew what you were doing. It was as if you'd overtaken me, and I started to think: she'll just keep on like that, going on and past me, and she won't want me any more; I won't matter. And then when you started talking about work, or about doing more exams and that – A-levels – I dunno. It does something in my head. It's like a great big . . . panic. Like I've done nothing, got nothing, and there you are, all set to just speed off into the distance – without me. I never really *knew* that was what I was feeling because, well, I'm crap at that sort of thing. I just started to feel all tense and angry because I couldn't control any of it. I wanted to lash out. It was weird – the way it'd just come over me at odd moments. After you left, I was blind with it, to start with. As if I had to smash everything, try and control everything ... And then I realized I couldn't even control myself.'

'I never wanted to leave you, ever,' she said miserably. 'Not even when you started on me, or not at first anyway. But it was when you went for Amy ...'

'I know, I know ...'

They held each other in silence, each of them in tears.

Feet approached up the stairs, cups clinking.

'I've brought you a cup of tea,' Wendy said from behind the door. It was like something breaking in from another world.

Joanne got up and opened the door, wiping her face. Wendy eyed her warily.

'All right?'

'Yeah, thanks Wendy.' She took the tray from her mother-in-law. 'Is Amy okay?'

'Oh yes, she's fine. Good as gold. She's got the cartoons on, and she's had a drink and a biscuit.'

'Thanks,' Joanne said, trying to smile before she shut the door. 'I'll be down in a bit.'

They sat on the edge of the bed sipping tea. Neither of them wanted the Bourbons that Wendy had brought up.

'Mom's all right, isn't she?' Dave said. He looked like a little boy, his face blotched from crying.

'Yeah, she's great.'

'Jo?'

'Yeah?'

'Are you going to come back? I mean, can we . . . ?'

'I'm already back,' she said slowly. 'It's you who's not there at the moment.'

There was a long pause. She knew she could not just say 'yes'. Not just like that. She still felt cold inside, detached, as if something needed to grow back.

'Let's take it slowly.' She saw anger flicker across his face for a moment. He stared at her, then looked down. She could see his disappointment. He had wanted her to make everything better.

'You did something too big, Dave. I don't know if I can trust you. And it's not just us – there're other people involved now, social workers and everything. You need to get better. *We* need to get better. I just don't know yet if I can live with you again.'

Fifty-Four

The librarians ushered them enthusiastically towards the circle of chairs.

'That's it; do sit down wherever you want!'

Margaret hesitated, more accustomed to the idea of chairs in rows, where she could hide at the back, but seeing the librarian's eager smile, she picked one as far away from everyone else as possible. Joanne sat beside her, with Amy on her lap.

'Is it all right: me bringing her?' Joanne asked the librarian in charge, a homely lady with neatly coiffed brown hair and pink lipstick. She was wearing a badge that said AUDREY. 'I'll take her out if . . .'

'I'm sure it's perfectly all right,' the woman said, leaning down to talk to her. 'She's lovely – and people will be happy to see her.'

Margaret kept her handbag on her lap, gripping its familiar brown handles in case her hands got the shakes. She longed for a cigarette. What the hell am I doing here? she thought grumpily. Her enthusiasm for starting a new life had dwindled now that she was faced with the reality of it. But she wasn't going to back out, now that she'd said she'd come. And she saw it as a way of trying to make it up to Joanne.

It was good that it was Joanne here with her today, now that she had done the sensible thing and come home. Margaret had felt a sense of amazement, as she walked along the street beside her, that her daughter could have done such a thing. Shameful! Yet timid little Joanne – who would have thought she'd have the nerve? You didn't *do* that, up and leave like that. It was unthinkable; yet Joanne had done it! She still didn't *approve*, not of running out on your husband. But the lad had evidently been out of order. And she had to admit, the thought of it gave her a prickle of excitement, like a window being blown open on a view of things that was new to her.

Then there was this group thing. It'd be old folk who should know better maundering on, she had said to Karen. But she was here, wasn't she? Though she'd lowered her dosage of Valium, she was still never free of a variety of symptoms, which had built up over her years of dependence on it. Would she ever sleep properly or feel normal again? But in one way she did feel a bit better – just a bit more *here*, in the world, instead of standing on the outside looking in. Now she was ready for a dose of new life.

And the truth was, she was curious. The war was long ago, dead and buried – so why were they suddenly digging it all up again, when for years no one had wanted to hear it? What was there to say? *She'd* certainly got nothing to say about it. But as Karen had pointed out, she didn't have to *say* anything – she could just listen. All right then, she'd do that.

The room was filling up, so much so that the librarians were scurrying about finding extra chairs.

'All right, Mom?' Joanne asked.

'Yes, ta. Why wouldn't I be?'

She felt Joanne looking at her. She could tell her daughter wanted reassurance of some kind, to know that her mom hadn't really turned against her. But she was here with her, wasn't she? What else was she supposed to say about it all?

Audrey, the librarian, opened up the session. Beside her was a flipchart, a list written on it in green: *The Day War Broke Out, Evacuation, The Blitz, Kiss Me Goodnight Sergeant Major, Joining Up, Smiling Through on the Home Front, The Day it was All Over!*

'We're delighted to see so many of you're here today. As you can see, we've planned a few sessions ahead to give you an idea of what you might talk about . . . But these are only suggestions. This is *your* session, for *your* memories. We're very aware here, especially as librarians, that there's a lot of interest in the war and in the memories of well, *real*, people.' She laughed. 'Not just of people who write the history books.

'So many people in this city were involved in the war, one way or another, and went through a lot of things that the younger generation can't understand, or haven't heard about. Your memories are very precious – you can help people get a sense of what it was really like. At the end of all these sessions we're hoping to put together a little booklet, with your permission of course, to pass your memories on so that they're not lost. Now, after you've all had a chat, there'll be refreshments, which Pat is looking after.' She smiled at a blonde woman who was carrying a tray of cups across the back of the room.

Oh, get on with it, Margaret thought, then wondered why she was so irritable all the time, so nasty about people. It occurred to her that she wasn't a very nice person and she ached to be a better one. A painful throbbing had begun in her right temple and her right hand was trembling. She clenched it. Her thoughts drifted.

When she came to, a neat-looking woman across the room was talking. '. . . I remember my father was out the back, filling sandbags, and he was in a proper temper: "Here we go again! Those bloody Krauts, we should finished 'em off for good last time . . ." I was twelve then, and we'd heard it that morning on the radio – well, we called it the wireless then. Our next-door neighbours had one – course my father bought one soon after; nearly everyone had one, once the war got going. So we'd gone round and stood in the front parlour . . .' She sat up straighter and recited, ' ". . . and, consequently, this country is at war with Germany." '

There were murmurs of recognition as she talked. 'Ooh, it makes me go cold thinking about it now – more than it did then. I was too young to remember the First War, even though I heard it talked about. And you saw the men selling matches, with a trouser leg pinned up . . . But I don't think I really understood much about it – not then. Course nowadays no one wants to hear about it . . .'

Margaret started to regret coming. The last thing she wanted to be reminded of was the morning war broke out. That, and the day her father came and dragged her away from everything she knew and loved in Buckley, had been two of the worst days of her life. But despite herself, she was drawn in. She found herself listening avidly, hungry to hear what had happened to other people.

Everyone seemed to want to speak at once now. 'One at a time, please!' Audrey called out.

Memories poured out, people speaking who had been at varying ages when the war broke out – some adult enough to go straight into munitions work or join up; others who were children. One after another, voices piped up, eager to be heard. Quite a few said that their families weren't interested, and they never really talked about it much.

After a time a quiet, thoughtful voice spoke: a man among a group made up mainly of women.

'That day was different for me: I was evacuated the very day the war was announced.' His voice was tentative at first. 'We were taken to the station and put on a train to south Wales ... Course no one told us where we was going. Loads of us – some were quite young, poor little buggers—'

'I don't really want to stop you there,' Audrey cut in, gently, 'because I know we'd all love to hear what you're going to say. But we're hoping to have a whole session on evacuation next week. Would you be able to save it for us?'

'Oh, well, the thing is, I can't come next week – I'll be at work.' He was a stocky, kindly-looking man with dark eyes and a shock of bristling brown hair, cut in a short, neat style. 'I had to take the day off special today. To be honest, it's no good really, putting this sort of thing on in the day when there's so many people at work. I've got my own little firm, so I managed a morning off, but I don't know why you don't put it on in the evening, so more people can come.'

Audrey looked stricken. 'Well, I suppose we could ... It could be on a Thursday, when we open late. What do other people think?'

There was a buzz of voices. Quite a lot of the ladies were pleased with the daytime session, but all agreed that it wasn't fair on people who were at work – it ruled out a lot of men. Audrey said they would see if they could rearrange it, and soon afterwards it was time to break for tea.

'Just in time,' Joanne said, releasing Amy, who cavorted around joyfully. 'Madam was just beginning to get restless.'

Margaret turned to her. She had almost forgotten Joanne was there. 'She's been ever so good,' she said vaguely. Her mind was still involved with the stories she had heard. She felt a bit queer and swimmy in the head.

'I think I'll take her over to the children's books while we're having a break,' Joanne said.

Margaret crossed the room to where the blonde librarian was making teas and coffees from a silver urn. There was a plate of custard creams and she helped herself to one. She had a strange feeling, amid all this talking, a need rising in her so urgent that she felt she might burst. She kept an eye on the man who had spoken, whose name she gathered was Alan, and when he'd got his coffee he looked up and caught her gaze. He hesitated, then smiled and walked over to her. She was so caught up in her thoughts and her need that for once she wasn't conscious of her bad eye, or what he might think of her.

'Hello,' he said. 'This is a nice idea, isn't it? What d'you think of it so far?'

'I . . .' Margaret hadn't known she was going to say it, or anything like it. Words just seemed to gush out of her mouth. 'I was evacuated too – same day as you,' she said breathlessly. 'I was only five, and it was terrible. They took my brother away and I never saw him again; well, only twice, but that was that . . . Oh, my name's Margaret by the way,' she said, trying to recover herself. She was blushing and confused now, but somehow relieved.

Alan's face creased into a pained expression. 'My

God,' he said. 'I know it was terrible for some people. My wife had some rough times where she was sent. I suppose I had quite a good experience really. But what happened to your brother?'

Thinking about it made Margaret's chest tighten. Her heart was racing, it was horrible, this feeling, but if this stranger whose name was Alan had moved away at that moment and ceased to listen, she felt she would have screamed. She had to say it – *had* to, to someone.

'They took him to a farm and he never wanted to come back,' Margaret said. She felt herself becoming emotional in a way that hadn't happened for years – or ever. She had to fight to keep it under control. 'I came back here; he never did. He was *stolen* from me, that's what he was. And the first lady I was sent to was very cruel – I think she was off her head; but then, after that, where I went was lovely and ... and ...' She was shaking now, so that her cup was rattling on the saucer, and he could see it.

'Dear, oh dear,' Alan said, and the kindness in his voice was almost her undoing. She wanted to fall to her knees and weep and weep. 'Would you like to come and sit down over here?' he suggested.

But Margaret shook her head, because she spotted Joanne coming towards them slowly, holding Amy's hand.

Alan followed her gaze.

'That's my daughter,' Margaret said, trying to control her trembling. 'And granddaughter.' Quickly she added, 'I've never even told them – none of it.'

The man nodded as if he understood and greeted Joanne and Amy kindly. Amy ran to Margaret, brandishing a custard cream and calling out, 'Nanna! Bikkit!'

'I probably should be getting off, Mom,' Joanne said. 'D'you mind if I go ahead of you? Amy'll need her dinner.'

'Oh, I'll come now,' Margaret said. Any more and she would be overwhelmed.

Alan stopped her, a hand on her arm. He bent slightly to look into her face.

'Look, I hope they'll be able to move it to the evenings next week. I shall have to miss it otherwise. But you will come, won't you? I don't want to be the only one!'

Margaret looked down, trying to compose herself. What a kind look he had! She felt so foolish. 'Yes, I expect I will,' she said.

As he moved away she had to sit down for a moment anyway, because her legs would not hold her.

Fifty-Five

It was a week since Dave had left hospital and Joanne had found it very difficult.

She had been to see him with Amy three times, taking him extra clothes and things he needed. He seemed so broken and helpless, and wanted just to sit beside her holding her hand. He kept begging her to let him come home.

'You're my wife – my family,' he kept saying. 'All I want is to be near you both.'

Seeing him so vulnerable tore at her. She wanted to comfort him, but she was still afraid of giving into it all. His need was too much for her.

On Tuesday she had taken Amy back to the toddler group. She felt a bit nervous turning up, realizing that Tess probably knew from Sooky what had happened. Would she have told everyone? But of course Tess hadn't. As she pushed Amy into the hall, Tess caught sight of her and waved. She came over, carrying her new baby. Joanne could see that Tess looked more back to normal, her face thinner again.

'Joanne!' Tess held the baby with one arm and gave her a hug with the other. 'It's so good to see you.' She lowered her voice. 'How're things? Are you okay? And Amy?'

Joanne nodded, blushing. 'Yeah, I'm back home – my husband's not, though. Taking it, you know, one day at a time. Amy's all right, I think.' She smiled at the sight of Tess's baby. 'He's gorgeous.'

'Yes,' Tess looked down fondly. 'He's great. Really easy so far, thank goodness. Anyway,' she patted Joanne's shoulder, 'great to see you. And don't forget – if you need any help with anything . . .'

It was really nice to be back. She missed Sooky a lot, though they were trying to get together every Thursday. There was no sign of Kieran, either, and Tess told her when they chatted again later that he had gone back to work. His wife was at home now with the boys.

'He's hoping she'll feel confident enough to bring them here soon,' Tess said. 'She's getting there, gradually.'

Joanne was glad to hear it, though she missed Kieran too. But she got chatting to one or two new people, and Amy made another little friend called Clara. It felt good to be one of the ones who knew what to do, and to show other people. There was also a new volunteer, a skinny white girl, who was sweet, but much shyer than Mavis.

Once the toddler group had finished she walked up to the library on the Soho Road. As well as getting out some books for Amy, she picked up information about the local colleges where you could do A-levels.

The phone was ringing. Joanne stood in the middle of the back room holding a basket full of wet washing, tempted just to ignore it. Which one of them would it be this time? Sighing, she dropped the basket and went to answer.

'Joanne?' Dave's mom sounded really flustered. 'Look, I really need an answer from you as to how much longer ... I mean, it's been nice having Dave back here for a bit, but it can't go on. It's driving me round the bend, him forever under my feet. It's upsetting the whole energy of the house. He's gone out for a little walk now, just round the block, and I feel *so relieved* not to have him in the house ...'

Joanne closed her eyes for a minute.

'It's been a week now, and I know you need some time, but this can't go on. You're going to have to have him with you ...'

A wry smile turned up Joanne's lips. Wendy's delight in having 'my boy' back at home hadn't lasted for long. In between her phoning there were Dave's calls, which ranged in tone from imploring to petulant.

'Look, Jo, I need to come home. There'll be no trouble, I promise. You *know* I've promised – it'll never happen again. I mean, *what more can I do*?'

'Just give us a couple more days, Wendy, all right?' She tried to keep her voice calm. 'I'm sure we can sort something out.'

It was grey outside, but not raining – just about worth putting the washing out. Amy was dozing, so she was rushing to get things done. There was something soothing about pegging out washing, the pegs kept in an empty ice-cream box. She breathed deeply in the breeze, hanging up one of Amy's little shirts.

She knew she wasn't ready. The thought of having Dave here filled her with dismay. It wasn't just the violence she was afraid of. Just as much it was the thought of sinking back into things as they were before, when she knew now that she needed something to change. She kept thinking about Sooky. How would it be if she went and did some classes, started on her A-levels, and just lived here with Amy: alone? Sooky had her mom, of course. Moving back in with Mom and Dad was out of the question – it would drive her crazy.

She imagined it, finding someone to mind Amy, learning, getting a good job. Her heart flipped with happiness, then landed belly-up in the realization of how lonely it would be. No Dave – the old Dave – coming home with jokes and kisses and playing with Amy. No Dave, full stop. She stood for a long time staring across the garden. She thought back fondly on the good times. Then she recalled the bad times.

Never before had she had to choose like this. Life had happened, and she had fallen into it: she had fallen into following Dave. But now she had to decide and pay the price for her decision, whatever that was.

All that week Margaret couldn't stop thinking about the group at the library in Kings Heath. The experience had shaken her up. At least while she was there she'd just about managed to keep her emotions under control. Once she was alone in the bathroom at home, where no one would hear, she let go. Perched on the fluffy cover of the lavatory seat, she put her head in her hands and sobbed and sobbed as if her chest would split open. It was all beyond her: she couldn't control it. Afterwards she felt exhausted, but lighter in herself.

Two days before the next one, she called into the library to check whether the time had changed. Audrey told her that it would be in the evening. She seemed delighted that the group had proved so popular.

Margaret went home jittery with excitement. She'd never known herself get in such a state over anything like this.

'What the hell's got into you, Margaret Tolley?' she

demanded as she made coffee back at home with shaking hands.

All she could think about was getting back there on Thursday. She wanted to see that chap she'd talked to. It was something about the way he'd looked at her, as if he really wanted to hear what she had to say. He had such a warm, lively look in those brown eyes. She couldn't explain it to herself – it wasn't as if she was ever going to say anything in the group, but she knew she just had to be there.

'So, are you going back to that reminiscence thing?' Karen had asked that morning. 'It sounded quite nice.'

Margaret took a long drag on her cigarette, taking her time to answer.

'Yes, I might.' She wanted to tell Karen to mind her own business. This was *hers*. She didn't want anyone else interfering. 'It's going to be in the evening now, though.'

'Oh.' Karen sounded disappointed, as if she thought this meant Margaret would never go to it now. 'That's a shame. Thing is, I've got my evening class on a Thursday.' This was said with importance. Karen had enrolled on a twelve-week course entitled 'Introduction to Counselling'. 'And Joanne can't really come out at that time.'

'It doesn't matter,' Margaret said. She didn't want any of them coming along with her. 'I think I can manage to get to the library and back without an escort. I'm not quite over the hill yet, you know.'

Karen looked surprised, then laughed. 'Oh! Well, that's really good. Great!'

*

On Thursday night she and Fred had chicken cooked in a tinned wine sauce, which he liked, then she left him in front of *Channel 4 News*, reading the *Evening Mail*.

'I shan't be late,' she told him.

Fred looked up, bemused. 'Where're you off to?'

'I told you. The thing at the library. About the war.' She knew he wouldn't ask if he could come.

'Oh ar, right then. Tara. See yer later.' He returned to his paper.

Margaret watched him for a few seconds. He was already completely oblivious to her being there. It had always been the same with Fred. He was a poor thing really. Sometimes she thought his mother had taken a piece of him with her to the grave. He was like a boy with his face pressed against a window, looking at the colours of life inside and wishing he could find a way in. Seeing this in him made her boil inwardly, because she knew that she had been just the same.

'Don't know why I bother,' she muttered, putting on her coat.

She got there too early and lingered out in the cold, waiting until a few others came and she could go in with them. She didn't see the man, Alan, among them. She was afraid he wouldn't come.

Once again there was Audrey and a double ring of chairs. Margaret sat down and put her bag and coat on the chair beside her as if she was reserving it for someone. A stream of people came in, chattering, all about her age and older. Soon, among them, she saw Alan. She wondered if he had come with anyone, but he seemed to be alone. As he came in he spotted her and raised his hand in greeting. He came straight over to her and she was quick to take her things off the chair.

'Is that a spare one?' he asked cheerfully. 'Hello, Margaret.'

'Hello,' she said. 'Alan.'

He was wearing a navy raincoat and took a minute to get it off and folded, placing it under the chair as he sank down. She noticed his black trousers looked spruce and his shoes well polished. She was suddenly overcome by her own sense of dowdiness. She was tidy and clean, of course – always that. But her clothes, her beige blouse and brown skirt, were so shabby and old. When was the last time she had given a thought to getting some new things? And she was suddenly conscious that she stank of smoke. She found herself wishing she had kept her coat on.

'It was touch and go tonight,' he said, sounding pleased. 'But I've made it!'

He told her that he ran a small engineering firm, and there'd been a bit of a rush on, but they'd managed to get done in time.

Something in his stocky build and dark eyes reminded her for a second of her father, Ted Winters. Except that Alan was different in every other way. The Old Man had died from the drink years back, alone in his house. It was true he'd been a charmer, but he was an idle sod for most of his life, whereas Alan was active-looking, intelligent and busy, by the sound of things. She wondered what his wife was like.

'You said your wife was an evacuee as well. Didn't she want to come to this?'

'Oh,' Alan said, his face creasing sorrowfully. 'Well, she might if she knew about it. Thing is, we aren't together any more. She left me – two years or more, it is now – for a tour guide on a holiday we went on, would you believe.' He rolled his eyes. 'It was supposed to be our second honeymoon!'

'Oh, good Lord,' Margaret said.

Alan started chuckling at her reaction, and though she couldn't really see why it was funny, Margaret joined in. She suddenly felt wildly happy.

'Yeah, well, you have to laugh, don't you?' he said eventually, just as Audrey started calling everyone to order. 'That or go mad.'

Margaret recognized a lot of the faces from last time, but there were some new ones too. Her laughter with Alan had put her in a strange frame of mind. She felt safe, with him beside her, as if she was floating in comfortable warm water. She wasn't going to say anything of course. She just wasn't that type. But she could listen to all the others.

Audrey gave her introduction, then turned to Alan.

'I felt rather bad last week, stopping you from speaking – Alan, isn't it? So I'm glad you've managed to be here tonight. Would you be happy to start us off?'

'Well, yes, all right,' Alan said. He looked down for a minute, collecting himself. He rubbed a hand down his face and Margaret heard the rasp of stubble. It sounded loud to her, as if her senses were heightened.

'I s'pose I'd have to say I was one of the ones who didn't have it too bad with evacuation. Course, when we left Brum I'd never known anything else. I was from the Vauxhall area, and life was just – well, it was what it was. Pretty poor really. But when I had to come back . . .' He shook his head. 'I mean, it was only three years I was there. But it changed me all right.'

'Perhaps you'd like to say where you were sent to?' Audrey suggested.

'We – that is, me and my brother – were sent to Wales: Abergavenny.'

Margaret sat riveted as Alan told his story. Compared with her own, it was a straightforward one. Alan and his brother had gone to a kindly couple, who treated them well, kept his parents informed about him and even had a real bathroom in the house! He had gone to the local school and, apart from a bit of argy-bargy with the local kids for not being Welsh, he had thrived and fallen for the place. It was coming back to Birmingham, to his overstretched parents and an impoverished city life, that had been the biggest shock.

As soon as he had stopped speaking, others were eager to say their piece. Some had been evacuated in those early days, several only staying a short while before their families fetched them back. One man had made his own way back from Wales, walking most of the way just to get home. Others were evacuated later, in 1942, in another wave of concern for their safety. Their experiences had been very mixed. There was an attentive silence as one woman told them how cruel the family had been where she was sent.

'It wasn't even just the father, Mr Granger – he was a brutal man all right,' she said. 'But it was as if I was the enemy. I was the outsider. They all sort of ganged up on me. The worst were the children, because at least with the adults you could just keep out of their way. Mrs Granger was the sort who'd give you a slap for so much as breathing. But there were two girls and a boy – the youngest about my age. They were wicked, what they did. There was a well at the back of the house and they were always on at me, "We're going to throw you down the well. No one'll know – they'll think you jumped in." That sort of thing. One day they caught me and tied a rope to my ankles and let me down into the well head-first. It was dark and cobwebby, and all the blood went to my head. I was scraped all down my side, against the rough bricks. They kept it up for a while and then they got bored and pulled me back up. But I thought I was going to die.'

A whole catalogue of cruel bullying followed at the hands of the Grangers. There were murmurs of horror, but the woman herself told the stories in a flat way with no emotion. Margaret found herself wondering if she was on Valium as well.

By the time they broke for tea and coffee, she felt tired out with hearing it all.

'What would you like?' Alan asked her.

'Oh, I'll come over with you and stretch my legs,' Margaret said. She liked the way he looked after her and stuck with her. He was friendly and spoke to other people, but seemed to gravitate back to her. It made her feel special.

There was a buzz in the room.

'Some people want stringing up, don't they?' Alan said angrily as they sorted out their drinks. 'What that poor woman went through – well, child she would have been. And I bet there was no comeback on any of them, the whole vile lot of them.'

Margaret looked up at him. 'The first woman I was with was fined after what she did to me,' she said. 'My teacher called the police, because she kept locking me out in the shed all night – in the middle of winter, this was. They sent her to the asylum in the end. She had her dead husband up in bed, nursing him. I mean he wasn't really there, but she thought he was.'

'What – you mean . . . ?' Alan stopped what he was doing, eyes ablaze. He put a hand to his forehead, then looked back at her. 'Christ! What some people went through. All we hear about is people in the forces, but all those poor kids . . . Look, Margaret, don't take this wrong or anything, but – would you like to come out after this? For a drink or something? I mean this bit's over now, they're moving on to another topic next week. You should tell me about it, even if you don't want to say anything here. We could just pop into The Station or somewhere – it's not far.'

Margaret knew she ought to say no. She had told Fred she'd be back by nine or soon after. But would Fred notice? It was all above board. Alan knew she was a married woman. She also knew that nothing on earth was going to stop her going.

'That'd be very nice,' she said. 'Have you got time?'

'At this time of day I've got all the time in the world,' he said.

Fifty-Six

'That's a nice picture,' Sooky said.

She was looking at the photo of Joanne and Dave's wedding on the shelf in the back room. It showed them standing in front of the Registry Office, smiling at Pete, Dave's friend, who had volunteered to take photos.

'It was only two years ago,' Joanne said, handing Sooky a mug of tea. 'I've made it your way, with milk.' Sooky had taught her, and she liked the sweet, milky brew.

'That's lovely, thanks.' Sooky turned and took the mug. The girls were playing with Lego.

'I was four months pregnant with her,' Joanne said. 'Which was lucky, because I was just past the sicky bit.'

Sooky peered at it again. 'He looks nice,' she said cautiously.

'Yeah,' she sighed. 'Well, he was – is, really I s'pose. Come on, let's sit down. Oh, I've got some Jaffa Cakes. Is Priya allowed one?'

They were getting into a routine, visiting each other's houses on a Wednesday or Thursday. Joanne really liked going to Sooky's, the feel of there being a big family around. Her own home seemed lonely in comparison. She thought Harpreet, Sooky's sister, was lovely. Her mom seemed a bit out of it and she wasn't sure about Raj, her big brother. He was really uptight and unsmiling. Sooky had told her he was obsessed with politics. His wife Roopinder had been okay – a bit distant. Joanne simply saw that she seemed tired.

'So, how's it going: the degree and everything?' Joanne asked, when they were all settled.

Sooky gave her smile. 'It's good. Actually, I really love it – learning again. Getting out of the house. I know Priya's okay with Mom, so that's not a problem. And it's nice to have a challenge.'

'That's great.' Joanne watched her with admiration. She kept toying with the idea of going to college. There were even places with crèches. For some reason, though, each time she thought of it, her heart sank. It seemed a lonely road to take and she didn't want to leave Amy, not at her age and with strangers. Asking her own mother didn't feel like an option.

'How's your husband?' Sooky asked.

'Okay, I think. It's hard to tell. I've at least got his mom to say he can stay there till the end of the month. She keeps saying, "Oh, he'll be back at work before that, so he'll need to come home." But I'm not sure that he will – he's just . . .' She shook her head. 'He's gone to pieces. Completely. But at least now that Wendy's sure he'll be moving back here by November, she's calmed down a bit. She's stopped ringing me up all the time anyway! And he's been over a couple of times, on the bus, for a visit. In fact he's coming on Friday, if he's up to it.'

The first time he had sat where Joanne was sitting now and wept. 'Oh God,' he kept saying over and over. 'Oh God, God . . . I could've lost you. I'm such a fool.'

'You do want him back, though?'

Joanne loved Sooky's directness. It felt as if they could talk about anything now. And she knew Sooky wasn't a simple hearts-and-flowers romantic who'd just

say, 'Well, if you love him . . .' She did love him, still –
but it wasn't as simple as that.

'I think I do,' she said slowly. 'I know that the way
he was before he left is not really him. I've known him
years. It's more as if he's been having a long, slow
breakdown without any of us realizing.'

Sooky nodded. 'That's a kind way to look at it.'

'I do want him,' Joanne continued slowly. 'Only at
the moment everything about it feels like jumping off a
cliff. I don't know where we're going to land!'

Sooky laughed. 'That's the trouble with marriage in
general, I'd say!'

They spent a lovely afternoon, taking the girls out
for a little while when the sun came out, to play in the
garden. Sooky told Joanne more about her family.

'It's really nice the way you and your sister are so
close,' Joanne said.

'Yes, she's a sweetheart. When I got married and
went to Derby I missed her more than anyone – well,
Mom too.'

'What about your sister-in-law?'

Sooky made a face, then tried to be charitable. 'Well,
she's okay.' She bent to pass Priya the ball they were
throwing around. 'It's just – me coming home and
everything . . . She can be quite spiteful. It's almost as if
she thinks it's her duty to be nasty to me. The disgraced
sister-in-law, you know. She's quite traditional, but
then I don't know if she's really happy with that. Also,
she's not feeling well during this pregnancy. She seems
really down.'

Joanne remembered Roopinder's pointy, aloof face.
She hadn't looked very nice. But she said, 'Poor thing.
It's all nerve-racking, isn't it?'

'Raj is out such a lot – I think it's tough for her.

He's quite obsessed with what's going on in India. What with that and work, he doesn't spend much time with her. Oh, look!'

A huge, hairy ginger tabby cat had appeared on the fence-post further down the garden, and Amy and Priya had just noticed it. The two little girls moved closer, staring up at the cat, which sat with its head bowed, gazing down at them.

Joanne laughed. 'I wish I had a camera!'

'What the hell's got into Mom?' Karen said when she phoned later.

Joanne was in the middle of giving Amy her tea. It wasn't a good time to talk.

'What d'you mean? Is she poorly again?'

Karen laughed. 'No! She's asked me to go into town with her on Saturday. Says she wants to get some new clothes, and I'm a better judge of what's in fashion.'

Joanne grinned. 'Well, that's true. But . . . that's good, isn't it?'

'Yeah, well, I s'pose it is. She just seems . . . different. I think it's because of that group – the war thing. It's really perked her up. I mean, she won't say much about it, but it only goes to prove that letting it out's the answer.' Karen had got her 'counsellor' hat on again.

'Umm, I s'pect you're right,' Joanne said, trying to cut up Amy's toast with one hand. 'Or maybe she's got a fancy man?'

'Pigs might fly,' Karen said.

'How's the course going?'

She almost heard Karen stand up straighter down the phone. 'It's *brilliant*! And the woman running it says I'm a natural.'

'Oh.' Joanne was leaning down to the table with the phone jammed between ear and shoulder, scraping out Amy's egg. Amy giggled. 'I expect you are. You're getting plenty of practice anyway.'

'How's Dave, Joanne?'

She righted herself again.

'Fragile,' she said.

They had agreed that when he came, it should be for a limited time. An hour and a half, Joanne had said at first. She had to set a limit, to make sure he would leave, and not spread his difficulties like an oil slick all over the house. The time had extended now to two hours. Megan, the social worker, had come for one of his visits to see how they were getting on, and Joanne found her presence comforting.

He arrived at two-thirty on Friday afternoon, planning to get a bus back before the rush-hour. Joanne had taken his keys off him and he had to ring the bell. To her surprise Dave had submitted to all this without a fuss.

Amy was asleep when he arrived. Joanne opened up to find him talking to Jim Coles over the fence. Jim was brisk, but friendly.

'Go on then, lad – there's yer missis,' he said. 'Mustn't keep her waiting.'

As soon as they were inside, he wanted to hug her. They stood for a few moments in the hall with their arms round each other. He felt different from how she remembered. Still solid, but somehow slacker. He made a small sound of relief, as if being in her arms was all he needed. She breathed him in.

'Where's Amy?' he asked, still holding her.

'Having a nap. She's been down a while, so it won't last much longer.'

This was the moment she expected to step back, but he still held her close and nuzzled the top of her head. In a moment she realized he was becoming aroused and she tried to pull away.

He looked at her pleadingly. 'I miss you. I need you, Jo.'

She wanted him too, in those moments, longed to be held, naked and warm. But she also knew it was too fast. Things had to go a certain way, slowly, carefully and on her terms, or she would be lost.

'Not yet,' she said. 'You know what we agreed. And Amy'll wake anyway.' She stepped away from him in a business-like way, protecting herself. 'Cuppa tea?'

He sat waiting as she brewed up. When she went to sit with him he said, 'I was thinking. Those albums you've got – shall we have a look at them?'

'What, the old ones of us?'

'Yeah.' He seemed eager.

She hesitated, not knowing if she could stand going over it all again. 'D'you think that's a good idea?'

'I just . . .' He looked down as if embarrassed. 'The counsellor woman said about looking at the past. Trying to see it differently – feel it. I just thought if I looked, with you . . .'

Joanne was moved by this admission. She could see he was working at something – really trying.

'Okay then.'

There were only the two albums that she'd looked at not so long ago. She sat opposite him as he went through them. She didn't really want to see them, or sit next to him. He lingered over pictures of his mom and dad.

'Mom looks older now,' he said. 'Doesn't she?'

He didn't say anything about his dad.

There were the triumphant pictures of him as a young, promising footballer. He stared for ages at the one of him at the Villa ground, foot on the ball.

In the end he looked up at her. 'That was a dream all right, wasn't it? But that *was me* – there in that picture.'

His face crumpled and again he was weeping, but gently. She could see that grief was washing its way through and out of him.

Fifty-Seven

That Sunday, after the dinner was cleared away, Margaret went up to the bedroom and shut herself in.

Opening the cupboard, she stood looking in at her shopping from yesterday, pulsing with excitement. There was a skirt and two pairs of slacks arranged on hangers, and beside them on the shelves, blouses and jumpers – colourful ones! – carefully folded. She put her hands to her face for a moment as a tremor of glee passed through her. All these nice new things! Last night, when she and Karen had got back, she had brought the bags up here, carefully cut off the price tags and hung and folded them all away. She couldn't stop thinking about them, so much so that she'd only smoked one cigarette all evening.

Taking off her skirt and blouse, which now seemed so drab, she slipped into a pair of navy slacks, a nice new white camisole – 'You might as well get some underwear as well, Mom,' Karen had encouraged her – and a pink jumper with a soft turtle-neck. Then the shoes, moccasin pumps in navy suede with a little gold chain across the front. It felt wonderful, as if she was clothing herself in a new life.

She combed out her hair, which was at a good stage after a perm (falling in soft waves, not too tight, but not yet grown-out and slack) and stood in front of the mirror on her dressing table. She could only see half of herself and leaned forward to look down at her feet.

Inside, she was trembling. She looked closely at her face. If only her eye was normal, instead of wandering off to the side! Nowadays something would be done to correct it. It made her look half-soaked, she thought. But otherwise, she had to admit, she didn't look bad at all. In fact she looked quite spruce – years younger! And she really must try cutting down on the fags as well; that would surely help?

She smiled radiantly into the glass.

'Hello, Alan,' she whispered. 'It's lovely to see you again.' Then she looked down, closing her eyes for a minute. 'Oh God,' she said. 'What am I doing?'

'Surprise!' Karen cried, opening the door to Joanne and Amy. She waved an arm towards Margaret, who came along the hall feeling suddenly bashful.

'Mom, you look lovely!' Joanne said.

'There's no need to sound so flaming surprised.' But Margaret was gratified to see that Joanne looked really impressed. She found herself grinning. 'D'you like it?' She twirled a little in the narrow hall. 'Me and Karen had a bit of a spree. She was a big help.'

Karen had, to Margaret's surprise, been marvellous. She had expected to be bossed and snapped at by her younger daughter. Instead, Karen had been helpful and encouraging, and seemed to have a good eye for what would suit her. They'd even had a bite to eat, just a baked spud and coleslaw and a coffee, but it had been a treat, making a day of it. Margaret realized she hadn't enjoyed herself so much in a long time.

'We got her some nice things,' Karen said. 'You

know – classics really. It was high time you sorted out your wardrobe,' she scolded, but jokingly. 'Bit of a late birthday present for you.'

'It's lovely,' Joanne said. Margaret was surprised to see that they found her transformation very cheering. What had she been like all these years? She could barely remember.

Joanne took Amy into the back room. Fred was sitting smoking, as usual, and looking at the sports results on Teletext.

'Doesn't she look nice, Dad?'

'Eh – what, bab?'

'Mom, she looks nice, doesn't she?'

Fred glanced round and took in the sight of his wife. 'Ar, she does.' He frowned. 'You been shopping?'

Margaret rolled her eyes. 'I *told* you. Where did you think we'd gone all day yesterday?' Shaking her head, she turned to Joanne. 'So, is Dave coming over?'

'No. I went over to see him yesterday. I did ask him, but to be honest, he's not coping with things easily. He said thanks, but he'll be round another time. He's trying to get himself ready to come home this week.'

'I dunno what's up with the lad,' Fred remarked, clicking off the TV.

'No,' Joanne said, 'I don't suppose you do.'

'I mean, I'd've thought he'd've snapped out of it by now.'

Margaret saw Joanne roll her eyes at Karen.

'Come on – I'll get the kettle on,' she said.

Every time she moved, Margaret was aware of her new clothes. Standing in the kitchen, she admired the delicately knitted cuffs of her sweater. She had never had anything as nice before. From the front room she could just hear Joanne trying to explain to Fred what a breakdown was, what had happened to Dave.

What was the point? Margaret thought. She felt such a long way from Fred. All these wonderful new experiences made her feel she was riding a high on a beautiful wave that had risen right over Fred's head, taking her to a magical place where she couldn't even see him any more. It was as simple and brutal as that.

Altogether now she'd been to three meetings at the library.

At the end of the second one Audrey had announced, 'Next week's session we've called "Joining Up!" Now, this doesn't just mean the men. It means the women who joined up too, whether it was you or someone you knew – a relative perhaps.'

Margaret and Alan stepped out together into the dark street. A mizzling rain had started, but they only had to walk round the corner into Station Road. It felt strange to her, walking along with this man. The only man she had ever walked beside before was Fred. She was nervous, yet also very excited. There was nowhere she wanted to be more. She'd also promised herself that she wouldn't smoke in the pub. She didn't want to go about stinking like an ashtray.

'What'll I get you?' Alan asked once they were inside.

Margaret asked for half a lager and sat down. She examined Alan as he went to the bar, his broad, square shoulders, the way his hair bristled out at the back, then stopped suddenly to reveal a band of flesh above the collar of his coat. His skin was a sallow colour and looked soft. An intense feeling came over her as she looked at his solid outline in his raincoat, of a sense of rightness, of being drawn to him.

As he turned to bring back the drinks, she realized in confusion that she hadn't even taken her coat off and stood up hastily to do so. She'd put on the navy slacks to come out and felt self-conscious, but of course no one else had noticed. She was glad Alan hadn't commented, that he seemed to take her as she was, whatever she was wearing. But did she imagine the admiring look that he cast over her as he walked back to the table?

'There you go,' he said, placing her drink on a beer mat. He shouldered off his own coat and laid it over the chair-back beside hers. Then he leaned over and fished a packet of cigarettes out of the breast pocket, went to open it, then made an impatient sound and laid it on the table. He turned to Margaret with a wry expression.

'I'm trying to give them up.'

She smiled. 'Snap! Me too.'

Reaching for the packet, she moved it over to her side of the table. 'Out of harm's way then,' she said.

'What about you, though?'

'I don't feel like one at the moment.'

'That's all right then – you can keep an eye on me!' Alan gave a laugh, took a sip of his drink, then said, 'I was just thinking about what Audrey said about women joining up. There was this wench – and she was a wench, if you know what I mean – up the old end where I lived as a kid. Molly Fox, that was her name.' He shook his head. 'God, she was trouble, she was! Blonde bombshell sort – always in a scrape of some sort. Her mother was like a prize-fighter – a drunk, no good to anyone. Anyhow, Molly went off and joined the army. I'd love to know what happened to her. The army must've wondered what'd hit them!'

Margaret smiled. 'Well, good for her. My Old Man spent the war avoiding doing anything, if he could possibly help it. They caught up with him, though – got him working in munitions.'

Alan looked across at her. He had a way of looking so interested in what she was saying.

'Tell me about your family, Margaret?'

'Not much to tell,' she said. 'There were five of us originally – my mother was widowed and remarried. She had a girl and two boys, then my brother and me the second time round. I only ever saw Elsie, my stepsister, after the war – in fact, I lived with her for a fair while. She was good to me. She passed away rather young, though, and her daughters moved away. But the other two: Edwin got killed somewhere in Belgium; and Cyril, well, he was a bad lot. We never heard another thing from him. And then Tommy – well, you know about that.'

Alan was nodding encouragingly. 'Just tell me,' he said. 'You know – how it was.'

She stalled. 'You really want me to?'

'If you don't mind.'

Margaret looked back at him: that rarest of people, someone who would listen and wait to hear what she said.

'The thing was,' she began, hesitant to awaken the painful memories. 'The day war broke out, our mom was very poorly ... She was dying. It was terrible to see ...'

She told him everything, about never seeing Mom again, about Tommy and about her stay with Nora Paige. And then she talked about Buckley, about the sisters and all the animals and John and Patty, and how it had been. And about that terrible day when Ted Winters had come to fetch her, and about getting to Birmingham. She had never spoken about any of it before, not to anyone. To him she seemed to be able to talk and talk, and when she looked across at him, with tears running down her cheeks, she saw that his face had creased and he was wiping his eyes as well. The sight moved her so much that it made her cry all the more.

'Oh, I'm sorry!' she exclaimed, reaching in her bag for tissues. She gave him one and wiped her eyes. 'I never meant . . .'

'It's all right.' He dabbed his eyes and cheeks, and tried to laugh. 'Look at me – honestly. Only, what you said, about coming back here, it just set me off . . . D'you know,' he looked sorrowfully at her, 'I've lived my whole life here in Birmingham, other than that bit of time down there – less than three years. And yet that's the place I think of as home: Abergavenny. I think I always will.'

Margaret nodded. 'Fancy,' she said, 'I feel exactly the same. D'you know, down there, Miss Clairmont and Mrs Higgins always called me Maggie. I belonged down there. I went to the school, and I knew everybody and they knew me, and I did well. I know I look . . . Well, my eye – people think I'm retarded. But I'm not!'

'You certainly are not,' Alan said. 'You're—' But he stopped himself saying any more, giving a cough instead.

'When I got back – since then – I've never let anyone call me Maggie. Not Fred, no one. That was my Buckley name. Here I was someone else. But that was where I was happy.' More tears came then, she couldn't stop them.

'When I went back to Abergavenny—' Alan began.

Margaret's head shot up. 'You've been back?'

'Well, yes. A few times. It feels like going home, even though the people I was billeted with are long gone now.'

She stared at him, amazed. 'I can't imagine ever going back!'

'Well,' Alan sat back smiling at her, 'maybe you should.'

The next week, during which she had been longing to see him ever since they parted, they went to the pub again. They talked and talked. Alan told her his giving-up-smoking campaign was going well.

'I've only had a handful all week – weaning myself off gradually, sort of thing.'

'That's good,' Margaret said. 'I'm cutting down as well.'

Alan told her, that evening, about his own family: his four older sisters and the one brother who had been evacuated with him. How his parents were struggling so hard to earn enough to keep the family housed and fed that they never seemed to have time or energy for anyone.

'That was something I was determined to do differently with my own kids,' he said, frowning. 'I've a son and a daughter. For one thing, that's enough – two – I think. Everyone was overstretched back in those days and ended up with too many kids. I wanted to be able to give them things I'd never had. And spend time with them, make sure we had holidays, that sort of thing.'

'In Abergavenny?' Margaret asked. She found herself, just for a second, feeling acutely jealous of Alan's wife and children.

'Actually no. We went to the south coast quite a bit.' He stopped, seeming to hesitate, then looked up at her. 'What about your family – your husband?'

'I've got two daughters,' she told him. 'And my husband . . .' She stopped. How to talk about Fred? For so many years she had felt nothing, gone through life like a robot. What had she ever felt for Fred, or he for her?

'Fred and I knew each other as kids,' she said eventually. 'We met again later and I married him. She looked at Alan and shrugged. She couldn't seem to be anything other than honest with him. 'I suppose I thought he was the only person who would ever ask me. So that was that.'

'I see.' His dark eyes seemed to look closely into hers as if to work out what she was saying and feeling. But he didn't say any more.

When they parted that night, after he had walked her most of the way home in the drizzle, he said, 'Will you be coming next week, Margaret?'

'Oh yes,' she said. 'I wouldn't miss it!'

'Good.' He looked down, seeming confused, as if he might say something more. But he just looked up again and smiled. 'Good – well, see you next time.'

And he was walking away from her down the street.

Don't go! a voice cried inside her. But in a moment, after a glimpse of him passing under a street light, he had faded into the darkness, like the end of a dream.

And she had to go back to her real life.

Fifty-Eight

Sooky was hurrying across the upstairs landing when she heard the sound of distraught weeping.

She'd overslept, and was now in a frantic hurry to get to college after giving Priya her breakfast. But she knew the rush was worth it. She loved Tuesdays. And then on Thursday she'd meet up with Joanne. She and Mom were getting on better – life felt so good these days. She had come up to gather her files and notebooks and pick up her jacket before running for the bus.

Harpreet came out of her room. Both of them stopped, listening.

'What's going on?' Harpreet hissed. She had her coat on already.

'I don't know – you go. You'll miss your bus.'

Mouthing 'Thanks,' Harpreet ran off down the stairs.

The noise was coming from Raj and Roopinder's room. The men had already left for work, so Roopinder was in there with the children and, by the sound of it, they were crying too. Sooky frowned. For a moment she listened at the door, then knocked. For a second things went quiet, then she heard Jasmeet start gulping and sobbing again.

She opened the door, wary of being shrieked at by her waspish sister-in-law.

'Roopinder? *Bhabi-ji*? What's happened? Can I help you?'

Amardeep and Jasmeet were standing close to the bed, both crying and looking scared. Their eyes were fixed on their mother, who was lying hunched under the covers, sobbing, below Raj's blue-and-yellow Khalistan flag, which was pinned across the wall.

'Oh dear!' Sooky went over and put her arms round the two children. 'There, it's all right,' she told them. 'Why don't you go down and see *Nani-ji*?' She knew Meena was in the kitchen. 'She'll give you some breakfast. I'll talk to your mommy.'

She dabbed their faces with a tissue and they trustingly stopped crying and toddled out of the room. Sooky perched on the edge of the bed and waited, trying to quell her impatience. Soon Roopinder emerged from under the sheet and looked at her with tragic eyes. Her hair was loose, she had no make-up on and she looked young and vulnerable.

'Has somebody upset you?' Sooky asked carefully. She was so used to Roopinder being nasty to her that she waited to be snapped at and rejected.

Roopinder sat up, reaching for a tissue and shaking her head.

'No, it's not that. I'm just . . .' More tears ran from her eyes and she rocked back and forth in distress. 'I'm so worried about the baby! I tell Raj, but all he says is, "You're just being anxious – it's nothing to worry about. You've done all this before." But that's just the point!'

She struck her forehead, working herself up again.

'I've had two babies and I know there's something wrong. The baby is not moving! You know, when it's at this stage, it's always moving about like an octopus inside. But he has gone quiet – I'm sure he hasn't moved for days. There's something really wrong, and I'm so frightened!'

Her face crumpled and she put her hands over it, rocking violently back and forth, working herself into a state.

'All Raj thinks about is politics, politics and the *Khalsa*, and what's happening in India. But what about what's happening right here? What about me and the baby?'

'Well, maybe you should go to the doctor, or the midwife,' Sooky said, seeing in her mind's eye her bus to college disappearing off along the street without her. But she could see that Roopinder was truly frightened. Leaning forward, she touched Roopinder's arm. 'Look, I'll tell *Ma-ji* and maybe today the two of you could go to the clinic?'

'She doesn't listen to me,' Roopinder cried resentfully. 'She keeps telling me: just wait a bit, everything is okay, no need for the doctor. Oh, Sukhdeep,' she reached forward and grasped Sooky's hand, 'will you come with me? I'm so scared.'

For a moment Sooky felt she might explode. This was her day at college: she was supposed to be leaving now! Why did she always have to be everyone's dogsbody? But she tried to speak kindly.

'What about your mom? Wouldn't you like her to come with you?'

'No, not for this,' Roopinder said. 'She'd fuss and worry – she's not calm like you.'

Sooky told herself not to be selfish – she could probably make it in for the afternoon anyway.

'Okay,' she said and gave what she hoped was a reassuring smile.

Sooky had never seen Roopinder so subdued. She was soon glad she had skipped the morning at college because her sister-in-law was in a terrible state – she would never have reached out for Sooky's help if she hadn't been. She sat in the GP's waiting room red-eyed, her pink *chunni* pulled over her head, staring down into her lap, her hands clenching and unclenching.

'Come on, that's us,' Sooky said softly when they were called in. Roopinder shuffled along almost like an old lady, her misery preventing her from standing upright. Sooky took her arm.

The midwife, a white woman with ginger hair, listened repeatedly for a heartbeat with her ear trumpet, frowning. After numerous attempts she said calmly, 'Just one moment – don't worry, I'll be back.'

She returned with a doctor, a young woman with long blonde hair, who also made several attempts. She straightened up.

'I think,' she said slowly, 'we had better admit you to hospital – just in case.'

Roopinder lurched up into a sitting position.

'The baby's dead, isn't it?' she cried wildly, tearing at her hair. 'I know it is – something is terribly wrong. Just tell me the truth!'

Everyone did their best to calm her down and be hopeful.

'It may well be quite all right,' the doctor said. 'Don't assume the worst at this point. It may just be the way the baby's lying inside you. It does happen. But I am having difficulty locating a heartbeat, so we really need to get it checked out, don't we? We can do a scan and keep you under observation for a bit.'

Sooky saw, though, how worried she looked as she moved across to the phone.

'I'm going to call the hospital and make sure they're expecting you, okay?'

Roopinder nodded, sobbing. Sooky supported her out of the room, feeling suddenly sick. She could well imagine how Roopinder was feeling, how desperate and full of dread.

'Let's phone your mom, shall we?' Sooky said gently.

With her head drooping, Roopinder nodded.

Roopinder was admitted to Dudley Road Hospital that afternoon. Raj was called home from work, and Roopinder's mom came over. Sooky stayed at home with Meena to help look after the other children. They sat in the front room, Amardeep, Jasmeet and Priya all playing with toys. Then Sooky put some cartoons on for them to watch. She and Meena didn't speak much. All they could do was wait, restless with nerves.

Eventually the phone rang: Khushwant, asking for news. Sooky heard her mother tell him they had none, not yet, and promising to call as soon as they knew anything. Her voice was quiet and upset. Sooky went to the kitchen and made them both tea. They had no appetite for anything more. As they sat sipping the frothy milk, the phone went again. Meena uttered a brief prayer.

'You answer,' she said.

Sooky wanted to argue: *If it's Raj, he'll want you* – but she did as she was told.

'*Mata-ji?*' Raj was already sobbing before he could get any words out. He sounded like a little boy.

'It's Sukhdeep,' she said, preparing herself for insults and curses – I'm not speaking to you, *Besharam*. But her brother was too upset.

'The baby's dead,' he sobbed, in English. 'There's no

461

heartbeat ... And it's a boy ...' He broke down again, unable to speak.

'Raj-*ji*,' Sooky said, her own eyes filling. Her chest filled up with pain. 'I'm so sorry. So sorry – that's terrible ...' She was crying too. 'Look, d'you want to speak to Mom?'

'No, it's okay – you tell her. They say she has to stay in, to have the baby. They are going to induce her tomorrow.'

'Oh God!' Sooky said. She could feel the horror of it, the fear and pain, knowing that the baby was already dead. She wanted to put her arms around both of them and hold them tight.

'Look, I'll call later,' he said. He was crying too much to continue.

Sooky replaced the phone, choked with emotion and put her hands over her face.

'Sukhdeep, what is it?' Meena had come to the door.

Sooky turned to her, wiping her eyes. She shook her head. She saw her mother lean against the doorframe, her face creasing with distress.

Fifty-Nine

They waited at the hospital all the next day, while Roopinder went through her ordeal. Raj was with her some of the time, and Roopinder's mother. The only one not there was Pav, whom they had told not to miss lectures. Harpreet stayed home and Sooky waited with her and their parents, Roopinder's sisters and all the children, taking it in turns to be in the side room or the corridor, or taking the children for walks outside.

Sooky found she had to try not to think too closely about what Roopinder was experiencing. It was too horrible, too heartbreakingly sad. Prayers were said, hushed conversations, attempts to keep the children occupied. Now and then Raj came in, looking haunted and exhausted, and they crowded round.

'It's taking a long time,' he said. 'But she is strong.' Suddenly he seemed older, softer.

Roopinder had been given an epidural and was dozing. Meena brought Raj a cup of tea and, when he had drunk it, he went back to the labour room. Now and then a midwife would look round the door and say something reassuring.

'What did she say?' Meena always wanted to know. Otherwise she sat hunched with her arms folded. Sooky could see it was all an agony for her, and the way Meena dealt with agony was by falling silent.

Eventually it was over. Raj came down and they could see the change in his face. He seemed stunned.

'You can come in for a bit and see him, if you like,' he said.

They all trooped over into the delivery room. Roopinder was sitting up, holding the little boy's body wrapped in a blanket and gazing down at him with glassy eyes. Sooky could see she was in shock. Her mother stood one side of her, weeping quietly, and a midwife waited on the other. She moved tactfully out of the way when the family appeared.

His voice cracking as he spoke, Raj said, 'We've called him Hari – it means "the one who belongs to God".'

As everyone looked at the tiny baby, Roopinder began to weep at last. Sooky took in the sight of Hari, his creased, strained-looking little face. He was a mauve colour and it was easy to tell there was no life in him. Tears filled her eyes. She thought he was the saddest thing she had ever seen.

'He's so lovely,' she whispered to Roopinder, and touched her shoulder, before moving away to let Harpreet look at him. She heard her sister's sobs break out at the sight of the tiny little one.

Everyone hugged and wept with the couple. As her brother approached her, Sooky saw the deep hurt in his eyes and all she could think of was giving comfort. Silently she reached out to embrace Raj, and they hugged and she felt his body convulse as they cried in each other's arms.

'I'm so sorry,' she said, her lips close to his ear.

'Thanks, *Veer-ji*,' he murmured back.

And Sooky knew she was crying all the more because, after all this time, instead of his cold insults,

Raj had called her by the affectionate name that he had not used for her in such a long time.

Sooky's call in the morning had been a disappointment for Joanne. She had really been looking forward to seeing her – especially as it might be the last time for a while that she could come to their house.

'Your poor brother,' she said. 'And his wife, of course. That's really awful.'

'It is.' Sooky sounded very subdued. 'She's just going to have to go through it. Look, I'm sorry – maybe we could meet next week?'

Joanne hesitated. 'I hope so, I'll have to see.'

'Is he still coming home?'

'Yes – tomorrow.'

They wished each other luck.

The day stretched ahead empty in front of Joanne. She wanted to go out, not sit brooding about how things might be the next day and the day after. Once the chores and Amy's nap were over, they'd go into town, she decided.

In the end she didn't get out until nearly three o'clock.

'Now,' she said to Amy, when they'd climbed off the bus and sorted out the buggy, 'we'll go and have a look round the shops.'

She headed for New Street, hoping the sights would distract her thoughts, but round and round went her head. She could think of nothing but Dave coming home. Some of the time she was full of dread. Several times she nearly collided with people along the crowded pavement, she was so lost in thought. She took Amy to buy a jumper for the winter.

'You're growing too fast, young lady,' she said, pushing the jumper, in its bag, under the buggy. 'You'll soon grow out of everything.'

Off went her thoughts again. She had a surge of energy and optimism. She loved Dave – he was her husband and she wanted to see him! They could do this; they could start afresh. And it was up to her, not just up to him!

She managed to buy herself a new pair of jeans, keeping Amy happy with a bottle of juice. The time seemed to pass quickly.

'Right,' Joanne said. 'We'll go down to the Bull Ring and get some fruit and veg and then we'll get home, okay?'

As it was near the end of the day, some of the stallholders were reducing their prices to sell stuff off. She wheeled Amy round to take in the sights and sounds, the piles of cheap crockery being sold, the toys and watches. All the time there was the smell of oranges, crushed underfoot, and the loud shouting about apples and mushrooms, carrots and spuds. One stall was piled with pumpkins, as it was Halloween. Joanne held out her bag for them to tip in a pound of carrots, a cabbage, some knock-down mushrooms. Most of them called out to Amy in a friendly way and she watched, fascinated.

At the top of the slope the lady with the flowers was selling off her last bouquets. Joanne leaned over Amy's buggy.

'We'll get a bunch of flowers, shall we?' She found she wanted the house to look nice tomorrow. One minute full of dread, the next a good wife. It was all part of the confusion.

As she went to walk past Woolworths a short, grizzly man shook a tin at her.

'Help for striking miners' families,' he said. Absent-mindedly she slipped fifty pence through the slot.

Nearby the newspaper-sellers were calling out as well, 'Get yer *Mail*!' One of them stood holding a copy of the paper. The headline caught her eye: INDIRA GANDHI ASSASSINATED.

Hesitating, she thought of Sooky. In their conversations Sooky had talked a bit about India and politics, but Joanne didn't feel she knew much about it. She wheeled Amy over and bought a copy, before heading up to buy the flowers.

Later, while unpacking the shopping, she took out the newspaper. The Indian Prime Minister, Indira Gandhi, had been gunned down that morning by her Sikh bodyguards. Joanne read the report, frowning. The assassination was said to be in revenge for her ordering the Indian army to storm the Sikhs' most sacred temple in Amritsar.

Realizing she did not really understand the whole thing, Joanne switched on the TV. There were Sikhs rejoicing at the news, fists raised high. She switched it off again. She would have to ask Sooky.

Then realization returned to her, making her insides clench. Dave was coming home. In just a few hours.

Sikhs. She was murdered by Sikhs.

Even in their grief, this news overrode everything. It was all they could think about. They sat round the TV, watching report after report.

Roopinder was still in the hospital, in a drugged

sleep after her ordeal. Raj would have been asleep too, had things been different. As it was, he was glued to the images on the screen. The Hindus were distraught with grief at the death of 'Mother India', the Sikhs rejoicing at the death of the loathed woman who had ordered the desecration of their most sacred temple and the slaughter of so many of their people.

'She's gone!' Raj kept saying. He was still tearful, full of grief, but now also of triumph. 'That filthy bitch has gone!'

But there would be a backlash. What would happen now? Meena thought that she had never in her life felt more helpless. She sat tensely on the sofa, Harpreet beside her, stealing distressed glances at her mother's reaction.

All of them had their emotions pulled in so many directions: grief, triumph, horror.

At last Nirmal had managed to book a call from Delhi. He had no telephone in his house. Meena wept with relief, hearing his affectionate voice down the line.

'It was early this morning,' he yelled. He always shouted into the telephone, even though there was no need. 'She was walking in her own grounds. It was her bodyguards . . .'

'I know all this,' Meena said impatiently. 'We have it all on TV. But you . . . I am afraid of what is going to happen. You should leave – get out of Delhi. Come to UK, to us . . .'

'We are okay,' Nirmal said. 'I think everyone is shocked. To tell you the truth, I am worried, but what can I do? I don't have money to come to UK.'

'I send you! We are frightened for you. We will get a ticket for you.'

'Nothing is going to happen,' he said. 'I cannot leave.

I have my business – everything. You are worrying too much.'

Meena listened to his jovial tones, the voice of the man she had looked up to and loved for so many years.

'I wish you were here,' she said desperately. 'I am so worried for you.'

She sent her love to Bhoji and all the family and rang off. He had sounded so sure – too sure. But had there not been a tremor in his voice? Forever after, she never knew if she had imagined it.

Sixty

Thursday. As soon as she woke, Joanne had butterflies in her stomach. *He … is … coming … home …* Without waking Amy, she managed to creep down, make a mug of coffee and take it back to bed.

She sat with the duvet pulled up round her, sipping the coffee. Tonight he'll be here with me, lying next to me, she thought. And tomorrow Megan is coming to see us again. Dave had had the shock of his life when the police turned up on his doorstep. Surely he'd learned his lesson and things could get better? A rush of longing filled her. Let it be okay. Let it work out, *please*.

Once she was up, she found herself wanting to make everything nice. She fed Amy, then dashed round tidying up. She even put the oven on and baked a cake, grating orange peel into it so that the warm, fruity smell seeped round the house.

The phone rang, and with her heart pounding she rushed to answer it.

'Jo, what time's he coming back?' It was Karen, phoning from work.

'I'm not sure. This morning – soon.'

'You okay?'

'Think so. Bit nervous.' She couldn't think of anything to say. Her mind was jittering all over the place.

She must go and make the bed, pop out and buy some milk . . .

'Well, I hope it goes okay,' Karen said cautiously.

'Yeah . . .' Before her sister rang off, Joanne managed to pull herself together and say, 'Look, Karen – sorry. I'm just a bit out of it. But thanks, you know, for being such a help and everything.'

'Oh, that's okay,' Karen said. The words *Someone's got to keep it together in our family* were left unsaid, but implied in her tone. Joanne smiled as she rang off, thinking: At least we're giving practice to a budding counsellor.

But as she rushed round doing chores, her thoughts stayed with her family. She was surprised by her mother's reaction. Of course she'd had the lecture, to start with. Margaret had always been old-fashioned, up in arms when anyone stepped out of line, broke up a marriage or had a baby out of wedlock. But somehow she seemed to have come to terms with what had happened more quickly than Joanne had expected. She had her own things to deal with of course – getting off the Valium. But in fact . . .

Joanne stopped for a moment, standing in Amy's room. Mom seemed different altogether these days. She had been so wrapped up in her own problems that she hadn't given it much thought before. But all that business with the new clothes . . . It dawned on her that for the first time she could ever remember, her mother looked happy.

Dave had to ring the bell again when he arrived.

Joanne hesitated behind the door for a few seconds.

Would the Coles be twitching their net curtains, seeing him come home?

'You know we're here if you ever need us, bab,' Mrs Coles had said. And it was reassuring to know.

Now, she thought unlatching the door. *It's the beginning*.

There he was, spruce as ever: well-ironed jeans, navy jumper, hair freshly cut. He had his things in a zip-up bag of Wendy's and a bin-liner tied neatly at the top.

Joanne smiled, feeling as if they were on a first date. His face was full of uncertainty, but he smiled back, in a humble way.

'Can I come in then?' he said.

Once they'd closed the front door, he put his bags down and held out his arms and she, a bit awkward at first, stepped up to him. Silently they held one another. From the back room they could hear Amy chatting to herself.

'Amy, look who's here,' Joanne said after a minute.

Her little blonde head appeared round the door. 'Dada!'

Dave leaned down and scooped her up so that the three of them were all in one hug. He kissed each of them and held them tight.

'Home,' he said. 'Oh God, it's good to be home.' And in front of Amy he managed not to dissolve into tears.

That day reminded Joanne of the time after she had first brought Amy home from hospital, when all normal routines had been suspended. There was a floating quality of everyone just being together and taking no notice of time or anything else.

Shyly she offered Dave a cup of coffee.

'That looks nice,' he said, standing at the kitchen door and seeing her cake cooling on the rack.

'I'll put some icing on later,' she said. 'It's too warm now.'

They spent the morning just sitting together, playing with Amy, giving her lunch, letting her watch *Sesame Street* when it came on. She asked him when he was thinking of going back to work, but he shrugged and avoided answering. So she asked what he'd been doing at Wendy's.

'Not much,' he said. 'Watching telly – helping Mom out a bit.'

Her spirits sank. He still seemed so punch-drunk, as if all his spark had gone, even after several weeks. Was he ever going to get better again?

He seemed happiest when she was talking, so she told him what she'd been doing while he was away, about her friendship with Sooky and going to meet her family. No more pretending, she thought. I've got to have friends and go out – I'm not going to be stuck in the house just with him. Everything's going to be in the open.

'She's ever so nice,' she told him. 'You'll like her – she's really kind and chatty. And her daughter and Amy are best friends.' She felt proud that Amy had a little friend. 'Sooky's started a degree: she wants to be a social worker, so that's why she can't come to the toddler group. She's very clever.'

She waited for Dave to ask about Kieran, but he didn't, so she said, 'You remember that guy we met up Soho Road that time – with the red hair? Well, he's really nice too, but he's not around any more. His wife's come out of hospital, so he's been able to go back to work. I'm glad things are working out for them – so far as I know.'

Dave nodded, seeming to listen. Joanne realized, with a moment of worry, that at the moment she could say or do almost anything. He wouldn't dare to challenge her. But would it last, when he was feeling stronger? Would his old, possessive ways come creeping back?

All he seemed to want to do was sit beside her. She noticed that even when she got up and left the room to make sandwiches for lunch, he seemed anxious and wanted her back beside him.

As *Sesame Street* ended, she got up. 'Come on, Amy, time for your nap.'

Amy looked round and said cheekily, 'No – Amy stay!' She stuck her lip out. But in a second she was rubbing her eyes.

'Come on, young lady.' Joanne took her hand. 'Give Daddy a kiss.'

The sight of Amy reaching up with pursed lips to kiss Dave brought sudden tears to her eyes.

'I think she'll settle,' she said, coming back down a bit later. 'She's quite good at the moment.'

Dave looked up at her, his eyes full of need. He held out his hand and after a second she took it. They looked at each other.

'Can we . . . ?' He looked down for a moment, then back up at her. 'Can we go up as well?'

They undressed shyly, on opposite sides of the bed. It felt to her such a long time since lovemaking had been loving that they had in some way to begin again. Yet there was his body, long and lean, creamy-white, every inch of it so familiar. For a moment they stood apart, each taking the other in. He was already stiff, ready for her, and the sight moved her. She walked round the bed to him, conscious of her own naked body and how she must look to him, a woman with long legs and heavy breasts.

They lay down on the cold sheets, which soon grew warm under the weight of their bodies, and made love, tentatively at first. He touched her with a look of wonder. Then it became urgent and finally tearful. Words poured from his lips as he moved in her, 'My babe, oh my babe, my woman . . .' He lay on her for a long time, still inside her, she holding him close with her arms and her legs cradling him while he sobbed, his wet cheek pressed close to hers. The warm closeness of it, of being reunited and having hope and love, made her cry as well. He kept saying he loved her, he loved her so much.

At last he pushed up on his arms and wiped his eyes with the heel of one hand. As he looked down at her his face was tender, but she could see how lost and scared he looked as well.

'I don't know what's happened to me.' His voice was thick with tears.

'I s'pose you had a sort of breakdown.' Her nose was all stuffed up. It was hard to breathe.

'Here, I'll get the tissues.' He withdrew from her and reached for the box on the table on her side.

They drew the cover up and settled side by side. Dave pulled her into his arms.

'Sometimes I feel so scared. I feel as if I've come to pieces and I don't know how to . . . you know, like Humpty Dumpty.'

Joanne laughed. 'I'm sure you can – put yourself

back together again.' She was beginning to realize, only now, just how long this might take.

'I just feel so bloody pathetic. It's like I can't *do* anything. Everything's a massive effort – even making a cup of tea. That's what the counsellor said: it's like injuring yourself, cutting yourself or breaking a bone. It takes time to heal up, so why should our minds be any different? But even coming over here on the bus every time, all those people – it feels like one of the hardest things I've ever done. I mean, that's not me, is it? I've never been like that.'

'No, but this is different.'

Dave rolled up onto his elbow and looked down at her. 'All I want is to be here with you – for you to be my missis. You and Amy, you're everything to me. I know that now: you know, how stupid I've been and everything. I never knew what was going on, why I felt the way I did. I didn't know what to do about it. But it's all going to be different now, I promise you. I love you, Joanne, you're my wife and – well, that's it. That's the only thing.'

He lay back beside her, kissing her again and again. 'Oh. You're gorgeous, you are.'

It was lovely, to be loved and kissed and held. But in her mind she could hear the warning voices, women from the refuge, Gina and Doreen and Linda. 'He always says he's going to change – he promises me the earth, and I think he means it when he says it. But after a day or a week or more, he's up to his old tricks . . .'

It was her turn to lift up onto her elbow. Things were loving and sweet and all she really wanted, but she had to say it now – to make it clear.

'I love you, Dave,' she said. 'I really do. I want you home and for us to be together, with Amy and everything. But it can't go back to the way things were – not for any of us. I'm not going to stop in all the time like a prisoner, that's one thing. I'll decide for myself whether I go out or not. And I won't have any violence. If you ever, *ever* lay a finger on either of us again – Amy or me – even just once, it's over. I'll leave you and take Amy; and I won't come back. Not again, ever. That's it.'

Dave stared back at her. He seemed to be struggling with something. Joanne saw that that something was her strength. Well, she thought, too bad. That's how it is.

'You do understand, don't you?'

He closed his eyes. 'Yes. Course I do. It'll never happen again. I promise.'

'Dave?'

'Yeah?' His eyes were still closed.

'I love you. I do.'

In a subdued voice he said, 'Love you too.'

She lay back down and they rested together, close and warm.

Sixty-One

The next reminiscence session at the library was on *The Blitz*. Margaret sat beside Alan as everyone talked about air-raid shelters and the sound of the planes, the cold, terrifying nights of the bombing, and emerging at dawn to see which bits of Birmingham had been flattened this time.

'I don't remember any of that,' she told Alan when the tea was being brewed up afterwards. Alan handed her a cup and saucer in his usual gallant way. 'Miss Clairmont and Mrs Higgins always listened to the news on the wireless. I remember when they bombed Coventry – everyone was talking about it. And there were planes over us sometimes. Everyone was scared they'd just empty out whatever they had left on their way back! But it was nothing like they had in Brum.'

The evenings stirred up their memories and feelings, which made it all the easier to talk about the past. As the session ended, Margaret was alight with excitement. Surely he'd ask her again this week? They'd be able to go to the pub round the corner and have the bliss of sitting in the warm, talking and talking! They scarcely ever thought about smoking – they were far too involved.

As everyone was gathering their coats and bags Alan turned to her.

'Have you got time for a drink this week?'

Margaret was touched by the fact that she could see

he was trying to seem casual, to insure himself against disappointment.

'Ooh, yes – I wouldn't miss it,' she said. 'I've been looking forward to it all week!'

A delighted grin spread across his face. Margaret blushed. Had she sounded too forward? Still, it was the truth – she had been!

Once they were settled in their favourite corner of the pub again, they talked more about the war and the things they'd heard.

'That poor woman,' Margaret said.

Alan immediately knew who she meant. One woman, from Balsall Heath, had been a young teenager. Her house received a direct hit and everyone in her family was killed, except her. From then on, her life was spent in children's homes. Her voice had been full of unspent grief, even after all these years.

'Everyone carries a bit of it all around in them, one way or another,' Alan said sadly. 'Whatever it says in the history books about battles and tanks and all that. For most people it's about a mom or a dad or a brother – or a house.'

Margaret nodded, feeling the truth of his words.

Alan hesitated. 'Your husband . . .' he said, then stalled. She knew he needed to know about Fred. 'You never talk about him – not unless I ask.'

She looked at him. *Fred doesn't matter*, she wanted to say. *It's you – you're the one who matters.* But of course she couldn't say that. She told Alan about Fred, about how they'd met and about Fred's mom.

'Fred and I were like two lost souls, clinging onto each other. It's been years since we've ever really said anything to each other. We're like ships that pass in the night – only in the daytime as well. He's not a bad man, but I s'pose he just didn't have a very good start. Neither of us did.'

She thought for a moment, then went on, 'I don't know if he ever loved me. I don't know if I loved him. I don't think I knew what it meant. Not until—' She stopped in confusion. She couldn't look at him, not for a moment. But when she did pull her gaze up to meet his, he was still looking at her intently, hungrily.

There was a long silence and then Alan cleared his throat. He seemed in some way unsteady.

'I . . . I'm in trouble here, Margaret, I have to tell you. I just . . .'

Everything inside her seemed to swell until she could hardly breathe. She didn't need to ask herself what he was saying. It was clear in his face. For the first time in her life she knew what she was seeing: someone looking at her with the force of love in their eyes. She knew that the way she was looking back was the same.

As she gazed helplessly at him, Alan reached out and laid his hand over hers. She could not resist, had not the slightest will to do so. It felt as if everything – all she needed – was here.

'Oh,' she said tremulously. 'Oh dear.'

'Yes,' Alan said. 'Oh dear. I'm – I don't know. This has all happened a bit fast – for me, anyway. I haven't thought about anything but you for weeks.'

'Yes,' she agreed, throbbing with happiness. 'Me too.'

Again they sat staring at each other. They smiled with utter joy. They fell serious again.

'I'm . . .' Margaret began. She had to stop and think. 'I'm a married woman. Not happily married, no. Just married.'

She frowned, looking at him to help her work this out.

'Why don't I feel that's enough? That's the way it's supposed to be, isn't it? You get married, you stay married. Then when I'm with you, Fred and all my other life – it doesn't seem to mean anything. It's as if I'm living in two different worlds.' She put her hand to her head. 'When I'm at home it's the same as it's always been. I mean, we've had our problems. My youngest daughter's been having difficulties in her marriage. She walked out with the baby because she said he was . . . Well, he'd started knocking her about. I didn't believe it at first – Dave's been a good lad, and we've known him since he was quite a young'un. But evidently it's true. But when she just upped and left – I thought: You don't *do* that. I mean, you just *don't*. In our day you put up and shut up, didn't you?'

'Well, no, not everyone . . .'

'No, all right, but in the main, people just stayed. After all, the law was all on the man's side . . . But the thing was, it was her getting up and going. *Choosing* to go. I mean, she was protecting Amy – and herself. But it was her feeling that she could *choose*. I was so angry at first. I thought: How *dare* she?'

Alan was listening attentively. 'The law makes a hell of a difference.'

'Well, *yes*. It's all changed. Now you can make your own decisions more. All my life I've never felt I could choose anything – not even new clothes,' Margaret said. As she spoke, she was learning about herself. She hardly knew that she had felt such things. She had never known she had so many words in her. 'Let alone anything else. But now . . .'

She looked at him, searching his face, not yet daring to say it.

'Is this my fault?' Alan looked stricken. 'I don't want to cause harm.'

She looked levelly at him. 'There's always going to be harm – one way or another. If you turned round and left now, and we never saw each other again . . .'

He closed his eyes. 'No, don't say that.'

'Exactly. That's what I mean.'

'You're the best thing – the *only* thing – that's happened to me in ages.'

She nodded. 'And you are to me.' She wanted to say something better than that, but it was too big to say.

'Look,' Alan said. 'I'll walk you home.' He always did, or most of the way, even though he'd left his car in a nearby street. They liked the time together.

Outside, without a word, they linked arms and she felt him pull her close. Before long, at the corner of the road, he stopped, in the shadows.

'Oh, Margaret.' He turned to face her. There was a second's hesitation and then, also feeling natural, they stood cuddled in each other's arms. 'I just want to hold you close,' he said. 'Every waking moment that's all I think about, I swear to you. I feel like a flaming teenager. I don't know what's happened to me.'

She giggled into the collar of his coat, feeling his rough chin against her left temple.

'I think about you too. All the time.'

She turned her head up. In the darkness, she could just see the moist gleam of his eyes; smell the warm beer on his breath, the smokiness of their clothing from the pub.

'I think I must love you,' she said.

'Oh – I love you all right, girl.'

Laughing with amazement and joy, they moved closer, lips touching, pecking and playing, until they had to stop laughing to kiss properly.

When she got home, what felt like a century or so later, Margaret was alight with desire and happiness. She felt as if it must show all over her, as if Alan had planted vivid red kisses all over her face and neck for anyone to read there.

'Can we meet sooner – than next Thursday, I mean?' Alan asked.

She longed to, could hardly bear not to see him every day, every hour.

'The evenings might be a bit tricky,' she said, thinking of Karen's eagle eye on anything she did.

'What about the daytime?'

'But you're at work!'

'Yes, but I do get a dinner break – well, sometimes anyway. I could make sure I do. And your husb—?'

'Yes, Fred's at work every day.'

'What about Monday? I'll need to see you after the weekend, I can tell you – it tends to drag a bit, to tell you the truth.'

They arranged to meet at a pub a little way away from Alan's firm in Rea Street.

'We don't want to be too close to the works,' he said, 'or all the lads'll be in there ogling us. Sorry you've got so far to come, though.'

'Don't be daft,' she said. 'I've only got to hop on the bus.'

They parted with a long, lingering kiss. Afterwards she felt she had been ripped away from where she truly belonged.

She slid quietly into the house. Fred was where she had left him, in his chair, his head back, mouth open and fast asleep. Margaret went through to the kitchen and put the kettle on. Her sounds woke him.

'Oh!' she heard him say. She went into the front room. He was rubbing his face. There were empty cans of bitter on the table next to him and he looked a bit muzzy. 'Must've fell asleep,' he said. It took him a moment to remember that she'd been out. 'So – you're back.'

'Yes,' she was saying, trying to quell her fizzing, beaming exaltation when a key turned in the latch and Karen came in, back from her counselling course.

'All right?' she called from the hall, taking her coat off. 'I thought you might be in bed. We went for a drink after.'

'So did we,' Margaret said. 'I've only just got in. D'you want a cuppa tea?'

'Ooh, yes, ta. It's cold out.' Karen came in, looking pleased. 'That group of yours seems very friendly,' she said, taking in her mother's pink cheeks and eyes, which suddenly seemed full of life.

'Yes,' Margaret said, turning away. 'It is. I'll brew up the tea.'

Sixty-Two

They were days of horror, of helpless watching and waiting for news.

Indira Gandhi had been dead for less than twenty-four hours when the news began about revenge killings, angry mobs on the streets of Delhi, attacking and burning Sikh homes and businesses.

Meena felt as if her eyes wanted to burn through the images on television, for her to be transported into the picture so that she could go to Nirmal and Bhoji, help them and their family and get them to safety. And she cursed her lack of English.

'What are they saying?' she kept crying, desperate for words that would contradict the reports of flames and screams and death.

Everyone went to the *gurdwara*, needing to wait together, to exchange news and share their fears. Meena and Khushwant barely even discussed going – they just headed there automatically, and Sooky, Pav and Harpreet went with them, taking the children.

Meena moved among the other women, who were talking and praying. She met Banita, who instead of her usual jolly, ebullient self was drawn and pale, her *chunni* pulled tightly round her head as if to warm her. She saw Meena and they embraced.

'My sister,' Banita wept. 'She is in Delhi with all her family – in Trilokpuri. And my mother in Amritsar . . .

May God protect them! What can we do? That is what I am asking, every moment, what can we do to help them?'

'I know,' Meena said, her tears flowing. 'My uncle also and all his family. And Khushwant's brothers.'

Nearly everyone had someone in India. None had telephones in their homes. How were they to know what was happening?

Still weeping, Meena told Banita about Roopinder, that she had had to give birth to a dead baby boy.

'A double misfortune!' Banita cried. She asked after Roopinder. Meena shook her head.

'She is very sick, with a fever. Raj is staying with her at the hospital and we are all going back and forth to visit.'

'Poor Raj,' Banita said. 'To lose a son – and in the middle of all this as well.'

The two women sat together, comforting each other. Later they all went home and kept the television on, hour after hour. Meena thought constantly of Nirmal and Bhoji. Harpreet kept making cups of tea, offering snacks and biscuits, but Meena could not eat. Her heart was heavier than she could ever remember.

The stairs in the hospital felt so steep and endless as she and Sooky climbed them. Meena clutched onto Sooky's arm, feeling as if, overnight, she had become an old woman.

'Are you okay, *Ma-ji*?' Sooky asked, eyes full of concern as Meena stopped at the top, leaning against the wall to catch her breath.

'Yes – just give me one minute. I'm tired, that's all.'

She was glad her eldest daughter was with her. Pav had said he could mind the little children that morning.

She saw that Sukhdeep was looking pale as well, darker rings than usual under her eyes. With a grunt of effort she pushed away from the wall and took her daughter's hand. Together they walked along to the ward, passing a blaring TV set.

Raj was sitting beside the bed with his head in his hands. He wasn't facing the TV, and even if he had been, it was only showing adverts, then someone having their hair styled. Roopinder lay on her back with her eyes closed. Meena saw that she looked younger, rain-washed somehow, without make-up – prettier in fact, not frowning, and with her hair a dark frame against the pillow.

'Rajdev?' she said softly.

Raj stirred and lifted his head. He looked dazed and rubbed his eyes. 'Oh, it's you, *Mata-ji*. I think I was asleep.'

'How is she?' Sooky whispered.

'They said she had a bad night,' Raj said. 'Very high fever. I think the antibiotics are kicking in now. But every time she wakes she just keeps crying. She just seems so broken . . .'

His voice cracked and he put his face in his hands again. Meena felt her own distress rise. She laid her hand on Raj's heaving shoulder.

'Look, son – I've brought her some fruit.' She laid the little bag of grapes and bananas on the bedside cabinet. 'Sukhdeep and I will sit here for a while. She will be better when the fever passes. You go home and sleep.'

Raj struggled to his feet. His wiped his eyes, his

cheeks and beard. He was like someone punch-drunk from too many emotions all at once. Meena wanted to hold him close and protect him, like she had when he was a tiny boy.

'India,' he said. 'What is happening? What is the news? This TV shows nothing but garbage. Have you heard from *Mama-ji* Nirmal?'

Meena shook her head. 'I have not heard. The news is bad, very bad. But there is nothing we can do, only wait and trust in God. Go home now – sleep. Your wife will need you.'

When she turned to the bed, Sooky was sitting holding Roopinder's hand.

There was no call from Nirmal.

As the days passed, Roopinder's health improved and she and Raj had to face their grief.

The news from India was horrifying. By the time Mrs Gandhi was on her funeral pyre on 3rd November, more and more news was getting out. The number of Sikhs massacred in Delhi alone was reckoned to be in the thousands. Many had been butchered in the street, their homes set alight; trains arriving in Delhi and Amritsar contained the corpses of Sikhs, beaten and burned. In one suburb alone, to the east of Delhi, there was an area where the streets ran with blood and could hardly be passed, so choked were they with bodies. The area was called Trilokpuri.

Where were the police? everyone was asking. The bitter, enraging answer came: They had turned a blind eye, joining in the slaughter. As the facts sunk in, it started to be called a massacre, a genocide of the Sikh people.

Banita never heard from any of her relatives in Trilokpuri again. And as soon as Meena heard the name of the suburb mentioned, she knew Nirmal was dead. They knew Khushwant's brothers were alive; they had telephoned. Nirmal would have called by now to reassure her. Somehow he would have been in touch.

The call came very early one morning. Meena heard it ringing from the hall below and she knew instantly it was from India; their timing was five hours ahead. No one in Britain rang you at this hour. She was out of bed and down the stairs almost before she was aware of it.

'Meena?'

It was her aunt Bhoji's voice, sounding close, so close.

'*Mami-ji*? Oh, my God, yes – it's me. Oh, at last! Tell me everything – Nirmal?'

But she knew. She knew. Why would Bhoji be calling; Bhoji who until now had never touched a telephone?

Bhoji was almost incoherent, she was weeping so much.

'I am all alone – they killed him! My husband, my Nirmal! And they killed Manjit ... They dragged Nirmal out of his car, and they put a tyre round his neck and petrol and they set it alight...'

A howl of anguish came down the line, which made Meena double over herself, feeling as if she had been kicked.

'You are sure?' she managed to find the breath to say. Could it have been someone else, some other taxi driver – could it?

'Yes, yes,' Bhoji sobbed. 'And Manjit, they murdered

my Manjit – just killed him in the street. Everything is gone: fires, everything destroyed, only me left and the girls. What are we to do? How can we live?'

'Your house is gone, your apartment?'

'No, the house is not gone. Many are burned, not ours – but we have no father, no brother . . .'

'We will help you,' Meena gasped. She became dimly aware of people around her, others coming down the stairs. Suddenly Khushwant was beside her, making signs to her: *What is it?* Sukhdeep and Harpreet were there in their nightclothes, their arms round each other.

'We will . . .' Meena was shaking now, couldn't think what to say. 'We will help you, *Mami-ji* – don't despair . . .'

She put the phone down and turned, and her legs gave way.

Sixty-Three

'But surely you don't want us round – not with all that on your plate?' Joanne said. 'You must all be really upset.'

'Yeah, it's been horrible,' Sooky said. 'But it's okay, honestly. Mom said she doesn't mind. We have to look after the kids whatever happens, don't we?'

'Well, if you're sure.' Joanne sounded doubtful. 'I'm sorry, I'd invite you round to ours, only it's just not a very good time here, either.'

'No, come,' Sooky assured her. 'It'll be really nice to see you – and it'll take our minds off it.'

It was good to hear someone else's voice, someone outside the situation, Sooky thought as she put the phone down that morning. It had been a desperately sad week. For all those days, her heart had felt like a stone.

They'd kept Roopinder in for observation, but she was now recuperating upstairs. She was very low and weepy, and while Sooky did her best to keep her company, she could only stand so much of it. Her mother had been curled into herself with grief ever since Bhoji's call. Sooky was upset – for all of them; for the horrific way Nirmal and his son had died, and for his daughters and Bhoji. She knew how much Nirmal had meant to her mother. She'd loved him like no other relative – and he had been her connection with home.

Now Meena seemed so lost and sad. On top of that, no one could stop thinking about the situation in India and all the anguish and rage that the events had caused.

Sooky had been to college on Tuesday this week and it had been a relief to get away from the grief-stricken atmosphere of the house. She realized most people weren't taking too much notice of what was going on with the Sikhs in India, and this both angered her – such a bloodbath! Imagine if it happened in England, the uproar there would be! – and was an escape from thinking about it all, just for a while. One thing she did do, which was unusual, was to go to college dressed in Punjabi clothes. Putting on jeans, fashion clothes, and leaving her head bare had felt wrong that day. She couldn't work all of it out emotionally, but she just felt she had to be a Sikh and show she was a Sikh: Sukhdeep Kaur Baidwan. She wasn't the most religious of people, but it was part of where she belonged.

She went to find Priya, who was with her cousins by the TV in the front room. Everyone was taking it in turns to look after them all this week – even Dad. To her surprise she'd come down on Tuesday, ready for college, to find him on his hands and knees on the rug, one arm swinging merrily in front of his face as he pretended to be an elephant. Smiling, she had stood and watched for a moment.

Khushwant had looked up at her, his hair all rumpled. He wasn't dressed for work and she knew he was doing this to allow her to go out.

'How the elephant got its trunk,' he said rather bashfully.

'Go on,' Sooky said, leaning on the doorframe. 'I don't want to interrupt.' It was a relief to laugh about something.

'This is much harder than going to work,' he grinned up at her. He took in, suddenly, what she was wearing. She had toyed with wearing a bright orange-and-yellow suit, but that felt wrong too. She had put on one in a sober green.

'You're going to college?'

She nodded.

'Dressed like that?'

Again, she inclined her head.

'Okay.' He had smiled suddenly, with understanding. 'I see. You look nice.'

Tears sprang into her eyes.

'Thanks,' she said.

This morning the three children were glued to a cartoon. Too much TV, she thought. They watch too much.

'Priya, Amardeep, Jasmeet – shall I read you a story? Some rhymes?'

Jasmeet, who was standing quite close to the TV, shook her head, bewitched by what was on the screen. Amardeep shouted 'No!' very decisively. Priya, looking torn, came across and settled on Sooky's lap, sliding around on the silky material. She picked out her favourite book of nursery rhymes.

Sooky read 'I do not like thee, Doctor Fell' and 'Sing a Song o' Sixpence' ... Her mind wandered as she did so. The image of Nirmal's burning necklace wouldn't leave her mind. She knew it wouldn't leave her mother's, either. Meena didn't weep a great deal; she just seemed winded, wordless, as if whatever was going on inside her had to be worked out in silence.

For want of a nail, a shoe was lost ... Priya was rocking to the rhythms on her lap, pointing at the pictures.

For want of Khalistan ... Off toddled her mind

again, then stalled. What was it all for – Khalistan? For safety, for a place we Sikhs can call our own.

For want of Khalistan, a temple was occupied.

For want of government control, a temple was desecrated . . .

For that desecration, a Prime Minister was gunned down.

For the murder of a Prime Minister . . .

For that murder, thousands more . . . And angry demonstrations and hatred and more anger . . .

And even before that, death upon death in the spiral of violence leading up to it: Hindus killing Sikhs, Sikhs killing Hindus . . . Horror upon horror, *for want of, for want of . . .* what? Her mind looped and bucked, could not cope with more.

'Come on.' She stood up decisively. 'We're all going to the park. Turn off the TV.'

To her amazement they obeyed. Auntie obviously sounded as if she knew what she was talking about. 'We'll get some fresh air, and then this afternoon,' she told Priya, 'your friend Amy is coming round!'

Joanne expected Sooky to answer the door, but instead it was opened by her mom. In that instant she realized that she had no idea what to call her. She had forgotten Sooky's actual surname, apart from the Kaur bit.

'Oh, hello,' she said awkwardly.

Sooky's mom looked different: tired and thinner. Of course she would, Joanne thought. There'd been so much bad news. She was dressed in pale mauve today. But she raised a faint smile, said 'Hello' and stood back to let Joanne in. She pointed to the front room and said, in English, 'Wait here, please.' Joanne realized that she probably understood quite a lot.

The room was very tidy, no toys scattered on the floor. Joanne heard Sooky's mom call up the stairs, 'Sukhdeep!' Then words she couldn't understand. She thought what a nice voice the woman had, smooth and gentle.

A moment later she heard Sooky coming downstairs, telling Priya to hurry.

'Hello!' She appeared, smiling. 'Sorry – I had to change her clothes. She got in such a mess with her lunch.'

Amy went up and solemnly kissed Priya's cheek, and Joanne saw Sooky's mom, who had come into the doorway, give another slight smile.

They settled with cups of tea, but this time Sooky's mom did not stay in the room. Sooky said she had gone up to sit with her sister-in-law for a bit, with her kids up there too. Roopinder's mother was due to arrive later.

The two of them sat on the floor close to their daughters and some toys. Sooky talked about the baby and how cut up her brother was about it. She seemed relieved to be able to tell someone. Then at last she said, 'Now, tell me about you. How's your husband – and everything at home?'

Joanne sighed. 'Well, it's okay. I mean okay in the sense that there's nothing angry or violent about him, not like before. I suppose I just never thought he would take so long to get better. To tell you the truth, I'm really glad to have somewhere to get out to today. I have to get out sometimes. The thing is, he can't cope. He follows me round everywhere. All he really wants is for me to sit on the sofa with him, hour after hour – as if the sofa is an island and everywhere else is a sea full of man-eating sharks or something!'

Sooky laughed at this.

'I can see why his mom was keen to get him out of her house. We've hardly seen her since! I suppose eventually he'll go back to work, but it's going to be a slow business. He'll have to go back part-time at first, I think.'

'Can he do that?'

'It's his business.' Joanne took a sip of the sweet, milky tea. Sooky offered her ginger biscuits and some spicy snacks. 'Ooh, I'd rather have those.' Joanne pointed at the bowl of spicy bits. 'Thanks. Yeah, it was his dad's little business – he inherited it sort of thing, so he's his own boss.'

Sooky's eyes were sympathetic. 'He's really been in a bad state, by the sound of it.'

'Yeah, I know.' Joanne softened. She had been talking rather jokily, not showing her real sympathy for Dave. 'Poor old sausage. I love him to bits really, even after all this. It's terrible seeing him the way he is, but I think he'll get there. I just feel like everyone's mother at the moment. How's your mom? She looks really worn down by it.'

'Yes – well that, and my brother. At least it's taken Raj's mind off politics for a bit. The thing is . . .' she said reflectively, 'one thing I really realize through this is how much my brother loves his wife.'

'Well, that's nice, although . . .' Joanne whispered, 'I thought you didn't get on with her?'

'No, I didn't. She wasn't very nice to me at all. But somehow everything feels a bit better. You know, she asked me to go to the doctor with her when she was worried and now she's different – a bit softer – just nicer.'

'Well, that's good.'

Sooky grinned. 'Let's hope it lasts when she's back on her feet.' She nodded at the girls. 'Look at these two!'

Amy and Priya had pulled out a cardboard box full of odd silky bits of clothing in a variety of colours. They were piling them all on, wrapping things round them and giggling wildly at each other, and this set their mothers off laughing too.

'Heaven help us in ten years or so,' Joanne said.

'Oh, my goodness,' Sooky laughed. 'Teenagers!'

Their eyes met, each warmed by the thought that in ten years' time they would like still to be friends.

Sixty-Four

Margaret went to every single one of the Second World War reminiscence sessions at the library that autumn. They stopped running in mid-December, with promises of more in the New Year.

Alan was there at every one too, and between them they made new friends in the group. There was a little party at the end of the last one, with people bringing nibbles along and the librarians made some mulled wine.

They barely had to discuss it. Instead of going to the library, Margaret went out anyway the next week and met Alan at the pub.

All those weeks they had met twice, three times some weeks and talked endlessly, gone for little walks in places where it felt safe: around the block from Alan's works, or in the dark around Kings Heath. They shared all their memories of their evacuation experience. It seemed to Margaret that they shared everything, finding out more and more about each other's lives. Anything she needed to say she could, to Alan, and he listened. He never dismissed her or turned away. Fred had never been able to talk or listen much. He was locked deep into himself. He didn't like talking about feelings in any way. Margaret, who had already had plenty of practice in denying her emotions, continued to do so throughout her marriage. But now everything was different. It felt like a huge discovery.

'I just never knew,' she said to Alan one day as they walked along arm in arm. 'I never had any idea it could be like this. People talk about love and all that, but I sort of thought they were just pretending. All those feelings everyone goes on about in the films and that . . . Now I know they're real!'

'Oh, love,' Alan would say, sounding as pleased as punch. He leaned round to kiss her. 'I know just what you mean, though. It feels like a miracle to me, finding you at my time of life!'

Margaret walked round in a haze of happiness. She wore her new clothes, found herself speaking out more, even sang around the house. Singing – *me*! she thought. The only songs she knew were a few hymns from going to church in Buckley, and she hummed the bits she couldn't remember the words to. There were songs they'd learned in the school there too: 'Greensleeves' and the one about Uncle Tom Cobleigh and all. And a few Beatles numbers . . . She made sure no one else was in when she started warbling away.

She knew Joanne and Karen had noticed. Joanne had been over a few times with Dave and Amy. The lad seemed to be getting himself together again, she saw to her relief. Maybe Joanne going off like that had shocked him out of it? Who knew? Nothing was ever simply right and wrong – not like she was brought up to think. There was always more to things.

And every day she dreamed about Alan, about being in his arms, while she cleaned the house and made Fred's tea and all the things she'd always done – well, not everything. Not *that*. She and Fred had twin beds now. There hadn't been any of *that* to speak of for years. Not that she'd got to the stage of *that* with Alan, either. It wasn't that she didn't want to. Sometimes she burned with it, and knew he did too. But there was nowhere much to go, and much as she loved kissing and cuddling with him, *that* was another stage. It meant facing up to things, and Margaret was old-fashioned enough to believe that *that* was something you did only when you were married. And getting married to Alan would mean owning up to everyone. It would mean trouble, it would mean divorce – oh, heavens above! It was so much nicer just to go on as they were. And being the gentleman he was, Alan never pushed it. She was the one who was already married, after all. He didn't want to be the one to force anything.

'I'd do anything for you, Margaret,' he'd say sometimes. 'Anything at all. Even if I have to wait forever.'

The last time he'd said it they were standing out in the dark, arms round each other. She was smitten with guilt. Surely she *should* be prepared to go through all these things for him? All the things she'd spent her life condemning in other people: marital break-ups, affairs, stepping out of line. What would her daughters say? What about Fred? She trembled inside, her heart sinking. She was far too much of a coward for all this.

It was the week before Christmas. That Thursday was the last time she would be able to meet Alan for some time – at least until Fred was back at work after the holiday.

The tree was up in the front room and Karen had bought a wreath for the front door. She'd come home with some fancy new decorations and hung them round the house, as well as paper streamers. Karen, Margaret realized suddenly, seemed full of it too. She had started talking about a man called Geoff whom she'd met on her course.

When Joanne called in, Margaret brought out some chocolate decorations for Amy to tie on the Christmas tree, keeping just one to eat. Margaret smiled, seeing her granddaughter's wide eyes as they decorated the tree.

'Have you written your letter to Father Christmas?' she asked her. 'Sent it up the chimney?'

Amy frowned, puzzled.

'You'd have a job in our house, with the gas fire in the way!' Joanne said.

'Oh, I expect he'll be happy if you just leave him a note in the fireplace with a mince pie to eat,' Margaret said. 'Father Christmas likes pies. And a carrot for the reindeer.'

Amy was tickled by this. 'Carrot!' she giggled. 'Mommy put carrot!'

'Oh, I s'pose so,' Joanne agreed.

'She's talking more now, isn't she?' Margaret said. Amy had recently had her second birthday.

'You're telling me,' Joanne said.

Margaret thought Joanne looked rather pale and strained.

'Things all right, are they, love?'

As Joanne turned, Margaret saw her surprised look. Was it such a new thing, Margaret wondered, that she should notice something about her children, should think to ask? Where had she been all these Valium-stifled years?

'Not too bad,' Joanne said. 'I mean, it's not bad like it was before. He's all right – he's being really good. He just needs me a lot, that's all.'

Margaret was at a loss for what to say. 'I expect it'll pass,' she brought out eventually. Joanne seemed reassured by this.

'Yeah, I expect so.' She looked directly across at her mother. 'What about you? How're you feeling?'

'Oh.' She was about to be evasive – they didn't have these conversations normally – but pulled herself up. 'I'm not too bad, really. I've cut down on the pills, slowly. Very slowly, but I'm on much less than I was. I never feel a hundred per cent – but much better, yes.'

Joanne smiled and Margaret saw her little girl as she had been, pink-cheeked, sunny. She experienced a pang of deep sorrow. How much had she missed in all this numb time?

'That's great,' Joanne said. 'It must be really difficult after all this time. But you look better. Dad seems a bit happier too.'

'Does he?' Margaret said. Guilt washed through her. What the hell had being married to her been like for him? Married to zombie-woman. Maybe that was why he was the way he was.

Later that afternoon, once Joanne had gone and before the others got back, Margaret sat by the fire in the front room with a cup of tea. She put on the Christmas-tree lights and it all looked lovely and cosy. Karen, organized as ever, had already wrapped a few presents and laid them under the tree, and the gold stripes in the paper glowed with the colours of the lights.

Margaret sat and looked round her. She had lived in this house since just after Karen was born. Every inch of it – the lay of every board, every bulge in the walls, the squeak or rattle of every door handle – was almost as familiar to her as her own body. She thought back to when the girls were small, getting them to sleep of a night, having them play outside in the garden; paddling pools and leaf-sweeping and snowmen; Fred coming in from work; and meal upon hundreds of meals when they all sat round the table in the back room. Then Christmas, each year with the tree in the same spot in the window, lights gleaming welcomingly as you came home and saw it shining behind the nets.

For the first time she faced up to what she was doing. Alan! Could she and Alan go on like this, meeting up, courting – for that was what it was – and never decide anything? Was that the right thing to do? Or should she own up, tell Fred, leave all this, her home, everything she was used to?

She was so filled with panic that she couldn't carry on sitting. She leapt up from the chair and walked back and forth across the little room.

'I've been in a dream world,' she said out loud.

She thought about poor old Fred. He hadn't been a bad husband. He'd earned his wages, brought them home and not drunk them away, like some. He'd just been there. That was all. Not much more, but not less, and he had always been much the same, whatever she had been like. Even if there was nothing much left between them, he didn't deserve to be left, to be betrayed with broken promises.

Alan's face swam into her mind, his eyes full of love and longing, and her panic increased. She was supposed to be meeting him the next evening.

'Oh, dear God, what am I to do?' she said. The walls were silent, giving no answer.

Sixty-Five

I've got to be strong, very strong. All day she kept saying this to herself, getting more and more wound up as the time to meet Alan drew nearer. *Alan, there's something I've really got to say . . .*

'I'm just off to my library group again,' she told Fred after tea, of which she had scarcely managed to swallow any at all.

'All right, love,' Fred said, from behind the *Mail*.

For a moment she paused in the doorway with her coat on, looking at him. With a pang she remembered the boy she had first seen, shivering, with no shirt, on the way to the wharf. It seemed an eternity ago. Where had all the years gone? Where had she gone? And Fred? What did he think about all the time, she wondered? She felt as if she was seeing him from far off, through the wrong end of a telescope.

'TTFN then,' she said softly.

Fred actually looked up. He smiled. 'Oh – thought you'd gone! You look nice, bab. Tara!'

Tears stung her eyes. Of all the times he had to notice her and pay a compliment! She was glad of the walk, of having time to think. At that moment she was full of the past, of memories of Fred. She thought about that day she had seen him again in the cafe after the war. He'd been so pleased, in his quiet way. He had felt like a rescue to her. She might have spent her whole life stuck in Elsie's house, playing housekeeper to her elder sister. Fred had offered marriage; a way to have some sort of life.

She tucked her scarf tighter in round her neck in the cold wind. Some of the shop fronts in the High Street had Christmas lights in their windows. She passed huddles at bus stops, pubs spilling out the sound of voices as doors swung open and closed.

The last time, she said to herself. This must be the last time meeting Alan. Then I'm going to put my life back in order. I don't want to be a . . . what do they call it? Divorcee. That's never been me. I've got to do the right thing. I owe it to Fred. And what do I really know about Alan? I've never even spent a whole day with him, or a night. And what sort of man is he, who would keep on walking out with a woman whom he knows is married, disturbing her life? It could be a disaster from start to finish, and then where would I be?

You've been living in a dream, she told herself sharply. Again she pictured her home, the cosy front room. She knew her mind was made up. No big changes for her. She wasn't one of these overturning-the-apple-cart types. She didn't allow the misery of her decision to take over. She had to be firm, tough even: tell Alan, then walk away.

'I can't do this – not like this,' she murmured, rehearsing. 'It's got to stop. I'm not that sort of woman.'

She was seated at a table in the warm pub only seconds before he arrived, with no time to collect herself. There he was, coming across the room towards her, seeming in a hurry, his coat swinging open. Immediately she saw in his expression that there was something wrong.

'Sorry, love,' he said, out of breath. 'I just had to come and tell you, but I've got to get out to the car again. There's been a bit of bother – the police are coming. I just didn't want you to think ... Look, I'll have to get back – it's my car, you see ... You could wait here in the warm.'

'No!' She didn't hesitate, buttoning her coat up again. 'I'm coming with you!'

It had happened further along, not far from the library. Alan had slowed to let a van in front of him turn off to the right, and the car behind had smashed hard into the back of him. The driver had turned nasty and was insisting it was Alan's fault. As they hurried outside, a police car was drawing up, to Alan's evident relief.

They all stood in the dark and freezing wind amid the lights of the traffic struggling to overtake and the flashing blue from the police car. One officer worked to calm the irate driver, who was clearly all the more worked up because he was in the wrong. The other officer directed the traffic. Eventually the towing van arrived to haul Alan's car away. The back was badly smashed in. There were lengthy discussions.

Margaret stood watching, her eyes on Alan.

Eventually he came to her, looking very fed up. 'I'm sorry about this,' he said miserably. 'It's gone and spoiled the whole evening.'

'Don't be daft,' Margaret told him. 'It wasn't your fault. That bloke just wasn't looking where he was going.'

'No, and the speed he was going – ridiculous!' For some reason he chuckled, as if at the craziness of fate. 'Look, shall we have a drink anyway?'

'Yes,' she said calmly.

She followed him back into the pub.

'I'm sorry,' Alan said again. 'I've wrecked the evening.'

'No,' she said. 'No, you haven't.' If he only knew!

He seemed sad as they settled down with his pint and her half.

'Your car's quite a mess,' she said.

Alan shook his head. 'I don't think they'll be able to salvage it – it's a write-off, I think.' He shrugged. 'Never mind: no damage done to life or limb anyway.'

She realized this was not what was bothering him. Even though he started talking in his normal way, there was still an underlying feeling.

After a while she said, 'What's up?'

'What d'you mean?'

'You seem a bit – down. Is it the car?'

'Oh, no not really. That's just one of those things.' He paused to think. 'I s'pose it's just – maybe it's Christmas. It brings things out, doesn't it? You know, you can't help looking back, thinking of how things were, how you might have messed them up. It comes back to haunt you.'

'Yes,' she agreed. 'It's a family time.'

There was a silence. Alan looked down for a minute, then away across the pub. It felt to her as if there was something he wasn't saying, couldn't say. She knew it was up to her.

'Alan? Do you – I mean, d'you think much about the future?'

He turned to her. 'How d'you mean?'

'Well, about how things might be.' She swallowed. All her blood seemed to have turned into one of those jacuzzi things, swirling round her body. 'About – us?'

'I think about it, yes,' Alan said cautiously. 'I

just . . .' He shook his head. 'I don't know that there's all that much I can do about it. I suppose I don't feel I have the right – to ask anything.'

Margaret gazed into his eyes. *I can say it now*, she thought, *or not say it . . . And it will make the whole difference to everything . . .* In that split second she knew all of it, could see it opening out in front of her. She would speak now, the truth that she knew, as she had known following him out to the street, to the wrecked car; hearing his voice as he spoke in his quiet way to the police, while they probably assumed she was his wife: she knew she belonged with him, that she just couldn't imagine life without him. He *was* life – a new life full of wonder that she had never experienced before and hardly dreamed of. She had moved on too much – he was her love, and things could be no other way.

And she knew that this would lead to other things. She would have to find strength and courage to gather her family together: Fred and Karen, Joanne and Dave. And in front of them she would open her mouth again and make her choice, and cause things to change, and from then on she would have to take on that change, whatever it meant.

I have something to say, she would begin.

February 1985

Sixty-Six

Sooky sat at the desk in her room, finishing a college assignment. It was late in the afternoon. Harpreet was downstairs helping Mom. Roopinder was looking after Priya.

Sooky sat back for a moment, pausing to think, and realized how dark the room was, apart from the light from the angle-poise lamp. Like a planet floating in space, she thought. If that were the case, how would it be to land, alone in her spaceship, on an unknown planet? What might she find there when she climbed out and looked around? Captain Kirk had always had all his space crew . . .

Dragging her mind back to the task in front of her, she looked down at the lined page, her biros and textbooks, her curling handwriting, blue across the page. She experienced a moment of acute happiness and possibility. Even the act of writing was pleasurable, marking the white page. Her handwriting was nothing special, but a whole page full of it looked nice. And here she was, learning things, going to college, with a future in mind. She was only twenty years old and had so much already – a daughter, a place at college, friends from before, from school and college; and Joanne, who had been round with Amy that afternoon. And what was more, slowly, miraculously, things had improved at home. Even she and Roopinder got along better these days. They were more of a team.

She looked down at herself, at the pink Punjabi suit she was wearing. Funny, when she was younger Mom was always trying to force her into suits, and all she wanted was jeans, trainers, denim skirts and platform shoes like the white girls wore.

'But you are an Indian girl,' Meena would say, her brow puckering with bewilderment. 'You look so much better in our clothes, with a nice plait – not this hair – in pink and green, like these girls are wearing.'

'But I'm *not* Indian, am I?' Sooky would protest. 'I've never been to India!'

'One day we will be going . . .'

'Yes, but that doesn't make me Indian – not in the way you mean.'

One time Meena pulled her over to a mirror and stood behind her, pointing. 'So, look at your face: what do you see? Are you a *goree*? No! You're Indian!'

'But why can't Indian girls wear jeans?' Sooky demanded stubbornly.

Over the years Meena had softened about this and let Sooky choose for herself. Just now, though, she found herself opting more for Punjabi dress. What had happened last year had made her see things differently. Everyone was still full of anger and a sense of betrayal – no one had been prosecuted for all the killings in Delhi. It felt as if it was willed, even organized, by the government. If I was really English, Sooky thought – white English – I would just see it as another piece of news. 'Oh dear, how awful!' Until the next piece of bad news, which as it turned out came in December, when an American company called Union Carbide had allowed a chemical leak so catastrophic that it had poisoned thousands of people in an Indian town called Bhopal. This too felt personal – it felt part of home.

I'm not Indian, but India is part of me, Sooky thought. That's how it is. It's not part of Joanne, but it's part of me.

And just as she had been coming to terms with these things, her mother surprised her, as she sometimes did.

Meena had been in deep mourning. The loss of Nirmal had touched something very deep in her, as she tried to explain one afternoon as she and Sooky sat in the front room minding the children. Sooky was on the floor and Meena behind her on the sofa. She suddenly started speaking again, as if a tap had been turned on.

'*Mama-ji* was always so kind to me. Always my favourite uncle – before we left home, and after.'

Sooky swivelled round to look at her. Meena was hunched forward, rocking very slightly back and forth, a pained expression on her face.

'He was so funny and such a good man. No one should meet a death like that – but a man who was so kind and amiable, who brought joy to people . . .' She shook her head. 'Now I feel I have nothing left of home – nothing at all.'

'What about Bhoji?' Sooky said.

'Yes, Bhoji . . . But I hardly know her really. She and the other widows will have to give each other comfort. Nirmal I knew from a child. Now – it is all gone.'

There was a long, sad silence. Sooky was trying to think of something comforting to say, but then Meena started again.

'All these weeks I've been thinking. I came here to this country when I was very young. I had no ambition to come to England for myself, but it is the duty of a wife to follow her husband. And at home there was not much for me, living with my mother-in-law. She was not the worst, but she was not very nice. Rajdev needed his father. When we got here, all everyone could think of then was to make enough money to go home. At first. Then we realized we were not going home: we had too much here; we had changed too much to go back. So I wanted to make India here. Always I was dreaming of home.'

She looked at Sooky.

'It took me too long to notice that my children do not dream of home like this. Rajdev did – does still maybe – but he and I have been talking a lot. He is changing. I try to make him see that his life is here, with his family.'

Sooky was surprised by this. It was news to her. Though Raj did seem softer, less burdened, even despite the rage he shared with everyone else over the Golden Temple, the killings. He seemed more peaceful in himself.

'Now I am starting to see that I have been foolish. Even if I went back home, everything is gone.' Meena made a sweeping motion with her hand. 'Too much has happened. They are there – we are here. And you children: you are English . . .'

'Indian-English,' Sooky said, smiling.

Meena inclined her head. 'Indian-English. Yes, that is true. But I have decided . . .' She sat up straighter to make her announcement. 'I have children who are intelligent and do well in school. Now, I don't mean to be rude to your father, but I don't think you can have got one hundred per cent of your intelligence from him. Perhaps I have a little helping too?'

'You do, *Mata-ji*!'

'And I have decided that it is time I learned English,

so that when your *goree* friend comes round she does not think I am an ignorant Indian peasant.'

'Joanne!' Sooky laughed. 'She doesn't think that – of course she doesn't.'

'Hmm,' Meena said, unconvinced. 'And so I can talk properly in shops and – and health centres . . .'

Sooky laughed at this, pleased and excited at the determined look on her mother's face.

'Banita told me they have volunteers who will come and teach English in the home,' Meena said. 'An English lady is coming.'

'You mean you've already arranged it?' Sooky said, astonished.

Meena inclined her head again. 'Banita helped me.'

And ever since the middle of January a plump, jolly young woman called Rosie had come to the house each week, wearing baggy dungarees and red, flat shoes. With her she brought books and picture cards, and Meena was ensconced in the front room with her for an hour or more. Afterwards Meena would make her tea and snacks. Sometimes they even cooked together and laughed a lot. They seemed to get on like a house on fire.

'Your mother already understands a lot of English,' Rosie said to Sooky after the first couple of sessions. 'After all, she's been here a good while. It's just putting it all together and helping her to speak. She's a fast learner.'

Sooky liked Rosie. She seemed genuine and lively. Raj found her bewildering. 'Why does she wear those awful clothes – and her *shoes*!' But he too seemed pleased to see his mother progressing. Khushwant also appeared proud. It was all rather surprising.

Sooky breathed in deeply, smiling to herself, and

bent over the desk again. Picking up her pen she was just writing the next sentence of her essay when the door opened. She turned, squinting, only just able to see Harpreet's outline in the doorway.

'Sorry, Sukh,' Harpreet said.

Sooky was alerted by the tone of her voice. There was worry in it, and warning.

'It's just – Dad's home. He and Mom want to talk to you, downstairs.'

Somehow she already knew. It was something that had been nagging at the back of her mind, like the pain of a boil that has not yet reached the surface. When she saw them both, she knew for sure.

The two of them were in the front room, sitting side by side on the sofa as stiffly as if they were posing for one of those old-fashioned photographs where, on pain of death, you mustn't smile. If it hadn't been so serious it would have been funny, the way Mom's *chunni* was so neat, and Dad was sucking in his belly and trying to sit up very straight.

It suddenly occurred to Sooky that they were very nervous, which made her stomach clench with dread in sympathy.

'Shut the door, Sukhdeep,' Khushwant said with overdone cheeriness.

She obeyed and sat down like an interviewee. Mom and Dad looked at each other.

'You want me to get married, don't you?' Sooky said.

They exchanged glances again.

'We-ell,' Khushwant said. For the first time ever it occurred to Sooky that they were a bit afraid of her, of her strength and her ability to do what was best for herself, if necessary. 'It's not so much that we *want* you to . . .'

But his eyes were begging. *Please, Sukhdeep my daughter, don't fight this. Please do the right thing, put us right again with the community, with tradition, with what is right . . . Don't continue in a state of disgrace forever!*

'It is a chance for you,' Meena said, sitting bolt upright. 'There is someone who has asked to meet you.'

'Okay,' Sooky said cautiously. 'Tell me.'

'The thing is, he lives in Birmingham and he would be prepared to allow you to go on studying,' Meena said, all in a rush.

Sooky frowned suspiciously. 'Doesn't he want children?'

They looked at each other again. It was Khushwant who explained. The man in question was called Arun. He was a Jat by caste, of course, and had a good job working in insurance. But he was thirty-two years old and a widower. His young wife had died of a brain haemorrhage more than a year ago. He had two children already, a boy and a girl.

'Oh,' Sooky said. 'I see.'

Even though she had been expecting something like this, she still felt stunned and a bit sick. She found she was shivering. *Arun.* A man called Arun. Longing and dread threaded through her, confused.

'How old are the children?' she asked.

Khushwant looked helplessly at his wife.

'The boy is ten years old, he is called Deep,' Meena said. 'The girl, Leela, is eight.'

Sooky swallowed, looking down. All the possibilities of her life rushed through her mind. Study, a career, a husband, a father for Priya, sex, love even – no, that might be asking too much. But one thing she saw with horrible clarity: the alternative. She would stay home, the divorced, disgraced one. This would keep happening: men would be brought for them to view each other. As time passed she would get older, and the men might get older too – or a lot younger than her. It would become more and more agonizing as the years went by. The pressure would never go away for her to make things right. *Arun.* She tasted his name. He had had grief and bad luck, just as she had. He might be all right, who knew?

'There is no need to be deciding anything too quickly,' Khushwant said into the silence.

Sooky looked up. 'He's really okay about me doing my degree? And he knows about Jaz – and Priya?'

Khushwant and Meena were nodding as eagerly as toy dogs in the back of a car window.

'Okay then,' she said slowly. 'I'll see him.'

Sixty-Seven

Margaret sat beside Alan as the car sped smoothly along the M5.

'Valentine's Day treat,' he'd said, even though it was two days later, as they'd had to wait for the weekend. The bouquet of spring flowers that, to her amazement, he had presented to her on the day were still brightening their living room with vivid yellow, white and blue.

'We could wait until it's warmer – in the summer?' she'd suggested.

'We can go then as well, if you like,' Alan said. 'Rationing's over now, you know.'

They'd developed a joking way of talking, a banter by which he often teased her out of her gloomy, glass-half-empty view of life.

'You're just putting it off,' he challenged her.

'I'm not! It's just . . .'

'You're frightened it's not going to be the same.'

'Well, it's not, is it? Let's face it, it was forty years ago – it'd be pretty peculiar if everything had stayed the same.'

'But it's the same in your mind.'

'Yes. It is.'

She knew that was what she was scared of – losing the images of paradise she had held onto all these years. And of being overwhelmed by emotion. But she didn't mind Alan's teasing. She knew he had been through just the same with Abergavenny. That was the thing with Alan. He understood. She looked round at him with a surge of love and gratitude. There he was, miraculously beside her, concentrating on the driving, his salt-and-pepper hair neatly clipped round his dark-eyed face. The face she loved abundantly.

'What're you looking at?' There was still teasing in his voice.

'You. Because I can. And you can't look at me.'

He chuckled. 'Oh, I see. Well, I'll make up for that later, Margaret my girl, that I will!'

They were in a green Montego saloon, which he had bought with the insurance on his other smashed-up car.

'Is it new?' she'd asked, awed, when he first drove up in it.

'No. Not quite. But the "not quite" makes a big difference to the price, I can tell you!'

It still smelled new inside. Margaret rested her head back and closed her eyes. *I'm here*, she said to herself. *I'm really here.*

She could hardly believe the process that had brought her to this day: the upheavals of the past – six? – yes, six or so weeks since she had announced to Fred and the girls that she was leaving, to be with someone else. Margaret Tolley, yes, she, Margaret Tolley, had sat at the table with them just after Christmas and said it. She thought about talking to Fred first, on his own, but that just felt impossible. The shameful truth was that she could not have begun to talk to him, not on their own – that was the sad fact of the matter.

'I'm sorry,' she said to them. Something drove her

on. She had thought and thought about it and never imagined she would get the words out. 'Something's happened. I've fallen in love. And I want to be with him. I have to – it's just how it is. I'm ever so sorry. I don't know how else to say it.'

The girls were both there, and Dave and Geoff, Karen's new boyfriend, whom they all liked. Margaret felt like someone else. Who was this new person in new clothes, who for the first time ever felt so sure of something? It wasn't that she was proud of it, not of causing such hurt. But she simply had to be with Alan.

They all sat staring at her. For a few seconds Margaret wondered whether she had said it at all, or whether she had been hallucinating. If they had just carried on drinking their tea and eating cake, she wouldn't have been unduly surprised.

'I thought . . .' It was Karen who spoke first. Karen who, God knew, had grown up so much in the last year! 'Well, I thought there was something different about you, Mom.' But Margaret could hear a tremor in her voice.

Margaret saw Dave reach for Joanne's hand, to offer comfort. Then all of them looked at Fred. He was holding a cup of tea and his hand began to shake, so that the remains of the tea started to slop. Joanne reached over and took it from him. Fred's eyes never left Margaret's face – his expression cut her to the heart, and she was glad of this.

'I . . .' he started to say, then ground to a halt. He seemed to be finding it hard to catch his breath, and tears rose in his eyes.

'I'm sorry, Fred,' she said. 'I've not been much of a wife to you.' Suddenly she was weeping; they all were. Dave and Geoff put their arms round their partners.

'Oh, Mom!' Joanne said. Then, not seeming to be able to find any other words, she turned to Fred and said, 'Oh, Dad!'

Fred pushed back his chair from the table and stood up. 'Are you serious?' he said in a choked voice. 'You look serious.'

Margaret wiped her eyes, nodding.

'After all these years. I never thought . . .' He shook his head. 'I need to get out.'

They heard him put on his coat, sniffing, then the front door opened and closed. They let him go, let him be alone for a while.

When he had gone, Margaret told the others what had happened.

It had taken time to sink in – for all of them. One of the most humbling things that had ever happened to Margaret in her life was to witness the reaction of her daughters. Karen was full of psychology. She said it was best to get things out into the open; how the Valium had allowed her to stifle her feelings all these years, when it had been obvious that she and Fred were not especially happy. Her coming off the drug, Karen said, had allowed Margaret to find herself.

'And Dad's so cut off from himself,' she said. 'I mean, when was the last time you two ever really *talked* to each other?'

Margaret said she couldn't remember. Before, she would have said it wasn't about talking. She and Fred had, as Karen also said, 'ticked the boxes'. They had had two children, brought them up right, worked hard for a living and never sponged off anyone else or had any handouts. What else could you expect from marriage? Fred had never laid a finger on her in a harmful way – that counted for a lot. But now ... Oh, there could be so much more, so much!

Fred, as ever, said nothing. For a fortnight he came and went, barely speaking, as if nothing had happened. Margaret began to think he would never react to what was happening. She felt guilty and sad, but his silence did not help. It just felt as if he didn't care, when she knew he probably did.

Joanne was so kind it brought tears to her eyes.

'It's taken me a while to get over the shock,' she said. 'I mean, we weren't exactly expecting it. Especially with the things you used to say about ... But never mind that. I really do hope you'll be happy, Mom. I've never thought you were very happy. You never seemed to have much of a life, to be honest. So I hope it works out for you.'

Both the girls said they would help look after their dad – keep an eye on him. They met Alan, and though it would take time to get used to each other, all had gone well. They said they liked him. After a month at home, giving everyone time to get used to the idea of her leaving, Margaret had moved into Alan's house, further out of town.

'In the long run, I think we should move,' he said. 'Get a new place of our own – but we'll sit tight for now, shall we, get used to things? We could move a bit further out, nearer the country?'

Sitting in the car beside him, she was filled with sorrow and joy and gratitude for everybody. Even Fred, in the end, had told her he hoped she'd be happy. This had made her cry for a long time.

'I hope you find someone,' she told him. 'I'd like to know you're happy too.'

Fred nodded in a vague sort of way that had also wrung her heart. But she had to go.

They parked in a quiet spot in Buckley, just along the road from Orchard House. It was a bright day, the sun trying to burn through the haze, and there was a cold wind blowing, which whipped Margaret's scarf out behind her. They wrapped up well, and Alan took her arm.

'Ready?' he said. He put his hands on her shoulders for a moment. 'It'll be all right.'

'I know. It just feels . . .' She shrugged.

Alan took her hand. No one else was about. As they walked along, seeing the house come into view, she said, 'Ooh, this feels really queer.' Then, further along, full of wonder: 'It looks *just* the same! Well, almost.'

They stood outside as past and present collided. It felt so strange to be standing here again.

'The drive wasn't like that – it was rougher, of course. I remember standing here waiting for Tommy: he came just once. He got down, just there. They fetched him on a cart . . . no cars – not like that, of course.' She nodded at a smart blue car on the drive. 'The trees have grown – oh, and there are some new ones. Course it all looks in better nick, painted up and everything. Not like in the war . . . My, oh my!' She stared up at the windows. 'Now, which one was my room? John and Patty were at the back – that was mine, I think, the second one along.'

She put her hand over her mouth, musing. It still felt as if Miss Clairmont or Mrs Higgins might come bustling out of the house, with Dotty barking madly beside them. That was the last thing she'd seen – the house receding, Dotty barking – as Ted Winters dragged her away. She remembered the boots she had been wearing, the holdall as Ted Winters flung it away over the gate . . .

She gazed at it all for some time. She had never written back to the sisters. Could things have been different – could they have kept a thread going after the war? Might she have come for visits, the place becoming a part of her life instead of a lost dream?

Tears didn't come as she had expected. There was nothing she could change now. She felt resigned and sorry, that was all. And very sad for the lost child she had been, for the wife she had been. I may not have been the best mother ever, she thought. But my two never had anything like that happen to them – nothing like. And they'd been so kind to her lately. She couldn't have been all bad, could she?

'Ah, now this is different . . .' Further along there had been a rickety iron fence through which you could see into the paddocks where they had played for so many hours. Now there had grown up a beech hedge, well tended and blocking the view.

'That's a shame,' Alan said.

'No,' she said. 'I'm glad – to see something definitely different.'

'D'you want to knock on the door?' he suggested. 'I'm sure they wouldn't mind, if you said why you're here. They might find it interesting, show you round.'

Margaret hesitated. 'Did you – when you went to Abergavenny?'

'I did. The old couple had passed away by then, but I did see the son. He just about remembered me.'

Something about the way he said it seemed melancholy to Margaret. She squeezed his arm. Already she felt lighter in herself, with a sense of relief.

'No, I'll leave it. It's nice to come back, but I'll keep my other memories as they were. It all feels ever so long ago now.'

She walked up to the tree at the front and picked a sprig from its boughs. Its buds were just appearing.

'A little souvenir,' she smiled, looking into Alan's eyes. 'You know, what matters is now. You – and me.' She reached up and kissed him, and he held her for a moment. 'Alan?' She looked up into his face. 'Will you do me a favour? Would you call me Maggie?'

She saw a moved expression in his eyes and for a moment he placed his hand, warm on the back of her head.

'Maggie? Yes, love – it suits you. My Maggie.'

Closing his eyes, he leaned to her and kissed her forehead.

Passing back through other villages, looking for a pub for lunch, suddenly everything was familiar.

'Hold on, this is the other place where I was! No, don't turn through the village – just go straight on down there a minute. I think it was down here; we used to walk up to the rectory to have lessons.'

For a second she felt herself tighten inside with fear and loathing at the vile memories that returned as they neared Nora Paige's cottage. But change aplenty had come here.

'Oh!' she exclaimed. 'It's gone – completely! Well, I suppose I'm not surprised; it was quite ramshackle then.'

A well-established modern house stood on the site, enclosed by trees and hedges. You could just see into the drive, between the winter branches. A child's red bicycle was propped against the front of the house.

'Well, I'm glad that's gone,' she said. 'It's all right, you can turn round now.'

'Yes, ma'am,' Alan said.

Laughing, she touched his hand. 'Sorry – ordering you about. Shall we go and find some dinner now? I could eat a horse.'

'Are you glad you came then?' Alan asked.

They were at a cosy table in a pub, side by side with their drinks, waiting for the hot pies they had ordered. Everything felt exciting, just sitting in a pub, eating lunch. Margaret kept reminding herself that she was fifty years old, not fifteen, but it didn't seem to make any difference to the way she felt.

'Oh yes, I am. It was good to see the old place. That's the funny thing – nothing's changed much, but it did look a bit smaller than I remembered.'

'Yes, I remember the Abergavenny house seemed a cramped little place when I went later on. Always clean as a pin though, of course.'

Margaret sipped her drink. 'I just held onto the memory of it because everything was so bleak and horrible when I got back.' She put her glass down and turned to Alan. 'I don't need to now. Everything's wonderful.'

'Thanks, Maggie May,' he said happily. 'It certainly is.'

She beamed back at him, but then her face sobered. 'It's all right for me. I just hope, in the end, that Fred's better off without me.'

Alan shook his head. He looked sad for a moment. 'God, I hope you don't regret—'

'No!' She stopped him, reaching out her hand. 'I regret hurting him. But I couldn't have stayed. Not now I've met you.'

'It's funny . . .' Alan sat back, releasing her hand. 'I know I'll go on running my business – some things will just stay the same. But now I'm with you, all sorts of things feel possible. As if everything's new.'

'Yes!' She felt the same, bubbling over with it. 'I feel as if I've spent the past twenty years asleep. I want to make up for it!'

He looked at her, interested. 'How?'

'Oh, I don't know!' She laughed, feeling foolish. 'I don't know if I really want to do very many things; it's just so lovely feeling properly awake while I'm doing them. But maybe we could go on holiday! Or I could take a course, like Karen's doing – and spend more time with Amy. Joanne and Dave could do with the support.'

'Yes,' Alan said. 'They seem all right, though. She's a brave young woman, that daughter of yours.'

'I s'pose she is, yes – though I didn't see it that way at the time. That opened my eyes all right.'

'My ex, Pat – sorry to mention her – but Dawn, my daughter, says Pat goes along with the little'un to the kiddies' playgroup, or whatever they call it, to help out. Doesn't Amy go to one of them? You could go with her?'

'What – over there? It's in Handsworth!'

Alan looked blankly at her. 'It's only just the other side of town; it's not the end of the Earth, you know.'

'No, but it feels like it! I mean, it's a bit *foreign* over there.'

'Foreign? Oh, you mean there are blacks! Well, yes. It's a bit different, but it's just *kids*, for heaven's sake! Your own granddaughter. Come on, Margaret, people are people – it all depends how you treat them.'

'I suppose.' She felt ashamed, and that he'd shown her up as mean-spirited. 'Maybe I will then. If it'd help Jo and Dave.'

'Sounds great,' he said, sitting up as their meal swept into view. 'And that's just the beginning. I expect there are all sorts of things you could do.'

Once the steaming pies were in front of them and the waitress gone, he looked at her again, his eyes full of love.

'Give us a kiss, Maggie.'

She turned to him, smiling, and reached up, as they kissed, to stroke his cheek.

Sixty-Eight

Joanne and Dave were both amazed when Margaret said she wanted to come to the toddler group. That first time, Dave said he'd drive over and collect her.

'I won't be able to, once I'm back at work properly,' he said. 'So I might as well. You walk round and we'll meet you there.'

He was talking more about getting back to work full-time now. So far it was three days a week, easing back into the swing of things. But he was staying at home on Tuesdays and coming along to the group with her.

At first Joanne had bitten back the comment 'But Tuesday is the one day I don't need anyone at home – I've got somewhere to go!'

That was completely the wrong thing to say, she realized. It was good for him to come along and get to know some of the same people as her. And it wouldn't be for long – he was already getting a bit bored with it. That was a good sign! He was recovering, not needing to be chained to her side at all times. He wanted to get back to the world of work and other men. But things had definitely changed. They talked about things more, instead of taking their roles for granted. They were trying to build something new. But Joanne didn't take anything for granted. We're together today, she sometimes told herself. And we'll likely be together tomorrow. That's all I need to know.

As she pushed Amy up to the Soho Road, she saw a familiar green-clad figure passing in front of the big *gurdwara* pushing a buggy. For a second she thought it was Sooky, before realizing it was actually Meena. They were almost the same size and shape, but of course Sooky's mom's face was older and a little more severe. Seeing Meena look across at her, Joanne raised her hand and waved. Meena waved back, checked for traffic and crossed the road.

'Hello,' she said amiably. 'Very cold!'

'Yes,' Joanne nodded. She pointed at the sky. 'Snow, I think.'

She wasn't sure if Meena knew the word for snow, but she smiled and nodded as if she did and they both hurried to get into the warmth of the church hall. Joanne felt responsible for Meena. She had been the only person Sooky's mom would recognize at the toddler group, and Sooky had asked her to look out for her when Meena first came, a couple of weeks ago.

'Mom's decided to bring Priya to the group,' she said, sounding surprised. 'It won't be very easy for her, but I'm really happy she's coming – Priya will be too.'

'She'll be all right, we'll look after her,' Joanne had said. And of course Tess was kindness itself.

In fact Joanne had been to the Baidwans' house a couple of days ago. Sooky had told her that she had met the man whom she might marry. Joanne had been shocked when Sooky said she was going to see another prospective husband, but when Sooky explained her reasons, it made more sense.

'Anyway, it doesn't mean I have to say yes,' she said. 'But I'm going to meet him.' She looked reflective. 'You know, the amazing thing is, Mom said to me the other day – when we were on our own – "You don't *have* to get married, you know. I don't want to force you." '

'Did she? What did you say?'

Sooky turned to her, and Joanne saw that she was moved. 'Well, I said, "No, I know. But in a way, I do have to some time, don't I? Maybe not this one, but sometime."'

Joanne had been very curious to know how it went. She found Sooky in an optimistic mood.

'Well,' Joanne began as they settled down with the children, 'what's he like?'

'What's who like?' Sooky teased.

'Oh, don't be daft!'

'Oh – Arun! We-e-ll . . . I think he's okay. On first meeting. I mean, I did actually quite like him, as a person. He's rather handsome actually, and the children seem okay too: quite sweet. He works in insurance, but he said he thought it was really boring – he made fun of himself – and he really likes cinema and books and stuff . . .'

'Hey, you do actually like him!'

She was sure she saw Sooky blush. 'Well, as I say, he seems okay.'

'You haven't said yes already, have you?'

'No – we're going to meet up again, take it slowly. I probably will, though; he's really okay about me doing my degree . . .'

'But, Sooky, *marriage!* You can do your degree anyway.'

'Yeah, but you know. I kind of have to get married sometime.'

'At least you'll be here and not dragged off to Derby or Bradford or somewhere. I'd really miss you.'

'Yeah,' she smiled. 'I'd miss you too. Anyway, I'll probably go for it.' With cool pragmatism she added, 'I'll give it five years.'

Joanne grinned to herself, thinking about this. Sooky made her laugh. She certainly wasn't marrying with overblown expectations.

Dave came into the hall with Margaret after the toddler group had got going, and Joanne introduced her mother to Tess. Joanne saw Tess putting her mother at ease. She stood back and let Dave and Margaret do most of the looking-after of Amy. It was nice to have a break, and they would have felt awkward without something to do.

Watching Dave for a moment, she saw him bend over, by the painting table, which was still Amy's obsession. Priya immediately came up as well, with Meena following shyly behind. Joanne smiled, seeing Dave and Margaret helping first Amy, then Priya on with their painting overalls. She watched him gratefully. He was still seeing the counsellor, was really trying. No guarantees – she still had that caution in her mind – but she had reasons to hope.

'Nice to see your mother here.' Tess had come up beside her. Her baby was asleep in the pram for the moment.

'Yes, she's getting out and about a lot more these days,' Joanne said. She was proud to see how nice Mom was looking in her neat trousers and a soft blue jumper.

'And your husband's looking much better.'

'Yes.' Joanne smiled. 'He is, thanks.'

Tess asked after Sooky, and then added, 'It's great that her mother's here, isn't it? She seems a lovely lady.'

'She is. Come to think of it, I ought to go and introduce her to my mom.'

They were all still by the painting table. Margaret and Dave were busying themselves with Amy; Meena stood near Priya with her arms folded, looking uncertain.

'Mom,' Joanne caught her attention. 'Come and meet my mate's mom, will you?' She steered Margaret towards Meena. 'This is my best mate Sooky's mother. Her name's Meena.'

Joanne felt her mother hesitate for a second.

'She doesn't speak very good English, so it's a bit hard for her.' And to Meena she said, 'This is my mother.'

Meena was smiling, pleased to be spoken to, and held out her hand. 'Hello. My name is Meena.'

Joanne saw her mother take in what a nice person Meena looked. Shyly she shook Meena's hand and smiled back.

'I'm Margaret.' She added, 'Maggie. You can call me Maggie.'

They were all getting used to the idea that she now actually wanted to be called Maggie. She had explained to Joanne why.

'Maggie,' Meena repeated.

There was an awkward pause, but then Meena sat down on one of the baby chairs near the painting table and indicated in a friendly way that Margaret should sit beside her. Margaret shot a panicky look at Joanne, but didn't like to refuse. In any case, they found quite a bit to keep them occupied, watching Amy and Priya, enjoying their antics with the paints, without having to talk much. The girls saw them sitting together and broke off from their painting to run back and forth to them, making them laugh as they tried to avoid getting covered in paint.

Joanne sat beside Dave, watching first the grand-children laughing, then the grandmothers. She just wished Sooky could be there too.

'It doesn't look as if we're needed for the moment, does it?' Dave said.

Joanne shook her head. 'Let's make the most of it!'

Dave reached over and took her hand, squeezing it. She turned to look into his eyes and they both smiled. She squeezed his hand back.

Margaret didn't like to say too much to Meena, because she didn't know what she would understand. Now that the ice was broken, she could see that Meena was a nice lady and they smiled and nodded and found ways to communicate, discovering that they were enjoying themselves and were both very pleased when they could understand each other.

'I am learning English,' Meena announced proudly as they sat together.

'Ah,' Margaret enthused. 'Good. That's good. Difficult!'

'Yes.' Meena nodded. 'Difficult!' They both laughed at this.

After a few moments Meena looked across at Joanne.

'Your daughter,' she stated. 'She is good girl.'

'Yes. Yes, she is.' It was only now that Margaret realized just how good. She was filled with a swelling sensation of pride, of joy and possibility, of life opening out.

'Have daughter is good,' Meena continued. 'My daughter Sukhdeep is good girl. She teach me lot of thing.'

Margaret turned to her new friend. Across the room, Joanne saw her radiant smile. 'Yes,' she agreed. 'Mine too.'

FOR MORE ON

ANNIE
MURRAY

sign up to receive our

SAGA NEWSLETTER

Packed with **features, competitions, authors'
and readers' letters** and **news of exclusive events**,
it's a must-read for every Annie Murray fan!

Simply fill in your details below and tick to confirm that you would
like to receive saga-related news and promotions and return to us at
Pan Macmillan, Saga Newsletter, 20 New Wharf Road, London, N1 9RR.

NAME

ADDRESS

POSTCODE

EMAIL

☐ *I would like to receive saga-related news and promotions (please tick)*

*You can unsubscribe at any time in writing or through our website where you can also see
our privacy policy which explains how we will store and use your data.*